The
Shadows
of August

The Shadows of August

Denis J. Linehan

authorHOUSE®

AuthorHouse™ LLC
1663 Liberty Drive
Bloomington, IN 47403
www.authorhouse.com
Phone: 1-800-839-8640

Cover Photo by Connie Bush
Cover Art by Crystal Wood

Published by AuthorHouse 03/26/2014

ISBN: 978-1-4918-7381-6 (sc)
ISBN: 978-1-4918-7380-9 (e)

Library of Congress Control Number: 2014905203

"You may keep the things of bronze and stone; just give me one man to remember me but once a year"

Damon Runyon

To the Reader: A keepsake before entering.

The Shadows of August is intended as a novel and may be read as such. However, it also can be enjoyed as a collection of short stories, each with a center and a purpose of its own. Either way, it is an offering of parables and parodies from The Spa that acknowledges the people, history, traditions, and mythologies this long loved sanctuary has become famous for.

While you turn these pages, remember how each tale was put to paper with disarming ease as all of the characters within may still to be found roaming the thoroughfares and back alleys of the city of Saratoga Springs this summer. No flights of fancy or arabesque inventions were required to recreate their adventures. All that was required, as the agent of these chronicles, was an acute ear, tuned to capture each jewel. Try it yourself some summer day. Alight in Saratoga, go through the racecourse's timeless gates, sit beneath a giant shade tree and listen; the stories will be all around you. And if you can not venture north into the foothills of the Adirondacks, take a settled moment within your own home and listen, grand tales will be all around you. Hear them?

Contents

September 21,

Dear Yvonne,

I hope this note gets to you before you are off to Puerto Rico
or Spain this year. Yes, I remember the spectacular tan lines.
You always seem to devour the sun and come back healthier and
happier than ever.

My Saratoga was fun, and more than somewhat, believe you
me. The racing was really good, like usual, and I had a little luck
late in the meet, at least enough to keep the old Buick on the road
for the drive back home. Don't laugh, the Invicta runs just fine and
it suits me; we had some good times with it. I even drove some
strangers around town and acted like a tour guide. Me and the old
Buick were like the newest taxi in town. Really. Everyone was
asking for you like always. My cousin Vinnie had his new wife
with him this summer, she would have enjoyed your company, and
Shiner was asking for you as well as Cotton and Jay and Ted and
Fat Frankie. Of course Nick was there having fun with his pals, you
know he can't resist pushing Ted's buttons and Ted is comical in his
own way, without even trying. It was quite a menagerie, the rich
and not-so-rich, the sharpies and the not-so-sharp, but everyone
seemed to be having a grand time.

Sure was great to see the old place filled with all those people
each weekend, it never gets old when you see young couples
pushing baby carriages around the picnic areas, or walking their
children toward the racetrack to watch the horses. Little girls
always love horses, no matter what. Patricia, Laney, and Cass
were all back bartending. From what I saw they must have made
a fortune this summer; the bars were packed, four and five deep
sometimes. And of course there was a cast of new faces from all
over the place, I met people from Texas and Boston and Long
Island that made the quiet days even more fun. It was even great
seeing the young kids trying to work their first job and make a few
bucks for college or car insurance or whatever.

But mostly I just missed you and wished you could have been
here so we could have walked in the sunshine one more time and
you might give me a chance to understand your new life. I took
some notes, they were fun to put together; I've attached them to

1

this letter so you can see some of what you missed. It was fun. The only thing that might have made it better would have been to see it through your eyes. Hope you like them.

Please write or call sometime, anytime. I miss you.

Heigh-Ho, Heigh-Ho!

It was a glorious Adirondack morning when I awoke in Saratoga Springs for the start of the new racing season. I felt refreshed, renewed and somehow all was right with my world, despite the long drive from Maryland the evening before. In truth, the great trek up Route 95 had recharged my soul and prepared me, mentally, physically and spiritually, to once again pursue the puzzle that is August in Saratoga. Saratoga, in deep summer, the Philadelphia Orchestra establishes residency just as The New York City Ballet steps aside, Café Lina welcomes folk singers from around the world, the Racino's doors stay open till dawn, and the ancient thoroughbred racetrack thunders alive; romance, riches, and adventure are sure to follow.

By noon the sun had steadied straight overhead and its warmth was a most welcome change from the misty dull fogs of my winter on Chesapeake Bay. Broadway was a wonderful sight to behold, thick with the subdued rummage and ruction that always anticipates opening day for the thoroughbreds. Gamers and gamblers stir the sidewalks and shop fronts with stories to tell, and each with a story that needs to be told. As for me, I had been away for nearly a year, and with so many of my closest conspirators yet to arrive, I remained something of a stranger to my fellow pedestrians. An anonymous condition I quietly enjoyed.

After a quick lunch at Compton's Diner and an equally spontaneous review of Mabou's latest trophies and chef-d'oeuvres, it was time to stroll up Lake Avenue and reclaim my 1957 Buick

Invicta from the clutches of a Phil Reina, my young, but well-intended mechanic.

"I take it my car is ready?"

"Yes, justa 'bout," Phil muttered as he perused the yellow pages.

"So . . . what was it, the temperature gauge?"

"Well no, sorry, you were almost out of radiator fluid. Your bottom hose was cracked. Didn't you see any fluids leaking out of this old boat?"

I could only grimace and admit my ignorance. The mechanic walked me over to the shade of a giant oak tree, opened the hood, and showed me the new rubber hose near the bottom of the radiator.

"Said you drove in from Maryland? Lucky you got here."

"Really?"

"But you made it. We flushed the whole system for you . . . top to bottom . . . and went through the whole sha-bang. Matt'll top off the antifreeze for you in a minute and you'll be good to go. Get you off to a fresh start."

I could only smile and hope my good fortune might continue. "How's your Dad?" I asked.

"He's doing well right now," he returned with a sway of his head. "He doesn't like being retired, that's for sure, but he's dealing with it."

"Ever come by here?"

"Humph, all the time . . . regular as clock work. He's got a big sun porch and we set him up with easy chairs and lounge chairs, so he could sit in the sun like they use to in old Italy, 'specially at this time of year with the sun so high, but no, he still has to come down and tell everyone what to do or how to do it. Still thinks he runs the place."

"Well, that's the old generation; they are a tough bunch. Say hi to him for me."

"I will. But if I do I know he's gonna ask about the car. He always asks about the Buick."

"Sure, he sold it to me way back when."

"How many miles on that thing anyway?"

"Not sure. I stopped counting in 1980," I said with a smirk. "Think the odometer's been around three or four times?"

"Really? Well, keep drivin' it and I'll keep it goin'. Give Matt a couple of minutes and Sandra will get your bill together. Shouldn't be too long."

Phil went back to his desk and I found a soft chair in his little waiting room. There, right in front of me, I found another reason to smile and, as the old writer used to say, more than somewhat. There, on the counter top, was a copy of today's Pink Sheet. For those who have never had the pleasure of losing at Saratoga's races you probably do not know or understand my excitement. This is easily understood. You see the local paper uses bright pink paper for their racing section during the month of August. Yup, that's right . . . bright pink. Nothing could have warmed my soul any better than finding this lovely little letter. There were a few articles about the races and the harness track's entries. Some earnest handicappers had written columns trying to predict the winners and the losers for the meet, even before it started. That made me laugh. It's always like that, experts selling information in order to make some money to pay their bills. Everyone reads these articles with a grain of salt because after all, if the writer really knew anything about the races . . . I mean anything about picking horses . . . he wouldn't have to write for a paper; he'd just go to the track and win. Such reading is always fun, and around the Springs, the Pink Sheet is a glorious time-honored tradition. When I had exhausted its resources, I turned to the crossword puzzle in hopes of exercising my brain when a smallish man entered the garage and sat next to me. He introduced himself as Mr. Mullins and within a few moments we were in polite conversation.

"Of course I'm here for the races."

"Oh, well then maybe you will see my son Andy over there?"

"Really?"

"He's a senior at Saratoga Catholic next year. I got him a job working the grounds."

"Good job."

"His first real job."

"Really?"

"Certainly. Poor kid had a tough day yesterday."

"Really," I said.

And with that innocent introduction, I found myself drawn hypnotically into my first tale of the summer meet. It was a charming little story, one anyone might identify with as every moment in life has a beginning, a middle, and some form of commencement. It was a simple story told with much pride and anxiety, so emblematic of the adventures I always discover in this tiny hideaway in New York State. The father turned out to be an understanding gentleman, blessed with the patience of a pine tree. He was both enjoying his son's confusion at the vagaries of his first new job, while trying to provide just enough guidance to help him settle in and be successful. We spoke and laughed and shared. It was a nice way to spend a few moments with a temporary friend and a fine narrative inside Phil Reina's Garage.

As it turns out, it is a tale worth telling, and as best I can reconstruct its finer details, with some sympathetic imaginings thrown in to keep me happy, it follows as such.

Andy Edmund Mullin was a young man who had enjoyed this earth for seventeen years and two months. In the gloom of an early sunrise he tussled with his first day of work in much the same way as he jostled with his pillow. His cloistered mind clawed at itself, trying to maintain a firm grasp on its latest fantastic inventions. Alone in a warm dark deepness, he tried to will himself back to sleep, and beat to submission the stream of doubts and questions that imprisoned his every thought. The clock couldn't be saying six, not six in the morning, could it? Why didn't it say two or three? Why is it light already, why aren't there more hours of peace and darkness? Worst of all, when he surfaced, close to consciousness, the ultimate unanswerable query surfaced. Why did he ever say yes to his Father when the idea of a job was presented across the dinner table all those weeks ago?

"Andy," Mother's voice called from the foot of the stairs, "Andy, six o'clock, you told me to call at six." Her voice was gentle, a mother's voice trying to be universally apologetic, salubrious, and punctual. This was a trial she shared with her son, a rite all mothers survive in their own way. This was her son's

passage into early manhood, the movement of the years, and
the inevitable empty room. She sensed the very quality of her
motherhood was on trial this morning, and somehow, his demeanor
would be the measure of all the things she had done to instill truth
and pride in him. Yes, her voice had been more than a whisper,
but it maintained its genteel air for reasons ~~the~~ that could not be
understood from the security of a warm bed and the walls defended
by Red Sox pennants, the Star Ship Enterprise, and so many of
Walt Disney's minute conscripts.

Once on his feet, the reality of this day was inescapable. His
shower was brief and breakfast meteoric. He pulled on his T-shirt,
located his wallet, and stepped on to the porch to face the day.

"Andy," his Mother said, "have you got your driver's license?"

"Yes Mom."

"And the directions they gave you?"

"Yeah, in my wallet."

"And do you want a lunch; can I pack you a lunch?"

"Mom, it's four blocks. I'll come home."

"Did you comb your hair yet, I don't want . . ."

"Mom, I'll comb it when I get there. They got rakes don't
they?"

"Smart-Alex," she whispered to herself as she stood behind the
screen door. She wanted to watch him cross Jackson and Nelson
Avenue toward the racetrack. "Thou shall not cry," she said to
herself, "Thou shall not . . . !"

At the Nelson Avenue gate, the first person Andy met was a tall
and truly imposing security guard. She looked tremendous, ebony
black skin, six feet tall, with enormous eyes that could see through
a young man's heart. Her stare made him back up a pace before
summoning the courage to ask for the service employee's office
and Mr. Stewart.

"Straight ahead, past the escalator and then keep on going."

"Keep on going?"

"Yeah," she said, posing like an enormous weather vane, "all
the way down to the end of the grandstand. You'll see the signs."

Andy tried to come up with a polite thank you, but the
queasiness under his belt made him scurry in case the Gorgon

pursued him. Everywhere people swept by him with huge brooms, metal ladders, and over loaded carts. Men spoke a Spanish Mrs. Cord never taught him, while young waitresses, in full Skidmores, scurried through white doorways, and everywhere there were the sounds of hammers and drills and the scream of electric saws. He kept wondering how the place got so crowded, there were hundreds of people here who all knew what they were doing, and he didn't. Always the question, 'Why did today have to be today?'

"Mister, mister. Where's Mr. Stewart's office?"

"Dunno," the man in blue grey overalls said as he pulled the flatbed truck with its load of televisions.

Then there was a tiny fellow, half running, and half skipping toward an old Ford pickup truck parked next to a stack of large picnic tables. He asked his question again.

"Dunno," was the answer, again.

Next to a large support beam Andy found another security guard tugging against a heavy belt. This one appeared quite unlike the imposing creature he had met at the opposite end of the grounds. Andy thought he looked like someone he knew from school so he asked his question again, but again all he got for his trouble was . . . .

"Dunno."

He began to think that no one living soul in the entire place had a vocabulary beyond, 'Dunno'. I'll have to remember 'Dunno', he thought out loud to himself, that's a good word around this place. He began to practice 'Dunno's' as he walked down the length of the grandstand.

From a sheltered hallway out of the sun's rude intrusions, traffic came and went, and for a moment he wondered if he should look in there. It was dark and scary, and not a place where he was welcome. The young man peered into the subdued shadows and decided he was better off sitting under the warm security and the comfort of near-by trees.

Two men in dark blue suits emerged, both balding and fifty with enormous waistlines.

"Where the hell is Aubry and that Mullin kid?" one man said.

"Mullin?" the other man said.

"Got a call from security that he was here and . . ."

"I'm a Mullin sir," he proffered meekly.

The two men stared, "You're Mullin?"

"I'm Andy Mullin, I'm suppose to have a job here today," he could hear his voice wobbling under the strain of their eyes.

"Your Dad works at the car place downtown?"

"Yeah."

"Well, come' ear, you're twenty minutes late already,"

Late, Andy thought, how the heck could I be late, I'm barely here? Can somebody be late when they're lost?

Mr. Stewart quickly scribbled off some notes on a receipt paper. He attached them to a badge and scribbled Andy's name on it with a Scripto marker. "There, you're done, all set; report to Davine Geroux, down in the breakfast area of the clubhouse right away, you'll be working for her this summer. Good little job son."

"What'll I'll be doing, sir?"

"She'll tell you, just don't get caught up in any mischief. Did you go to orientation last week kid?"

"Yeah, sure. That's where I got this paper."

"Yeah, yeah, sure, sure, OK. Anyway, Mrs. Geroux'll give you something to do. Hurry up now, she's looking for 'ya, down there, at the end of the clubhouse, scoot."

"Scoot?" he muttered under his breath, "Now I'm scooting. I don't know if I want to scoot? First I'm lost, then I'm late and now I have to scoot. Am I being paid to scoot? What the heck is scoot anyway? This place is weird."

Davine Geroux turned out to be as strange as the day itself. She was a little woman with no chin, soiled blue denims, tennis shoes blackened with grime, and the tattoo of a blue serpent on her right arm. Even her hair attracted remarkable attention; it seemed to explode out of her skull like an ancient Greek nightmare. To a high school junior, it was obvious it hadn't seen the business end of a comb since Eisenhower left the White House. She was sweaty and disheveled and soiled, and gave the impression of always being ready to loose her temper. She, with a pair of young kids, was stacking patio chairs and tables.

"Opening day's tomorrow, and we got a lot 'a winter to get rid of," she kept saying, "gotta get winter out 'a here."

Andy finally introduced himself, and repeated Mr. Stewart's instructions. She looked at the signature, scowled, wiped a thick track of perspiration away from her eyes, and then shoved the papers back into his hands.

Mrs. Geroux introduced James and Patrick and told them to get to work. Patrick was a tall skinny kid he had known around school, but Jim was a smallish stranger. Soon they were hauling truckloads of picnic tables out by the walking circle and then, with no explanation, Mrs. Geroux made them bring the tables back where they started. Nobody knew why. For another hour they raked lawns and loaded wheel barrels with clippings, brown grass, twigs, and old plastic grocery bags. Andy wore out one pair of gloves and then got a rake burn at the base of his thumb. His shirt stuck to his back. Patrick talked about their old algebra teacher, while the other kid, Jim, entertained them with stories of his broken down high school, and a gym teacher who demolished the English language on a daily basis.

"When do we get a break?" Andy asked.

"Soon kid soon. But first we got some special stuff for you to do. Matter of fact, here, quick, go into the clubhouse area and get the guys downstairs, you know, in the basement, to give you the left handed monkey wrench."

Andy used his free hand to shade his eyes and peer into Patrick's eyes, "Monkey wrench? Why a monkey wrench? My dad only uses them for plumbing and . . ."

"Sure, but we need it to put together these picnic tables."

"They are together."

"Some, some, but we gotta tighten up the bolts and stuff, you know, keep'em from wobbling."

"Sure," Hayes interjected, "going to run the Schuylerville tomorrow. Gonna have lots of people here, little kids'll be climbing all over these damn things. Don't want anybody getting hurt." His eyes flared open, and he nodded his head up and down trying to pull some level of acquiescence out of Andy.

Andy grinned, "Well, I suppose."

"Right in there, inside the building, just ask for old Joe. He'll tell you how to get to the basement where they keep the wrenches."

"Ok?"

So Andy was off to find the basement, and old Joe, and the left handed monkey wrench.

The first fellow he met was a giant of a man whose nametag read 'Wolfie', which made Andy laugh a little. But when he asked 'Wolfie' for a left handed monkey wrench, all the guy did was laugh so hard he showed his back teeth. Andy stood there, under the shadow of an awning in a kaleidoscope of confusion. 'Wolfie' never said a word, he just walked away shaking his head. Then a balding man with a ponytail stopped to listen to his question and smiled. He rolled his eyes, which made Andy even more uncomfortable.

"Kid, ka'mere," he said, "It's under the dietetic dog food in the kitchen, but don't tell no-body." The guy chuckled and walked away.

Andy's head was beginning to ache, and gnawing suspicions were growing in his imagination. His throat knotted and his confusion returned. He couldn't understand why his eyes were burning.

Near the stand where bettors rented binoculars during the racing season, Andy found a large ponderous red door that looked promising. There was no doorknob or handle, but it was big. He knocked on the door, pushed, and knocked again. Nothing. He turned away, but heard a noise behind him. The door, just that fast, was gone, and a powerful looking man in a stained sweatshirt with a pencil in his teeth, was standing where the door used to be. His great square jaw set his enormous teeth against the pitiful pencil and his red eyes glared at Andy. Andy's throat knotted into a tourniquet.

"You knock?" he asked.

Andy was suddenly scared.

"Hey you, kid, you! You want something?"

"Ahhh," was Andy's only recovery.

"I'm busy kid; this damn elevator is a pain in . . ."

"My boss and the guys, they want the wrench," he stammered.

"Wrench?"

"Ah," Andy was fighting desperately with his stomach to collect words, "the guys I work with need old Joe's wrench."

"Huh? I got no tools here, these are all mine. See the nametag, Scholenbach. Do I look like my name is Black or Decker?"

"No, no, I mean Jimmy and . . . and . . . Patrick, ah, they want the left handed monkey wrench."

The man standing in the doorway spit out his pencil. "The what?"

Andy repeated himself, suddenly feeling even more self-conscious, and tried to resist the faint whisper in his mind that told him he was in the middle of a very bad joke. "It's in the basement. They told me to get the wrench for the tables."

The man stepped out of the elevator, reciting the names of an entire litany of religious prophets, icons, and heroes. "Kid, look, you're being played for a chump, and we ain't got no time for chumps to-day."

"Chump?"

"A chump. Look pal, 'Dare' ain't no such thing as a left handed monkey wrench." He paused laughing, "There ain't no such a thing as a right handed monkey wrench. In fact 'dare' ain't nothing in the world but monkey wrenches. Sometimes you need a regular old monkey wrench, or sometimes a bigger monkey wrench, and a once in a long, long while you need a really, really huge monkey wrench. But that's it; kid, you are being played for a chump."

"Really?"

"For sure. And worse than that, the basement in this joint, the one you are looking for."

"Uh-huh."

"It does not exist neither."

"No?"

"Sorry kid, there is no such thing as a basement full of tools here. Your buddies are playing a joke on you."

"There's no . . . ?"

"Nope. Tell me, is this your first day?"

"Yeah," Andy muttered sheepishly.

"I thought so."

The man put an arm around Andy's shoulders and nodded to him, "Come on, show me where you're bosses are. We're going to have a little conversation."

Andy's clouds of confusion swirled.

After Mrs. Geroux stopped screaming, she lined the three boys up against the Travers porch bar like the bright yellow bulls-eye of an archery target. She was letting out a river of the hottest language Andy had ever heard. He never knew, would have never guessed, that a woman's mouth could make such sounds. The fire did not go out of her voice for a full minute. The burning in his eyes was scaring him again, and he didn't know why.

Finally Mrs. Geroux was out of breath. She stood there slapping her palms together as if she was brushing off the grime of the day. The glare of triumph burned through the boys but Jim Hayes wouldn't stop chuckling.

"Stop laughing," Andy protested when they finally got back to their rakes, "What's wrong with you, didn't you hear how mad she was?"

"Yaaa," Jim smirked, "boy was she hot. Did you see the way she kept spitting on herself?"

"And the way that stuff was running out of her nose," Patrick howled. Both boys laughed so hard they dropped the table they were carrying.

"You guys are crazy or something," was the best retort Andy could devise.

Ten minutes later a half dozen young women came down the clubhouse steps and stepped out into the daylight. Their voices were buzzing and sharp over the sounds of power tools and stereos. Some looked into mirrors, one lit a cigarette, but mostly they stood and chatted and laughed. Jim put his broom down.

"Ay. Ay, things are looking up Bo-Bo!"

Patrick turned, following his friend's eyes, "Holy Hannah, look at all that talent."

"Oh man," Jim kept saying, "where's my knife and fork, dinner is served."

"Kid, look," Patrick said elbowing Andy and chanting like some bewildering television salesman, "Tom-Tom, look over there, over there. Oh my God, I've died and gone to Heaven. Thank you Lord for my deliverance!"

Andy thought this guy Patrick shouldn't be speaking about God and stuff right now, especially in a racetrack.

"Kid," Patrick said again, "Look."

Andy didn't move.

"Come here and look, we got something good for you."

Andy knew what was behind him, "Why, you going to tell me those girls have got the left handed monkey wrench?"

Jim smirked, "Good one. Maybe we could take'em to the basement too. That could be fun."

"Poor guy's scared of the girls, I guess," Patrick said with his best mocking tone.

"Ha-ha," Hayes laughed. "You're not. Are you, really? You scared 'a girls? Well this should be fun, they're coming this way."

"I'm not scared of girls, I know lots of girls."

"Yeah, your sister."

"What's the matter with my sister, she's only ten."

"We ain't looking at your sister though, we're looking at the real deal, these girls ain't 10 and they're heading right for y-o-u."

"You're rotten," Andy protested quietly.

"Letting all that talent go to waste would be a real rotten if you asked me?"

"Criminal, I say," Jim announced, "criminal. I shall throw myself on the mercy of the court and beg for a public . . . public . . . . What do they call those cheap lawyers?"

"You dope," Patrick smiled, "public defenders."

"Ha . . . that's what I need. I must take the fifth, damn I wish we had a fifth to share with these young ladies . . . but I'm gonna need a lawyer right now if this crime is committed."

"What crime?" Andy asked, "You guys are going to get us into trouble again."

"We are not. We're just talking to some of the new girls here. Probably the new waitresses, right? No harm there." And with that he began to wave at a small clutch of the young women who were walking toward the offices. The ladies were laughing out loud and chattering away. Some covered their open mouths, and others seemed to be gasping for air.

Andy put his rake back to work, "Going to get us in trouble."

"What's the matter Crystal?" Patrick said hesitantly, sneaking a peek at the woman's nametag.

The women looked at each other and renewed a new chorus of shrill screams.

"Sounds like something good to me," Jim offered.

"Oh, it's nothing," another girl said, catching her breath.

"Come on," Patrick begged, "let us in on it, please."

"Don't," a raven haired girl shot out, "Sandy, don't you dare, don't say anything, we don't know these boys!"

Jim and Patrick looked at each other, knowing they were near a break through.

"Meghan, please, I mean I can't keep this bottled up, it's the most unheard of thing ever. Oh my God!"

The squealing returned.

The raven haired Meghan stepped forward as if petitioning the three strangers for some relief clearly lacking in her feminine friends. Finally, with one last burst of impudent pride she decided to share her story with the all male jury. "Come on, you've seen a can of Hawaiian Punch haven't you?"

Patrick, Jim, and Andy were held in a vice of silence, "Course." The girls screamed anew.

"Well," she continued, "and have you ever noticed the label? You know the label with the volcano and all the red stuff pouring out of it. Well . . . well . . . doesn't it look like the juice is coming out of the volcano, doesn't it?"

Crystal was rocking back and forth, about to explode, "Meghan, be real!" She turned to look Andy in the eyes. "She told the chef upstairs, the chef for God's sake, and told him he should have Hawaiian Punch on the menus 'cause it would be sexy. Can you believe it, she said sexy. People would think it was sexy drinking juice that came straight out of the Kilauea, the volcano. Oh, my God!" The woman was close to expiring she was laughing so hard.

"Don't believe them," Meghan said to the three boys, "don't believe them, that's all I have to say."

"Oh Meghan," a third girl said out loud over her laughter.

"And don't you start, don't you start Janet," Meghan protested, "You're the one; I remember when you thought you had counterfeit M & M's."

The roared returned. Andy was dazed.

"Counterfeit M & M's?" Patrick had to speak. "What the heck are counterfeit M & M's?"

"Her," Meghan said, with a surge of new found confidence, "Miss Smarty-Pants, Janet. I can remember the day she thought her M & M's all had E's on them, 'E's'. Gave some poor little guy hell in the mall. Some poor little guy from Pakistan, or India, or some place. Didn't know what she was screaming about, or saying, or nothing. Miss Smarty Pants."

"And even when we turned the things around to show her the 'E's were 'M's, she still wouldn't stop barking at the poor guy. Probably was on a plane the next day."

"Splush," was the only defense Janet could muster.

Even the boys had to laugh now. Counterfeit M & M's. Bystanders were chuckling . . . and then . . .

Mrs. Geroux reappeared. No sedative known to medical science could have displaced the mirth of the moment as quickly as her phlegmatic face. The ladies smirked, made faces of mock sympathy, and began to slide away. She gave the waitresses a dirty look and watched them move away. She glared. She didn't mention the feminine distraction once, just summoned her best stern voice, and told Patrick and Jim to get up on the third floor and ask for Louie. There was a freezer that needed moving, and it had to be done right now.

Then she turned to Andy. "You, get over to the breakfast area and . . ."

"The what?"

"Breakfast. What are you stupid or something? Breakfast!"

His eyes were filling and his jaw tightened, "Breakfast?"

"Don't you know nothing?" she growled. "They run a big breakfast here, lots of fancy people; they eat here, and watch their damn horses run around."

"Oh."

"You don't know anything do you? Damn kids. Come with me."

Andy felt his knees go numb for a second. The onslaught had set him back, and he didn't know how to react, he just followed in silence. She walked him as far as the gate beneath the red and white awnings. There were women there in fancy clothes and great hats, many with meticulously dressed children in tow. Other groups of people were alighting from large white limos in their Sunday best, chattering away and looking curiously lost. They all seemed to be stumbling around in a daze and staring at some prodigious monument or some wondrous apparition. Andy was stunned trying to understand why all these people were here at this hour?

"Here, back here, behind the hedge. For the next couple of hours, you, Mr. Know-Nothing, you have to help Mr. Peters here with the backstretch tours. Now take this counter thing." She put the small silver machine into the palm of his hand. "The backstretch tours start here. You stand here and use that thing to count the people as they get on."

"Count? On?"

"Yeah count. You know how to count don't 'ya?" No more than 75 people per trip. Understand?"

"Ah . . . well?"

"Jesus . . . there are tours of the backstretch, the people ride around in a tram, you know, a bunch of stupid little carts, they go all through the horsy stuff over there in the stables. You stay here and help Mr. Peters, you count so he knows when the trams are full." Her voice was becoming slow and mocking of his intelligence. "No more than 75 people get on. Get it? There's only 75 seats, so we only let 75 people get on. Kabish?"

"I think so?"

"What's not to get?" she was nearly screaming. "Just count the people and tell Peters."

"Who's Peters?"

"Ah Christ," she growled out loud, "thick as a plank. Mr. Peters is the guy who runs this area."

"But who is he?"

"Just read the nametags, he'll be the one who's wearing the one that says 'Peters'."

"And then what?"

"Then what? What? Well then get on with it. Today's tours start in a coupl'a minutes and they end about noon. When they're done, you work with Peters keeping the place neat and swept up. After the damn trams stop running, he'll send you back to me. Ok?"

Mrs. Geroux charged off. Andy exhaled. Fear was an overpowering principle, especially when it storms your battlements during the very first hours of your first day of your first job. Andy looked past the great walking circle peering between the elms to see if he could catch a glimpse of his home. He considered leaving, but was unable to master his inertia. Then Peters, with his official nametag, materialized. "Ready to get started kid?"

Within minutes masses of humanity began collecting under the awning waiting their tour of the backstretch. Just that quickly there was an explosion of confusion and angry voices darting across the Traver's Porch. A tall impressive man in a shiny gray suit was charging out from the porch area. He had two smaller people scurrying to keep up with him.

"Peters, Peters, have you seen this Mrs. Geroux?"

"She was here a while ago," was all he could say.

"Damn!"

The group dashed off toward the clubhouse escalator. Peters looked at Andy and shrugged his shoulders. Another new face appeared: small, seventy, rotund and strained.

"Hey Peters, Mr. Carden, have you seen him?"

"Yeah Billie, just a minute ago, looking for that Geroux lady."

"Which way did he go?"

Peters gestured toward the escalator, "That way I think. What's up?"

"You won't believe it. Depalo got sent home and Aubry's in the hoosegow downtown. Got into a fight last night and . . ."

"So?"

"So, we got no driver for the second tram. Look at this mob, the place is filling up already, damn Governor's here, all the newspapers and TV idiots. This could be a real mess. With all these big shots around they didn't want anything going wrong and . . . ."

"We've gotten by with one tram before," Peters mused, returning to his broom, "no big deal."

"Oh yeah, tell that to Carden?"

Andy played with the little silver counting device and pushed some crushed stones about with his feet.

A tram clattered up to the clubhouse and rumbled to a stop. Seven small carts all tied to a motorized lead. A man in a green polo shirt and jeans jumped out and waved at Andy. "Hold'em kid . . . count out the first group, but don't let them on yet. Hey Peters, did Carden get a hold of you?"

"Of course, but I mean what the hell am I suppose to do?"

"Another driver?"

"Who for Christ's sake, who?"

The men began to argue and kick small stones around and finally they seemed to throw their hands in the air and admit defeat. It was all the hottest kind of language anyone had hear in quite some time, even Mrs. Geroux would have blushed. Every time someone came up with a way out of their dilemma someone else reminded them of another reason why their idea didn't apply, at least not today when every living creature the New York Racing Association could gather was somewhere else trying to catch up with tomorrow's opening.

People were scurrying every which way, ducking caustic blasts, taking on unknown tasks, and generally looking for a place to hide. Tourists admired the confusion but only snickered.

And that was how Andy, the small boy in a man's body, came to be the driver of the second tourist tram that day as the old racetrack got ready for yet another racing season. He protested, but was denied. He tried to run away, but was stopped by the visage of his disheartened mother. His eyes watered a little, testimony to fears, but no one noticed; he had a driver's license, and, according to the bosses, that meant he was the driver of the tram today. They threw him a bright white shirt with gold trim and told him to pull it on. It smelled funny, like Dad's work shed, and had a long brown stain on the left sleeve, but it was his, at least for as long as he drove the tram.

Colin Brockway, the actual guide, jumped backed into the lead car right next to Andy, microphone and loudspeaker in hand. He was suppose to tell Andy where to go, where to stop, and then give the customer's anecdotes or abbreviated histories about the way real racehorses live on the backstretch. He gave Andy a pat on the back and with a quick nod, tried to reassure him that they were going to be just fine.

"How'd you get stuck with this gig kid?"

Andy shook his head. All he could think of was, "Dunno."

"Where'd you get that shirt?"

"They told me to put it on. I don't really like it, but . . ."

"Yeah, its one of old man Depaolo's shirts," he said with a laugh. "Must be two sizes too big for you! You could use it for a freakin' circus tent. Fits this place today."

Andy could only raise his eyebrows and shrug again.

"The old man ain't gonna like this, but I don't care if he don't. Well, I'm Colin, my Mother calls me Colin, but my friends call me Hap, cause I'm always happy. I mean, I don't give a damn 'bout nothing, so don't ask me to get worried or care. I won't. I teach school all winter long and this job just gets me out of the house so the lovely Mrs. Brockway can't tell me what a bad guy I am. So, for better or worse, let's get this crate up where it'll do some good and we'll see what happens."

"Sure."

Hap showed Andy where the 'forward' lever was and reminded him of the throttle and brakes. There was terror in these knobs and dials. Andy put the machine's go-lever into forward and quickly managed to get the empty tram around from behind the fountain. The machine growled and snapped while the car heaved and bounced beneath them. "Is it suppose to do that?" Andy asked with his brain in a freeze. Hap started laughing.

"What's the matter?" Andy asked at the sound of grinding wood.

"Ha, kid, didn't you hear that? You took out the stop sign. Knocked it flat. Look!"

"Oh no," Andy whispered. "Am I gonna be fired or something?"

The broken sign was removed and Hap and Andy waited while the first tram loaded and departed. Andy tried to relearn the routine of breathing. He was shaking, perspiring, and still wondering if there was any way he could escape and just go home. He didn't dare take his foot off the brake. If he did, he just knew something horrible was going to happen. A little girl in a bright pink dress with dramatic black trim walked in front of their tram. Andy tried to get her to go away. "Please don't walk in front of this thing, please."

"Our turn," Hap whispered in his ear, "Watch'em load and smile a lot." The cars lurched and jumped and growled again. When they arrived at the loading area, Hap used Andy's counter and the tram began to fill. The more people came forward, the more Hap laughed and commented on the stream of tourists they were going to entertain.

"You a school kid Andy?"

"Sure, I'm a senior."

"Well, keep your eyes peeled, you're gonna get an education."

Andy looked over his shoulder to watch the unsuspecting victims assume their position. He looked into each person's facade, petitioning relief somehow, but none was coming. Each seemed enwrapped in the cool indifference that over-confidence always brings. Andy kept thinking,' If they only knew'. None returned his glances. He sighed deeply and prepared to face his destiny.

"Where, oh where, did they get this bunch?" Hap kept repeating under his breath.

Andy didn't want to look anymore.

"Look at this collection! Are these cats out on parole?"

The first tenant to load sat right behind the Andy. He was an older man, wearing a loud plaid jacket and a strange little double billed hunter's cap that highlighted his extensive sideburns and two enormous ears. He was holding an oversized meerschaum pipe and a small notebook. When he settled in, he crossed his legs and adjusted a pair of bright argyle socks. He was the picture of a language professor on sabbatical.

Right behind him came a smallish round faced man with bulging eyes, a fire hydrant neck, and a jacket that glowed in the sunlight. He took up most of the seat next to the first. His great girth spread out like an angry oil spill. His eyes were swollen, nearly closed, and his mouth rested on layers of heavily-tiered chins that poured out of his shirt collar. When he sat down, all he could manage was one great desperate gush. Stevie Wonder could have found his hot pink sport jacket in a coal mine.

"Did you see that one kid," Hap whispered to Andy, "must weigh 400 pounds . . . better count him twice huh?"

A tall man with bright red hair and beard of similar shade jumped into the second car. His buddy was more athletic looking with thinning salt and pepper hair. He was wearing a blue polo shirt, cargo slacks and green tennis shoes that gave Hap a chance to make rude color blind jokes. Sitting next to each other, they were hard to ignore; they were arguing. The tall man no sooner stepped up into the second car when he whirled, and pointed an angry finger at the man next to him.

"You are a dope, you know that, a dope." he said so anyone could hear.

"Please, you hurt me; I thought The Coach might want to come with us, that's all. I didn't know he was waiting for a pal. How was I supposed to know that? Please, I'll bring my crystal ball next time, we can use it to pick some winners," the other man said laughingly. Andy was confused.

"Just stay away from me. You sit back there and try to be an adult."

"Come on," the second man said, "have a beer, I got lots of'em in my pockets right here. Here, here have a beer, you'll feel better."

"Nick, you are sick. You know that, sick. Beer, at this hour of the morning? Just stay in your own seat and watch the pretty horses. Maybe you'll learn something . . . but I doubt it."

"Why are you so unhappy today? This is a vacation, don't be so grumpy. Come on now, what's better than a beer? Tell me. Come on, I've got four or five brew-skis in here, one has your name on it. Come on! It would make me feel proud if I gave you your first beer of the summer."

"Sit down!" was all the tall man could say to end the debate.

A fifth man, who appeared to have been born in the previous century, squeezed into the next car and sat behind Nick. Immediately he had to hide his face as he began to cough and sputter until suffocation seemed at hand. The man enjoyed just a momentary reprieve when another encore of adenoidal wheezing evolved into a metronomic sneezing performance. The afflicted creature buried his face in a handkerchief just to keep from coating his new neighbors with debris. His face was turning rainbow shades. Nick and his sidekick looked back at the desperate gasps as if expecting the appearance of a lung. Even the professor turned to observe the performance. Finally, when the retching had subsided, the man came up for air wearing a curious smile, happy to have simply survived. Nick offered him a beer.

"Help yourself," Nick said with a gigantic grin "Go ahead, this'll kill that nasty cold . . . beer is the solution."

His red-headed cohort turned around, but shook his head in defeat.

"Oh no, I'm sorry, I'm not sick . . . really" the little man said from behind his grimy handkerchief, "really, it's my allergies . . . my allergies."

"Oh sorry, you sure sound sick. Here, beer is good for allergies too, here; it'll knock it right out of you."

"Well thank you, I think, but I'm not really sick. Do I look sick?"

Nick peered over his Foster Grant's. "Let me see, truthfully you do look a little pinked. I've seen sick folks that looked better than you."

"Oh dear," the little man groaned as he withdrew into his handkerchief for another round of asphyxiation.

"Do you mind," the redheaded man growled over his shoulder. "Just leave people alone . . . mind your own business. Just mind your own business."

Nick smiled back at his accuser. "Come on Professor Life-Coach, I got the cure right here. Twelve beautiful ounces of Dr. Coors best work."

"What a dope!"

It was just as the passenger's exercise in empathy had subsided that a striking young woman, in a dramatic black dress and white linen blazer, appeared from beneath the Traver's Bar canopy. Diamonds shimmered beneath cascading black hair that tumbled over her shoulders and flirted with the morning breeze. A small swarm was following her, each with a camera or microphone in tow. She strode toward the tram with the effortless nonchalance of a Marchen princess.

"Who the heck is that?" Hap whispered with breathlessly.

Andy remembered his lesson from the morning, "Dunno."

"Well you should man. Don't be shy. You should be finding out these things."

"Dunno," seemed the safest place to be right now for Andy.

"I wish I did. Hey, isn't that Liz Bishop from the TV station over there? That dame in the black outfit must be somebody famous. Hey, we're gonna be on the evening news. Isn't that great!"

The woman turned and spoke into a microphone for a moment and then was joined by two slender young men in meticulously tailored dark suits. They all carried something useful in their left hands, a valise or notebook, and seemed to be riveted on the woman's every move.

"Maybe she's a queen or something, you know, from Siberia or one of those little 'stan''s outside Russia, you know," Hap murmured to Andy, but Andy didn't dare offer an opinion.

"Hey kid, this is big. Look at those servant guys she's got following her. Look at'em." Everyone seemed to have little to do but watch this woman take center stage. She moved confidently toward Andy's tram, but turned one last time to wave to the assembly behind her.

"My God kid," Hap sputtered, "did ya see the skating rink she's wearing on her hand? And, and, the bracelets . . . the earrings. Did you see that?

"No what?"

"'Diamonds kid, 'da diamonds. If those things are real they gotta be worth millions. Hole-ee, size of golf balls. That doll is worth a fortune. You oughta find out who she is kid. Want me to introduce you?"

"No," Andy muttered, he had already endured enough embarrassment around women for one day. "No, thanks."

"Will you look at that? Will you look at that? Miss Fancy Pants is getting on our tram. What is a rich doll like her doin' riding a tourist tram? Some publicity stunt?"

Andy could only shrug his shoulders in a minuscule gesture of ignorance as the lady in black, and her followers, slowly boarded the last cars. The young men hurried about and settled into their seats with all the polish and poise of juvenile penguins about their hen.

"Maybe she's looking for a new boyfriend kid? Maybe you could be her knight in shinning armor? Huh? Whata'ya thinks? Wanna be a Prince? Nothing ventured as they say, nothing ventured . . ."

The other cars loaded, children in their Sunday best, grandmothers guarding chunky third graders with cameras, and a small group of men, each wearing blue pins with a large letter 'A' in the middle. A voice yelled from the back of the tram.

Andy put the drive lever into forward and bounced softly as the tram emerged from the security of the canopy into the glaring sun beaming directly over head. The day seared his neck and his back dampened with sweat. Just that quickly the shirt had an odor.

"All set, let's go kid, and watch your speed . . . hey, hey . . . slow down . . . slow down. Ah damn, there goes another stop sign!" Andy flinched and looked behind, desperate for good news. All Andy could see was the man in the plaid jacket, engaged in vigorous conversation. Andy couldn't help but hear.

"My good fellow," he was saying, "I am a doctor, and I am sure you are dealing with some of the usual allergies, not a cold, given the time of year and all."

Nick, after swilling down twelve ounces without interruption, leaned across the car and inserted himself into the exchange, "Me too, I thought so!"

"What the hell do you know?" his red-headed friend said.

"Well I am a doctor and the pollen . . ."

"I'm not talking to you," the surly red-haired man growled, "I'm talking to this dope here."

"Who's a dope?"

"You're a dope!"

"I'm sorry sir, but I am a doctor."

"Who are you? Am I talking to you?"

"I am a physician."

"Yeah, and this guy next to me here is a dope. So what?"

The doctor in the plaid jacket tried to look past the two combatants and speak directly to the other gentleman who was having such a difficult time breathing.

"Do you need some help, sir?"

"Maybe he swallowed a bug?" Nick interjected, "a beer would wash that right down, believe me, right down."

"My dear man," the good doctor offered in a genteel manner.

"You are a dope. Bugs, be real," growled the red-head.

"Hey," said Hap quietly, "look, the guy in that blow torch jacket, he's snoozin' already. I think he's passed out. He must be wasted to snooze on this tram."

"I can't look," Andy whispered, "which way do I go?"

"Horse Haven. No, not that way, left kid, go left, toward Horse Haven, left."

"Where?"

"Horse Haven."

"What's that?"

"This is great," Hap said over and over again in mock derision. But from the back, "Go on Doc, give him a beer."

The sneezing and coughing recommenced from the third car. The gagging was becoming melodic. Hap started laughing in Andy's ear and the distraction was getting annoying.

Nick turned around and, with a wave of a new beer can, found the eyes of the lady in black, and started a new conversation, "Don't mind him," he declared with a magnanimous smile, "my friend's always a little peevish when he's around pretty women." She nodded politely.

"Will you stop," his friend barked, "leave the women alone, they don't want to talk to you."

"Stop what?" he replied with perfect naïveté. "This is your Uncle Nicky, I'm trying to help you folks. I like helping people, that's my calling in this life. Here pal," he said to the unconscious traveler behind him, "have a beer."

"Yes I'm sure, but . . . ," the doctor was trying to offer more suggestions about asthma and the effects of tree pollen when Nick looked him in the eye.

"Doc, hey doc," he said quite loudly, over the racket and clatter of the tram wheels, "you a person doctor or a dog doctor or a shrink kinda doc?"

"I am a medical doctor, if that is what you mean?"

"Well then, tell my friend here about the medicinal uses of alcohol, tell him. I heard it on Oprah that alcohol is good for you."

"Well in moderation it can . . ."

But the doctor's directive was interrupted by the taller man.

"Moderation, save your breath mister, he can't spell moderation."

There was an argument amongst strangers before they left the shadow of the clubhouse. The tram cleared the clubhouse turn and, near Horse Haven, Hap took up his microphone and tried to explain how and why thoroughbreds are routinely walked in endless circles by a machine, weighed directly after exercising, and given haircuts by a barber. From one of the cars there were voices. Within seconds a new featherweight battle of wits renewed.

"No way. No real, honest to goodness, gonna-be-a-queen-someday-fancy-pants-movie star-type-broad, is going for a line like that. You are wasting your time." It was Nick again. He was standing up in the car, talking to his red-headed friend while trying to retrieve another beer can from the bottom of his cargo pants pocket. He was laughing and trying to make eye contact with the other residents of the tram. He reached behind him to one of the young men, and presented the can. "Hey, kid, here, give that lady a beer. If the sick guy don't want it, maybe she's got a thirst?"

The man looked astonished.

"Go ahead, she'll like it."

"Will you stop," his friend chimed in again. "Stop!"

Andy was startled and he took his eyes off the tram path for a second to look behind him. He could hear Hap laughing through his microphone. Apparently the spectacular lady who had been getting all the attention earlier was still attracting more.

"Don't believe everything you hear, especially form a guy like this." The red-haired man seemed to be speaking to anyone who would listen.

Someone queried, "How do you know she's gonna be a queen?"

Someone else murmured, "All the queens were shot in the last war."

"Who the hell are you to be talking?"

Andy was trying to twist his ears to the back without turning his head. The fun seemed to be behind him. He could hear someone snoring loudly. Whoever it was, they were sputtering and gasping like Casey Jones's old steam engine.

"She wouldn't give you the sweat off . . ."

"Hey, it's a racetrack, you never know."

"I wish your wife was here to see this. You're just an old curl-smudgeon," Nick was trying to be coherent between bursts of laughter.

"And your ugly enough to wear a saddle, ya' big dope!"

The man in the plaid jacket interjected himself again. "I believe you mean curmudgeon."

"Huh?" was all Nick had to say between great quaffs of Coors Light.

Hap leaned in again, "Are you getting some of this kid? This is amazing stuff we got back here."

Andy shrugged and tried to miss an enormous pothole, unsuccessfully. The doctor lost his pipe. The red-head swore, Nick spilled his beer, but the sleeper never budged.

Dozens of mounted horses cantered past the tram. The riders were mostly young women and smallish men, enwrapped by heavy protective vests. One young lady displayed an enormous golden pony tail that shimmered in the morning sun across her back. She smiled at the tourists and Hap nearly lost his balance trying to wave back at her.

There were more laughs as Andy steered the tram around a trash near a barn. A horse was being bathed, steam spiraling off long layers of muscle and bone, curling into an ancient oak tree. Andy was watching so intently, as the grooms cleaned under the tail and rear legs, that he didn't hear Hap until it was too late. The tram slammed into a steel drum garbage can and ricocheted into a large wooden horse crossing sign. The wooden posts cracked like artillery fire. The horse jumped to its left and the groom's garden hose splattered into the length of the tram. Everyone was caught in an unexpected shower. Some screamed, others laughed. The assistants jumped, trying to cover the lady, and the tall man with the red hair swore.

"My goodness!"

"Oh God?" Andy sputtered in bitter panic.

"Stop the tram kid, brakes, hit the brakes!"

"Who's the idiot"

"Son of a . . ."

Water was everywhere; another cloud burst flooded the cars when the groom dropped the gushing hose.

The horse reared up and whinnied, a desperate frightened call. The groom yelled and grabbed for its halter, but it was already up on its hind legs. The horse was tipping over on its back, frantic legs crawling through the air.

"Steer kid, steer, over there, get out of here!"

"For Christ's sake!" The horse had jumped up on all fours and was off at forty miles an hour. Grooms were swearing in Spanish and broken Cajun English. Security guards blew whistles and sirens began to scream. Everywhere people were yelling.

Nick was laughing despite the confusion raging just yards away, "You're all wet! Does that mean you are going home for the day?"

"Kid you gotta listen!" Hap said as the tram came to a jolting stop with one wheel stuck in a storm drain. The cars crashed together and the engine stalled.

Andy's eyes were burning, he didn't want to cry, but he knew he was about to when Hap yelled stop again. Andy turned to look at the passengers. The tall man and his friend were pushing and shoving and just about to get into an old fashioned punch up. The doctor was cringing and crouching in front of his seat. Andy saw the spectacular lady in black and white crawling over the back of the car, not wanting to risk another dowsing. Her assistants scurried to lend a hand and appealed with their eyes for some deliverance. Even the man with the cold had found a way to hide under an upturned collar, but tripped and fell flat on his face; he was catapulted headfirst into mud and hay. New rounds of swearing!

Andy looked into the second car. There was one man fast asleep. His chin was on his chest and his eyes were closed shut. Andy smiled for the first time.

"Somebody call the supervisor will you," Hap said, "This damn thing's stuck good."

Later, inside the clubhouse, Mrs. Geroux was pushing garbage cans around and dragging small white tables across the Travers patio. Andy approached in silence . . .

"They sent me back here," he said.

"Who's they?"

"Some guy."

"Some guy?"

"Yeah, he said I couldn't drive the tram anymore, I had to help you with . . ."

"The tram," she was almost yelling, "who told you to drive the tram?"

Andy remembered his morning lesson well, "Dunno. Some guy said if I had a license I had to drive the tram."

"You're kidding, right?"

"Naw, some guy."

"With passengers?"

"Yeah,"

"Real people?" Mrs. Geroux collapsed into a chair with her head in her hands.

Later that night.

"Mom, it's OK, I'm gonna get out of these wet things and shower."

"Sure Andy. What did you do today?"

The boy thought a minute, "Stuff. Different stuff."

"Like what?"

"Aw, nothing special, you know, cleaning stuff up. Mom, I want to get cleaned up."

"Just throw those clothes down the stairs Andy," she fretted, "Oh, poor Andy."

"Ma, I ain't poor. Remember this job is going to get me rich."

"Just throw them down the stairs, I'll take care of them, and I'll get your supper together."

"Good," was all he could say as he lunged into the shower. For the first time in his life he understood the word tired.

In fresh underclothes, he sat on the edge of his bed to consider the task of pulling on clean Wranglers. Some mathematics snaked into consciousness. Eight dollars an hour meant maybe sixty-four dollars plus some overtime. He wondered out loud if that was the way life was measured, in overtime. The July evening was still bright, and he spent some moments looking out his window at the peaks of the old racetrack visible from his room. Those people he had met today, some of them were still there, still sweating, still breaking their backs with saws, and shovels, and wheelbarrows.

"Supper's ready," she called from the foot of the stairs.

"Right there," he answered.

Andy reviewed some of the college pennants that decorated his back wall, Colgate, Hamilton, Colby, and Drew. He kept thinking that these places better be worth all this trouble. He absentmindedly traced the face of Andy Kirk on his 'Old Yeller' poster and looked across the shelves at his collection of Disney souvenirs. His 'Disney-Friends, as Aunt Helen called them, were suddenly relegated to a distant arena of vapors and murmured echoes. Mickey was smiling at him from his perch on the dresser, but with a smile that would go unanswered today. Even Snow White and her miniature attendants were oddly stilted in manic poses. He rearranged their place on the mantelpiece. He brought the evil queen, and all her ceramic terrors, to the front of the bookshelf. "Even looks like Mrs. Geroux," Andy said smiling. He finished dressing.

Supper was a labor. His Mother's ability to ask questions seemed inexhaustible, and he was having a difficult time remaining polite. She was worried, and a mom, and well, he knew she was supposed to do this. This was the biggest thing in the world for him right now, and if she hadn't shown some interest he would have been hurt.

"Yeah Mom, six o'clock tomorrow morning. Mrs. Geroux said I worked OK, and that she wanted me in early for the breakfast crowd and stuff like that."

"That will be fine Andy. What will you be doing?"

He thought a moment, "Dunno?" he said with a sheepish grin.

Too Tall's Tale

You must understand that thoroughbred racing has always been a poet's paradise, an arena filled with majestic themes worthy of a Marlowe or a Racine. Those that leave their automobiles in parking lots and cross its threshold, breeders, owners or betting fans alike, become instantly immersed in a drama much larger than themselves. They are, each and every one, both gambler and gladiator; brave, intelligent, and most importantly, astute metaphysicians who must touch the agents of tomorrow.

And for the most adventurous of these purveyors of prognostication, few places on earth carry with it the same reputation for both high adventure and even higher romance as the summer madness of an August in Saratoga Springs. With more larceny than virtue behind their eyes, these brave souls leave the peace and safety of homes in Ascot, Dubai, Lexington, or Kildare to brave a migration into the pastoral elegance of the Adirondack foothills. There they gather in legions, when the calendar is right and the shadows of August return, to stake their claim on 'the Golden Fleece'.

So as I sat behind the wheel of my trusty old Buick, waiting for 'the ex' to reappear from another futile visit to the local herbalist, I could not help but to relive the strange convergence that led to last night's adventures in the thoroughbred sales ring on East Avenue. You see every night of the Saratoga sales is worth noting, with both enormous fortunes and egos at stake, but last night's performance proved to be exceptional. It even generated a small article in the morning's newspaper. Yes, it had been a great night, but it took some doings, some genuine metaphysical shenanigans to get all the players into place playing their parts. I witnessed some of this, overheard others sharing chapters here and there, and as best I can reconstruct I think I got the story straight, mostly. It started many days before, up in New England, as best I can make out, and, to the best of my information, this is how it went.

Central to all this was Ranson Hightower of Newport, Rhode Island, a gentleman who had long been part of these summer gambits up the Hudson. For decades he and his friends had anticipated the 'season' in Saratoga with great happiness. The Spa was always the high point of each summer, a string of chilled balsam nights framed by warm summer days that shimmered over expansive lawns and panoramic piazzas. The season had always been curative, leaving him renewed and optimistic about the fall.

But this year, as he reached for his favorite comb, he found himself wondering if this would be his last trip to play the races. His recollections had become wonderful warm memories, but now, sadly, just memories and little more. His ancient plastic comb, the one he always carried with him in his jacket pocket, was the last sentimental thing he owned to remind him of his wife. They had found it on the Orient Express, a dream vacation Janice wanted after reading Ms. Christie's novel in 1974. The next spring she would suddenly, and secretively, go back to France, never to return. His son, the professor, lost his life-long battle with Crohn's disease some time ago, and finally, when his best friend and business partner passed away, Ranson found his mornings becoming shorter and shorter. For a time, the season in Saratoga became solace of a kind. Cloaking himself in summer to both grieve and smile, he used this holiday to renew himself for the challenge of living. Three such Augusts had maintained him, but now the grieving was done and he was simply alone.

In about two hours the train for Saratoga would be leaving Newport. These 'special' trains are hired each year for the run to the Springs during the thoroughbred meet. They have long served as a grand reunion and revel of the first order. Old friends introduce new friends to even older friends, while champagne and kisses play their part in larceny and laughter. The enthusiastic banter never stops until the cars arrive at Saratoga's city station, where bags are jammed into Volvos or taxi cabs, and promises are made to share even more stories 'later in the meet.' Ranson knew this non-routine routine of the Racetrack Special, and for the first time he was not looking forward to it. He found himself grimacing and drifting toward his shaving mirror, not hurrying, just drifting, oblivious of the time.

From his bathroom's window, Ranson watched tourists rambling along the rocky shoreline with picnic baskets and Nikons. Newport's low tide is always an invitation for adventurous souls to gather amongst the enormous rocks, smile in the sun, rehearse many practiced gestures, and mug for the camera. Unconsciously he found himself watching the exploits of one particularly intent young man who was jumping from one great stone to another and then, suddenly, was in the Atlantic. Just as suddenly Ranson understood. The would-be gymnast hadn't slipped; he was trying to pull yet another man to the safety of the shore. An older gentleman had taken a nasty fall and was clearly injured. He was thrashing at the water and the waves, fighting through pain to regain control. Passerby's joined the triage while others keyed cell phones, and each found places to lend a hand.

Ranson watched the production unfold with almost scientific detachment. He bounced the comb against his knuckles and allowed the rescue to continue beyond panes of unmoving glass. The mini-drama ended as quickly as it had begun with good Samaritans escorting the casualty to solid ground.

"My land," he spoke to the walls, "snap out of it. Come on, get with it."

Ranson reached for his phone to dial 911 just as a police cruiser arrived. He slowly replaced the receiver, looked shamefully around his room, and then walked pensively to his kitchen. He considered leaving some last-minute instructions with the maids, but was lost in thought and never spoke a word. It was the third time in less than a week a situation had arisen that should have impelled him to act somehow, but instead apathy and inertia had left him numb. He found himself standing before another mirror in the great hall. He examined his reflection from several different angles until Mrs. Kaitlin passed through the image and stirred him from seclusion.

"Sylvia," he called.

"Sir?"

"Yes, a little something, but please speak your mind."

Sylvia was still.

"Don't look like that, it's not that bad, just a little something. Could you tell me . . . do I seem different lately?"

"Mr. Hightower?"

"You know, different, not really myself anymore?"

She never hesitated, "Mr. Hightower, please, I mean we've all changed, but you, no, not really, you're still Mr. Hightower, the best employer I've ever had." The woman stared at him with the eyes of a forensic pathologist. During her eleven years of service to Mr. Hightower, such personal exchanges had been reserved for Christmas, Easter, and funerals.

"Plainly now Sylvia, just listen. Anything at all over the last few . . . months . . . years?"

"Mr. Hightower, don't, please. You have always been the perfect gentleman and you still are. But tell me; is there something I should know?"

He regarded the woman before him intently. He trusted her eyes. "You are sure? You don't have to spare my feelings or anything like that. You see, I just had a peculiar . . . well you see, I've been thinking a bit and I'm afraid I'm a little disappointed . . ."

"Now, now, now, must be nervous or excited about your holiday. I know you still think so much about your son, but I wouldn't say it has changed you in any real way. I think you are just . . ." She found her voice dropping off as she realized the gravity of the conversation she had fallen in to . . . "Well anyone would expect a few ups and downs. Don't you see?"

He found the plastic comb in his pocket and turned to look out over the driveway. "Maybe I do need this vacation more than I thought?"

He watched the summer sun spread brilliantine on the silver maples along his drive and listened to a cardinal chirp below a window. Far past the highway, far past the half drawn curtains of his hall windows, sails of racing yachts bent against a northwest wind and garnished the horizon with elegant white diamonds. The peacefulness of his own home was making him self-conscious.

"Hurry Mrs. Kaitlin. Help me with my bags. I'm afraid I've over packed and I don't want to be late for my train."

As it turned out, the excursion to the Springs was all right; a first rate performance. It started out quietly for Ranson, a bright singular review of the New England coastline and the Connecticut hills. But then Martin Ewing found him in the club car and invited him to sit with his family for a round or two. And as soon as he left that group of happy people, Mrs. Dean McCall crept up behind him and pulled him, with a rude bear hug, toward her table to meet the 'folks.' Everywhere he looked, grand glowing faces displayed that countenance humans wear during pristine moments when family and friends reunite. Handshakes and kisses introduced stunning narratives, and each had effervescent tales to share of the moments that populated their lives.

Ranson felt quite peaceful by the time the car jangled and bounced to a stop. He had enjoyed so much Canadian whiskey, and the wake of so many cigars, his head was quite woozy. Much of his melancholia was gone and a tiny frye of hope was swimming somewhere in his brain. Maybe, he mused, this little trip will prove a blessing after all.

Tuesday passed snugly. The sun was warm and lunch on the patio of the Gideon Putnam Hotel reunited him with the son of another old friend, Bill Watterson. Some years ago Bill's father had trained a small stable of horses for Ransom and his partner. They had had some success together, winning their share of races at Hialeah and Aqueduct. He knew the racing operations had been turned over to young Bill two or three years previous. He was looking prosperous, a little too well fed for a man his age, but he was still one of the most genuinely likeable and magnanimous young men Ransom had ever met. Bill was also lunching on the great porch, waiting for his family to find him. His wife was at the baths, enjoying a massage and his two children were playing tennis. They had plans to attend a special performance the New York City Ballet was offering that evening at Saratoga's Art Center and, without so much as a wink, he was inviting Ranson to join them.

"Well, thanks, Bill, but I don't appreciate the ballet the way I should."

"Aw, come on, neither do I. I just close my eyes and listen to the music. If there is anything really interesting I need to know, I just ask my Marissa. She knows everything about ballet."

"Thanks, Bill, but there is one thing you might tell me. Maybe it's the air or the waters, but somehow I'm feeling a little lucky. I'm going to go to the races tomorrow, but I don't have a seat."

"Your box?"

"No, gave it up some time ago. My wife was always the one who wanted the box so, well, you know."

"Then join us. We'll be there, section AA. We'll be there by noon and you will be sitting with us."

Ranson smiled.

Thanks to a little guile and a dusting of luck, Ranson had whittled himself a place to sit on his first day at the races. He smiled as he crossed the enormous manicured lawns of the park. He liked the way his face looked in the reflecting pool outside The Springs Restaurant. It told him that he would have a delicious read that evening, and not with Gideon's Bible.

The next morning Ranson taxied to the track quite early. The Victorian splendor of the old place impressed him once more as it glowed through the summer humidity. The refrigerator white clubhouse was again greeting ebullient travelers as it had for over 135 years and he felt instantly at home. Ranson climbed the freshly oiled wooden stairs and quickly found the Waterson's box. Bill and his family were all there and they seemed quite happy to welcome this new member to their cast of characters. After an hour of laughing and story-telling, Ranson couldn't help but notice how his smile was beginning to ache.

Even the wagering was good to him. Handicapping must have something in common with bicycle riding he thought to himself. Of course, if little Billy Watterson hadn't been so eager to exhale in his ear while chomping his way through sauerkraut and hot dogs, he might have been a little more comfortable. And if Mrs. Waterson's recently divorced sister had kept her hemline a little closer to her knees, he might have been able to summon some additional reserves of concentration for the Racing Form. And worst of all, he might have hit the early daily double if he had seen Sunrise Dancer's recent three-furlong workout in 35 and 2/5 seconds, but his host insisted on whispering embarrassing jokes and back-slapping him dizzy with every punch line. Yes, he had missed his chance with Sunrise Dancer and the daily double, but in retrospect, a pink complexion and a few mild subluxations seemed a miniscule price to pay for this perch with friends, good cheer and a majestic view of the thoroughbreds.

However, in the fourth race, when Galaxy's Child held off Crimson Lady at 14 to 1, Ranson found his pockets stuffed with unexpected cash. The Wattersons roared with such rabid approval that the congratulations became a bit embarrassing.

"Dove Bars anyone?" Ranson offered, and after the hands were counted, Ranson was off on a merry mission of chocolate and philanthropy.

A happy attendant told him where to find the nearest ice cream van and Ranson began weaving his way through the clubhouse. Just before turning toward the Carousel Restaurant, his eyes were joined by an image only a privileged few might know. There, at the top of the clubhouse steps was one of Saratoga's great traditions, the unmistakable visage of Too Tall Teddy Beset. Ranson stared for a moment in light wonderment. If ever delusion or hallucination could persuade an observer that Saratoga's clubhouse was the harbor at Rhodes, well, clearly, here was its Colossus. Closer to seven feet tall than six, with a mane of flaming red hair and a manicured beard to match, Too Tall stood, arms crossed, guarding the comings and goings of each player as they climbed the stairway to the betting bays. Everyone who passed his way was observed, registered in his memory bank and, when needed, interviewed with advantage. In fact, at this very moment a new visitor to section B was in the penultimate stages of his interrogation.

"Hi, I'm Theodore Beset . . . Who Are You? . . . How long have you been coming to Saratoga? . . . Had any luck today? . . . What have you got? . . . . Holding any seats for later in the meet?"

It was an interview Ranson had survived many times, but it was a welcome face filled with the energy, hope, and honest excitement only the true horseplayer may easily understand.

"Theodore," Ranson called when the interviewee escaped.

"Hightower, you're here . . . we thought you were dead," Ted exclaimed.

"Good to see you. How are things?"

"Don't ask, do not even ask, I just got beat out of a thousand bucks, a thousand bucks by a lip, do you hear me, a lip. Look," he said over and over again holding up a losing ticket, "I got the pick three, but . . . but that bum, that B-U-M Mullen, whatever her name was, can't get past that other horse and there you are, I get beat again. And I even thought of putting that Child horse, what's her name, on my ticket, I wanted to, but . . . . Do you believe it?"

Ranson nodded; he knew the dialogue all too well. "Well, you'll have to get the next one, won't you?"

"I don't know, I don't know, maybe I should quit this game, I'm down to my last fifty bucks and . . . Maybe . . . Ah heck. Anyway, how are you, how have you been, are you here for the sales?"

"No, heavens, I haven't had a stable for years."

"Getting back in? The sales start tonight."

"Land, I doubt it."

"Well, still, the sales are tonight. Ya oughta go . . . lots of fun, always something to see over there."

"I'll bet on that. I hear Trump and Branson are in town."

"Along with the Sheik and what's his name . . . what's his name from England?"

"Oh I'm sure they are all here, and they all have their little parts well rehearsed."

"Absolutely, the next few nights should be fun, eh?"

"I'm sure . . . I'm sure."

Ranson smiled and over the next few minutes the two exchanged abbreviated biographies and worthy philosophies.

Ransom soon realized he had been away from his hosts a little too long and began to feel uncomfortable. "Look, I better get some ice cream back to my friends. Come down if you want to sit in the box, I'm sure Bill wouldn't mind." Ranson beamed as he slipped away into the waves of spectators.

"Who was that?" Too Tall's friend, Nick, asked from his park bench seat.

"Ranson something or other, some rich guy from Rhode Island."

"Really?"

"Good guy, used to be a real good guy when he owned horses."

"Really?"

"Oh, yeah, he always knew when his horses were ready, always. Man, he used to live at the $50.00 window, and if you asked, he would always tell you if his horse had a chance. He was beautiful when he owned horses."

"Too bad, we could use some luck right now."

"Come on, who have we got in the next race? I gotta cash one today."

"Not me," his other toothy friend replied, "no maidens for me. Look at this bunch, seven first time starters, ya gotta know blood lines to do anything with this bunch . . . look at'em."

"Gotta find Travis." Sam said, "He knows these maidens."

So, the avaricious entrepreneurs set out to find Travis, and as luck would have it the gentlemen himself, looking dapper in his tailor-made suit, as all former jockeys appear at the races in tailor-made suits, was emerging from the escalator just as Ted and his two friends turned the corner. A debate ensued.

"Teddy," Travis whispered within the rustling crowd, "I've got this race 3, 4, 10 . . . those are my numbers."

"You don't like the one horse?" Sam insisted.

"Not here, not with the ten. Zeno's whole stable is as cold as the hinges of a Siberian refrigerator . . . no way, I gotta play Clemens's filly here, the ten."

"Well," the toothy friend said.

"What'ya think? Travis likes the 10, but I like the one, with the three and the four."

"Let's box all of 'em. Who knows?" Nick offered.

"How much does a four horse trifecta box cost?"

"Forty eight bucks."

"Too much."

"So?"

"So!"

"So?"

And so, the three intrepid friends pooled their funds, boxed the three, four, ten in the sixth race, and promptly wore out their welcome in section B when Theodore's first choice, the one, gave its competitors the slip in the turn and won by over eight lengths. The cursing was terrible . . . enthusiastic and creative . . . but none the less unacceptable.

"That's it, I'm done, I am broke . . ."

"Again?"

"Let's go to Siro's for a beer. I gotta save some money for supper and the sales tonight"

"We can't win no money over there."

"Yeah, like we're getting rich here."

"We're still going to the sales?" Nick asked.

"Course," Ted said, "the sales are great, great show."

"I don't know, maybe we should go tomorrow night after we win some money?"

"Tonight," Ted bossed.

"But what if we want to buy one of those plugs?"

"Idiot," was all Too Tall would offer, "Siro's, and you're buying."

The stouthearted trio pressed through Siro's feminine revue of spectacular hats, cleavage and heels. They squeezed past the entrance gate, around the cigar stand, the simulcast TV's, and the awninged portico with its ranks and files of gleaming champagne-covered tables. Ultimately, they found a shred of elbowroom beneath a great tent where they paused to enjoy some music and admire the view.

After the second round was purchased and well abused, the chatter drifted to the evening's adventures.

"Come on," Too Tall insisted, "the sales are terrific."

"I don't know, Teddy, let's go downtown and maybe meet somebody,"

"The Sales."

"Let's leave it up to your friend here."

"Well, actually," their toothy companion offered," I've never seen the sales."

"You're kidding?"

"No, never, but somehow it doesn't seem like a good idea."

"You're from around here, and you've never been to the sales?"

"Never."

"Well, that settles it," as the three raised their glasses, "to the Sales."

And indeed the Faisg-Tipton auction is one of the highlights of Saratoga's social season. The horseshoe shaped pavilion with its art-lined walls, attracts some of the most famous personalities from America, England and beyond. It is a spectacle of wealth and style, with trains of limousines circling through East Avenue, North Broadway and back again, delivering well-heeled bidders to search for next season's Triple Crown. They assemble for three glorious nights of pecuniary excess and play their parts in a grand game of one-up-man ship, strategizing and maneuvering, looking for that unfair advantage which might promise fame, wealth, and a place in history.

When the last opportunity for romance escaped Ted's friends, the three chargers hiked across Union Avenue, stopped at Bruno's for a light supper and, as the hour of eight arrived, made their way to the sales pavilion. There was more than money in the crush of the curious; there was larceny and intrigue and enough histrionics to make Shakespeare proud.

The trio became part of the show with another round at the bar, a visit to the office to procure some programs, and a moment at the entrance door to the sales floor. Everywhere there were so many grand faces to cherish. Ted's toothy friend stopped to acknowledge an old college roommate. Speaking with him relieved the qualms and discomfort he had been experiencing all evening. They spoke of their days in history class, Dr. Reintz, Pop Griffith's sailboat, and some classmates whose names had faded over the years. His smile was renewed, but it quickly disappeared when he found himself quite abandoned. The corral, the bar, and the coffee shop beneath the trees were void of anyone resembling Ted or Nick. This sudden shock of freedom was not totally unwelcome; it gave him time to lean on the wooden walls of the entry corral and admire the magnificent yearlings' parade to the showroom while the loudspeaker barked out the frantic bidding inside. Still there was this odd nervous twinge occupying his stomach and he could not, for any amount of effort, understand where the uneasiness was coming from. A tall chestnut yearling kicked and railed against his hot walker.

"Aren't they wonderful," a tiny lady in a Panama hat said to him.

"So like children," he confided.

"I know," she replied, "they're so scared and, well . . . something else too."

"Yeah, kinda scared and curious and . . ."

"Full of themselves."

He thought a second, "Yeah, they are all of that, full of themselves, just like the people here."

He continued to review and patrol the exterior of the pavilion, all to no avail. He looked at his watch and reviewed the program. The TV monitor recounted the ferocious bidding on hip number 73 that was going on inside. Number 81 was a General Assembly filly he wanted to see, and as his watch told him it was almost 9:00 PM, he reasoned it was time to go inside and enjoy the show, with or without his friends.

He strode toward the doorway leading to the interior and wondered, almost aloud, why he had been experiencing this strange feeling of dread, as though some peculiar disaster was awaiting him. He was excited and uncomfortable all at once; but he was ready to enjoy an evening in the Sales, within the show itself, and the fate of Hip Number 81. He passed through the North door and stood on the ground floor, listening to the auctioneers admonish the bidders for their reluctance concerning a roan colt before them. Around the floor several assistants carefully eyed the participants in their seats and kept the head auctioneer sharp. The room sparkled with diamonds and suspense; he was ready to exhale, if only he could stop the squirrel's wheel spinning in his stomach.

"Nine hundred thousand, Nine hundred thousand," the loud-speaker called.

"Damn," was all he could muster privately.

"Nine hundred ten, nine hundred te, . . . do I hear twenty?"

At each radius from the podium, well dressed daredevils reclined in red velvet seats consulting trainers and friends about the diaphragm of the chestnut colt on the elevated platform that was the center of everyone's attention. These were the faces of intrepid men and women whose presence spoke volumes of their silver-certificated grandfathers, great homes, and egos willing to risk failure.

After he followed hip numbers 77 and 78 through the arena he patrolled the faces one more time. No Sam, no Nick. He was anxious to find them, but he wanted a seat and a chance to follow the General Assembly filly. He ascended the stairs as the auctioneer acknowledged growing interest in Hip Number 79.

"Nine hundred seventy two-thousand, seventy-two. Do I hear seventy-five?"

Deliberately he climbed the stairs. The lights glared more brightly somehow and the auctioneer bellowed on. Two steps from the top of his climb, on the far side of the balcony, he spotted Ted and Nick, beers and programs in hand, sitting with the look of contented, if not, slightly inebriated cows.

"Nine hundred seventy-seven thousand, do I hear . . ."

And at just that moment, with foreboding still racing beneath his belt, he made eye contact with his friends. They returned his look, paused, and, as if on the edge of a great moment, Teddy slid toward the front of his seat . . .

"Do I hear seventy-seven?"

. . . and, wanting company, lifted his hand, an inch or two at most, to mouth across the gallery, "Hey, over, here."

And just as deftly, just as succinctly, the auctioneer, responding to the wave of a hand, pointed with unerring precision at Ted and bellowed,

"Nine seventy-nine, Nine hundred and seventy-nine thousand. Do I hear . . . ?"

Nick's eyes flashed open and rammed Too Tall in the ribs, "Holy crap, Ted, you bought a horse."

Eyes turned to the mysterious bidder who had appeared in the top row; Ted's friends froze in disbelief. With fourteen dollars and forty-three cents in his pocket, he looked back and forth from the auctioneer to Nick and back again, petitioning relief.

"No," he hollered, in the middle of the Fasig-Tipton auction, "NOOOO!"

The auction went silent! Ted jumped up, waving his arms like a wounded heron. He lost track of his beer and it spilled into his lap, all twenty ounces dripping rudely out of his khaki shorts. Six foot seven stood straight up to yell again, "NO!"

Dear Reader, you must take a second to understand some small matters of decorum here. You see people do not yell *'no'* at the Fasig-Tipton auction, but then people do not pour beer down their pants in front of Mary Lou Whitney and her friends at the Fasig-Tipton auction, and they most certainly do not offer specious bids on a thoroughbred with 'Graded-Stakes' blood lines in the middle of such an arena. It is just not done.

The spotter realized in an instant the mistake that had been made and cringed in disbelief. The auctioneer lost his ability to swallow as Ted's moose-like protests informed him about the disaster at hand. One of the bookkeepers summoned up the memory of a fabled story concerning a false bid back in 1954 or 1955 where, it was rumored, some poor sap made a similar mistake at the Sales and ended up getting stuck with a bill. Such is the mythology of the Spa.

For an instant, things bordered on the ridiculous. Teddy could only protest and stare at hip number 79 with an open mouth and torrents of perspiration cascading down his back. A woman seated in front of him couldn't help but notice that the beer had escaped his khaki shorts and found its way down to his socks. The lead auctioneer cast pleading eyes toward the stunned assemblage, tourists giggled at the embarrassment on hand, and security guards emerged from back rooms with bewildered eyes. It was a remarkable show all around.

Just then, when the arena was pivoting on a fulcrum of anarchy, a smallish gray haired man, sitting with his horse trainer friend, looked up into the crowd, and found the face of the humiliated protester. Instantly, he understood. He raked a fingernail over the teeth of an ancient plastic comb and realized that in the fate of his unfortunate acquaintance and this magnificent animal, he might be looking at his own destiny as well. He hesitated only a second and then quietly told his friend, "Bill, take this yearling."

"Here," barked the auctioneer.

A few observers chuckled under their breath and the auctioneer exhaled, but the security guards continued their bewilderment. Nick just laughed and Ted charged out of the limelight to complain to his toothy friend that he knew this was going to happen. When Nick comes to town something bad always happens, they always get into trouble.

Disaster had been avoided; Ted was off the hook, free to walk away with fourteen dollars still in his pocket. He mustered as much dignity as he could, but soon realized why the ladies were looking at him. The immense beer stain looked like something else, too terrible to think of in public, and he quickly retreated to stand before an English oil landscape painting, hoping the display lights might dry out his clothing and allow him a humble exit.

By midnight, most of the adventurers were tucked safely in bed. The lights of the arena were dark, the curtains pulled shut, and clean-up crew hard at work. Some of the evening's players slept close to their racing forms, warmed with avarice; others cruised through embattled nightmares, fueled by memories of so many lost opportunities; while a few simply snored off the evening's excesses in hopes of a better tomorrow. But on the third floor of the Gideon Putnam, Ranson Hightower was wide-awake and on the phone with his secretary. He kept looking down at the receipt for his filly and a smallish colt, Hip 107, Bill Watterson had also taken for him a bit later in the sale. He was telling Mrs. Kaitlin about the evening's performance and directing her to call Martin Small, his old veterinarian friend, and see if there was space available at the Florida training track next spring. Ranson Hightower was thinking only about tomorrows and, when passing a mirror, marveling at his own smile.

"What a day!" he spoke out loud. "What a day!"

And indeed it had been quite a day, quite a day for Too Tall Teddy, Nick, the Waterson's, and the auctioneers, but mostly it had been a very special day for Ranson Hightower and his tomorrows. A special day indeed, but just another day at the Spa.

The Test

No matter what propagandists promote, the state government does not love you or your automobile; no sir-ee, not on your Nellie. Miserably misguided travelers may think that the G-man along side them in the outside lane is simply a fellow admirer of our miraculous interstate, but that would be a fallacy worthy of Aristotle. Truth be told, the thought that one of their citizens might be cruising around, trying to be as little of a burden upon their fellow man as possible, is simply an opportunity for the state to renew its kleptomania and raid the vaults of their savings account. And believe me there is nothing petite about this petty larceny. I am witness to such muggings many times during my stay upon this here earth. This is an undeniable truth.

However one remarkable adventure came my way this summer, rather ironically, thanks to just such a gesture of the state's bigheartedness. It began on Union Avenue, just west of exit 14, when an enormous officer emerged from her deep blue patrol car and, after generating an extended conversation concerning the color of my 1959 Buick Invicta which, was listed as 'blue' on the registration, but had faded to a rather quaint shade of 'algae-green' due to its penchant for sunbathing in so many racetrack parking lots, glibly handed over a collection of tickets that indicated various reasons why my vehicle should not be driven when innocents were about. These were bulletins most unwelcome, as you may imagine, and while I deferred sharing my umbrage with the sergeant, I tried to remind her that I had been trekking around the state quite peacefully for quite some time and more than somewhat without complaint or injury. In reply, the good officer went so far as to tell me I should take pity on the poor thing and donate it to some worthy children's charity, a suggestion I found most distasteful. Our conversation ended when she reminded me that my inspection sticker hadn't been renewed in five years, but she would overlook that out of the goodness of the State's heart. I was not impressed.

And that is how, in my disturbed state of unloved ignominy, I ended up, once again, in Phil Reina's Garage with my 'sorta blue Buick, in hopes that the good Mr. Reina could unravel this Gordian Knot of bald tires, missing rear view mirrors, and inoperative brake lights, without sending me straight to the poor house. This Mr. Reina found to be vexing, to say the least, as this mechanic was 'up against it', as they say in the clubhouse, working overtime to get the proper sticker that would keep the gendarmes at bay until I got back to the Chesapeake.

So there I was, sitting in the waiting area, utterly devastated, on the very edge of clinical depression and teary-eyed destitution, because after all it was a Monday, and they race on Monday's and tomorrow was a Tuesday, and Tuesdays are dark with no racing. What could be worse then that? I looked to my watch, but it had stopped and I began to think that the machines in my life were conspiring. Distasteful as it might seem, the position of the sun told me it was nearly noon, and I knew I had but one choice in the matter; if I was to enjoy the afternoon, I would have to walk.

In fact I had gotten as far as The Parting Glass and was negotiating my turn to the south when a automobile horn called to me and a smallish black Chevy pulled up to the curb.

"Why are you walking?" It was the welcome voice of Laney Collins, one of Saratoga's storied bartenders. She and I had become well acquainted over the years and the sound of her voice told me I was getting a ride to the races.

"Going to work lady?" was all I said as I dropped into the passenger's seat.

She smiled, "Well yes and no."

"Huh?"

"I'm going to the races today, but not working."

"You're not working? The place won't be able . . ."

"It's a long story."

"Really? I'd love to hear it."

We shared a laugh or two about past escapades with the state police, my car, her job, until she dropped me off in front of the Union Avenue gate. I was saved. Providence was once more my guide. I collected my papers and racing form and told her I would meet her inside. Coffees were on me today. After reviewing the scratches and saying hello to Patrick, my teller in the lower clubhouse, I found my way to the lower club snack bar to thank my rescuer. There was advantage in that she had a story to tell, and as there was still nearly an hour until the first race, I promised no single thing on this earth could make me happier, at this moment, than being her audience.

We found a small park bench, not far from her old work station, and she proceeded to share with me a remarkable tale which I must share with you. It is a tale worth telling as, in retrospect, as it is a romance, and one that could only have happened under the elms of Saratoga.

Her adventure took place the week before on the day of The Test. Traditionally, Saratoga Racecourse features this race on the first Saturday of the August meet. It is a grand contest, pitting the very best against the very best in a rare Grade I sprint for older mares at seven furlongs. It is the kind of race rarely written at any other track but the Spa. And at the same time it is regarded with almost religious zeal by racing fans as it marks the heart of the Saratoga season. Everywhere there is an atmosphere of unending adventure and opulent hope, fortunes to be won and lost, and being part of it is sometimes a reward in and of itself.

Amidst the mirth and mayhem of that morning's preparations, Laney had reported for her first full day's work. For over ten years she had bartended during the month of August on The Travers Porch, a small open-air service area sequestered near the clubhouse turn. For Laney, it was a part time job she had grown to love over the years simply because she relished being immersed in the spectacle. During the other mundane months of the year, her infectious laughter and tapster skills warmed various cantinas and cabarets on the islands of St. John and St. Kitts. Hers was a well planned life. Yes she thought, as she first entered the park, despite one poorly planned trip to Jamaica, and a rather tartared romance with that lawyer from Tokyo, it had been a good year. That was all behind and of no matter now; it was summer, it was Saratoga, and The Test meant the heart of the meet was at hand. All was right with the world . . . for at least four more weeks.

With bartenders credentials in hand, and a new back pack slung stylishly over her left shoulder, she passed quickly through the clutches of other employees, and a few impatient patrons, to the white cubicle that had been her summer home for eleven years. It was a brilliant day. Early-birds were filtering in to see old friends, while much of the day crew was collecting under the grandstand's great eaves, safe from the noon day heat.

She stopped to say hello to some remarkable faces and noticed how everyone was smiling; the jockeys were clean, the railings were freshly painted, the gambler's pockets were full of money, and everywhere there was an intimation of romance that never fails to find a home in the hearts of those who cross Union Avenue.

"Morning love," Stan said from behind their bar area, "great to see you. Working with me today? How've you been?"

"Yeah, I'll be here till the feature. You?" she cheered.

"Great to be back, eh, and look at this day. What'ya think, thirty thousand?"

"Maybe more, after all that rain last week? Everybody will be looking for a little action."

"Think so?"

"Ha," she said with her incandescent smile, "know so!"

The support crew slowly showed up; boys to retrieve ice and supplies, security guards to sweep away the frustrated and angry, union reps to ensure jobs and placements, and of course, a few dewy-eyed fans who still believed last year's meet had never ended, and all their romancing could be renewed exactly where it left off.

Martha, her supervisor, leaned across the bar, "So very good to see you Gloria. Everything all set. Ya got everything?"

"Looks like. How was yesterday?"

"Good, from what Sam and Patrick said, the till was good."

"How many people did they have?"

"Twenty-five, a good Friday."

Gloria smiled at Stan and they both nodded, "It's gonna be a good day."

The two innkeepers renewed their friendship by exchanging abbreviated versions of winter's exploits and narratives. The anthem was played and when Tom Durkin finished announcing the program changes, Stan and Laney bent wits to the eighth race. Wagering on the feature was their traditional exercise frosted in voracity.

"Nobody's gonna beat Jersey Girl in the Test today, even my Dad told me to bet her, and he never bets."

"Think so?"

"Know so," Laney stated with emphasis, "This one's going to be easy. I'm gonna bet her, pretty good too, as soon as I get off work."

"Yeah, but what about the price?"

"She'll be the favorite. We'll have to find someone who knows something. You know, to go with her for the exacta or the tri." She always adored being the lead conspirator in a Dick Francis novel.

She leaned against the back bar and reviewed the panorama of elms, maples, and summer that sheltered the barns of the backstretch. The stone patio was emerging from its shade and the warmth of the sun found her cheeks. Faces, many well remembered, were emerging from the milling regiments of railbirds and punters, and the soft residue of their life's stories was a pleasant distraction. Some were unchanged, others showed the plunder of a year's excesses, but she never grew tired of saying hello and listening to the people she knew.

Shortly after noon, most of the traditional players were in place; Martin, the newspaper guy from Boston had arrived, along with, Dick, the beer distributor from New Hampshire and his bouncing blonde wife, and, of course, Mr. Cornelius Randolph Smith from Spring Lake, New Jersey, the immaculately dressed banker who could have taught Eddie Bauer a thing or two about sartorial splendor, as well as that anonymous guy, balding and toothy, from Buffalo, who always had the worst tips on 'scalding hot' horses. Even Stan was slouched across the bar between 40 ounce Budweisers, chatting with two 'old' friends he had known for years. Like Gloria, these people had become some of Stan's closet confidants; people he exchanged intimacies with, the kind that are usually reserved for brothers or wives, but they were also friends he never saw beyond the racetrack. Doctor Dan, Mad Mike and the Shiner were sharing great adventures, for as Stan often said, people never bring anything small into a bar.

It was a wonderful reunion, but something was missing. One of Saratoga's great modern mysteries was strangely absent, and when the first race broke from the gate, Stan couldn't resist tweaking Laney just a bit.

"Laney, it's getting late, one o'clock. I guess you're not getting your flowers this year?"

Laney checked her watch, "Yeah . . . wait a minute. Where is Robbie, where are Robbie and my flowers?"

"Looks like your run has . . . run out." he quipped with a smirk.

"Wait a minute; don't give up yet, eleven years is supposed to stand for something. He might be late or something?"

"Who might be late?" Robert asked.

"An old friend," Laney said as she pulled three beers from the ice chest, "just an old friend."

Stan grinned, "And for over ten years . . ."

"Eleven," she interrupted.

". . . this guy has sent Laney two dozen red roses on Test Saturday."

"Really, this somebody we should be jealous of?" asked Mike, emerging from his Racing Form.

"He is just a friend, he loves the races, and he never forgets me."

"Until this year."

"Shush!"

"Get real, a guy doesn't send red roses to a lady just for . . ."

"Careful buddy, don't get me mad. He's a good guy, but we're just racetrack friends, whether your old cynical heart believes it or not."

"Baloney! Come on Laney," Shiner said as he winked at Stan over his beer, "come on, fill us in. A little romance means there is hope for all of us."

A look of mock disgust almost buried her quick smile, "You guys are heartless, you've got no faith, none at all, and faithless men do not belong at a racetrack. You'll see, my Robbie won't forget me, he'll show."

The day continued, a parade of happy faces, old friends, and befuddled losers. Reunions continued, the cheering grew louder, while the whiskey flowed like the Hudson River in spring time. Doctor Dan became one of the happiest and started dancing when he hit the double and cashed a very generous ticket. A small crowd gathered to admire the celebration and applaud. Stan and Laney stifled laughs while others cheered from their tables. The sun grew stronger and the day sang.

About two in the afternoon, just as the third race left the starting gate, a man in his early forties, needing a haircut, carrying a large paper bag, and wearing a badly worn suit appeared at the bar. He leaned in and looked, with long yellowed eyes, at Laney. He did not speak at first, just looked at her. There was something about the face she knew, and yet it was a face she could not remember.

"Mister?"

"Are you Laney?" was all he said. His voice was gentle and soft, not at all like his face.

"Yes."

Her dark visitor looked away and studied the floor as five very loud and very happy fraternity brothers cheered their winnings with a round and a chorus of 'So you think you've got class'. Everyone laughed, but Laney's quiet patron just waited for the bar front to clear.

"You're Laney?"

"That's me, what would you like?"

"Nothing, nothing yet," he said as his feet shuffled and his eyes continued to trace the outline of her face. Stan watched the man and exchanged a serious glance with his partner.

"Stan," Max Croski boomed as he skipped down the steps to the Traver's porch, "Stan baby, how 'bout a beer Boo-Boo."

Laney, leaned toward the stranger, "Mister, this is a service bar, you buy your beer and then go back to your seat or something." She looked at him and shrugged.

"Oh sorry, you see, Robbie sent me. I have something to give you, but it's kinda odd in a way and, well, I was hoping you'd be alone so I could tell you kind of plain and straight. I'm not much at speeches. I wish Robbie hadn't asked me to do this."

"Robbie?"

"Yeah."

"Robbie Taro?"

"Uh-huh."

"Well, where is he?"

The man paused, "He ain't coming lady,"

"Robbie miss The Test, is he okay?"

"I'm sorry lady, he ain't OK."

Laney felt herself bolt straight upright. She hadn't moved or tried to pull away, but cold steel captured her spine. Stan saw his friend's sudden move. He looked at the dark stranger and then to Laney.

"Sorry to have to say this to you, I gather you two go back quite a ways, but I guess I've got to do it."

"Didn't die or anything, did he?"

"Three days ago, Thursday morning."

She spoke a nearly silent no that sat in the back of her throat and ground its way into her eyes.

The man leaned into the bar and spoke with a slow reverent voice, "This past winter, he went to the Doc with some stomach pains and, well, they found nothing but bad stuff inside him and, well, I guess it was down hill after that."

"No," she whispered again.

"Sorry," he repeated, "he really wanted to make it to the races, at least one more time, but things got real bad about two weeks ago and well, Thursday he was gone."

Laney's face was distorting; her eyes filling. The rush of redness made her face burn and after a moment, teetering on an edge, she turned away. Stan moved to her and tried to ask a question, but her hand stopped him, "Gotta take a break Stan."

"What's going on Laney," he asked and then turning his eyes to the man at the bar repeated, "What's going on here?"

"I'll handle it Stan," she said as she pulled her pocketbook from under the bar, "it's OK, I'm all right, just give me a minute."

Laney moved around the back of the bar and confronted the messenger as the crowd roared its approval of the stretch run of the third. The sudden uproar distracted her for a second and gave her a chance to catch her breath.

"Do I say, thank you, for telling me or something?"

"Course not, but I've got something for you, something from Robbie. Is there some place we can talk?"

"In this place?"

"Anyplace."

The pair wound their way through the tables to a small grassy prominence by an imposing red and white canopy where she found the best position to shade her eyes. She was only distracting herself, and trying to see his face more clearly.

"Like I was trying to say, this isn't my idea of a good time, but last week, after Robbie had a really bad night, his nurse called me and, well, when I got to the hospital . . ."

"Which one?"

"Rome, Rome Memorial. Like I was saying, when I got there he made me promise to run some errands for him."

"Errands?"

"Yup, that's what he called them, errands."

"Have I seen you before?"

"I don't know, maybe? I was Robbie's friend, helped him with his farm . . ."

"Farm?"

"Sure?"

"He really had a farm?"

"Sure, nice one, out in West Winfield."

"You're kidding?"

"Everyone knows about Red Sands, at least everyone out there."

"Red Sands?"

"The name of his farm, Red Sands Thoroughbreds, in the winter during boarding season, maybe a hundred head might be on the grounds."

"Really," she said quietly. She was relaxing and beginning to trust the face before her.

"Yeah, quite a spread. Hope the new owners keep it nice the way he did."

"You know, he used to tell me stories about his farm, but I never knew for sure if he was telling me a tale or not, maybe, exaggerating a little. There are a few people around this place that can tell tales, if you know what I mean."

"Well, he could tell a tale or two as well, that's for sure, but he probably didn't have to very often, least not around horses . . . race tracks anyway."

"I'll be damned," she mused leaning her weight on her back leg, "all this time he was telling me about his farm, he wasn't just throwing some bull at me."

"Don't think so? Probably not. Whenever he came back from the races, he always told great stories about his afternoons up here and you always had some part in 'em."

She looked away and feigned interest in a passing blue jay. For years she and Robbie had shared a quiet distant friendship that entertained her in August and held her close on winter evenings. After a season on the Travers porch there were always stories to tell and they made her friends both whimsical and a little envious.

Robbie and she had a ritual of sorts. First thing on Test Saturday, there would be roses. Then, near the fifth race, Robbie's bright, strong, smiling face would appear with a small gift-wrapped bottle of aspirin, and a bad joke about her needing them. They would tease each other about who had the better time the night before and then she would give him a kiss on the cheek for her bouquet. Her thank-you's were genuine but guarded. Her eyes said, 'thanks and that's all.' Why she had turned down so many of his dinner invitations escaped her at the moment. She didn't know why she had never allowed herself to get to know him.

Every weekend for the rest of the meet, Robbie would appear at her bar accompanied by an endless train of faces, both feminine and otherwise. His parties always seemed to be having great fun, but before the day was through he would stand near the end of the bar and repeat an offer for to join his party downtown at The Parting Glass or The Olde Bryan Inn for drinks, dinner and 'who-knows-what-else'. He never growled when she said no, never showed the least anger, or even seemed to be discouraged. He used to say 'You better practice saying 'no' lady, cause if you don't . . . I'll be buying dinner this year.' Standing in the sunlight, she could hear his voice as clearly as if it had just spoken. They would laugh and flirt and share wisdom about the game they loved, but they had never sat together.

"I'm sorry," the old man said quietly.

"Hard to believe, that's all."

Laney's eyes went looking for her blue jay, "We were friends I guess? He was always nice to me, very good to me, always wanted me to understand the races, taught me a lot, and he always took care of me, with tips and all, nothing cheap about Robbie."

The man began shuffling his feet through the grass and caught his breath.

"Look miss, I considered Robbie more than a friend, he was my best friend, the real deal. Maybe the only one I had left. He took real good care of me too, always had a job for me if I had problems 'ya see," his voice was growing quiet, but determined, "and this is the last thing he asked me to do for him so I feel I've got to do it right."

A sense of mystery and intrigue instantly silenced her tongue.

"This is supposed to go to you," he said after a moment lifting a rumpled paper bag to Laney.

She watched a trace of pain wave through the stranger's face; it watered his eyes. He slowly lowered his jaw and pushed out his lower lip. Thoughts began to assault the back of her mind, thoughts that challenged, and then bludgeoned her cautious resolve.

"I just know that Robbie asked me to do this."

There was an extended pause. She nodded, "I understand."

"I don't know much else of what to do. It don't make a lot a sense to me, but then Robbie always was one for jokes and things." He took four packages from the bag and held them up. Each package was labeled, one for Tina, one for Karen, another for Sondra, and the last one had her name scrawled across it.

"Well, here's the deal, this one here, on top, the one that says Laney is, well . . . yours. Open it."

Laney snatched a quick glance at her watch and then did as she was told. "This isn't going to explode or something is it buddy?"

In the package was a second package, gift wrapped in bright silver metallicized paper and a pale off-white envelope. With the package tucked beneath her arm, she read the card.

'*Dear Laney,*
This is my only way to ask you out this year as these
stupid doctors are keeping me a prisoner in this awful

*place against my will. i hope you have been practicing your
'Yes's', you'll need them today, because today i'm making
you an offer you can't refuse. today you get to sit with me in
my box, as soon as you get off work. that should put you up
stairs just about post time for the Test and just in time for
me to buy you dinner.*

*now assuming you haven't fallen madly in love with
me by then, the only thing I need you to do is this; please
deliver these other gifts to some other friends of mine
when they come to your bar. They'll ask for me and you'll
recognize them when you see them, you've met them all
before, and i'm sure they'll remember you. each package
is marked with their names so it will be easy and maybe
even fun. do this for me and later a present will be yours.
we will all get together in my box, A-13, for a great time
and everything will be all right, I promise. remember what
i used to tell you—a promise made is a debt unpaid, your
biggest fan, robbie."*

"I don't get it," she quipped as she pulled the gift box open.

The old man shrugged his shoulders and waited for her to
finish the unwrapping. She pried it open with all the assiduous
concentration of the bomb disposal squad. Inside, she found a large
ostentatious pin in the shape of a thoroughbred. It was big, oddly
shaped, but very well made. She grimaced a second and held it up
in a state of disbelief to see it in the light.

"What's this?" Laney whispered as she looked back in at the
box. Under the pin was a second note sheltered neatly beneath the
clasp. She read it out loud, "This trinket may be redeemed for one
reserved seat in box A-13 this very afternoon, see you there."

Stan couldn't withhold his impatience, "Do you get it?"

"I'm not sure."

"Well I'm supposed to be going; Robbie's got me doing more
errands for him this afternoon. But do you know who these other
people are and what it all means?"

"Not sure," she muttered shaking her head. "Brother, that
Robbie was a darb, a real darb."

"Thank you miss," he said as he tipped an imaginary hat and quietly withdrew into the crowd near the stairs to the upper clubhouse.

"Mister," she called after him, "I didn't get your name. Can I buy you a drink or something?" But he was gone, off on Robbie's 'errands'.

When she finally reappeared at her station the place was mobbed.

"Sorry Stan," she muttered, as she put the packages under the bar for safe keeping.

"You OK?"

"Yeah, at least I think so," she offered as she pulled two more Budweisers from the ice chest, "I'll tell you later, let me get caught up first."

Just after 3:30 the two barkeeps found a moment to relax.

"Just like you called it lady, this is turning out to be some day."

"You can say that again," she sparkled, eyeing the three mysterious packages beneath the bar, "and these are the icing on the cake."

Stan communicated only with his raised eyebrows as she lifted them up so Stan could see the packages

"That guy, that old guy that was here earlier, he left them with me. Seems Robbie wanted me to deliver them." She hesitated. "This place is getting nuttier."

"You're joking aren't you?"

"I wish I were. I'm supposed to give these three packages to three people I don't know, and I am supposed to hope they find me. This used to be my favorite day here. I used to love The Test. I haven't even done my handicapping to find a long shot to go with Jersey Girl yet."

"Do I dare say it, but where are your flowers?"

Laney was stunned and felt, for the first time, a wrenching knot pain her throat, "Didn't I tell you? Robbie won't be here this year."

They spoke for a minute, sharing stories from days when Robbie had entertained them.

Laney shrugged and rolled her eyes a little. She was sweeping dozens of old memories through her mind. She even caught a glimpse of the night she and Robbie had crossed paths out at Saratoga's Art Center during a James Taylor concert. Her friends had been impressed by Robbie's keen generosity. He had bought them a round of drinks at the champagne bar only to disappear when the music started up again. Her friends were convinced he was shy and they wanted to know more about him. Everyone liked Robbie.

"But now this old guy shows up with a story that sounds like Robbie."

"Sounds like fun."

"Goofy if you ask me, just plain goofy."

"And you don't know who these other people are?"

"Nope, no idea, I just got three little packages and they're going to, let's see, let's see, Sondra, Karen, and Tina."

The fifth race had Stan and Laney high-five-ing each other when Alpenglow nosed out the favorite. The ten-dollar exacta ticket she was sharing with Sandman and Shiner was well worth cashing and Laney immediately tried to get her partner to join them and let it ride on Jersey Girl in the feature. A debate ensued between deliveries to thirsty patrons.

"Nobody's beating Jersey Girl today Stan, nobody."

"You are getting greedy. Let's split it, get us something to go with the 11. We're ahead, let's play it safe."

"Come on, don't be chicken," she chanted almost as a taunt to her skeptical partner. "Let it ride! We'll put a hundred on her and front wheel the exacta. Come on!"

"You're making me crazy," was his only defense.

"Crazy-ER," was Laney's immediate laughing reply; she was beaming and throwing her eyes around, dancing a little, "Come on soldier, be brave."

"Let's split it, that way we come out ahead no matter what."

"No guts, no . . . ." but Laney never finished her homily, as a swollen, heavily rouged face appeared at the bar. She looked to her partner, but he was already watching. They both saw the woman, a bundle of dyed red hair that framed ample cheeks beneath layers and layers of makeup. The excesses of coloring introduced a size 22 hourglass figure that was having a difficult time staying in its dress. The woman positively jiggled standing still and it seemed there was no way simple stitchery could impound all that wayward flesh. It was difficult to look her in the eye.

After a second, Laney started to remember the face, and she knew it was a face that reminded her of Robbie. She was sure this woman had been here before. She suddenly remembered how Robbie would come up to the bar to order drinks and recreate a Jack Benny Vaudeville routine, followed by this redhead, usually with a whiskey sour in each hand, just to get between Robbie and the bar to demand attention. All unnecessary, but predictable.

"Hi," she said quietly.

"What do you need?" Laney offered professionally.

"Well I'm not sure, but do you remember me?"

"Yes, I think so."

"Do you remember an old friend of mine, Mr. Taro?"

"You mean Robbie?"

"Yes Robbie."

She hesitated, looking left and right just as two young fraternity brothers greeted The Travers Porch with a chorus of "We Won't Get Fooled Again." Laney reached into the ice to get their beer, but she never took her eyes off the redhead. Robbie's large friend was nervous, uncomfortable, and the enormous garden she was wearing wasn't hiding her disquietude.

"What do you need? Would you like a sour?"

This flustered the woman and by the time she had recovered and scratched out a 'yes', her complexion had gone from crimson to titanium white. She fumbled into her purse, but never stopped looking behind her.

Laney continued to serve one customer after another. The redhead just stood near the bar sipping her drink and watching the world through black sunglasses. The next lull inspired Laney.

"So you know Robbie?"

She came around slowly, "Yes, sure."

They spoke pleasantries for a moment and slowly the large lady began to warm to conversation.

"Well, that's just it, the other day I got a note from him in the mail. It says that I am supposed to meet him here, today, but I can't find him. I've been here an hour and well, he's not here."

"When was the last time you saw him?" Laney asked.

"Oh, well . . . I guess it was sometime after Christmas."

The problem sauntered through Laney's mind more than once, and more than somewhat. What was she suppose to say to her, what would Robbie have wanted, what did she need to know and would it make a difference? More questions. When she grew weary of the revolving interrogation she decided that the less she knew the better. This exercise in posthumous friendship felt unnatural. She got an idea.

"Are you sure Robbie wrote the note? What if it is a mistake or a joke or something?"

"I don't think so, really?"

"Well, I know Robbie's handwriting, let me see it."

"S'alright," the redhead mumbled.

There, at the top of the page was what Laney had been looking for, the note was addressed to Sondra.

"Sondra?"

"Yes, that's my name."

"Well then that reminds me, I have something for you."

She reached under her bar, retrieved one of the packages and held it up to the woman, "Here, a guy was here a while ago and well, he told me to give it to you."

Bewilderment was quickly replacing circumspection. "I don't get it."

"Well you will if you'll just put your hand out and take it."

"Where's Robbie?"

Laney just raised her eyebrows.

"I don't get this."

"I don't know. Come on, take it, I've got customers." There was a moment of silence. "Look, I'm suppose to give it to you, so here, it's something from Robbie and it's got your name on it." She laid the package on the bar top and went to refill a Bloody Mary.

The sixth went off after a long-gossip-filled delay when Jerry Bailey was dismounted in the starting gate. All the gamblers had an opinion that was punctuated with keen intelligences concerning cancelled wagers. Some returned to the bar for another round, while others had their eyes crazy-glued to the starting gate. When the race finally got under way it was proved to be worth the wait.

At the finish line, four horses were within a nostril of each other and everyone roared exquisite approval.

"The five horse got'em," Sammie cheered, "But man it was tight!"

Laney looked at her partner but he wasn't smiling. She looked for Fat Frankie but he was swearing. She even looked for Jay-Bird, but there didn't seem to be any of her friends she could congratulate. Sammie broke the mood with a well rendered laugh and beckoned his friends to join him in his new handicapping seminar. A few seemed to think he was serious.

"Where'd she go?" Laney asked. Stan pointed toward the hedges that divided the rows of park benches from the racing surface. The woman's red hair glowed in the sun. Both bartenders watched as a unique pantomime unfolded amidst the hushed cacophony that always follows a photo finish.

The package was opened, and the gift box was retrieved. Even from her perch she could see that the woman was holding up a large pin. A paper was taken from the box, exactly as Laney had done, but then things changed. The woman with the blast furnace hair, right there in the middle of a huge crowd of patrons, right in front of God and everybody, threw a fit, an absolute fit, a genuine jump up and down, curse at the top of your lungs, fit. The two bartenders had to stop themselves from laughing, while the gamblers stopped and stared. The woman threw her head back and hollered something foul to the heavens, then looked around to see if there was something she might grab, and failing that, slammed the gift to the ground and began jumping on it like she was crushing a bug. She came within one tiny elastic band from disrobing. Some people looked with open mouths; mothers covered children's ears, and the fraternity friends roared with approving laughter. Even a tall, dark and rather imposing security guard started moving in the woman's direction, as outbursts like this are rare and unwelcome in the clubhouse.

"What is that about?" Laney asked.

"What an idiot." someone said between smirks.

"Where's the loony-bin?"

"Get the little white wagon, that is a coo-coo bird."

"Oh God, she's coming back," Stan remarked.

"Damn look at that face . . . uh-oh, isn't it my break time?"

But before either could move a foot, the woman was on them.

"What the hell is this?" she said as she held up what used to be her pin, now mangled beyond recognition, "what is this, is this your idea of a joke?"

"Hey wait up there, I just delivered it, I don't know nothing about nothing except I was asked to give it to you."

"I can't believe this, I can't believe this." Her cursing was renewed. "This is it, nothing else?"

"Lady!" Laney said, her eyes asking the security guard to stay close.

"Crap, pure crap, he drags me miles and miles to this lousy place and, and for what?" She was shaking the thing in everybody's face. "Crap," and after a final assault on Club Profanity, she flung the golden souvenir over the bar into the seating area where it landed in John Martin's bucket of beers. The security guard was getting closer, but without another word, fair or foul, the redhead charged off toward the exit gate.

Laney and Stan stared after her departure for nearly a minute and then, as if properly choreographed, both burst into gales of laughter.

"Do you believe it?" he said through his teeth.

"Did you ever?"

From every corner of the Travers Porch regulars gathered to review the show. Frankie, Too Tall, Fat Frankie, Casey, Powder even Big Stew, all had been within earshot, and all wanted their own private interview.

The security guard approached the bar's front. She spoke with a soft strong voice that still carried a hint of the South. "What was that all about?"

"I'm telling you," Laney was pleading through her watery laughter, "I'm telling you, jewelry. A pin, like a broach thing. Look at it, that guy gave it back to me; she threw it in his beers. No, no bet, no lost ticket, no cheating boyfriend. I'm telling you a pin." More laughter followed.

"You for real?" the security guard asked.

"Absolutely," Stan added. "Laney here was asked to give her a package . . . it had a pin in it and . . . I don't know, she lost it."

The guard opened her eyes even wider and, shaking her head, told Stan and Laney she would make sure the woman left the grounds. The bartenders applauded, but Laney couldn't help but think that some comic relief was exactly what her day needed.

The smile lived on until she discovered another face, both seen and remembered in the same moment. First, it was the only one in the crowd that was frozen, deadpan, uncolored and without a smile. In fact, it was while she was reenacting the jewelry attack for Jay and Fat Frankie that the face returned to her mind's eye. It was a pretty face, with long sharp features and lengthy dark hair; a face she had seen with Robbie.

Laney went on her break and spent a second under the scratchboard outside the Jim-Dandy bar reading a friend's Racing Form. The Test was going off in less than an hour and, while she had nothing but confidence in Jersey Girl, still this was Saratoga, the Graveyard of Favorites, and if that ancient dirt could drag the soul out of Man 'O War and wither the legs of Secretariat, well, you never know, there might be a sniper lurking in the bushes, as the old-timers use to say.

"Laney?" a soft voice spoke close to her ear.

A big blonde greeted her with a soft smile. Her once pretty face was now bloated with age.

"Hi," she almost whispered. "Haven't seen you since last year . . . been a while."

Despite the heavy sunglasses, Laney could sense the furtive eyes darting back and forth behind the lenses. She was either a very good actress or a soft gentle injured heart, shy to a fault. "Yes, last year, how are you doing?" Laney felt herself wince a little; falling into the charade of friendly pretense.

"OK, I guess, I mean . . ."

"Just got here?"

"No, no. I've been here a while," her voice was getting very faint, almost secretive as the woman continued to look around and draw Laney closer to her.

"You remember Robbie don't you, Robbie Taro, we use to come to your bar. Have you seen him today?"

Laney winced again, "No, I haven't seen Robbie today, no, but if I knew your name . . ."

"Tina, I'm Tina," she offered quickly and tried to force a smile. Laney offered her hand, but the woman refused to shake.

"I got something for you, from Robbie; come over to my bar."

Tina answered with silence.

The two returned to the Travers Bar and stood across from each other when the exchange was made.

"What's this?" was all she asked.

"Yours."

"I don't get it?"

"Neither do I. I was just asked to give it to you." She resisted the temptation to retell the story of the old man and his mysterious errand.

"But Robbie told me to meet him here."

They spoke for a moment until the bar became thick with customers again. In between a giant round of martini's and margaritas, Laney caught a glimpse of the blonde slowly moving toward the hedge rail and surreptitiously unraveling the gift.

The light gray case emerged as impeccably manicured nails unraveled the string. The contents were exposed and Laney watched the hollow look in the woman's eyes become dark and muddied. She found Laney looking at her.

The note was located and read. The blonde looked around, put the note back, and then closed the case. She walked toward the bar, as unmoved as stone.

"Can we see?" Laney asked.

The woman never looked back at her, "Does this mean I have a problem?"

Laney was confused, "Problem? Put it on, maybe . . . maybe it's a good luck charm?

The blonde looked down for a moment, then around at the crowded patio, and finally pushed the trinket away. Without a gesture, without saying hi, goodbye, or kiss my foot, she simply walked away.

Stan looked at Laney, Laney looked at Stan, and they both shook their heads. To her unbelieving eyes, the woman was disappearing, walking off the grounds in utter silence.

"Amazing,"

"Wow, what a friendly one you found there. Bet she flunked her Dale Carnegie course."

"Bet they wouldn't let her in."

"She's leaving?"

"Gone, yeah, I mean gone, out the door."

"What about the package?"

"Gave it back to me. I'm stuck with it again. Guess I'll put it below in case little Miss Personality comes back." They both laughed.

In the crowd the other faced loomed. The long sharp features and the thick columns of dark hair were hard to miss. She kept looking between customers; not moving, just standing beneath the awning, out of the sun, next to the hedgerow that defined the parade route to the track.

The face brought back a moment from last year, exactly one year ago to the day, Test Saturday, when this woman, wearing a similar black summer dress, was sitting at one of the little white tables with Robbie. Laney had thought her a little too young for Robbie, and oddly aloof. They had seemed an odd couple, but Robbie was clearly smitten.

While talking with Powder and serving a large group, she remembered how she hadn't liked the woman that day. She remembered thinking that Robbie could have done better, and how the woman was distinctly territorial when Robbie spent some time at the bar. There was none of his bad jokes or clumsy attempts at flirting as long as this woman was nearby. Before the feature went off that day, the two had gotten into a bit of a tiff. Their exit had been marked with some noise and chair slamming. It was an uncomfortable scene, and Laney had felt badly for her friend.

Stan whispered to her, "What now?"

"Easy Stan, I'm watching someone."

"I can see that. Who?"

She served two more customers, and tried to answer while her head was down making change, "Over by the hedge, the tall woman, pearl necklace."

"Black dress?"

"Yup, I think that's my third mystery lady, must be Karen."

"Ooooh, a mystery lady. Mata Hari herself maybe? I love a good mystery."

"So do I, so do I, but I'm getting just angry enough at these women to really get into this."

"What's she doing?"

"That's just it, I've seen her more than once today, but she hasn't come up to the bar."

"Ah, the strong silent type."

"Creepy if you ask me."

Impatience was set aside when the mystery lady looked toward the bar, quickly Laney raised her hand to wave. Gently, she made the most unassuming gesture she could muster. Nothing! Laney waved again. No response! She waved one more time and the charm almost took. The woman stood still and became quite rigid. She turned away for a second and then looked over her shoulder. The two women made eye contact a second time.

Exactly at that moment, as if cued by Busby Berkley himself, a wall of humanity, composed of at least twenty members of the Troy City Fire Department, moved through The Travers Patio. They were chanting happily some ancient tune most thought extinct with Vaudeville. Everyone at the tables laughed, but when the chorus moved on, the mystery woman was gone. Gone, as if she had never been there, gone without a trace, or acknowledgement, or a clue. Laney pulled herself up on her bar to look around the corner. She looked out toward the racing surface, up toward the dining area, and again throughout the tables. The mystery woman was not to be found, a desperate winter hare, giving her pursuer no chance to pursue.

"For Gosh sake," she said with a laugh, "for Gosh sake."

"Now what?"

"I don't know. I mean that woman ran away or something, as soon as she knew I'd seen her, Poof!"

Stan refused further involvement, he was too busy. He simply shook his head and rolled his eyes.

"Stan, what should I do?"

"Enough! Ten minutes to post time. Laney, it's your quitting' time and I'm done with this other stuff. Let's get down to something important . . . like picking' winners and making some real money."

She began gathering up her purse, keys, and the unclaimed gifts.

"Going to stay for the Test?"

"What do you think? Course."

"Did you play it?"

"I will as soon as I get out from behind this bar."

"The one horse?"

Laney smiled and shook her head at Stan.

"Go ahead, give your money away, You're on your own this time. I told you the eleven, Jersey Girl." and she punctuated her selection by pulling the trigger of her imaginary pistol. Stan smiled.

She stopped by the ladies room on her way to the clubhouse stairs. Next to the sink she looked down at the packages and her broach. She remembered the note within the wrapping paper and the offer to use Robbie's box to watch Jersey Girl win the Test. She held the pin and looked at herself in the mirror. She had to smile when she caught sight of a woman reviewing her futile attempt at modeling. Mind your own business Laney thought.

Spurred by an instinct more of chutzpah than courage, she rehabilitated her lipstick and emerged from the ladies bespangled with Robbie's bit of glitter. She smiled at her own self-consciousness. What the hell, she thought out loud, he was a good guy and he wanted me to have this and well, if that's all I have to do to sit in his box and get a bird's eye view of The Test, why not?

"OK Robbie, you got me," Laney said out loud as she made her way toward the box seats.

She pushed her way through a thick crowd milling before the section E betting windows. She stopped long enough to place a twenty dollar exacta bet on Jersey Girl and two long shots, the 'five' and the 'three'. As she stepped away from the window she gave the people around her a careful review. Half of humanity seemed to be here. She leaned on the rail and laughed a little. Damn pin is heavy, she felt silly in the middle of the crowded clubhouse with this lead weight tugging at her blouse, but amazingly enough no one was looking at her, not even a passing

glance. Every where she looked she found enough material for
a doctorate in sociology. Right in front of her was a large round
man wearing bright white athletic shoes, grimy slacks, and a great
glob of mustard on his sleeve. She passed between twin 400 pound
divas in purple moo-moo's, a 75 year old grandfather sporting a
Chiquita banana blazer and holding hands with a 19 year old cutie,
who, in turn, was wearing little more than a stitch of spandex, and
false eyelashes longer than her skirt. There was even a circus clown
jumping around, passing out promo coupons, doing his very best to
avoid security.

"What am I worried about?" she thought.

Beyond several rows of patrons, the sad and heavy visage of
Robbie's sadly dressed friend entering the box seats caught her eye.

"Why's he still here?" she thought out loud.

She half skipped through the clubhouse and found Julie, the
section usher, who remembered helping him find his seat. Julie
looked at her blouse and pointed at her pin.

"Opps, there it is," she said.

"What?"

"Yup, got the word, anyone wearing that pin can sit in box
A-13."

"You're kidding?"

"Nope, that's the word."

"Should I tip you?" she said with a smile.

"All taken care of," Julie said with a bright smile.

"I'll be damned."

Laney followed the maze of ancient wooden cubicles until she
found Box A-13 and Robbie's friend. His face was that of a man
both worried and fatigued. He was sitting quietly, slapping a small
racing program against his knee, and looking like a lost schoolboy.

"Hello again," Laney offered.

He returned her greeting with only a blank stare and a slight
nod.

"How's your day going?"

He shrugged but continued in silence, eyes sliding back and
forth.

"It was a funny day where I was."

He looked around and behind her.

"Really, it was, a funny day, especially without Robbie."

"You're alone?"

Laney, didn't hesitate, "Sorry, were you expecting the others?"

"They were supposed to . . ."

"Yes, I tried to give them the packages, but they didn't believe me or something."

"I know," he said quietly.

"Come again."

"I was watching."

"You were? I didn't see . . ."

"Sorry, don't want you to think I was spying; I ~~was~~ just wanted this to be done right, you know, the way Robbie wanted it done. I saw what happened . . . most of it. Not your fault they aren't here; you did what you could."

There was a long silence between them.

"Mister, this whole thing is kind of weird; I don't want to get into trouble. What do you mean?"

"You won't."

The two strangers sat together and watched the entries for The Test parade before the grandstand. Laney tried to watch both Jersey Girl and Robbie's friend at the same time.

"Great place to watch the race isn't it," she stated out loud, "I don't think anyone can touch Jersey Girl. She looks great, even from the 11 post she's untouchable today."

"You are a good lady," he said quietly as he reached beneath his seat. "Here, Robbie wanted me to give this stuff away." There was finality and weight in his voice. He held four envelopes and offered them to her.

"What's this?"

"Well, now, they're yours. Robbie wanted everyone who came to his box to get a present. I guess he thought there would be four of you, but one is better than none?"

"No, you're fooling with me."

"No, really, he wanted whoever came up to his box to have gifts, real gifts I gather, really, I mean it."

"What is it?"

He rolled quiet reserved eyes. "Yours, because, well, it seems you were really Robbie's friend."

Laney could only suppress a nervous laugh and look away.

"Robbie took care of all his friends. When he knew the end was near, all of us, except for his friends up here, got taken care of. He was generous. This little game was kind of his way taking care of these friends too." There was a silence in the midst of the crowd's crush and clamor. "I guess, you see, he loved this game and this place. He called it the greatest game, and he wanted people to understand it and love it. He was ready to tell anybody who would listen how great the game could be."

"I know, he taught me a lot about the races."

"So, I gather, this was Robbie's way of knowing who really liked the horses. That's the way it was to him; that's the way he explained it. I guess he wanted to know who really loved this game, you know, the thoroughbreds and all."

"Get out. Is that what this is all about?"

"Guess so. My wife, God rests her soul, used to call him a sketch. Yup, that's what she used to call Robbie, a sketch."

Laney shook her head and resisted a sentimental wave. It made her stomach nervous and her face burn. She looked out past the infield to find the starting gate.

"Take'em lady, they're yours."

"Really?"

"Yup, yours, because you're here, and that was all Robbie wanted. His way of saying thanks."

She sat with presents on her lap. Again she resisted an impulse to ask more questions, "How do I thank you, I mean for all the trouble you've been put through with all this? I don't even know your name."

He shook his head as if to say she couldn't. "I'm Mike, but no need to thank me lady, no need; Robbie took good care of me, besides you don't thank somebody for just being a good friend. A promise made is a debt unpaid, remember."

When she heard Tom Durkin call three minutes to post she relaxed into her chair. "Thanks," she said.

The crowd was chattering and murmuring and rustling toward their seats. Forty thousand fans, desperate to find out if the graveyard of favorites would deflate the dreams of yet another champion, clattered away as they regained their seats and peered through binoculars toward the starting gate. But none of them, none within earshot of the clubhouse, could ignore the absolute squeal Laney let out when she looked into the envelope. At first the noise from her throat mirrored a piccolo's C. Then the sound became a shriek when her disbelieving eyes went into the third package, and then the fourth. People stopped and stared at her, white caps stepped forward out of the background to see if they were needed. Even the ushers stopped watching the televisions to see what was the matter.

Laney's eyes were ablaze, "Is this real, this can't be real," she bellowed into the vacant box. The man was gone. She looked up and down, but her benefactor had disappeared into the crowd. She stood there, her hands shaking, her eyes tearing and her heart raging. "Robbie," was all she could say and she said it many times. "This can't be real; this can't all be for me." Tears were her only companion.

Tom Durkin called, "They're off!"

Shortly after Jersey Girl the won the Test Stakes, by a desperate nose, Laney, sensing the confusion in her heart growing into a bitter sweet fire, charged through the grandstand and parking areas to her car. Her hands were shaking so violently she couldn't unlock the doors. She leaned against its fenders and tried to weep. In would take her many moments to sift through her thoughts. She had no frame of reference for this, by herself in the crowded arena, and yet not lonely at all, somehow esteemed and sheltered. Suddenly rich in ways too numerous to count, she left the race track and drove toward The Posie Peddler's tiny flower shop on Broadway. Her one thought was to spend her evening home with a bottle of her best wine and place two dozen red roses on her mantle piece.

I was charmed. We sat there smiling until some old friends, Robert and Nate, appeared promising good news for the early double. My friend smiled and took her leave to visit other friends on the third floor. I was serenely aware of how my admiration for her had grown in just a few short minutes. As she walked away I was conscious of a crucial truth Laney's tale had shared with me. I understood that there are, in the game of thoroughbred racing, many tests, many challenges to be answered, usually nine times a day, but there are other ordeals that exist apart from the racing surface. Some are measured and scored at dawn by a hundred sweat caked grooms nursing stallions through exercise and repair, others are faced and evaluated in the mirror, after a day's wagering is done and damages understood, while others are challenged at 'the' sales barn with their checkbooks and egos. But on The Test Saturday, one private challenge had demanded a gesture of love and passion for the game, and one, only one, had passed.

A Lesson In Privacy

Time and again I am reminded that my Grandmother was a very intelligent creature. Over the years of my ill spent youth she managed to instill in me a thousand truths and wisdom's, often through the indisputable logic of a lilac switch. True. Amongst these empiricisms, she was the one who told me a zillion times that it was not only a big world out there, but also a private one. Everyone thought and did and said things they could never explain in public and shouldn't be expected to. This was a truth that applied to everyone, including myself, and because of that, she would always say, it was best to allow each of my neighbors their faults and mind my own business. Why I am unable to remember this bit of genius out of Poor Richard's escapes me, but it does. In fact, it does so, so often, I am a bit ashamed to have to tell this tale, but I will.

You see the details of this disturbing little saga are so incredulous, and at the same time, so repulsive, that I have not been able to sleep for some time, as I am one of those peculiar persons who are unable to snooze successfully when the stomach and cheeks ache severely, which they do each evening when this adventure is shared with close associates over dessert. In truth, the details of this affair are so bizarre, and my suffering so extreme, that I have been convinced by one of the local quacks who occupies the rail next to me near the finish line, that the only way to get over these aches and pains is to write it all down and share it with my special friends. So, despite my Grandmother's admonition to mind my own business and not get involved, here it goes.

It all started on the morning of The Whitney Handicap in old Saratoga and I am sitting on the hood of my ever faithful Buick Invicta, behind The Bread Basket Bakery, relishing the last fingertip morsels of a second maple twist pastry, when what to my wondering eyes should appear, but the six foot seven inch visage of none other than Too Tall Teddy himself. He is a most notable character amongst these parts during the month of August, and even from my automotive perch I am very aware that the good Mr. Too Tall is a man on a mission of some importance, which is something I am able to decipher, as the countenance of the good Mr. Too Tall is of course a mug I have reviewed several times in the past, although it must be said that I have never before seen him with such a miserable kisser as the one I must review at this moment. In fact, the redness of his mane and beard can not hold a candle to the shade bespeckling his face and nose. In short, he is quite the crimson sight.

Unfortunately, I am also a rather obvious hood ornament, as I have backed in to my parking spot and Teddy sees me. This I know is not a good sign and the fire in his eyes tells me I am in for quite a tale, which is true. We exchange quick glances and immediately conversation evolves that goes something like this:

"Theodore," I says through the last dram of my coffee, "to what do we owe the pleasure?"

"Stranger, do not be so cheery, you are looking at a homeless bum, I am abandoned and alone on the streets of this here burg, and I am in a bit of a, a . . ."

"Quandary?" I suggested.

"What?"

"You're in trouble?"

"Precisely, I am in trouble, big trouble and . . ."

And then against my better judgment I spoke before engaging my brain. "What trouble?" I said, disbelieving the very sound of my voice, and all the time wondering why I had opened my big mouth.

"Worse I am telling you, worse than you can ever imagine. What am I going to do?" he kept repeating with the regularity of a grandfather clock as he paced back and forth, "I've been thrown out of my cabin, out, do you hear me, out," and these words were shared with much gusto and gesticulation, "out on my ear, and now with no place to go, and I am suppose to be here at least two weeks, and, and, Sally will be in town next week . . ."

Now Sally is Too Tall's ever loving little squeeze, a mysterious lady blessed with a particularly powerful portion of pulchritude and who has, it was rumored, warmed Teddy's extensive arms for many years and more than somewhat.

"Come on," I offer, "you cannot be out, not just out, you've been at Captain's Cabins for years."

"Seven, this was my seventh year in my room, seven years and I am bounced."

A strange little man started rasping away on an equally little 'tom-tom' in the back of my brain, but foolishly I resumed the conversation, "What has happened, pray tell?"

"It was the damn dog, the little yapping dog and the Captain's wife."

There was a poignant pause, "Continue," I said.

"Son of a . . . . I got into town a couple of days ago you see, and I went to the track and checked out the landscape and then went straight to the Captain's to begin moving in. I had just finished unpacking my things, boxes of essentials, you know, mustard and olive oil and bandages and stuff such as that, when I hear the barking of this annoying little dog."

"And you pays this creature no attention at first of course, because it is the middle of the morning and dogs have been known to bark and make such noise."

"Precisely! So I finish unpacking and I hang many of my shirts on hangars and generally make myself comfortable. I even take a short stroll through the shower just because I can, as it has been a long drive from Punxsutawney, Pennsylvania, and I am feeling on top of the world, clean, warm and with the Racing Form in front of me. What's better than that?"

True, I could find no demerits in the image he had painted for me, so I simply bid him continue by saying, "Nothing!"

"But just as I am about to start doing my numbers for tomorrow's first race, I can't escape the racket of that dog, still yapping away. By the time I have got a handle on the third race, the dog's barks have gotten on my nerves most thoroughly and so I investigate."

"And you found?"

"Well, wait till I tell you. I look and look, and after many minutes imitating Sherlock Holmes, I discover that this nasty little noisemaker belongs to the Captain's neighbor, a Mrs. Conley. And to make matters worse it is one of those disgusting little rug-mops-on-a-leash kind of dogs, with a big lower jaw and shaggy hair and just generally disgusting to look at."

"To say nothing of hear."

"Precisely! A high pitched yap like nails on a blackboard, only worse, and it's been gagging away for over an hour. So I calls up my landlady to find out if this dog is going to be ripping away at my ears for very much longer and what do you think I gets in return but a bit of an attitude from the wife, Mrs. Captain herself."

"Attitude is not good."

"Precisely. She says to me it's only a little dog and all women her age love these little hair balls as she has one herself, and to which I remind her it maybe little but it is making a big, big racket, mostly in my ears, and doesn't the city have a noise ordinance or something, and by the way what is the phone number of the police department."

"This, I might guess, got her attention."

"Yes, in a way, she gives me more attitude, tells me I wouldn't dare get the police to her house on a complaint, I wouldn't dare embarrass her before the neighbors, and something about men learning to love helpless creatures."

"Most provocative."

"Huh?"

"Nothing, nothing, keep going."

"Ah, yeah, but about a minute later I hear a screen door creaking below the big window in my room and the yapping stops. I investigate. I can see an old woman next door, walking around inside her sun room, holding the little noise maker and hugging it and kissing it and such, and I know all the right calls have been made and I am at peace, although a bit ill seeing the old woman kissing such an ugly dog so . . . so . . . ."

"Ardently?"

"Huh?

"Never mind, but none the less, a difficult vision to be sure."

"Precisely! Anyway, the next day I goes to the races and it is most profitable. I hit the double and three pick threes, but when I return to do some joyful accounting, that obnoxious, shaggy, glorified rat is once again leashed next to the porch and barking its little skull off. I call Mrs. Captain, no answer, I call again, no answer; the Captain's car is in the garage, but they are not home. I have a brain storm, I will go downstairs and give the dog something to do, like eat; so I find a few slices of baloney in the fridge and I take it down to the little monster and throw it over the fence. Well this Conley woman comes charging out from the porch making almost as much racket as her dog, and she is saying the most violent things about me, about how I hate animals and I'm trying to poison her little Roger. Do you believe it she calls the damn thing Roger? Roger; a cowboy star or a pirate maybe, but that ugly mutt, Roger . . . whoa!"

"And did this end amicably?"

"I thought so, especially after she started talking about calling the police herself because I had poisoned her freakin' little shoe polisher. So I tried to make peace with her by giving her a little bull, and I was finally able to escape and withdraw to a little peace in my room. But wait, about eight bells, Mrs. Captain calls up and she is in a most foul mood as apparently this Mrs. Conley has called her up and . . . well . . ."

"Given her a most unfavorable report, should we say?"

"Precisely . . . Yes, we should. She is really quite angry, this little old lady has painted quite an unflattering picture of me, me Theodore J. Beset, a gentleman from Punxsutawney, Pennsylvania, a high school graduate, and generally well respected at every racetrack from Florida to Maine. All of a sudden I am a bad-guy just because I wish for a little peace and quiet. So I sue for peace and the call ends as well as it could I suppose."

"But you do not get removed?"

"Precisely, but wait till I tell you. So I gets to sleep and I sleep the wonderful peaceful sleep of a winner, and when I wake up about six or so I go for a long walk through the alleys and quaint little avenues of Saratoga, up to Sarge's Diner for my usual breakfast. I pick up the Form and return to my lodgings as happy as you please, but when I return and sit at my kitchen table to do my numbers it starts."

"It?"

"It, the squealing and yapping of a little barking dog. Rap, rap, rap, the most disgusting yelping and croaking and rasping you ever hear."

"Oh dear," I offered, "I think I can see it coming."

"Not really, wait till I tell you. I phone down to my landlady, but she does not answer. I phone again, no luck. I then goes to the phone book and find this Mrs. Conley's number and I give her a jingle-jangle on the Alexander Graham Bell and what do you think happens? She starts hollering at me, this little old gray haired bag of wrinkles starts yelling into the phone that she is tired of me picking on her doggie, as her dog is perfectly quiet and a wonderful little companion, and I am of course a really bad dude for bothering her while she gets her beauty sleep. To which I inform her that she is a . . . a . . ."

"Fabricator of the truth?"

"I think so?"

"Oh dear, you called her a liar?"

"Precisely."

"Oh . . . this is not going to end well is it?"

"Wait till I tell you. So I finish our phone call as I am now compelled to tell her what I think of her and her obnoxious little ugly dog and we hang up. There is a second of peace and quiet so that I think I can return to my Form when the cats-are-calling starts up all over again."

I was confused for a second until I realized he meant caterwauling. Why had I parked my car in this lot? Gram, where are you?

"Well by now I've had it, up to here, as they say. I charge to the window, throw up the sash, I sticks my head out and, even though I cannot really see demon-mutt, I can certainly hear it. So I let it fly; I mean I fill my lungs and fire off a full barrage. I mean I didn't need a megaphone, they probably heard me on the backstretch. 'Shut that 'blankety-blank' dog up, and worse, three spectacular volleys."

There was a pause so I knew we were reaching the unfortunate conclusion of this most unfortunate tale. I was limited to offering, "So?"

"So," he began, suddenly assuming a sheepish posture, "so, just as I finished the last blast I looked down and there, right beneath my window, is my landlady, Mrs. Captain herself. She had been coming up the walk carrying a brown paper bag filled with groceries, and she was not pleased. She looked at me with such fire in her eyes that I knew, well, I knew I was in it deep."

"Deep?"

"Very deep indeed, you see it turns out," he paused here and looking away found momentary distraction in moving small pebbles about with his foot, "it turns out that the dog that was barking was not Mrs. Conley's shaggy little toilet face, no, I'm not that lucky. The lousy little noise maker actually was my landlady's mutt. I did not know it, but I had been hollering at the little dog that belonged to Mrs. Captain, and Mrs. Captain was not happy."

This I found difficult to embellish.

"Yes, we had quite a confrontation. She claimed I was rude and had embarrassed her before the neighbors and she used words like selfish and thoughtless and crude, and I returned the compliments with some choice offerings of my own and . . . well . . ."

"The end result is . . . you are out on your ear."

"In a nutshell."

"And your rental money?"

"She put it under one of my windshield wipers in an envelope with a note saying she was going to give me an hour to pack my things and vacate or she . . . she . . . would call the police."

"Oh dear, oh dear, the police in this town do not know how many close calls they have had."

'But now what do I do? I mean my car is parked over there by the Brew Pub, filled to the mirrors with my summer stuff, and my little lady is due in to town very soon and . . ."

"Well, this is a busy town; there must be another place you could rent?"

"Say, could I use the phone in your room?"

"Sure Tom," I said reluctantly, wondering again, for the umpteenth time, why I had never listened to my Grandmother.

II

It goes without saying that the rest of this fine Saratoga morning is spent indoors listening to WGY radio and eavesdropping on Too Tall's many and varied conversations. The local rag supplied several joints within driving distance to the track, but few seemed either affordable enough for Ted to do any serious gambling with the residuals, or comfortable enough for his ever-loving Sally to hang her hat and shower with both confidence and hygiene. It was a most vexing conundrum, but the thirteenth call produced a ray of hope at the end of this housing-shortage-tunnel, and suddenly Too Tall regained his enormous smile.

"Ted?" I asked.

"Maybe, just maybe. The Gerald's, ever hear of them? They have a B & B just off Route 29, this might be the one."

"Where on 29?" I ask, as this is a highway that goes all the way to Syracuse.

"The lady said their road is three miles outside of city limits, short of Greenfield."

"Promising," I replied with more than a smattering of relief secreted in my syllables.

Instantly the gentleman in question was off like a two-year filly without a jockey, and I was returned to the rather Victorian silence of my simple room.

The rest of the day went properly enough as I arrived at the race track in time for the fourth and soon found that my pick-of-the-day, Runyon's Pride, had finished up the track in the third. By not betting I was up 100 clams; I had not lost. I considered this a most fortuitous sign. I cashed a few small tickets in the sixth, saw my selection in the eighth scratch at the gate, and left the premises quite a few dollars ahead. I was happy.

The evening was also quite pleasant when, after a light meal at Hattie's Chicken Shack, I received a phone call from a former lady friend of mine. This was a lady most pleasant to know as she was always what the old-timers used to say, 'all girl' and most pleasant to be around. Just the sound of her voice rewound many provocative and spectacular images through my suddenly shaken brain, which grew even more unstable when she informed me how utterly disappointed and depressed she was with her new husband. He was a louse! Now I could not escape the pained memory of the day she informed me she was running off to marry this new dream of hers, but I also could not help but relish the thought that this 'louse', who had been the cream in her coffee, was now reduced to grounds for divorce. I mean, she had married the wrong man, clearly, but one mistake does not make one a bad person, I always say, so I succumbed to a 'charitable' urge and told her she was more than welcome to come to Saratoga for the weekend; where I would gladly put her up. Our dreams can be our happiness, sometimes. Again I slept the sleep of a winner.

The next day I was able to arrive in the clubhouse before noon and what do I find there but Too Tall Teddy. He is talking most energetically with, a retired jockey turned betting clerk, known to one and all around the Spa as Prince Travis. I listened.

"Well I took the damn room, I took it," Ted was saying, "But I think it was a mistake. The road to this place is about three miles out of town, but the house is at least another four or five miles up this old dirt road . . . That's why they can't rent it to anybody, nobody knows they're there, they're too far off the road, too far."

"But how about the room?" Travis kept asking.

"Oh, oh, the room is fine, really very nice, all decorated in that fancy wallpaper and old antiques and mirrors and all that. And the bed is new I think, queen size I think she said, and it's OK, really OK."

"So you took it," Travis reiterated.

"Yeah, but I think it was a mistake."

"Stop fussing, you got a place and you got it in one day. Your lady friend will like it right?"

"Yeah, Sally likes all that old frilly stuff."

"So you did all right, ten miles is nothing in a car, you just drive in every day, no big deal."

"But you should see it; it's a real farm, a real farm with big fields of corn and wheat or something, and cows in the fields and everything. They've even got a donkey."

"A what?"

"A donkey, you know, mule, jackass thing. It leans its head over the fence and brays and bellows just like on Hee-Haw." With which Teddy begins to flap his elbows and imitate the sound of the ostentatious pack animal; quite a sight to see, a six foot seven inch red haired donkey with a brazen voice in the middle of Saratoga's clubhouse. Even a few near-by security guards had to stop and pay attention.

"I think I had a ticket on that donkey in yesterday's Daily-Double?" someone said.

"Yeah a donkey, they use it to pull this little cart, you know, give hay rides to kiddies I guess, Halloween and stuff like that."

"Yeah"

"And they got a bull, a real big huge kind of chestnut colored bull they keep in a pen all by itself . . . real mean I gather, Mrs. Gerald told me three times to never, but never go near the freakin' thing . . . like ever-never."

"Oh yeah," Travis interjected, "a real breeding bull can be trouble with a capital 'T'. Rip you up big time with those horns man, rip you up and spit you out."

"So she said," Ted repeated several times, "I'm not going near the thing, not even thinking about it."

His review of Old MacDonald's continued with a full report about some chickens, three goats and a retired standard bred race horse. In fact he had to recreate the comings and goings of the llama's that inhabited a corral on the farm when a collection of Ted's friends assembled and each in turn received a colorful portraiture of his new digs. He must have created and recreated his pastoral vignette five or six times. It was good to see the old boy happy.

The day settled in to a most relaxed and comfortable routine. After the races a group of five or six of us met briefly at Siro's to toast the day's profits, and debits, admire the fine ladies with their extravagant hats, and at sundown parted company with promises to meet at Shiner's bar tomorrow.

All of which was followed up by a most charming and rewarding evening. My former flame called once again to discuss her plans for the weekend. This, at least on my end, I assured her was 'in the vault'. Next, my examination of the Racing Form uncovered a Barclay Tagg maiden with a 43 second workout, a sure sign of future profits, and quite late at night, a phone call arrived, just before Black Velvet time, from a most unscrupulous character known to the inmates of Tampa Bay Downs as Big Headed Bill. Now Big Headed Bill is without question a person who is rarely welcome in the Jockey Club, as he was burdened at birth with a most unlikable mug and a most inhospitable personality. Children in malls have been known to burst out in tears if he approached, and often his own mother was known to preach long passionate sermons to her many friends about the dangers and pitfalls of adoption. However, he is also a character who has spent years wining the favors of talented and devious horse trainers. So when Big Headed Bill calls long distance with information about a 'very well intended filly running in tomorrow's third race', it does not behoove an avid plunger like myself to ignore such fertile and high quality inside stuff.

In fact I am about to rest my weary head upon my pillow, and dream the dreams only avarice and greed can muster, when I am struck by a charitable thought. Seeing how he has had such a run of bad luck lately, I think I should share this little Florida jewel with my good friend, Too Tall Teddy. And as luck would have it, he is just entering the Gerald's residence when I call. So we quickly exchange the information, and Teddy is extremely excited, almost wildly ecstatic so to speak, as he has not been enjoying his usual run of bad luck, but lately he has been more like an old dinosaur at the windows; we congratulate each other, (prematurely), and return to our pillows, cool summer sheets, and the promise of tomorrow.

III

Well the next day at the racecourse is a most comfortable one. Rarely can I remember a time when Saratoga has supplied us with a more beautiful day. A bright blue sky and pleasant soft air make me so contented such that I am the King of the World. I find a fortuitous bench before the Travers porch and begin my reign. Perry Mason, a lawyer from Vermont comes by and then Dick, the beer guy form Boston, and finally Chattering Sal, all looking for some happy gale to blow them in the right direction which, I am happy to share, as today, armed with Big Headed Bill's intelligences, I believe I am smarter than a tree full of owls. So we form a quiet Chautauqua under the elms, share our information, and with knowing nods, smiles, and handshakes go our separate ways toward our favorite betting windows. But when I go to Travis's window in order to 'early-bet' the third, I can not help but notice that something is bothering me.

Travis greets me with his usual smile and I am quick to adopt the horseplayer's secret—spy posture so as not to allow some interloper to over hear my good news. Travis is a bit bewildered himself, but quickly removes his caution when I tell him, "I got it form Big Headed Bill last night; he called from Florida."

"He called you?"

"Yeah, he knows I will bet it for him, he can trust me, most assuredly, and if I get a little for myself . . . he will not be offended."

"Big Headed Bill?"

"Himself."

"Hmmmm," says Travis.

"Hmmmmm," I say as well.

"And did you tell Ted?"

Immediately I realize why I am uncomfortable, why my soul is not at peace.

"As a matter of fact, I did tell him last night, and he was much excited at the possibility of picking up some much needed scratch so he can entertain his ever-loving little sweetie-pie, but I have not seen him today, honest to Pete, I called him, he should be here."

"Strange," said Travis.

"Very strange," I replied

"Hmmmmm!"

"Very hmmmmmm," I repeated.

Well just minutes before the third race, just as Reggie's Red Hot Foot Warmers stopped playing their Dixie Land tunes, a terrific uproar came thundering from the paddock area below my hitching post. People were laughing, and bellowing, and calling out strange names. The grandstand area near the escalator of the old racetrack began to sound like a regular circus. I was intrigued. I even ventured to leave my perch and examine the riot when I saw the unmistakable image of Too Tall Teddy leaving the mechanical stairs and whisking through the breezeway, heading for the windows, which is where I found him, desperately out of breath and most uncomfortable looking.

"Ted?" I said, "Where have you been?"

"Don't ask!"

"Huh?"

"Don't ask!"

"What is going on, you Ok?"

"Shut up!" he squawked, suddenly throwing his arms in the air.

"Problems?"

"Precisely!" and with that he pulled out his wallet to get his bet in just as Marshall Cassidy called out, "They're off!"

Ted is shut out, as they say, as one can not bet on a race after it has started, and his face is now an open book, testimony in the flesh that he feels lower than the buttons on the vest of a mud turtle. It only gets worse when Big Headed Bill's lightning fast filly wins by open lengths at nine to one. I am rich, Bill is rich, but Theodore is another story all together. I dasn't look Mr. Too Tall in the eye, as I would not have been able to hide my glee which would have made his dismal state of mind much worse. In fact, out of politeness, I am beginning to direct my interests toward the seventh race when I realize Ted has disappeared.

Here I must reiterate my inability to follow Gram's lead and simply 'mind my own business' . . . Heaven forbid such common sense be applied to the life of a simple horse player. God knows I should use my head for something other than a hair farm. For at this most fortuitous moment I should have withdrawn and buried my oft broken nose in The Form, but did I? You'll see.

I walked past Travis's window and gave him a philosophical shrug, when he motioned to me.

"Seen Teddy?"

"As a matter of fact I have not. He disappeared after he got closed out. Poor guy can't get a break. Last I saw of him he was running out toward the paddock."

"He said something crazy to me about cops and getting busted and then he ran off."

"Truly? He's probably mad about getting shut out."

"Probably?" Travis said.

I found a vacant beam to lean on and returned to the next race. I had just put my numbers together when a new derisive roar went rolling through the paddock. Again, this was followed by Thomas clamoring up the escalator. This should have been my cue to adjourn, it should have been a reminder that nothing good was to come from Ted's misguided experiment in animal husbandry, and it should have served to confirm my instincts that the anonymity of the grandstand would have been the proper place for me that day. It should have, but it didn't.

I took a peek at Too Tall and found him looking even more pathetic and frantic than before. In fact I was just beginning to construct an excuse and withdraw to the rail when Teddy made eye contact with yours truly.

"I'm in trouble, I need helps." He whispers at me. My charitable urge weighing heavily on my shoulders.

"Huh?" I offer.

"I messed up this morning."

"What?" was my only reply.

"Seriously, I've screwed up, big time."

"Again?" (I wanted to speak with my ever-faithful Grandma.)

"I've lost their donkey."

Silence and a declining jaw was the best I could do.

"Ya gotta help me look for it."

"What?" was the best I could do.

"Come on, help me, I've lost Mrs. Gerald's damn donkey."

"Theodore, you know not what you say . . . say it is not so."

"Come on, I need . . ."

And with that Too Tall begins to relate another tale, and it is such a bewildering anecdote that I can only hold on tightly to my sides and bite the tip of my tongue, nearly off, or I will bust out howling and fall down prostrate on the floor. Such was this story which goes like this:

Earlier Ted jumped out of bed with a glad heart and an
expansive smile, having received my tip from Big Headed Bill and
further notice from his ever-loving sweetie, Sally, that she was all
excited to be joining him in his new digs for a romantic weekend at
the old Spa. In fact, such was his confidence that Ted slept in and
finally rose a little before nine. He found himself to be 'lord of the
manor', so to speak, as the Gerald family had packed up the entire
brood and headed to Lake George for a day of relaxation away
from the farm. Ted found Mrs. G's note about helping himself to
anything he needed and to expect a friend to be over after noon to
tend the animals.

All was right with Too Tall's world, until he discovered that his
car would not start. Dead it was. He tried and tried, but all it did
was make strange clicking noises. He went to his room and called
several friends, including myself, but no one was in, which was
true, as most known aficionados of the turf spend their mornings
at the track noting the workouts. He tried the Saratoga Taxi, but
they only laughed saying even the snowplows didn't go that far
from civilization and they were so busy, as it was a racing day, they
could not be out to the Gerald's farm for at least two hours. Even
the Automotive Club refused to help because he wasn't a member.

He then lost his temper and threw some things around the
room and began screaming, which of course is never a very
profitable venture. So in desperation he began walking down the
dirt road toward Route 29 and had gone a good mile or so when he
remembered the Gerald's had no neighbors and such a hike as this
would take hours and he would never make the third race anyway.
Again he began swearing and throwing things, rocks mostly, and
stamping his feet in the dust until he conceded defeat and returned
to the house. There he sat on the front steps wrapped in confusion,
hot and sweaty, crushed and forlorn, a posture known all to well
by most railbirds. He cursed, he swore, he tried to start the car one
last time, and in the end resorted to kicking the floor boards and
blowing the horn. The horn squawked.

Later, when he looked back on this moment, Ted convinced
himself that the strange bleating sound the horn made is what
really did it, what really was to blame for getting him into his
appalling mess. His horn had made a sound not unlike the sound of

the donkey. He remembered the kiddy cart and his mind began to sputter, to reach, and there were consequences.

"How hard could it be to make this happen?" he kept saying as he poked his head into the pen and examined the harness with its leather straps and brass couplings, "How hard can it be? I am a high school graduate. I grew up on my Dad's farm, I've done stuff like this before. Eureka!"

Now a real working barn, with a real living donkey, and a genuine antique rolling hay wagon might be no place for such a character as Too Tall Teddy, but that is what happened. He kept thinking that Ben Franklin had it all wrong, desperation was the real mother of invention and somehow, after some difficulty, and gnashing of teeth, Teddy managed to connect the animal and its cart, climb aboard and set off, with the crack of the reigns, for Route 29.

In fact the pungent animal seemed to know his own way down the road, but unfortunately, when they got to the highway in question, Ted realized that he had not thought his peculiar plan through. Hitchhiking the rest of the way meant he would have to leave the cart and the animal alone on the side of the road, which would certainly disappoint his new landlady, and getting thrown out of two places in one week, because of his inability to get along with God's dumb brutes was, needless to say, unacceptable. So once he got to the highway he sat there several moments trying to digest his conundrum, while cars honked horns and insolent teenagers barked discourteous abuse his way.

Yes, he soon realized, there was only one thing to do, he would simply take up the reigns the way he had seen Roy Rogers do it a hundred times on television, and go to town in the wagon, which is exactly what he did.

The trip into town scared him to death. Buses missed him by fractions, trucks practically pushed him into the ditch, and his nerve had been severely tested when the jackass exercised a laxative urge right in front of the Saratoga Hospital.

Now while Ted was relating his story, which was certainly wildly important to him, yours truly is having a difficult time listening and remaining poker faced. An image kept creeping into the back of my mind, the image of Too Tall Ted, six foot seven or thereabouts, in a tiny kiddy cart made for children, behind a jackass with indigestion riding through Saratoga traffic; he must have looked like Ichabod Crane on a toy truck. But I did the best I could to stay mum and pleaded with him to finish his tale, which went like this:

"Dis ain't funny, I'm in . . . in it . . . I'm in . . . ."

"A fix?"

"Precisely . . . and worse."

"Worse?"

"Worse . . . I've lost the damn donkey."

Characters from the sidelines were beginning to collect and eavesdrop on the unthinkable escapade. Fat Frankie even stood behind Ted and began to make screwy circles over his head. Carl and Robert creased brows and quickly ordered beers from Shiner's bar, for it is well known amongst the plungers, there is nothing like listening to a great tale with some cold refreshment.

"Lost the donkey, is this possible?"

"Very possible."

"Are you sure?"

"What kind of a stupid thing is that to say, of course I'm sure, even you could not miss a donkey tied to a wagon."

""A wagon?"

"Yeah a little yellow cart, wagon, thing, with balloons and clown faces painted on it."

"Clowns, well this picture is complete."

"Huh?"

"Never mind. The donkey, where did you leave it?"

Thomas hesitated. "I got on to Union Avenue and the stupid animal was acting up and hee-hawing and not doing anything I told it to, no matter how hard I hit it with reigns and such, and the cars were all honking their horns so much and some stupid crossing guard started hollering to call the cops because I was blocking traffic or something . . ."

"Oh dear, the police again."

So I made a quick left and this mule and I ducked through the gas station toward the sales pavilion. I found a little corner behind the hay barn nobody was using and tied the damn thing to a telephone pole.

"And?"

"And now it is gone, not there, not tied to the pole," he said with great energy and enthusiasm almost tearing out his hair, "and if I don't get that damn animal back to the Gerald's I'm done for . . ."

"Blue and tattooed as they say."

"Preeeeecisely. Come on, you got to help me look."

"For the donkey?"

"Yes, what else is there to do?"

"Missing persons . . . call the cops . . . how about the dog catcher; this town must have a dog catcher. Maybe he could help?"

"Dog catcher," Ted exploded in outlandish frustration, "it's a damn donkey, they don't have a donkey-catcher in this town and . . . damn it . . . and . . . . I've . . ."

To which I was unable to withhold my tongue any longer. I could see the image of my beloved Grandmamma forming faintly behind my eye's imagination, but I couldn't hear her, not one syllable, not one phoneme. In fact, even if I had heard her pithy aphorisms about privacy and mind-my-own-business, I doubt I would have resisted the temptation to open my big mouth, so I said it;

"And now you've lost your ass in Saratoga."

"Again," Shiner chimed in from behind his bar.

The place howled. Fat Frankie lost his beer, Mary ducked below her service counter so as not to be seen, Jay slapped his knees and Robert just walked away, desperate to tell the story.

Ted stood straight upright and shook. He stared at the convulsors around him, former confidants, suddenly convinced of their animosity. The howling persisted, more beer was spilled. He finally turned away, forlorn, friendless, and withdrew toward the paddock without saying a word.

"You can't make it up," someone kept saying again and again.

"Hitchcock wouldn't make the movie," someone offered. The laughing never stopped until police sirens were heard in the distance and the cheering was replaced with feigned concern and thoughtfulness. No matter how good the windows were to each and every player in the clubhouse that day, Ted's misadventure was the top gossip. By six that afternoon, I found myself sitting beneath an umbrella near the Shake Shack bemused by the extra cash I was carrying, but still worried about Too Tall's troubles. Somehow I knew he was gone.

Later that evening I was sitting on a bench, waiting for a table at Bailey's little eatery when two grooms from Jimmy Brad's stable walked past. I was unable to keep my ears to myself when I heard bits and pieces of a story involving a mule. I inquired and we shared a quick laugh when they told me Saratoga Police had found a donkey, hitched to a cart, somewhere on the back side of the Oklahoma training track, munching on grass between two horse trailers. A security guard discovered the Gerald's name stenciled on the cart, they were called, and a worried, but relieved family, drove into town to retrieve their prize.

When they left I couldn't help but wonder, since the donkey was truly safe, what had happened to Ted? It was a tale most bewildering, as we never did see the likes of his depressing kisser again. The next day at the racetrack rumors quickly spread amongst the players in the Clubhouse. The less charitable gossips proposed he had been arrested for animal cruelty and spent the night in the slammer with some very unsociable mugs. Others said the Gerald's entire family, including the children, had taken turns beating Ted with large sticks when he returned to retrieve his automobile. Still others were convinced that a tall and rather undistinguished gentleman with red hair had been seen entering the local hospital seeking emotional asylum.

But the most believable version of this story states that Ted was able to hire a mechanic, who accompanied him to the Gerald farm long before the family returned from their day trip, jump-started the mischievous vehicle which had precipitated this misadventure, and then had shrunk away and returned to his quarters in Pennsylvania, a much wiser, albeit poorer man. As to who might have been at the railroad station to greet the ever lovin' Sally, that is a story which should be told another time.

As for me, I had expectations of a visitor myself, but sometimes the odds are against you. This visitor I was hoping to see, the one would have bent my ear about the terrible things her not-so-new husband does to her, and how she must get clear of the dope, and how she was a fool for sending me over, which, of course, I would have done my best to console her injured ego. Who could find fault with such an arrangement? So I waited many days for the phone call, but somehow I missed it. I had the phone company check and double check the line and circuits to be certain they were in proper working order and even checked with my landlady, the good Abigail Wentworth, but she disavowed any knowledge of such a phone call. Apparently there was none. My happiness waned. Such is the fate of many a horseplayer, but hope springs eternal, as the poet said. And as they say in Saratoga . . . 'Hey, you never know'!

To Bet or Not To Bet

So, there I was, early one morning, warmly ensconced in my favorite little booth far at the back of my favorite little eatery in the entire world, Mother Goldsmith's of Saratoga, doing my level best to work my way through a half dozen of the good chef's mini-corn muffins and get the news from Phil Reina that the battery in my ever-loving Buick had been revived at minimal cost, when my perspective on the day was thrown totally awry. Fat Frankie from Florida and Jay Bird, the lawyer from Newark, entered with all the aplomb and ascendancy of Napoleon himself. No two happier faces could be found anywhere in this berg as these two appeared to be wearing some rather well financed hearts on their sleeves. They were glad handing everyone at the bar and waving hellos like a pair of Macy's Santa's out of costume. I was intrigued.

And just as I finished enjoying my last morsels, the pair found me in my little booth which seems to maintain the only vacant seats in the joint. They smile at me. I smiled at them.

"Jay Bird," I called. "Over here, come and have a seat or two."

"We are welcome Stranger?"

"Most certainly you are welcome . . . come sit."

"Thank you again," Frankie exhaled as he sat with a great sigh. "Oh. Thank you so much, I was afraid I was going to have to eat standing up and my old legs do not do standing as much as they used to."

"I understand," I returned. "We will get you a waitress and some breakfast perhaps?"

"Perhaps is right," Jay said as he pulled the laminated menu out of the sugar holder, "we are starved, starved I am telling you."

"Really, you gentlemen have not been able to earn an honest meal in this here little town, which is full of named restaurants and more than a few greasy spoons?"

"Naw, that is not it Stranger. Ask Jay, he will tell you. We have been out celebrating a little too much and as 'Desperate Annie's' does not serve breakfast we thought we should come here. We are very lucky to have found you, this is for sure."

"Annie's?" I asked. "Annie's?"

"Well that is where we ended up," he said with a chuckle, "after we wore out our welcome at The Professor's, the Old Bryan Inn, and The Adelphi Hotel."

"Lillian Russell's," Jay offered through a quick smile. "Don't forget Lillian's. And the bartender, my God, the prettiest woman I have seen in years . . . magnificent . . . and she's been working there the entire meet. Where have I been?"

"We were very lucky to meet her. She put up with our bad jokes and kept the bar open after hours just because she liked us."

"Us," Jay said with a laugh, "us? Who are you kidding? She liked one of us, but I am afraid . . ."

"Go on," Frankie said, as he punctuated his objection with a soft elbow in Jay's ribs.

I had caught on. "Do you two mean to sit there and tell me you have been up all night?"

"Of course, I think we drank ourselves sober," they chimed simultaneously.

"Well, I must assume you had something to celebrate."

Frankie only nodded and grinned.

Jay's eyes appeared over the menu, "We had a very good day."

Frankie nodded again and again.

"Well let me congratulate you two. What was it?"

They two gamblers looked coyly at each other. "Should we tell him?"

"Should we?"

"Of course."

Jay bent across the booth so as to whisper and said in a very quiet voice, "We hit the last race."

"The ninth?" I was shaken as I knew yesterday's ninth race had been won by long shots, and as such, any bet worth betting would pay off in 'automobile vin-numbers'.

Jay winked. "Had the triple . . . had it good."

"You had the 10-2-7 triple? You two do not need a breakfast, you need an accountant."

"Had it good," Frankie said under his breath. His smile was spectacular.

Now having it 'good' is a semantic peculiarity horseplayers use to tell other horseplayers that they bet the bet heavy, which means they did not risk two dollars or five dollars or even ten. Such denominations could not fulfill the definition of 'heavy' amongst the gamblers who truly gamble. Clearly, the two gentlemen seated across from me were very well oiled at the moment. When I gazed down at my pink sheet, the numbers stated clearly that yesterday's ninth race triple had paid over $6,000.00 for a two dollar ticket, and I was sure they had more than one ticket.

"Heavens help us, you two are rich." I exclaimed.

Frankie put a knowing forefinger over his lips, "Let us not broadcast it too widely Stranger, you never know who is listening, and I do not want any hapless loser putting the bite on me, at least not yet."

I sat corrected. My little outburst was understood and possibly appreciated, but clearly inappropriate. True gamblers are expected to win, and lose, with a certain amount of decorum.

"Amazing," I said in a hush. "But how did you come to pick those horses? All three were long."

"Well the truth is Stranger, we almost didn't," Jay said as the waitress took their orders, "Frankie found these horses the night before, and we went to the track to bet just them, but then things got a little out-a-hand and, well, we almost didn't. The day started out terrible, just terrible. We had no luck at all. Lost a photo when McCauley got DQ'ed in the opener, and then our next bet never left the gate."

"Most discouraging," Frankie offered, "almost gave up on the day, but then, ah-ha, but then, our luck changed and something just told me we were going to hit it big."

"Your luck changed?"

"It sure did," Jay said, "it was a strange day I am here to tell you, uncanny, but our luck changed in the third race, because you see, our luck changed when we did not lose." Frankie nodded his confirmation.

I knew the look on my face only spoke of confusion.

"We did not lose and when we did not lose, it was like a great big search light came on in my brain; I knew we were on the inside rail for sure."

"Well more like a night light," Jay said with a laugh.

All of which contorted the features of Frankie's rubbery face into a sardonic smile, "Ah, funny guy. Maybe a refrigerator light went on, but it went on, and I knew."

And with that my two well-heeled conspirators took great pain to relive all the varied details of a moment from their yesterday that turned their world around and put them on 'the money trail'. I listened with more than a small amount of polite jealousy to a story all horseplayers have known at one time, or another in their days. It is day of exquisite Gothic irony and for Fat Frankie and Jay bird, it went something like this:

"To bet, or not to bet . . . that's the question," Jay said out loud to no one in particular as he glanced up from his racing form to review the silhouettes in section B of the Saratoga Clubhouse.

"What is?" replied his friend Fat Frankie.

"Here, in the Form. Have they got these workouts right for Noble Danzig?"

"What do you want?"

"Haven't you been listening?"

"Listening to what? You talk too much; all you ever do is talk. What's the problem?"

"Oh, that's how you practice diplomacy in Florida, with name calling and . . . and . . . ridicule."

"After the first two disasters, why are you reading that paper? Clearly you can not read. What is it?"

"The workouts for Noble 'what-cha-ma-call-it', look, they look phony to me, they can't be right. How can you back a runner with any conviction when the Form's full of misprints and bad dope?"

"Listen, God gave you two ears and one mouth. That means you are supposed to listen twice as hard as you talk. Get it? So listen. The Form never makes a mistake; it is the Bible."

"Well, you and I must be reading different books from different Bibles or something, because this horse never went four panels in forty six seconds, ever, nothing close to that."

"Out of Polish Navy, those Polish Navy horses can run, just like the old man."

"Yeah, but he never went forty six and change with some whale of an exercise rider on his back, never, or I'm a Polish Prince."

Fat Frankie looked up from his beer and let his eyes review the frame, posture, and countenance of his redheaded friend. He said quietly, "A prince? You a prince? That would seem to end the debate."

The day's card was filled with maidens, young horses who had never found their way to the winner's circle, which also meant they had had very brief careers, and even shorter resumes. Only the fourth race they were looking at, as well as the eight, the featured The Albany Handicap, had runners that touts refer to as 'form-full', ones that had a record or a history a handicapper could study. Horses, it is rumored, are a lot like people. Without a past, they can't be relied upon in the future, and the future was right now for Jay and his beer-happy friend. They were in the deepest darkest throws of a prolonged loosing streak, and with the day's card staring them in the face; they knew instinctively this might be their only chance to appear at Bruno's for a deluxe supper of pizza and English Ale. No diplomat in search of a cease-fire ever negotiated with more fervor, rigor, and passion then these two. It was fifteen minutes to post and the speculations in row G of section B were intense.

"I got it, one, four, six, and in that order. What'ya got?"

"Well, I ain't got that, I can tell you sure. The one horse, Pairadocks, has lost both of its races by over thirty lengths, and your four horse, Dark Queen, hasn't been out in, what is it, ninety . . . ninety-six days."

"Yeah, but Pairadocks was in open company, these are New York breds, and he's got a five furlong workout in a minute flat just four days ago."

"So?"

"So plenty. Queen-what's-her-name had to go five wide in that last race, she pressed the pace the entire backstretch until they all blew the turn and . . ."

"And nuttin', they should have blown her up. I bet her that day, and she cost me money."

"Then, look at Noble Danzig, the six, look at those works, if they're legit . . . ?."

"Could be, could be? He finished a close-up third twelve days ago. How much beer we got left in the cooler?"

"Beer, we don't need beer, we need a clear head to get this next race."

"Clear head my eye. What good did a clear head do you in the last race? None. Understand, none! So, give me a beer."

When Tom Durkin announced there were ten minutes left until post time, the two calculators left their seats to stand beneath one of Saratoga's innumerable television monitors and review the odds. This posturing beneath the televisions is a required gesture each and every player must master if they do not want to appear a 'rube' or some bewildered ignorant tourist. Serious players spend most of their afternoons examining the odds and the exacta payoffs in an attempt to unearth a bizarre betting scheme, somewhere out there in electronic simulcast-land, which might indicate the nebulous plans of a notorious trainer in a nefarious betting syndicate. It was a ritual that Frankie had mastered years and years ago, but Jay remained cynical and stayed near his friend more as a gesture of tolerance than anything else. Somewhere in the back of Jay's mind he kept hearing an old law school professor telling the class "A Golden Rule" that conspiracy theories are the last desperate refugee of the dim and hopeless.

"See anything?" Jay whispered.

"Nuttin," Frankie replied.

"Nothing," Jay whispered, even lower.

"We are doomed. Maybe we should take this race off? Let's go see if Maria has any more beer at the hot dog stand."

"You haven't finished that one for God's sake."

"Yeah, but it is a long walk to Maria's."

"Hold it Frankie," Jay said with sudden resolve, "Who is that over there? Over there by the ice cream truck."

"Where?"

"There by the little blonde girl selling ice cream. See the guy in the gray suit and the old straw hat. Is that, no it couldn't be, is that old man Hamilton?"

"It couldn't be. I ain't seen him here in years, I thought he was dead."

"I don't know? I thought it was at first, but then . . . doesn't he look awful. God he looks like death warmed over."

"Death fondue, poor guy. Maybe it's his ghost? That guy'd be better off if he was a ghost."

"Don't be sick . . . that's sick or something. Come on, let's get closer and take a better look."

The desperados walked cautiously past the fifty-dollar windows and stood close to the man in the gray suit. From behind it was plain that his neck no longer filled the collar of his shirt, and his once blond hair was as thin and as translucent as spider webbing. Jay turned to Frankie and grimaced. Frankie grimaced back with a shoulder shrug.

"It's him," Jay said in a whisper, "or what's left of him."

"You sure?"

"Positive."

Old man Hamilton had been one of the game's great plungers for several decades. He had, in fact, put together one of the first betting syndicates that pooled money to go after large Pick-6 wagers. One summer, many years before, it was rumored that his organization had hit six Pick-6 wagers in less than three weeks with profits just short of half a million.

"Who's he talking to?"

"I don't know? Himself I think?"

"This guy's an odd duck. You sure this is Hamilton?"

"Come on Frankie, he's going toward Patrick's window, come on."

And just that quickly, the three men broke away from the ice cream stand, leaving the attendant confused, and wondering if she had done something wrong.

"Look Jay," Frankie offered in a whisper, "you get behind this guy, and pretend to be reading your paper, or admiring the dolls in the next line, or something."

"What! Why me? That's not my style."

"Look, you lawyers are always up to something, so get up after this; it might get us back in the black. Act as natural as you can, don't let on your spying; if it is Hamilton he's been through this a thousand times and he'll get wise. The idea is to get him to let the cat out of the bag without knowing the kitten is gone."

"I know, I know."

"You gotta be cool, cooler than Eskimo cakes."

"Eskimo cakes? Cakes? You mean Eskimo Pie don't 'ya?"

Frankie looked right through his bewildered friend, "Cakes, pies, muffins . . . What 'da hell is you talking about? Get in 'da line!"

"This isn't the way I do things."

"Will you get off your high horse just long enough to let the saddle cool? Stop being a putz. Just do it. Hurry, we only got a few minutes."

"No, come on. You do it. I don't want any part of this eavesdropping crap."

"You, a lawyer?"

So Frankie stayed under a television while Jay stood behind the old man in the gray suit. The two inched their way forward until the gray suit leaned into the fifty-dollar window and began to speak. Frankie could see his friend lean forward and he knew covert deeds were at hand. The betting line stood still for a second and then, without gesture, the old man moved slowly away from the window. Jay jumped into the space and, pretending to fumble with his newspaper, took in all he could from the betting screen before him. The teller, busily counting a stack of hundred dollar bills, had neglected to erase the screen's display. Jay apologized for not knowing what he wanted to bet and whirled away from the window to watch the man in the gray suit ~~read~~ reread his tickets. Jay never lifted his head from his paper, but his eyes never left his silent partner. Frankie waved him away.

"What'ya got? Come on, six minutes to post!"

"It was Hamilton for sure, he bet two hundred dollar exactas, straight and boxed, on the three, the five and the six. See, Noble Danzig, I told you so, Petals Forever, and The Parasol. The guy laid out thirty one-hundred dollar bills like they were napkins at a firehouse wedding."

"Noble Danzig, maybe I can see, maybe, but these other two, these other two . . . he's crazy, he's gotta be crazy. 'Petals' hasn't even been on the board in a year and 'Da Parasol, look, look at the book on her. A lifetime record of four races with one fifth and the rest, up the track. Christ she's dead on the board, thirty to one."

"And I'm telling you Hamilton bet her. He just threw a crusher of an exacta down with her in it, and that means one thing, something's up, and I don't want to miss it."

"I don't know?"

"You got a better idea?"

"Well . . . no . . . but."

"Are you in or not?"

And so Jay, armed with his friend's twenty-dollar bills and some of his own, charged and reentered one of Saratoga's time honored customs, the betting line. It must be understood that the betting lines at Saratoga are one of its least appreciated traditions, as they can easily be twenty or thirty people deep on a weekend. They often stretch from the windows back to the box seats. People are jammed together, elbow to vertebrae, breathing on each other, and sampling one another's cologne. The lines move, but never well enough, or quickly enough, to sooth fragile insecurities.

"Five minutes," Frankie recited again and again, "think we'll make it?"

"Stop worrying, we got five minutes and there are, what, only six or seven people in this line. Stop worrying."

They waited, rocking back and forth on eager feet.

Tom Durkin called, *"Five minutes to post time."*

"What's goin' on up there? We ain't moved an inch."

"I don't know? Some big bettor I guess."

They waited.

"Four minutes to post time."

"Ah no way, we're dead, come on, move it up there," Frankie bellowed in his best circus barker imitation, "four minutes, let's go!"

"Somebody sunbathing at Patrick's window?"

Others behind Frankie roared even louder and a man in khaki slacks trumpeted his displeasure by stamping his feet. The line began to grumble and look to other queues for advantage. It was swaying and curling on itself like some ravenous anaconda. More protests were followed by accusations of skullduggery, and the noise began to attract attention.

Just when the cacophony was reaching its feverish zenith, out from the head of the line emerged the most pathetic little human creature Jay could ever imagine. She was dressed in a bright blue sequin studded dress that probably fit some years ago, but now dragged on the floor while its arm openings sagged well below her underwear. She was adorned with a red polyester hat, threadbare with use, and topped by dusty plastic flowers. The sad decorations must have been accumulating debris since last year's appearance at the races. Both arms were shackled in orthopedic braces in a losing attempt to keep the arthritis from curling her hands into her wrists. Her red lipstick was too thick, smeared from the day's adventures, and it failed to obscure the seventy plus years of living that had ravaged what had once a pleasant strong face. She shuffled away from the window, unable to actually walk without her walker, and smiled the best smile she could muster in hopes that pleasantness would suffice as apology.

Jay was startled into stillness. The men in the line, inhaling for a fresh volley of threats and obscenities, were struck silent. Grown men, some with medals from foreign wars, retreated into their newspapers, others pretended to look around at the odds board, and still others examined the contents of their shirt pockets, anything, to avoid the judgment that awaited them. Only a woman at the end of the line stopped the little lady in the blue dress to ask her a question.

"Oh, you're a red-hat lady. Did you bet this race?"

The small eyes brightened and she tied to smile, "Yes, I bet two dollars, two dollars to show on number two; my granddaughter is two years old tomorrow."

"Oh yes," the woman offered, "I hope you win."

"I do too! I'm starting a bank account for her and when she goes to . . . ."

Jay's face was buried in his paper. It emerged with a swatch of black printer's ink in his red eyebrows, "Two bucks to show, to show and we're . . ."

"Let it alone," said Frankie in a low grumble, "that'll be us some day."

"*Three minutes to post time,*" rattled over the loud speakers.

"Call the mortician, we're dead," the man in the khaki slacks said to Jay.

"What's goin' on up there? This line reserved for politicians?" demanded Frankie.

Before them in the line was a tall thin man with ponytailed white hair and a vanity goatee. His face was erupting with crimson anger. "Some jackass has a bum ticket, and he won't believe the teller it's no good."

Jay watched the man throwing his arms around and calling for the supervisor. Some of the people in their line broke to the left, some to the right, hoping to find a quicker way to a window.

New faces were surrounding the teller, and finally the irate customer was asked to come inside the office to have his ticket examined. He moved away swearing under his breath. A choral cheer went up from the betting line and he replied with a raised fist.

"Jackass," Frankie said.

"Amateur," Jay responded, "probably a bet from two days ago he found in his pocket; he can't read dates or something."

The line inched forward. A smallish little man in a pin striped Nehru Jacket was next. He chugged toward the window, his cigar puffing away with paragraphs only an Iroquois chieftain could decipher. Jay and Frankie watched intently as he leaned into Patrick's window and lifted his head.

"You want to bet," Patrick said quietly.

The little man began to cough.

"Mister?"

The coughing increased with the cadence of a metronome. His head and shoulders were bouncing with each muffled blast.

"You O.K. buddy?"

The coughing increased. He sounded like an asthmatic camel, wet and thick. The man was gagging.

"Damn," Frankie said to his paper," How the hell did we get in this line? Did a bus from the nuthouse break down here?"

"Two minutes . . . two minutes."

The man before Jay turned and rolled his eyes as the coughing rose to a feverish pitch.

"Key-Rist," said Jay, "it's like Who's Who in Mental Illness. We gotta get to a better line."

"Where?" said Frankie.

"We'll never make it, we're mummies."

The coughing continued. The little man was near collapsing as he hung on to the sill of Patrick's betting window. The teller stood up from his stool and leaned forward, "Hey buddy, don't die here, there are people waiting to bet."

"Sorry," was all he could say in a raspy damp gargle. He moved aside and waved the next man forward, but the coughing wouldn't stop.

A short balding man in Bermuda shorts and dark brown leather sandals jumped ahead and leaned into the betting window. The man in the khaki slacks and Jay and Frankie looked at him, then the clock, and back to the lone bettor that stood between them and their future. Jay could hear him calling out numbers . . . one and three over the four and six . . . twenty dollar pick three . . . three and six with four and eight with . . . . and on and on and on. The tote board began to flash one minute to post time. Frankie poked him in the back, "Should we jump to another line?"

Jay looked furtively around, "They're all the same now. It was that idiot with his bum ticket . . ."

"One minute," Tom Durkin announced.

Again the murmuring and shuffling returned to the betting lines.

"Come on hurry up!"

"Move it!"

Finally the man at the window stood up, called out his last numbers and began to settle his tab. The teller looked like he was counting change. Jay bellowed his cheeks in an attempt to stay calm. Mr. Khaki slacks jumped forward and began to place his bets, exactas and trifectas and boxes and key wheels and . . ."

"We're deader than dead," Frankie said over Jay's shoulder.

A bell, indicating post time, began to chime methodically; clang, clang, and clang.

"Ah God, get it in buddy," was all Jay could say.

Jay and Frankie looked at the TV monitor and watched the 'minutes to post' window change from one to zero. They both exhaled.

"That can't be," the man in khaki slacks said.

"Sorry, its ninety-six dollars. Do you want the bet?" the teller said.

The man stood staring down at the screen.

Tom Durkin called out, "*It is now post time!*"

"Now what?" asked Frankie.

"For Christ's sake, they're arguing over the price of his bet."

"Do not tell me this. DO NOT TELL ME THIS!" Frankie growled through his teeth.

"Well I'm telling you," was all Jay could mouth in desperation.

"Mister, do you want the bet or not? It's post time," the teller said loud and clear. He was standing at his chair now. He needed the bettors in his line to understand what was going on at his window.

The man in the khaki slacks stood a second longer and then slumped toward the window reluctantly.

"Come on," Jay kept saying under his breath, "Come on!"

But just as the two earnest speculators were beginning to see a faint sliver of hope, a tiny ray of promise, the man in the khaki slacks did the unthinkable, the absolute unthinkable thing no horseplayer worthy of the title would ever think of doing, would ever dare to do, he reached for his wallet. Jay almost spit out his gum. The guy was reaching for his wallet, he was standing in the betting line all this time, preparing to lay down close to a hundred dollars in wagers, and he didn't even have his money out.

Frankie threw his paper in the air hollering, "Give me a break, just one little break, you gotta be kidding me."

Jay was too stunned to speak. The man was sorting through the bills and counting out exactly ninety-eight dollars. He counted it out like the teller was expecting change for his 'blue-light' special. He hadn't even finished examining his betting tickets when Jay, unable to restrain himself, shouldered his way past and leaned into the betting bay. The man took some umbrage at the way Jay had moved him aside, but Frankie stepped into the man's face and said, "You are done, understand! Your bet is in. Done!"

"Quick, I want twenty dollar exacts boxes. Give me the 3 with . . ."

And the alarm rang out.

It rang as loudly, and clearly, as any bell that had ever rung in Jay's ears. It rang as loudly, and as clearly, as a racetrack alarm can ring. The horses were bolting out of the starting gate. The race was on. No more bets.

Jay's eyes opened an inch wider. Frankie looked up at the television, only to see the horses scrambling for position at the first turn. Jay crushed the newspaper into his fist while Frankie threw his pencil to the floor. It bounced across four betting aisles.

"Closed out? I never get closed out."

"Hey, I'm the professional; I'm the one who never gets closed out."

"Baloney, I have never been . . ."

"Who's the knucklehead who put us in this crazy line anyway?"

"Knucklehead? I told you we should've jumped lines. I told you with five minutes to spare."

"You did not! I'm the one who told you we should have . . ."

"Don't get me started . . . I told you . . ."

The incriminations continued, volley after volley, until they heard Tom Durkin call,

"and at the top of the stretch, they're coming for home. Noble Danzig is looking for racing room, Petals Forever will not quit, they are nip and tuck every step off the way."

Twenty thousand voices cheered and cried out loud.

"It's Noble Danzig and Petals Forever . . . Noble Danzig . . . Petals Forever . . . The Parasol is looking for racing room . . ."

The two men gasped as they looked up at the image over the teller's head. It couldn't be, it shouldn't be, but there they were, just like Old Man Hamilton had bet them, charging down the stretch with an eighth of a mile to go, six to one and twelve to one and thirty to one, noses apart heading for the finish line.

"Do not do this to me," Jay spoke, quite out loud, as if addressing the racing Gods like old school chums.

"No way," Frankie was heard to say under desperate breath, "no way."

"Oh please," Jay's voice began to get pathetic, "no, please, somebody, anybody, noooooooo please."

Jay looked to his right and found his corpulent friend had clasped his hands in dynamic prayer. "No, no, no," he kept saying over and over again to no one, or anything except the back of his teeth and the tip of his tongue.

The two charged to the rail behind the rows of clubhouse seats. The horses should be right in front of them by now. People were standing and cheering. The noise made it impossible to speak. Tom Durkin's voice was rasping through the ancient loudspeakers, but not one word could be deciphered from where they were.

And then another roar, a dynamic exhausting cheer, and the old grandstand shook.

Each man cringed in ironic disbelief and turned to total strangers near them, "Who won, who won?'

"The one, got'em right at the wire." Someone from the seats said.

Jay looked at Frankie, Frankie looked at Jay, "Who the hell is the one?"

Their racing forms flew open and there it was, the one horse, Pairadocks, twelve to one in the morning line.

Suddenly, without rehearsal or cue, the most uninhibited and unrefined form of celebration exploded from the two men. They feigned collapse, and held their hands over their hearts. False beads of perspiration were wiped from suddenly unwrinkled brows, and smiles returned to their tortured faces. Tiny smirks of forgiveness began to escape tearing eyes.

"Oh, Thank God we were wrong."

"I'd'uve died if that damn thing had hit . . . Oh, 'dat was close."

"Too close," said Jay, "way too close."

"I never 'tawt being wrong could make me feel so good."

"I never thought getting shut out would make me feel so good."

Jay was looking at the racing paper. Frankie was looking for his beer.

"What's wrong," Frankie said quietly.

"Jay's desperate face had returned, "Pairadocks, I told you that horse was going to run today. I told you. I can't believe I let you talk me out of betting him."

"Me, don't blame me, I didn't talk you out of anything, and besides if you hadn't put us in that line with Elmer Fudd and Porky Pigg we might have had a chance."

The two men looked up at the board as the public address system announced the results as official. Pairadocks had won and the nine, a horse named Umbrageous had finished second. The exacta paid one hundred and ninety eight-dollars.

"Umbrageous?"

The two men began to laugh. "Where the hell did 'dat come from? The second race!" asked Frankie.

"Must've come out of the grandstand."

"Was there a horse named Umbrageous in this race?"

They couldn't stop laughing. They leaned against one of the racetrack's ancient wooden beams and laughed the laugh only a horseplayer might fully understand.

"We didn't lose," said Jay.

"We didn't lose," said Frankie.

"Our luck is changing?" said Jay.

"Maybe it is?" said Frankie.

"Let's get to work on the ninth."

"Hold it. First, Maria's, beer, and you're buying!"

It was as if I was sitting before Midas and Croesus themselves. The affluent nabobs polished off their breakfasts and retold the story again. Their voices were subdued, but their pride was boiling over. Later we stood on Phila Street in the morning sun and shook hands. I watched them meander toward Broadway admiring the laughter in their stride. Sleep or no sleep, they were walking on clouds, lovely big soft green clouds.

It took me only a minute to end my reverie; I had things to do myself, for one I had to get my car, and as I strolled through the side streets and parking areas I kept rolling the story of Frankie and Jay over in my mind with growing admiration. After all, there would be racing today and that meant I should have at least nine opportunities to prove how smart I was. If I brought all my talents to bear at the windows I might have the opportunity to make some lucrative decisions myself. I suddenly could not wait to get to the racetrack. After all, hope is a tenant, in the heart of the horseplayer that never wanders far.

Patti's Piggy Bank

Now it is true that the private history of most horseplayers has been shaped by Dame Fortune in more forms and disguises than New York's 44th Street ever imagined. There are chapters from Fate's diary that testify to eras of affluence and excess that might rival the opulence of India's emperor Shah Jahan, while there are other moments of deficiency and disappointment that turn into lessons of bona fide humility. Each of these moments, be they grand or gruesome, testifies to the resilient nature of the human soul, for those that throw themselves against the Gods of Fortune must face their own private Kierkegaardian moment and confront the ultimate 'either-or' each day brings. Often, on the darkest days, the sufferer questions his or her involvement in the game, their level of intelligence, or, worst of all, the very purpose of living. The machinations and variations of this game can strike deep. These are maxims all gamblers know to be true.

Unfortunately, I was enduring a similar era, and doing what I could to survive during the third week of Saratoga's racing calendar. Reviewing my bank statement, recounting the bills in my shirt pocket, and rummaging through the pockets of yesterday's suit told me conclusively that I had arrived at Destitution's Door. I was pathetic. And on top of that, the good Mrs. Wentworth, my landlady, was beginning to run out of patience waiting for my room rent, and, on top of that, I didn't even know if I had enough money to sneak out of town so that I could stiff her. I was despicable.

So just two days before the running of The Sword Dancer, I sat in front of Compton's Diner, watching a blast furnace sun seer its way over Broadway, when I decided to salvage my dignity and breath fresh life into my days. My insolvency was something of a morass, but I would not quit, not yet. Through force of will, or at least some inventive contrivance, I was determined to find my way out of the maze that had kidnapped me. I kept reminding myself that there are ways to survive hard times, others had done it, Bet-A-Million Gates, John Morrissey, Andy Byer, to name a few, I just needed one good idea.

The first thought that came to mind was the old 'bogus' tip sheet ploy. Printing a bogus tip sheet is always a good scam to encourage the gullible to reach ever higher levels of naiveté. It is a simple plan. All you need is a photocopy machine and a radio. The secret is to printout a tip sheet that looks likes you had picked many winners on the day's card. Let's say it's a Wednesday. You listen to the radio and get the winners of the first four or five races. Then you quickly print out a tip sheet, with your own special logo of course, indicating that you had picked winners that day, especially the first five. You finish the tip sheet with logical selections for the rest of the card and then quickly print out a few dozen sheets. Next you rush to the racetrack and leave your 'sheets' scattered around for the patrons to discover and enterprise will follow. After a few days of this, your tip sheet will be developing quite a positive reputation amongst the unknowing and some may actually be looking for more 'good' advice which is when you reap your grim rewards. You print out Saturday's sheet, early Saturday, and appear outside the racetrack, about eleven or so, carrying a bundle of the things ready to make these simple souls rich at five dollars a shot. Sell thirty sheets by noon and you have a hundred and fifty bucks in your pocket, sell 50 and you will need deeper pockets to guard the two hundred and fifty dollars you now maintain, but sell one hundred and Mrs. Wentworth will love you again, you will be dining in established restaurants, and an appearance at the betting windows might even be in your future.

I gave it some thought only to concede that such a dubious endeavor takes time to develop, and I needed greenbacks now.

Could I become a stooper? These characters haunt all the big tracks and the bigger the track the more stoopers it attracts. They spend their days walking around the grandstand looking on the floor and in the garbage cans in hopes of finding a 'good' ticket accidentally dropped or thrown away by careless or the inebriated. It happens more times than you might think. Such offerings are then hurriedly cashed or canceled for a refund and the profits pocketed. Saratoga has a dozen or more of these ne'er-do-wells dodging about on any given day. I figured one more wouldn't be noticed.

But then I looked into the rear view mirror and saw myself. Could I ever look myself in the eye again if I was to stoop so low? Such citizens are generally considered amongst the lowest forms of life on earth, often categorized in the same breath as slave traders, politicians, and those that would rob a child's piggy bank. A true plunger, seeing a tourist drop a newly purchased ticket, would naturally return the dingus to its rightful owner in hopes of little more than a smile and a sincere thank you. But stoopers, not these grubs. I looked at myself again and despite the reality of my position I knew I would not lower myself to stooping . . . kick my bones to the gutter, famine would claim me first.

It was then, as I cranked down the windows of my rolling sauna, the way out was shown to me. It was the rear view mirror that showed me the way forward. It was my car. My mechanic had the old Buick running like a top, purring like a kitten as they say. I was saved; I was sure. There was balm in Gilead; all I needed was a simple roll of the handy man's secret weapon, duct tape, to fashion my safety net.

I dashed over to Allerdice's hardware store and picked up a roll of black duct tape and then sequestered myself in the parking lot of Ellsworth's ice cream factory. There I used my scissors to form an artfully lettered signs for the doors and trunk. They read 'TAXI'. And since my old Invicta had some years on it I decided to name this newly formed livery service "Classic Trails Taxi Co.". An hour later, encrusted with perspiration and wetter than I'd ever been, even when swimming, I was able to step away and admire my handiwork. "Brilliant," I said out loud to myself, "brilliant". The clouds were parting in my gloomy soul. I added a bogus phone number with magic marker and I was in business. The taxi, I thought, would be my salvation, but wait till I tell you. By the end of the day my new business, and one of my passengers, without even trying, had reconstituted my frame of mind and restored my faith in tomorrow.

Knowing that the more established operations might be a bit envious if I intruded on their domains, I decided to head toward the various smaller hotels and motels that are scattered about on the outskirts of the Spa. To my delight people jumped in. Some needed to be taken to the local airport, others needed to catch the train to Montreal, and one young lady waved me down in order to get her ancient grandfather to the hospital. Altruism bloomed and money followed.

Late in the day I parked my taxi beneath a giant maple tree near the corner of Wright and Jackson Streets, as near the regular taxi stands as I dare get, when a woman named Patricia approached me. She appeared unhappy so I asked if she needed a lift.

"My car, it's my car."

"Trouble?"

"It won't start. I must've left the lights on or something. It won't start."

And as benevolence and munificence have long been my new middle names, I offered to help. We peered under the hood of her car, did all the usual wire checking and jumper cable routines one might expect, but all to no avail. A sad commentary on my mechanical expertise, but there were rewards as this is where our story truly begins. It was the last fare for Classic Trails Taxi Co. that day, but it was a drive that spoke of renewal, faith, and the promise of tomorrow's morn.

Patricia, The Buick, and I turned on to Nelson Avenue and we began to exchange biographies. Mine was rather abbreviated but hers was a long familial history that surrounded the races each August.

"God, my Dad loved this racetrack, the things he went through to get away from the restaurant and have a day to himself up here."

"Really?"

"My mother use to haunt him and check up on him."

"Really?"

Patricia was smiling, "But she would rarely come with him, didn't like the smell of the cigars I guess?"

"Really?"

"When I was a kid, some of my best days were the ones I used to come to the races with my dad. We had so much fun."

"Really?"

"Yes really," she said with a modest laugh. "I remember one day I was giving my brother a hard time because Dad was taking me to the races and . . ."

And with that simple introduction Patricia related a story that has been tumbling through my mind for days now. It has infiltrated my dreams and day-dreams so often I have lived it myself. So here it goes friend, as best I can muster, a tale from the back seat of 'Classic Trails Taxi':

"I'm goin' and you're not, Ma said."

"Big deal," Patti's older brother shot back, "big deal."

"It is a big deal, it is. Mom even said I can use the money in my piggy bank, and I can bet on horses she said."

"You can not," he hollered, putting down the rake to glare at his little sister.

"Yes I can, she put my piggy bank money right here in the change pocket of my favorite dress."

"You're too young, you're a little kid."

"Am not."

"You're too young and little kids . . ."

"Am not."

". . . can't bet or gamble ever."

"Ma," Patti called.

"Get in here child, quick now, you've got a lot to do to get ready to go."

Downstairs, Patti could smell the kitchen bubbling away, being readied for the lunch crowd that filtered in from Union College and the General Electric plant. They were a mixed group of round faced Irish and soft brown haired women who spoke with crisp East European accents. Patti used to entertain them with her dancing and singing from behind the bar of her parent's grill. She even giggled a little as she got out her favorite patent leather shoes and wondered if all of her friends, some of whom didn't even have names, would miss her today. Well, if they did miss her terribly, they would just have to wait to hear all about her stories of her big day at the races with her Dad.

Her dress was pink with little black dots running through it, and pink frills at the hem and sleeves. It was her favorite. Mother was fussing with the way it fell about her thin legs.

"You've almost outgrown this dress pumpkin."

"Naw, I can't, this dress is magic, you said so."

"Oh yes you have, almost. We'll have to go down to Barney's and get you something new for school."

"The same dress, only bigger."

"Well maybe, if they have such a dress this year?"

"They will, it's my favorite, it's magic."

Patti could see her Dad in his seersucker sport jacket and hat standing outside with his friends. They were pointing and laughing and making the strangest faces. She knew what they were talking about, horses and her day at the races. Of course the horses used to make her Mom awfully mad sometimes, and sometimes she said the most powerful things Patti ever heard, but today everything was OK. It was OK because she was going to Saratoga with her Dad. It worried her a little when she overheard the way Mom had lectured her Dad the night before. They had talked, and talked so loud she could hear them upstairs when she was trying to get to sleep. It was always like this when Dad went to the races.

Her brother was still cleaning up the yard when her mother got finished with her dress and darted out quickly to investigate some row in the kitchen. Her brother came up to her looking all sweaty, and dirty, and sad.

"See, I am going to the races, and Dad said I can have anything I want, even ice cream and hot dogs."

"Big deal, the races on a Thursday, big deal you little imp." She stuck her tongue out at him, "I'll be going with Uncle Bud on Saturday, and that means The Alabama Stakes."

"You're jealous."

"Big deal. And I suppose Ma has told you to keep an eye on Dad up there."

"Maybe, maybe not?"

"Did she tell you to try and keep track of how much money he spends?"

"None of your beeswax," she declared as she started to dance a little.

"Huh, well you better behave and not get lost or do anything stupid up there, 'cause you'll ruin it for all of us."

"Will not."

"Yes you will if you do something really, really dumb, like the time you put four pounds of sugar in Mom's spaghetti sauce and got all of us in trouble. I bet you remember that don't you, imp!"

"That wasn't all my fault, you were there, you should'a . . ."

"The only reason Mom is letting Dad go today is because you're along. She thinks you'll keep him out of the Jim Dandy and away from all the touts."

"The what?"

"Oh don't be daft, just don't ruin nothing."

Soon 'her' old Oldsmobile was rumbling away on Lennox Street, in front of their family's restaurant, big, and warm, and friendly. It was Patti's car, she just let Dad drive it. But Patti was getting worried, if her Mother didn't stop giving her Father instructions about how their day was suppose to go, and asking questions about why they were leaving so early, well they really would be late, and she wouldn't get half of all the good stuff her Dad had promised. Her stomach was already rumbling. Sometimes a rumble in her tummy made her laugh, but today this was a rumble in earnest, it demanded attention on this, her special day.

"Anthony, it's barely nine in the morning, and I know the gates don't open until eleven . . . I know."

"We're just gonna stop for breakfast. Give the kid a break, let her show off these fancy threads ya got her in."

"Where?"

"I dunno, maybe Rollie's up in Burnt Hills."

"Him, Mr. Fish, he's a bum, and probably so drunk last night he won't even be open."

"Well maybe Scotties then. Who knows?"

"Another bum, always broke playing cards; his children haven't had a new pair of shoes since Christ was a kid."

"We'll find a place, I promise we'll find a place run by saints and Rockefellers, I promise. How 'bout if I stop at St. Peter's and let the nuns make us some pancakes, how'll that be?"

"Smart Aleck. Don't start your nonsense now."

"Aw come on Ma, we want to go, I'm hungry. Dad said I could have anything I wanted today all day."

Mother looked into the car with defeated disapproval and a thread of dismay. "See that you're back by six," she said plainly with her ultimate air of maternal authority. "And I'll have the races on the radio all day. I don't want to hear any news of lost children from up there. Got your money honey?"

"Yup, right here," Patti beamed as she patted the pocket that was ensconced along one of the pleats in her black and pink dress.

"Be careful with it now, it's from your piggy bank."

Mom's eyes had drifted away from her daughter and were looking squarely into her husband's . . . "you want to be able to have enough money for a soda up there."

"Oh Mom."

Eventually the great old sedan lumbered up route 50. Standing up in the back seat, Patti could see the enormous GE sign glowing over the equally enormous brick office building outside the turbine plant. It was shrinking as they drove and that could only mean one thing, they were getting closer to Saratoga and lots and lots of good stuff.

"What did she mean by that Dad?"

"That means she'll be checking on us."

The Burnt Hills Diner was a raucous cacophony of clashing china, ringing silverware and lilting voices. An entire fleet of cars made parking a chore, and Patti was none too happy about making her special shiny patent leather shoes walk across the rubble of broken pavement. But inside things were better, and after a short wait near the door they had two stools at the counter between a large old man with a big rubbery nose, and little fellow in a red checked shirt who smelled funny.

A smiling waitress dressed in black and white, found them right away. "Hi Tony, good to see you. And who's this your daughter?

Oh my gosh how cute you look today, oh I just love the pink." The waitress gushed and Patti glowed.

"Mom says it's my go-to-the-races outfit; she says I'm magic in it"

"Well she's right and the races. Lucky you, going to Saratoga for the races, and all gussied up and looking so wonderful."

"Look, could we get," Dad tried to interject.

"Mom says I have to come home clean too, if I mess up it won't be good."

"You'll be fine, and look at those shoes, oh my gosh they are perfect, where did you get them? They go perfect with your dress."

"Miss," a whisper came from down the counter where an old man waved his coffee cup.

"And your Mom did your hair too, I'll bet. Not your sister."

"Naw, only brothers."

"Oh," she mused with a disapproving curled lip, "and I bet they spoil you something awful."

"I don't know, mostly they just bother me and are a pest. Doug likes to tickle me all the time and I hate it."

The conversation lasted and lasted. Other waitresses came over to admire the blonde bombshell in pink and black with the hot pink ribbon in her hair, and despite the contagious admiration society that had erupted in the Burnt Hills Diner, everyone eventually got their coffee, and chocolate milk, and scrambled eggs, and toast with jelly.

"You sit quiet a minute Patti," her Dad whispered suddenly close to her ear," don't move now, I gotta see Blake in the back."

"Dad!" She protested.

"Don't move. If you don't move, I'll get you some bubble gum on the way out."

She watched her Dad disappear behind the counter through a stainless steel door that led into the kitchen. It was warm here and the waitress always smiled when she passed by her. She refilled her glass with chocolate milk and gave Patti the 'shush' signal with a forefinger over her lips. She didn't know what that meant, but the lady's smile meant it was a good thing. Even the old rubbery nose man smiled and nodded from behind his paper. Nice place Patti thought, bigger than Mom's food place, and more people. Every time the door to the kitchen swung, open she could see her Dad talking to the men in the back by the grill and fryers. I'm keeping an eye on him Mom, she would think to herself. I'm lookin' out for him. The men in the back were having fun with volumes of happy talk, Patti could tell, and they were all so busy writing stuff down on Dad's newspaper and shaking hands. I'm watching Mom, she kept reminding herself.

"I'm going to the races," she said to the funny smelling man when he happened to glance in her direction. The funny smelling man had not been properly informed that in

Patti's world, a glance in her direction was an invitation to conversation. He didn't know this, and it wouldn't have mattered anyway if he did, Patti was there to tell him.

His eyes opened in mild surprise. "Ummpf," was all he answered.

"And we're going to have ice cream, and hot dogs, and hot pastrami sandwiches, and maybe a pizza pie too. At the races, not here."

"Ummmpf." The man began to gather his belongings; glasses, pen, newspaper, and change.

"And my Dad is going to get me to the fence, so I can see the horses run, and I'm gonna vote on the gray ones, and if they win . . ."

The funny smelling man glanced at his crossword puzzle, and then looked up just as Patti remembered . . .

"My Dad says we can even have soda and stuff, not just milk, and once he let me sip his beer, but it tasted 'ucky', but maybe it will be better today, because my Dad says this is a new day and well, you never know do you, I mean at the races, my Dad says you never know."

The funny smelling man rolled up his upper lip and once again began to consider 43 down. "Hmmmm, Carmen's' creator?"

Patti watched his head go up and down and up and down . . . he appeared to be looking at some distant speck on the back counter.

"And my Dad said that we should make a great big—score today, because he really knows the horses, and he knows which ones want to run hard, and that means we'll be goin' home with big potatoes . . ."

"Does this Dad of yours, he knows everything, huh? Does he know the answer to 43 down? 'Carmen's creator?'"

"Sure Bizet, B-I-Z-E-T, my Mom makes us listen to it all the time. I like country, but Mom likes the other stuff, you know, the big band stuff with lots of violins and stuff and . . ."

The funny smelling man kept looking at his puzzle and muttering, 'I'll be damned' over and over again as he counted the squares for '43 down'. He was trying to recover a thread of his dignity and confidence by offering another conundrum. "Hmmmm, 18 across, how about the capital of Lithuania, does your Dad know that one?"

"Sure, Vilnius" Patti smiled, "he's from there," but before she could explain the entire history of her ethnic heritage, Dad appeared from the kitchen and took her by the hand.

"Where we going?"

"Gotta hurry little lady, lets see what's going on up at Mario's."

"Hey, how about my gum?"

II

Mario's Ice Cream Hideaway, a bright red barn, shouted at Patti through the windshield. She loved Mario's. The entire affair sat next to route 50, bejeweled with a string of bright white umbrellas and even whiter wrought iron tables. It always looked like a second home to anyone under the age of twelve who sojourned between Schenectady and the Spa, and to Patti it had been a playground ever since her Dad had introduced her to Mario and his children, David, the youngest, Cindy, and Mark.

Her Dad rushed inside while Patti slid out of 'her' car to look for fun. Dave waved to them, but was too busy harassing a German shepherd in the backyard to come over and say hello. Cindy, rumor had it, was sick in bed upstairs.

"Where's Mark?" she asked.

"Inside," David yelped as the dog nipped and growled him into a temporary truce.

"Where?"

"In the back. Something's screwed up with the freezer."

Patti looked around a bit bewildered, "Why aren't you in there helping?"

"Cause," he said with a distracted chuckle as he smacked the dog's snout with a baseball glove, "I'm watching the dog." Instantly, as if the animal had been tuned into some force for instantaneous justice, the dog latched on to David's ankle, and with a ferocious growl, threw him backward into the dust.

Patti didn't know if she should help David, but she knew she was supposed to be watching her Dad, so she went inside. There she found herself in the middle of a creamy nightmare. She charged through the café entrance door and instantly 'heard/felt' a thick cold invading her socks. From both sides of the counter a river of white goo was pooling and running around Patti's feet.

"Dad," She cried.

"Patti, stay out of here."

"I can't, I'm in here," she hollered as she climbed up on to a chair.

"Stand still then."

Her Dad was taking big brown cardboard containers labeled strawberry and vanilla, and putting them on a flat red cart that she remembered riding one Halloween. It had been pulled by a pony and smelled funny, but she and all her friends had had a great time, and the cart was a friend.

"Dad?"

"Bum freezer honey, now just stay there and give us a minute. We've got work to do. Just stay there."

Patti's eyes boggled. Her Dad was putting some of these real big ice cream containers in her car, lots of them. He made three trips in all, loading up container after container into the cavernous trunk, while Mario and his son put heavy blankets and big sheets of plastic around them. There was more ice cream in her car than Patti had seen in her entire life. In anyone's entire life she thought. In an instant Dad came for her and took her down from her perch on top of the chair.

"I can't eat all that," was all she wanted to say. She knew it would make her Dad smile.

"You won't have to Patti."

Mr. Mario finished loading another enormous mountain of ice cream in the back of his own old brown truck, and then just stood there shaking his head a moment. Dad put Patti on the hood of the car and then walked over to his friend.

"Damn it Tony, if you hadn't come?"

"Forget it, gotta have some luck once in a while. How much do you think you lost?"

"Some of it can be saved but, not sure. Probably a couple hundred pounds, damn thing, that freezer's only five years old."

"Well you got to get it fixed. Get rid of that Holleran clown you've been using and call Chicanelli. I told you before, call Chicanelli and it'll be fixed. Your guy's an amateur."

"Yeah, yeah, I've got his number but, Patti your shoes."

"Oh man, your mother's gonna be upset when she sees them."

Instantly Patti's shoes and socks were off. Mrs. Mario got a cloth to try and save the patent leather shine, and someone mentioned pink socks in Cindy's bureau upstairs. She sat with her toes out sticking out and smiled. So much attention.

"Well I'll be damned," her father muttered, "I'll be." Patti looked at her Dad with her best smile. "Who in tarnation nail polished your toes?"

She could only giggle, "Me."

"When did you do that?"

"T'other night."

"And where did you get the blue nail polish?"

"From the big table."

"Which table?"

"The one downstairs, the big one with all that stuff on it."

"Patti, that's not nail polish, you used my house paint. Patti, that's the blue I'm using on the north gable."

"So?"

"Sweetie, would you like something? Is it too early for a soda?"

"I like strawberry ice cream."

So with new pink socks in place, Patti and her Oldsmobile hurried toward Ballston Spa. The assistant manager of the Stewart's Ice Cream store was waiting at the back with the delivery door wide open. Two high school boys jumped out and began pulling out the ice cream cartons, now wet with condensation.

"Mario gonna be OK Tony?"

"Hope so Billy. He'll be here in a minute with the rest of it. I told him to get Chicanelli up here to fix the damn thing. Say you got a phone inside? Maybe I should phone him."

"Yeah, over beyond the coffee service area."

"Thanks."

"How about your little girl?"

"Patti, come on in while the guys are unloading our car, I gotta make a phone call."

Old Bill came up to the car and leaned in. "I hear you and your Dad played hero down at Mario's."

"I sure got my feet wet. I never had wet-ice-cream-feet before."

"Want something? How about one of my ice cream cones?"

"Strawberry?"

"If you'd like?"

Patti used three napkins to protect her dress from the melting cone, and waited for her Dad to finish his calls.

"Yeah, I found Chicanelli over at L-Ken's, says he can be at Mario's this afternoon."

"What about Mario's?" Bill answered with a raised eyebrow.

"Didn't give him a choice to say anything. I just called and told him Chicanelli was coming. I think I heard him gag a little, but too bad. He'll get over it when that damn freezer stops spitting out milk shakes in the middle of the night." They shook hands and laughed a little.

"His stuff gonna be OK in your freezer?"

"For a day or two, the Supervisor won't be around till next week, you know, what he don't know . . ."

"Good. Well, we better hurry if Patti and I are going to make the first race?

"You goin' to the track?"

"Seems so."

"Say, Tony, ya gotta minute. Let me get you some cash, the guy in the paper likes that 'Moon' horse in the second."

III

Once they arrived at the racetrack, The Dad became impatient, "Don't pay any attention to those guys," he said quietly as he searched for the entry passes Bill gave them.

"What are they doin' Dad?"

"Selling tip sheets. They're the touts your Mother's always harpin' about. They're trying to sell you a paper that tells you who to bet on and how to loose your money."

"They're no good are they Dad?"

"We don't need'em."

"Naw. We know how to loose our own money."

"Uh, something like that."

"And Mom won't be mad because you told that one guy to spit up a rope?"

"Well, he's a louse. Picks four horses in a six horse field, and then claims he had the winner."

Patti wasn't sure what all that meant, but she was sure it wasn't good. What she did know was there was fun inside this great white building, and food, and friends, and a job to do . . . watch Dad!

Upstairs in the clubhouse, her Dad gave the tickets to the usher, and after her cheeks were pinched for the third time, she was perched on a gray seat in the top row of section B. The racing surface glowed warm green-silver in the sparkling sunlight, acres and acres of perfect lawn. White rails defined each of the three racing surfaces. The whole place seemed like a giant dollhouse, just about perfect.

"This is better than the drive-in," she told her father with exquisite confidence.

And Mom would be happy she thought almost out loud. Dad was being real good. She had had pancakes and juice and bacon in Burnt Hills, and ice cream at Mario's, and then more ice cream at Stewart's, and new pink socks from Mrs. Mario, and she had watched her Dad play hero, and the races hadn't even started, and she could only imagine all the good stuff that was going to be coming her way when they won all those big potatoes her Dad's friends were always talking about. Big potatoes!

Soon they were surrounded by friends she didn't even know. Big toothy smiles and round weighty faces, and all these old men patting her on the head and saying she was cute. Dad did the introductions in his own special way. Next to her sat Johnny D. and a big huge blonde lady called Queenie. Next to them was the guy her Dad called Perry Mason, a lawyer from Vermont, but everybody else kept calling him by his other name, Jay. And in the next row sat The Shiner and then there was Fat Frankie from Florida, and next to him was a smaller man in a bright white suit named Robert. Nobody called him bob or Robbie, his name was Robert and he told Patti that several times. Patti was thinking she liked Robert, he had a plastic yellow flower in his jacket lapel. They were all Dads' good friends, and that meant they were all her friends too. They talked, and read papers, and laughed, and 'oooh'ed', and 'aaah'ed', and kept up the craziest kind of talk about 'Laserbeam' in the first, and 'Deep Wells' in the fourth, and one that Patti instantly liked a lot, Rainbow Dreamer in the fifth.

"Here's a five dollar bill small frye," her Dad whispered to her, "it's yours if you stay still and don't move."

"Small frye? Where's Howard Tupper?" Shiner asked with a laugh.

"Huh?" She was more than a little frightened, because she knew this was what Mom didn't want to happen, and she was suppose to keep an eye on Dad and not let him play around with his bad-boy friends. But, at the same time, this was a five dollar bill.

"You heard me," he whispered close to her ear, "I gotta see a guy downstairs, so you stay put, and don't leave that seat, and if you do what I ask you can spend that money on anything you want a little later."

"Anything?"

"Yeah, just don't move. I'll be back, so don't budge."

And with that her Dad was off toward the staircase and out of sight into the rush of people.

Patti looked around again. So many people and so much green, and there were geese and swans, and all kinds of pretty birds flying around the little pond in the middle of the racetracks. She stood up on her seat to examine her shoes, and was happy to see that there didn't appear to be any damage from the morning's ice cream adventure. She looked over Johnny D.'s shoulder and tried to read as many of the horse's names as she could, Once Upon a Time, The Grotto, SunTown, Potent Penumbra.

"What's that horse's name mister?"

"Huh?" was all Johnny D. could muster.

"That one," Patti pointed out with a tiny pink finger.

"Resume Writer," he said with some annoyance, "it's a horse in the first race."

"I know that, they are all horses in the first race," Patti stated plainly, "my Dad taught me everything about horses."

"Go easy," Queenie whispered in his ear, "she's little."

"Are you going to vote for Ra-zoom Writer mister, are you?"

"Naw, he ain't running for Mayor?"

"Johnny," Queenie interrupted again, "he's not, but I am sweetie. I'm going to bet twenty dollars on him." And she reached across Johnny D. and patted Patti on the sleeve. This made Patti smile again, and she returned to pretending to read the Johnny D.'s program. Of course, she was really was staring at the rings on Queenie's fingers. Mom never wore anything like that.

"Are you going to hit the double?" she asked after a short pause, "My Dad is."

Johnny only glanced up at her.

"My Dad said that he's gonna hit the double, and then put in a, a-crusher on Long Lost something-or-other. It's in the third race, he said that." And then Patti waited for conversation that didn't come from her new neighbors. They were supposed to talk with her, but they weren't getting their cues.

"And he gave me five dollars to buy anything I want and maybe I'm going to vote on the horses too."

"Five dollars is a lot of money for such a pretty little girl." Queenie said with a smile, as she pulled and fidgeted with the bodice of her blouse.

"Hey, here kid, here's another five-er," Johnny said looking up with a rye grin, "go get yourself something. You know, a Pepsi maybe?"

"Oh I can't, my Dad would be mad. He said I had to wait right here."

"Queenie will keep an eye on you. Right there, the soda stand right back there, you'll never be out of her sight. Go get yourself something."

"What do you want, should I get you a soda too?"

"Soda," the man said with a mock shiver, "too early for that stuff. Just get yourself any'ting 'ya want."

Patti didn't believe him, she knew all he wanted to do was read that old paper and talk about horses. But the idea of another five-dollar bill was interesting. Mom had said to watch your money, and a well placed 'five-r' would mean that the money from her piggy bank would last longer. Yes, it wavered and fluttered in front of her like one of the morning's all-too-quickly melting ice cream cones.

"OK mister. If you mean it?" Patti said quickly trying every trick known to her young mind to block out the guilt and fear rumbling inside her, "Thanks."

A couple of minutes later Patti stood near the top of the stairs and surveyed the mass of humanity weaving through rows of gray seats. She liked it here already.

"Pumpkin," it was her Dad's voice, "what are you doing out of your seat?"

She froze for only a second and then looked up with her best 'Aren't-I-Cute' smile. She was sure that if she smiled a lot, Dad would never have to know about the other five-er. "Nuttin', just waiting for you."

"Well, let's sit down."

"Are we going to get something to eat?"

"Sure honey, soon as I'm done counting all this."

"All what?"

"Our bets, I gotta do some bookkeeping, just hang on."

Patti watched his furtive activity and somehow just knew that this was part of whatever it was that made Mom mad.

As her Dad wrote small notes on the back of small pieces of paper, Patti decided that Dad wasn't doing anything worth reporting to Mom and so, finding the world to be calm and friendly, resumed her assault on privacy. The Shiner was promptly interviewed for comments on the running of the first race, and then informed about the care her Mother had taken with her dress, and then Dad's handicapping perspicuity as well as a rather clumsy conversation about a missing shirt button that exposed a 'hairy tummy'.

"Hmmmpf." was all Shiner could say when he found out about his tonsorial faux pas.

"Maybe my Dad's got a safety pin and then you could cover . . ."

"Look kid, look, maybe you'd like a lemonade or a soda or something, would'ya?"

Patti stared, "Sure, love lemonade."

"Good, well here, here's a buck, all yours, go get yourself something good to drink."

"Can I Dad, can I?"

"Sure, sure honey," her Dad said without looking up from his arithmetic, "just don't go far."

And with renewed style Patti's day proceeded in earnest. Shiner gave her money for lemonade, and later, just before the third race, Dad's other friend, Jay, contributed some additional funds for bags of peanuts. But when Fat Frankie from Florida gave her a ten dollar bill to sit 'quietly' and say a prayer for number 7, Patti knew her special day was getting better than even she had expected. The weight of bills in her pocket seemed to be getting rather heavy.

Unfortunately, it wasn't starting too well for her Dad. The first race ended with a furious volley of the hottest language she could imagine, and all Patti could keep saying to her self, as she covered her injured ears, was 'it's a good thing Ma's not here'. And the more she thought about the look in her Dad's eyes, the more she was really glad Mom wasn't there.

"No good Dad?"

"Not that one Pumpkin. Maybe we'll catch one in the fifth?"

"How bout the fourth race, are you going to vote on that one?"

"Maybe sweetie, maybe we'll be voting on the fourth."

"How about a hot dog, you promised?"

"With all you've had today?"

"Dad, I'm really hungry."

During the next race Dad and Daughter found a 'not-too-busy' hot dog stand where they could relive the morning's adventures. Patti listened to another explanation of why the first few races had gone so badly. Soon they were back in their seats where her new friend's faces were pressed together in desperate negotiations. Patti knew she had missed something very important. She just knew she had failed her Mom, and Dad was already getting into trouble, and she knew going home might not be really nice. It was, after all, her job to keep things right . . . Ma said.

"Dad, I'm thirsty."

"Huh, yeah, here, go get yourself something to drink. Right there, don't go far and come right back."

And Patti went and came back quickly, not wanting to disappoint.

"Where's your Coke?"

"Finished it."

"You were thirsty. Where's my change?"

"What change?"

"Patti!"

The fourth race didn't go any better and the fifth was worse. And by the time the seventh came around, her dad was wearing a long grave face Patti recognized as 'not-the-best'. He was growling, and that might mean even worse times when they went home. She could see it all now, Mom at the door of their restaurant, one hand on a hip, and the other speared out straight, demanding the winnings form the day's adventures. Patti scratched her nose and kept thinking. She was getting anxious and didn't want anything to spoil this day. It was bad enough the day was almost half over, but if it ended badly with one of Mom's lectures, well that would just ruin it.

"Dad, I'm hungry."

"You can't be hungry; you must have a hollow leg."

"Huh? Your friends make me laugh and laughing makes me hungry."

"Want a pony ride, out back?"

"Naw, that's little kid stuff."

"How about a pastrami sandwich?"

"I don't really like them."

"Yeah but I do. Maybe they've got a hot dog for you downstairs?"

"I want popcorn."

"OK, popcorn, as soon as I get my sandwich."

Dad and daughter strolled through the masses of strange faces. She liked the way they smiled at her, and she liked smiling back at them. She only wished her Dad would start smiling again, but every time she peeked up at him she couldn't see his teeth.

The popcorn seemed to throw a blanket over her hunger pains. Her Dad stood next to the counter of the cutting board, peering out at the racing surface and tote board. He was breathing loudly.

"Are you catching cold Dad?"

"Huh? No, just thinking," he said as he lifted his hat and scratched his scalp.

"'Bout what?"

"Nothing."

"We're losing aren't we Dad?"

"A little."

"Mom gonna be mad?"

"Maybe a little, but, hey, you never know, we've got a back up plan; maybe we'll hit the feature, and then we're good to go."

"Yeah, a back up plan, me and Dad have got a back up plan, and hey . . . you never know."

IV

The ride out of Saratoga was interminable. Dad cussed at the traffic, under his breath of course, and sighed heavily.

"You OK honey?"

"Sure Dad, that was great. Where we goin' now?"

"Well, home mostly. Gotta stop at Mario's, and the diner of course, but we'll be home soon."

When they stopped, Patti stood up to keep an eye on Dad. She could see the faces of the people she had seen that morning, but this time they weren't smiling. Everybody shook their heads, and heaved heavy shoulders in mock resignation that said that's-the-way-it-goes-some-days.

"Oh well, maybe next time," Mario spoke through the open window. He shook her Dad's hand again for the twentieth time, and he reminded Mario to get his ice cream out of Stewart's by Saturday.

'I will, don't you worry about that. Your man was here this afternoon. He got the old freezer going. It'll be out tomorrow."

"OK," Dad said, "now pay Chicanelli what you owe him and I'll see you soon."

"I gotcha'," Mario said with a grimace even Patti understood. "Maybe we'll get'em next time?"

The last few miles of route 50 consisted mostly of songs Patti had learned in Mrs. Williams' first grade music class. She did her best to wrench a smile out of her Father. She even tried hand puppets, the ones David Geroux had shown her, but little worked. It was a good day she thought, a great day. But she wanted it to be all-good, every bit of it, from beginning to end and it won't end good if Mom's in one of her moods. Patti thought and thought, and finally resigned her self to what she knew she had to do.

"I'm sleepy Dad, can I lay down?"

"We're almost home sweetie, almost in Scotia."

"I'm sleepy."

Her Dad pulled over and let her crawl into the back seat. The straight eight motor rumbled them back on to the highway and while her dad was distracted with traffic, Patti found a corner where she couldn't be seen. She pushed her hands slowly into the tiny frilled pockets that busied the waist belt of her spectacular pink and black dress. Each was filled with bills, five-dollar bills, one-dollar bills, a ten-dollar bill, and of course the twenty-dollar bill her Mother had taken from her piggy bank that morning. She counted her money with the best arithmetic Mrs. Williams had taught her. She was as stealthy as any Ian Fleming hero. Her eyes darted from the rear view mirror to her accounting and back again. She counted eighty-three dollars. Pretty good take for one day at the races. She hadn't really wanted all that junk those guys tried to get her to eat, and besides she wanted to eat with her Dad, and besides, you never know how a day at the races is going to end, so it's good to be safe and have a back up plan, like Mario's ice cream going to Stewart's, just in case, 'cause you never know.

They pulled up in front of the tavern at 7:30. Mom was at the door. She carried the hard stern face usually worn by prison guards or brain surgeons. It was a face to be remembered. Patti knew.

The family trio met on the front sidewalk outside the bar and away from the customers. It was better for business that way.

"You're late."

"Yeah," her Dad muttered as he approached, urging Patti to stay close.

"And how much did you lose, how much?"

"Not so bad, honey, relax, not so bad."

"How much?"

"Actually," he drawled as he reached into his back pocket to pull out his beaten leather wallet, "OK, you know, not great, but OK."

"OK my foot, let me see the money."

Patti had never seen her Mother's face or voice quite so strained. She saw something in her eyes that frightened her a little and knew it was her time to do something. It was time for her to be the hero and save her perfect day. It was time for her back up plan.

Silently she reached into the pockets of her dress, into the frilly bank woven into her magic dress, and found her eighty-three dollars. The bills were carefully folded into a tight, hard cylinder, so as not to be seen by angry eyes, and with an enormous smile on her tiny face, slipped them into her father's hand. To Patti's amazement, it went into a palm that already was gripping paper money. Her eyes darted into his palm and she saw the number '50' on the corner of the bill he was holding. Dad had secreted fifty-dollars in his old wallet and never used it at the races. He was forfeiting it to 'The Mom' in order to save an almost perfect day. Patti giggled. Dad had a back up plan too, just like me. My Dad and me, she thought to herself, we're 'back-up-planners'.

"What's so funny Patricia?" her Mother demanded.

"Nothing, nothing Mom, we just had a great day. I had pop corn, and ice cream, and hot dogs, and sodas and Dad . . ." She was doing her best to keep her composure in the face of her Mother's intruding eyes, and do the math at the same time. Numbers were galloping through her head, fifty and twenty and ten plus eight.

Mrs. Williams would be proud. "And Dad won a hundred, a hundred and (Come on Mrs. Williams, save me) a hundred and thirty-three dollars. He showed me."

"Not a chance," the Mother said, "Let me see it."

Dad looked down at his daughter, an enormous smile streamed through a row of happy teeth.

"A hundred and thirty-three?" he said, looking down at her shinning golden face.

He hesitated only a moment, concerned about the consequences. Patty saw his eyes, and just smiled the biggest smile of the day. He never flinched again, but simply extended his hand to the family accountant and repeated his daughter's numbers. The audit was completed quickly, not once but twice, one hundred and thirty-three dollars, to the penny,

"Hmmpf," her Mom said, "Who'd you rob for this?"

Patti's Dad was too busy trying to comprehend the precision of the count, the source of the windfall, and the smile on his daughter's face to even concoct a feeble reply.

"Come on, where did all this come from? Don't tell me you won it at the racetrack."

"Well of course it came from the racetrack Mom. What do you think? Where else would we go in my magic party dress, Mario's?"

The plotters only grimaced a little and began the soft victory stroll into the happy confines of Rudy's Tavern. Almost everyone was happy tonight because it had been such a great day and happier yet because the two contrivers had done so many fun things together, and made so many other people happy. But the happiest smile of all, the one that shimmered behind enormous blue eyes, was the little touch of magic that had turned her wonderful party dress into a piggy bank and a back up plan.

"Hungry sweetie?" her Dad asked.

"Starving," she said jumping over a small puddle.

"Want a hamburger?"

"Sure!"

The drive to Ballston Lake had gone too quickly. I was smiling. I let Patricia out and stayed just long enough to see her go through her front door. There were lights on inside so I knew she was safe, and I hoped she knew her story was safe with me. It was then I realized I needed a quiet place, deep in the shadows, to count my day's rewards. The bulge in my wallet told me I was back in the game. My Classic Taxi had done exactly as I had hoped and somehow Patti's story had also done me a special kindness. Hope is a thing with feathers, as the poet once said, light and fragile, and sometimes it can be discovered in the darndest places.

One Furlong from Murder

Playing the horses, thankfully, is a game we can play all our lives; we are always welcome. Other sports, football, tennis, golf, even croquet, have expiration dates as time comes when the inevitable infirmities of the spine, knees, or eyes demand each player retire to the sidelines. But as long as a punter has a pulse, racetracks will leave out the welcome matt. You must understand that for the individual with an active competitive mind, one who needs a challenge each and every day, few things can satisfy like a day at the races. It is a game where post time remains a grand test of spirit, intellect, and fortune, just like life, for to love this game is to love living, and loving this game will reward your years. I, as you must know, am one of these intrepid adventurers who crave the intrigue that awaits when ever Saratoga's gates are ajar and racecourse is in play. It is not a game for the weak or meek, as it is not an easy game to play, but then if it was easy it wouldn't be fun. One must always maintain a sturdy soul and be prepared for the dangers that will most certainly be coming their way. A truism every horseplayer knows is that one must never celebrate too much when the Fates are with you, nor can you shrink when the game blows an ill wind.

Sadly, right in the middle of the summer meet, I was beset by one of these dark and rather stormy periods. In fact these ill winds were more like a nor'easter blowing me off my feet, so to speak. But at the same time the game knocked me headlong into an escapade that tested my courage, my intelligence and then rewarded me in a way I could have never anticipated. Spectacular. Hang on, let me tell you.

About the time Saratoga's nocturnals were basking in the glow of a full moon, it had become painfully obvious that I was deeply entrenched in one of these tempestuous times and my pecuniary resources were becoming unacceptably light. True, much of this financial atrophy was the result of sharing far too much charm and good cheer, along with many C-notes, on exotic feminine acquaintances around Siro's, or The Lodge, which of course, is capital well used by any measure known to civilized man. Alas, other dollars had been less diligently invested on some of God's finest four-legged creatures who seemed determined to finish well up the track, fourth, fifth, or worse. Such a run of luck is not unknown to serious punters but it must be handled with a surgeon's skill. So given my state of monetary affairs, I deemed it wise to decline an invitation to join a few well meant friends at the morning workouts and sleep in order to revitalize my lumbered brain. It was not to be. The timid raping at my cabin's door stirred me from my delirium, and the voice, yes the voice, got my attention.

"Stranger, you in there, Stranger, it is me, Diamond."

I was flabbergasted.

"Stranger, open up. Let me in."

I shook my brains in disbelief. I listened. It was the voice of none other than Diamond Earl, a most unscrupulous character known to skirt the perimeters of racetracks, and society in general, from Maine to California, as he was someone quite unwelcome beyond the walls of Sing-Sing. Truth be known, the legal name given to him many years before, at a rather ironic born-again baptism near Florida's Lake Jackson, was Earl Chelm, but owing to his penchant to earn legal tender by initiating profitable fires for unscrupulous landlords, he had earned the ridiculous cognomen of 'Diamond' simply because, as you may have guessed, he was a meticulously professional arsonist; he always started his fires with wooden stick matches, preferably the Diamond brand.

I hesitated and tried to clear my dull brain. Against my better instincts, I opened the door.

"Stranger, thank goodness you are here, thank goodness."

"What 'da hay? How'd you know I was . . . ?"

"Your car, old buddy, your car, it is parked out front, is it not? Who else drives a tank like that with Maryland tags, who else?"

I nodded and went back to sitting on the edge of my bed. "Good Lord, what time is it?"

"It is six in the morning, yeah buddy, six a.m."

I caught my breath and summoned enough strength to focus on the gnarly face in front of me. This scallywag had a lot of nerve calling me, or anyone, 'buddy'.

"What's goin' on?"

"I have troubles old friend."

"So what else is new?"

"No, no, I mean real trouble."

"Does Howdy Dowdy have a wooden butt? You're always in trouble."

"Oh man, let me tell you."

I rubbed my eyes and began to concede defeat. Here I was, nearly broke in Saratoga, trying to establish a slightly illegal taxi service, hoping against hope for a romantic phone call, with no prospects on tomorrow's card, and now Diamond Earl Chelm, one of the worst people on the planet, was standing in my room asking me to get him off a hook. In the eyes of the Gods I knew I was now lower than the buttons on the vest of a mud turtle.

I made some instant coffee with the hot water tap and sat. That was my second mistake for I soon learned this notorious ne'er-do-well had brought trouble itself to my very door. This was serious, very serious, and a hollow ditch was forming deep in my stomach.

It turns out that that Diamond Earl had acquired a client some weeks back when his friend Erwin introduced him to a lady at Wheatfield's Restaurant. And while they all enjoyed some light banter and good cheer, it quickly became known that Erwin's voluptuous friend claimed to be in need of cash, and the best way to remediate her immediate predicament would be to see part of her heavily insured farm reduced to charcoal, due to some act of nature or bad luck, like it had been hit by lightning during a thunderstorm, or possibly a leaky roof had shorted out the circuit breakers, or a spooked animal had tipped over a lantern, or some such sad event. This proved something all too easy for a miscreant like Diamond Earl and apparently a bargain was joined.

Earl quickly came up with a 'can't-miss' plan' that required a thunderstorm and then waited patiently for the August rains to pummel upstate New York, which they often do like no other place on earth outside of Bangladesh. He was following orders to the letter for according to his 'client', torching this thoroughbred barn had to be done with some delicacy in order to guarantee both complete customer satisfaction and full payment from the insurance company, as insurance companies are usually a suspicious and cynical group who despise paying premiums. So naturally the fire had to be seen as above reproach, but it also had to be done in such a way as to protect the animals for which the client's mercenary heart still held a soft place. Summoning all the professional acumen Earl had at his disposal, he proposed that the fire would start in the office end of the stable so the animals had ample chance to be saved and yet he assured her that within sixty minutes the entire barn could be picked up with a Hoover and a small broom. This was a challenge no artiste like Diamond Earl could resist.

Well last night the heat wave broke and the sky's opened. Diamond took his cue from the heavens and was off on his warm mission of philanthropy. His efforts should have had him rolling in Franklins, but then we all know what oft happens to the best laid plans of men. (Remember, I was residing in Umbra's cabins, where the mice seemed to have successful strategies.).

"What the hell do you mean dead?" I was immediately terrified by his tale.

"Dead Stranger. When I got there she was dead." Earl was suddenly pacing back and forth. "I got into this guy Tomlin's stable with no sweat at all, one guard for the whole damn operation, sound asleep at the gate. I went in at one end of the stable, you know, I wanted to walk the length of it, you know, so as to be sure no one was around, you know, tending to some sick plug or nothing. But I never got to check the joint out, I never get into the office."

I was confused.

"Yeah, the office is at the far end of the stable . . . that is where the good stuff was supposed to start."

"Good stuff?"

"Sure, my olive oil and butter . . . that's how we do it these days, olive oil and butter. Who could make a stink about stuff like that in a kitchen . . . it burns, five hundred and fifty degrees brother, that's when olive oil burns, five hundred and fifty degrees will get a fire going . . . and if there is a short in a stove or microwave or something . . . especially on a rainy night. Come on Stranger, don't you know nothing?"

I shook my head. Why had I opened the door?

"But she was dead, lying there in the middle of this stall. My god, I clicked on my flashlight and there she was, this Martha dame, all covered in blood and just dead."

I tried to take it all in. "The woman who hired you was covered in blood?"

"Dead."

"Martha who?"

"Victor, Martha Victor. Why?"

That got my attention all over again. Martha Victor's family had a long history with international banking, real estate, philanthropy, and thoroughbreds. If Diamond's tale was true, this could be the biggest scandal since Tea Pot Dome.

"So what did you do?"

"Do? Nothing. How do I do anything? I made a deal with this doll to torch the barn and now she is kaput. I am not going to get involved with any murder. I didn't even get paid. This is serious."

"Yeah. Like arson isn't?" I began brewing a second cup. "But murder, how do you . . . Are you sure . . . murder?"

"Must be, and probably worse, you know, molested her too, molested her sure, I mean it took a couple of seconds to not get sick or nothing, but when I got my act together I looked the whole place over and I saw how this doll had got it right in the guts, and there weren't no sign of a knife or a gun nowhere. Sure weren't no suicide unless she was doing hari-kari with an icicle."

"What the heck do you mean molested? Was she dressed?"

"Well yeah."

"Dressed?"

"Well she had on some kind of plaid shirt and blue jeans and . . ."

"You're dumber than I thought. How's anybody gonna molest anybody with all their clothes on. Dress'em and then kill them? Diamond, wake up and die right will 'ya."

"Well, maybe, I dunno, all I know is she's been murdered and I don't want to catch no time for something I don't do."

"So what do 'ya want me to do?"

"Isn't it obvious?"

"No, nothing is obvious to me except you came here, uninvited, and have put a giant mess in my lap."

"This is why I need you to help me find out if I was spotted at that barn or . . . or . . . something."

"Something? You are insane. Do you hear me? Lunatic." I pronounced the word with great relish. "You're nuts. What the heck can I do? Shoot 'you' maybe? The best thing you should do is just get in your car and get as far out of this town as your old wreck will take you."

"Stranger, do not be so. For the last hour I've been sitting at that little Stewart's Shop down the road trying to think."

"Must have been a new thrill."

"It is a very well lit parking lot. I could think there, you know, my . . . you know."

I looked at him, more confused.

". . . my sciaphobia."

I paused. "Still terrified of shadows?"

"Listen, do not make fun. I must find out if I was spotted at the barn is all. You got friends with the cops and newspapers, don't you? I mean, if nobody there saw me then, even if someone knew about the torching, which never happened, I am free and clear. Right?"

I wanted to be the invisible man. We talked, I spoke, he chattered, and in the end I gave up on trying to reason with him. By just hearing this story and not calling the cops, I might be knee deep in some trouble, or worse. As simply and firmly as I could, I told Diamond to stay where he was. I went to the main office. The good Mrs. Abigail Wentworth was there and she let me use her phone. The only thing I could think to do was contact an old friend who worked on the Pink Sheet for the local paper.

"Aaron?"

"Stranger," the voice in the receiver called, "it's not even seven o'clock. What's up?"

"Well good to hear your voice," I said as we reintroduced ourselves.

"Aaron, wanna story?"

"You stranded? My little Austin is waiting for a clutch."

"No, no. I got wind of something you might be interested in, or maybe know something about, a real newspaper type story."

We spoke and a rather happy arrangement was made even as I remained as reserved and non-committal as a teenager's prom promise. I mentioned the name Martha Victor and just that quickly Aaron was wide awake, sans caffeine, which led to some mention of her recent divorce from this big shot named Saunderlake. Aaron was intrigued, and more than somewhat.

He agreed to buy lunch, purchase a copy of tomorrow's Racing Form for me, and even fill my gas tank, as long as I supplied the automobile and a tale worth telling. I didn't say much more, there would be time for that later. I was stumbling my way through Dr. Braille's notebooks right now, but the thought of getting caught up in one of Diamond's disasters was enough to keep both halves of the old brain on the inside rail.

Thinking Earl had told me the whole story would have been a foolish thing to do, so I knew I had to distance myself from the good-for-nothing. Clearly I did not want the local gendarmes to find his car parked in front of my room so his old Thunderbird had to go. Now it is well known to characters who live some yards beyond polite society that the best place to hide a car is not on a quiet dead end or a lonely side street. Truth be told, the best place to ditch a 'hot' heap is near the repair shop of a large car dealership (Please do not ask me how I come to know this). After all there's suppose to be lots of cars there, one more just fits in, and every dealership has a security guard protecting the customers from vandals. What could be better than that? So I had Diamond follow me to the Ford dealership on Route 50 and we left his car amongst the others waiting for oil changes or brakes or what-have-you. One problem done.

I then took him down Broadway, turned left on to Putnam, and dropped his unlikeable mug in front of Saratoga's Public Library. He promised that once inside he wouldn't even stick his nose outside to smell the air.

Then it was time to find my old pal Aaron at the Saratogian on Lake Avenue, but I quickly learned that he hadn't arrived yet. An all-too-busy woman at a large desk told me to try him at home, which sounded for all the world like a great idea. If I caught him before he got out of the house, maybe we could save a little time.

So it was back to my car which took me down Henry Street which, in turn, turned out to be 'almost' a good idea. There was Diamond, out in public. The jackass was sitting on the brick wall that defines the patio of Bailey's Café, smoking a Chesterfield in the rain, just as calm and happy as a fox in a chicken coop, like he didn't have a worry in the world. I was furious; my dashboard barely survived the assault. Now this area around Bailey's, better known as Saratoga's "Gut", is a busy little intersection just a block off Broadway, and as such, it is no place for a ne'er-do-well arsonist, one who might be a murder suspect, to be showing his depressing kisser, especially when his face might lead the coppers directly to me. Cretin! Low-Life! Dirt-Bag!

I shot into the library's parking lot and without killing the motor, dragged the addlebrained dunderhead off the street to let him have it, and much more than somewhat. I dredged up all the metaphors, synecdoches, and metonymies I'd learned in hundreds of locker rooms and gin mills over the years. I couldn't believe the words were coming out of my mouth, but they certainly felt good.

"Look nitwit, if you don't want me to go to the police right now, right now, get yourself back in the damn library and stay there."

"Do I gotta?" he kept sputtering. "That place is spooky Stranger, spooky."

I stared at him, slowly re-realizing that I was dealing with a genuine reprobate, a mental cripple of the highest order. "Shadows again, that's your excuse, you saw your shadow and ran out."

He only paused a minute. "Not quite, not quite. I just wanted a coffee. But their coffee shop is dark and in a corner and the lights were . . ."

"Pathetic . . . pathetic . . . you lily livered catastrophe. Your face isn't worth a good sunburn. No one could be this stupid and breathe. If you were any dumber you'd be entered in a dog show . . . and you'd loose the talent competition."

"Sorry Stranger . . . but the place gives me the willies."

"Great, good thinking, and if someone had spotted you out here this morning they'd have told the police, and then they, the cops, would've found you sitting out here, right in front of God and everybody, just like a boil on a big dog's butt, and then somebody would ask you how you got here, and how did your car get parked on the north side of town, and knowing you, you would've told them all about me. Idiot . . . I'd like to give you the willies, yeah, Willy McCovey's baseball bat . . . right between your bloodshot eyes."

He pretended to be contrite. "Sorry man, sorry, I just wanted a coffee, and maybe a cookie or something, and it just got to me. But did you find out if I was spotted, did you?"

"You greasy little toad, in fifteen minutes, I haven't had time to do anything. I've got a lot of things to check before you can ever, ever, ever, show your face in this town. Now get your sorry self inside, sit under a bright light or go to sleep, but one thing, while you are there maybe you can do something worthwhile."

"Anything Stranger, anything." I looked into his hollow eyes and my skepticism was growing. I'd seen stuffed animals on mantel pieces that looked smarter.

"I want you to look up the Saunderlakes and find out anything you can about these people, and I mean anything, kabish? Anything you can find about . . ."

"Ah, how do I do that?" he said with vacant grey eyes. I swear to you they were vacant, it was like looking into a cloud.

"I mean I will do it, sure, anything for you pal, but you want me to do what?"

"Look up stuff in a library? You look stuff up, reference cards, old newspapers and stuff. You know how to use a library . . . don't you?"

"Ahhh, I guess. Never been in one before."

The stupidity of this man was beginning to reach cosmic proportions, and it was no accident, it was his stock and trade. I found a piece of paper in my shirt pocket and wrote down the words Martha Victor and Saunderlake. I stuffed it in his shirt pocket and jabbed my finger into his face. "Here, take this and give it to a reference librarian, got that, ask for a reference librarian, and let one of them do the work."

I had him repeat the instructions twice before I made him go back inside. He actually did it four times, but the first two tries didn't count. I watched him trudge up the ramp to the main doors, mildly surprised that he had enough brain power to organize his foot work into a stroll. Only when the doors slid closed was I able to drain the red from my eyes. Problem Two solved, maybe.

Then a new neuron awoke and a scheme began to solidify. Knowing Diamond's a lying coward meant we would probably have to find out if this Martha Victor woman was actually gone, which meant we were going to the Tomlin farm, to get the facts, and that meant we would be somewhere inside a genuine racing stable where, yours truly, should be able to acquire some inside information about a few well meant runners intended for Saratoga's starting gate. Larceny should have been my middle name, Prudence just never fit me. I tried to ease my worried mind by giving my lumbered heart permission to dream once again; could the horn of plenty be playing my tune?

I drove out Lake Avenue, past the Doc's, Pepper's Market, and 'Rec. Field' until I turned right and made my way to 5th Avenue and Aaron's little place. For as long as I could remember, Aaron had maintained a small bungalow apartment behind the Victorian splendor of Mrs. Nellie Trainor's Bed and Breakfast Inn. The property sat next to the Oklahoma training track and offered a romantic view of the thoroughbred's early morning exercises. I parked my car and passed down a hedge-lined walkway toward the back of the property where, I discovered, my friend Aaron losing a round of canine hopscotch with his landlady's collie. I had to stop and enjoy this.

Now attack collies might be a rare commodity in a 'burg populated by leash laws and dog shows, but an attack collie it appeared to be, with all the accoutrements of canine warfare you might expect including slashing teeth, rivers of saliva, and impatient trench-clearing paws. He was trying to fend off the smallish dog with his umbrella and appeared to be losing.

"Mrs. Trainor, your dog, please!" Aaron was pleading as he jumped up on to a patio chair.

A tiny shell of a woman emerged through a screen door, but her smile dissolved as she assessed the situation, "Don't be so shy Mr. Burke. You mustn't be so shy around a harmless dog; they just want to be sure you mean no harm."

"Me? No harm! Me?"

It was hard not to laugh and give myself aware.

She muttered softly and pulled the door open, "So shy . . . come back in Buttercup." She slapped her thigh and smiled as her little hellion darted beneath her apron. "You can get off the chair now Mr. Burke, I've got him, it's only a plastic chair. Poor man's a scare-dee-cat Buttercup; don't be upset, he's just a scare-dee-cat." Her screen door closed and I watched my beleaguered friend withdraw to safety. I caught up with him at his kitchen door.

"Stranger," Aaron called out.

"Ha," I quipped as I followed into the kitchen and found my way to the refrigerator, "What does our local dog trainer have for breakfast?"

"Dog trainer? Oh, wise guy! I can't even check my mailbox without that Buttercup mutt going after me. You saw that? Thanks for all your help."

"I didn't want to interrupt all your fun old man."

He muttered a few stray syllables then watched me rummaging through his refrigerator with a sardonic eye. "You didn't think I was coming all the way out here just for a few drops of gasoline and a snack? I'm famished after watching you overpower Lassie out there."

Again he shrugged.

I collected a mug of tea, a plate of Melba toast, and a stale donut, while Aaron waxed less than eloquently about his impossible landlady, her insufferable dog, an absurd work load, and the broken automobile that refused to stay running for more than a month at a time. I had no sympathy.

"I told you about the car years ago, things aren't always what they seem; not easy getting parts for an old Austin."

"You did."

"Well my old jalopy might be an American tank, but it is running just fine."

"So?"

"How 'bout s'more toast and then I can tell you all about this."

We stopped at Pepper's Mobil and Aaron did the right thing. He filled the Invicta with high-test, and had the attendant put a few drops of oil into the crankcase. The Buick was happy.

"We might need your credentials, my friend, your newspaper credentials and if what I heard is right I will have your marker, for life maybe? You could be getting an exclusive, a byline, maybe a job at The Times?" The mention of a byline got his attention. "Now, here it is, but don't ask, just trust me. I got wind this morning that Martha Victor was killed this morning in one of Tomlin's barns."

My friend shot straight up in his seat. "Martha Victor? You sure?"

"I am sure of nothing at this time; I am just telling you what I heard."

"Really, who told you this?"

"Aaron, you disappoint, no questions. But I got a whisper, from a source, that she is no longer of this earth. Might be worth looking into?"

"Might be worth looking into? Is that where you've got us headed? Look, Tomlin's a big operation, we can't just go barging in there because you heard a . . ." His voice drifted off for just a second. "Damn, I know a guy, a guy that works for Tomlin."

"You do?"

"Yeah, Terry Martone, good guy; he rides horses for Tomlin. Tell you what, let me give him a call and find out where he will be in an hour or so. This could be big." Aaron found a payphone and we were soon on our way. He kept telling me his friend sounded upset, but he couldn't talk on the phone. Something certainly was up at the Tomlin farm, and might mean a story. I smiled at the way Aaron kept rolling his eyes in excitement.

Tomlin's operations were located just north of Mayfield, some thirty miles west of Saratoga. Our outing would take nearly an hour and, as we rolled along, I began to enjoy route 29. The further we drove, the brighter the day became. Off to our north, the heavily worn foothills of the Adirondacks were trimmed with retiring farms and isolated ranch houses. There was a tender quietude here that made me think of my old high school English teacher, Mrs. Munson, who had been so adamant I learn the word 'furbelow'. This I took as another indication that the dormant organ hiding behind my eyes might be waking up. I don't know why, but I suddenly remembered her little vocabulary lesson, and it seemed to fit as the wistful dells painted a peaceful picture and the entire ride served to buoy my spirits . . . again, more than somewhat.

In the bright morning light we arrived at Richie Tomlin's farm to find the barn area decked out in its traditional green and gold colors. It was too quiet. I expected to see grooms and hot walkers leading 1200 pound charges about paddocks and fields, but the place seemed empty. At the center of half a dozen barns and stables sat the main house, an enormous white palace fronted by Ionic columns and a jumble of luxury automobiles. Only a single police car, and a second unmarked Crown Victoria, confirmed there might be trouble inside.

We were met at the gate by a thin old man named Martin who seemed impressed by Aaron's credentials and he waved us inside. The ground was muddy soft, and the air smelled of horses and hay. Aaron seemed to know where to find his friend, but he found it difficult to keep his new Rockport Walkers out of the swill that collected in ruts and hollows along the path. A small cat appeared from behind a hillock of feed bags followed by a small Sheltie that yelped at us. We tried to ignore the little noise-maker, but he followed us to the back of the shed row, yapping all the way.

"Even this dog does not like you." I quipped.

At the end of the first stable we knocked on a shabby green door that immediately leapt open. Terry turned out to be a short-ish but powerful looking man, one I'd seen before, under happier circumstances, at the Fasig-Tipton sales pavilion. He seemed to recognize me and we nodded hello. He looked like a former jockey, but not a retired one. The thick arms and powerful chest portrayed a still vigorous athlete. Handshakes and introductions were exchanged, and we quickly situated ourselves around an old table cluttered with coffee cups.

He looked at us with strained bloodshot eyes.

"Terry," Aaron offered in a controlled voice, "sorry to burst in on you, but we got wind of some problems out here. True?"

Terry put a finger to his lips, "Glad you called, really, I gotta talk to somebody but quiet now, the walls have ears and we have many helpers. Ok?"

"What's up? I mean do you mind talking." Aaron asked.

"Oh man, this place is a mess, what a mess. You know about Miss Martha? Damn, that poor lady? This morning I, me, I was the one who found her. I found Miss Martha's body, lying dead in Cloud Cover's stall. Oh God, what a mess, what a mess!"

Aaron looked back at me and then Terry. "She really is D-E-A-D?"

Terry's eyes opened wide and he nodded in pained concession.

"A heart attack or something . . . she . . . ?"

"Look, I don't know if I'm supposed to be talking to you right now?"

I interrupted, "Did anyone tell you not to."

He rolled his lips and looked to the ceiling, "Well, no."

"Then," Aaron said, "I promise you, man to man, your name will never be mentioned in anyway. Promise."

Terry pulled himself across the table and his voice fell into a muffled whisper. "I thought she'd been shot, but the cops are saying she was stabbed. I know who did it. I'm telling you right here and now it was that lousy ex-husband of hers. He did it as sure as I'm born. He did it."

A confirmation of murder wasn't exactly what I wanted to hear. Diamond had gotten me into a real mess.

"You see I got here about five this morning, but I knew something was wrong when I drove in. Cloud Cover was standing, all by himself in the first corral out back, saddled and haltered, like he was ready to train, but no one was around him."

"No good?" Aaron asked.

"Course not," he replied with some impatience. "Cloud Cover won a $50,000 allowance race two weeks ago; he'll be in The Vanderbilt on Saturday. Thoroughbreds don't just wander around

saddled. This horse has class, a real professional, you can't take
chances with a horse like that; he always trains with a rider and a
lead pony . . . sometimes a group of horses."

My education was continuing. I even remembered the day
Cloud Cover had beat me out of a very healthy triple. He beat me
by a nose, but I am not the kind of guy to hold an equine grudge.
He did it fair and square.

"So I got his saddle off him, you know, so he didn't get the
wrong idea about training, and then I went inside to see what 'da
hell was going on, cause I knew something wasn't right, but I never
expected to see what I saw, never."

"Bad?" Aaron asked.

"Bad. She was lying in the middle of the floor, blood
everywhere, just lying there on a blood soaked pile of hay. It was
Miss Martha, and she was the awfullest color of grey and her face
all twisted. Never will forget how she looked."

"Stabbed?" I asked remembering how Diamond had described
her back in my room.

"Yeah, but shot or stabbed, what difference could it make, you
could see the dark hole right in her middle, a thick dark hole. I
called the cops and Mr. Tomlin of course, right away, and the cops
got here quick, real quick. They looked her over and the one cop,
Quinn, said it weren't no bullet hole, it was a stab wound, and as
soon as I heard that I knew this bum Saunderlake had to be behind
it, had to be."

I began to relax, knowing that if nothing else, Earl's story
wasn't all hogwash.

"Who is this guy Saunder-whats-his-name?" Aaron asked.

"Saunderlake," Terry repeated, "Martha's ex-husband and
Tomlin's big owner, he must own half the stock in these barns."

"Her husband? She was married to him?"

"Was," Terry offered, "was. They were divorced over a year ago
so the big jerk could marry his new honey pot, Miss Patricia."

"Big jerk?" Aaron asked.

"The biggest. This guy bullies everybody around here, Tomlin,
the grooms, the hot walkers, everybody, but nobody caught it like
Miss Martha, nobody. He treated her like she weren't even human.
No matter what she did for him, or tried to do, he called her names

and said the meanest rottenest stuff you could imagine. I never seen a dog treated like Miss Martha."

"You liked her?" Aaron asked.

"Everybody liked her in a way. She was from Portugal or Brazil I guess, and she was great around the horses, treated everybody great, spoke Spanish and French just great, and loved the horses. Everybody liked her, everybody but her husband."

He had my attention now, "Ever see him hit her?"

"Well no, not really, but I seen her walking around her with big bruises on her arms. What does that tell you? A jerk, nothing but a bully."

"Anthony, I never heard you so angry about anybody. He's that bad?"

"He's worse if you ask me. A cold devil's heart. That's him, a devil. She's probably not the first person he's done away with, but I hope the poor woman is the last. I want'em to get this guy, put him away for good."

"Terry," Aaron kept saying in mild amazement.

Terry was only beginning, "And at the same time the two women didn't get along either. Miss Martha was always trying to do things for her husband, like she was goin' to win him back or something, but at the same time she was getting into it with Miss Patricia. She blamed her for the divorce. Miss Patricia usually seemed to be the peacemaker round here, but she and Miss Martha could get into it once in awhile, especially about the way Miss Martha was working with the horses. This barn has been a wreck all summer with all the squabbling and arguing."

'All My Children' was the only title to came to my mind. It was becoming clear to me that I suddenly knew more about Diamond's little business deal than he did. All you had to do was look around the place, the main house, the number of horses, the Bentley's parked out front, and anyone with half the brains God gave a squirrel would know no one in this operation needed money. The torching job probably had more to do with jealousy, ill will, and plain old spite than delinquent car payments.

Aaron stood for a second and looked around the room, "Well if she was divorced from this guy Saunderlook, why was she here?"

"Saunder-lake, L-A-K-E. And that makes this little disaster even more complicated. Martha owned some of these horses outright, owned some of them before she married the big goon. Her family goes way back, been in the racing game for a long, long time.

Aaron and I exchanged bewildered nods.

"This isn't good man," Terry said, "her body is over there, still laying there, under some plastic sheet thing the cops put over her."

I shook all over. The body was still here. "Aaaaa, where is the body Terry?"

"Over in Florida."

I didn't know where or what Florida was, but I found my self looking around and behind me, just to make sure I wasn't going to step on something ghastly. Again I thought of my old English teach, and wondered if she would be proud of me remembering Macbeth's gory locks . . . only I was the one who was shaking.

"Eh-ay, where is this Florida place?" I quickly demanded.

"Big barn on the other side of the main house."

"You mean," Aaron queried, "we are here before the coroner?"

"Apparently the coroner's down in Clifton Park working on a big auto accident and, well, he isn't here yet." Terry paused and then looked at us like some specimen in a Petri dish, "Say, wait a minute, hold on here, I've only found her a couple of hours ago, how did you guys hear about this so quick?"

This I took as a cue to adjourn but Aaron stopped me, "My friend here heard a rumor in town, he heard a rumor that there was trouble of some kind out here."

Terry chewed on his lower lip and then got up to look out into the main stable area. He shook his head and sat back again. "No one coming."

"You said she is still in there?"

Terry looked at Aaron and nodded.

"Can I see her?"

That was it for me. I raised my arms in the air and thanked all in attendance for having been such polite company in these troubled hours; I didn't even want to hear the rest of these negotiations. I knew there was no way on God's green earth that a newspaper guy was going to get past the police to look over a crime scene, but just the thought of viewing a genuine real live dead person was enough to send me over the edge. Nope, not on your Nellie was I going to be found traipsing around in some blood soak horse stall trying to avoid getting dreadful 'stuff' on my soles. I can put on as good a show as your average thespian, but I will never pretend that being inches away from a corpse isn't going to send me right to Poughkeepsie. I'm no Olivier.

"Ah, Terry, where is Cloud Cover now?" I said, tying to change the subject.

"I left him in the corral. That idiot old George is out there lookin' after him He's still there probably eatin' all the grass he can get to."

"Idiot George? George a friend of yours?"

"Use to be. We've worked together for years, but when we got talking a little while ago, we got into a hell of a fight about Miss Martha and Saunderlake."

"Why?" was all Aaron needed to say.

"Idiot George thinks Miss Patricia did it. Idiot. That woman wouldn't hurt nothing; you should see her around the horses," Terry's face was reddening and he was waving a sharp finger at us, "It's Saunderlake, he isn't worth a flea off a big dog's butt. Talk to him, see the way he treats the people around him, you'll see, you'll see."

I didn't hesitate, this was my cue to escape, "Well while you fellas are entertaining yourself with clowns and jerks and idiots," as I had spent too much time that morning with an imbecile of my own, "I am going to try and say hello to a race horse and see if he can give me some advice on . . . on . . . The Vanderbilt."

I liked the cool morning air and the brilliant morning sun; it felt even better when I was out of my jacket. The sheltie appeared again and began dancing around in front of me, petitioning entertainment. I bent over to pet him but he darted away and yapped back at me. I tried again; he sat and waited for me to reach out, only to dart away at the last second. This little imp had played 'Tease-The-Humans' before.

I wised up. I found a small stick, waved it in front of him and gave it a good toss. He was off like Nashua, but when he came back with his little prize he ran past me and behind the barn. Had to admit it, he was entertaining.

He came back for Round Two so I found a larger stick, gave it a toss, and he did it again. I wondered what was going on. The third time he confiscated a stick I followed him, and sure enough his trail led straight to a little doghouse. It was dark behind the barn, almost chilly. I laughed to myself and peeked inside. The little shack was big enough for a German Sheppard but the little klepto had it so jammed with rubbishry and sweepings he could barely fit in himself. I could make out a blanket, tennis balls, a shoe, a screw driver, and at least a dozen good sized sticks. This wasn't a dog, this was a pack rat. I took one step toward his warehouse and was immediately barked away. With a closet like this, they should call you Fibber.

I reached into my pocket and found what was left of my morning snack, half a donut. I offered it to him and immediately the little warrior went into the classic begging posture, polite yelps and all. He was too cute and he knew it. So, conceding defeat, I tossed it in the air, he chased it, caught it midair, and wolfed it down in two gulps. He was quite the athlete, but getting him away from his quarters gave me a shock. There, on top of a grungy red mechanics cloth was what I had thought was a screwdriver. It wasn't, but unless my eyes were failing, it had blood on it.

"What the hey?" I said out loud. I stepped closer. It looked like the real deal, it looked like blood, but that was all I was going to get. Toby was back, warning me away from his stash. I tried to think.

Needing a minute, I walked past the barn and Cloud Cover's corral. He was standing next to the fence looking into the rising sun as if he had secerned some everlasting understanding of the universe. He let me come right up to him and pat his broad muzzle. I watched his ears, they wagged contentedly, never close to pinning the way they sometimes do when their about to savage you. Even his enormous brown eyes looked peaceful and contented. After a minute or two he nuzzled my hands with his half open mouth. It took me a second to realize he was probably looking for a peppermint.

A hobbled old man came up behind me and leaned on the fence next to me.

"You a cop?" was all he said.

"Me? No, not me," I said.

He gave Cloud Cover a soft pat. "That's good. Name's George, George Knight, pleased to meet you."

I shook his hand, "Work here?"

"Certainly . . . eleven years I been working for Mr. Tomlin, eleven years from Saratog-ee to Florida. Heard what's going on here? Man, never though I'd see a day like this. I knew something was wrong last night, I knew it. That damn mutt Toby was barking and barking, wouldn't shut up. We could hear him from our place, next to the barn. I told my lady friend, Adonica, to check on him and shut him up, but she said she couldn't see nothing wrong. Sure wish I'd gone down myself, or called Marty, might've done something, should've gone myself."

"Bad business huh?"

"Bad? Tragic if you ask me."

"Tragic, hmmm, good word."

"You a cop?" he asked again.

"No," I said again, "I'm Mr. Burke's driver, he works for the newspaper. He's inside talking with folks."

"Ummm, that's good. Me and the cops never get along. Still I knew something bad was boiling up around here, just never dreamed it would come to this, never in a thousand years."

I never got a chance to ask a question, he just kept talking.

"Martha was the sorriest woman I ever see this past year. Sorry. She didn't like being divorced from her husband, I can tell you that, didn't like it one bit. Guess she still loved him though I'll never know why. But that new wife, Patti, she wouldn't leave her alone, not one second. Anytime the two were here together they'd be going at it, goin' at it, hammer and tongs. Yes-siree, Patricia couldn't understand how Martha loved those horses she owned, wouldn't let herself understand. Seemed to me like all she wanted was to be sure she stayed away from her husband." There was a moment of silence. "Don't ask me 'bout women, they're the best of me, if you know what I mean. She didn't give Martha an ounce off respect, didn't give her credit for nothing. Had some bad days around here, Patricia would get into it with her every time Martha showed her face. Poor Miss Victor, awful sad eyes, always watering like she'd been crying; sad eyes, with little rainbows in'em."

I tried to think of something.

He smiled a little. "Patricia could be nice in her own way, pretty as picture, but when Martha was around, stand clear. I sure hope she didn't do this."

"Do you think she could have?"

He shook his head, "Not good to speak bad of anyone, till you're sure, but well, I hope she didn't. I tried to talk with my old friend Terry, you met Terry I'm sure, but when I mentioned I was worried Patricia might've done this he jumped down my throat like I was crazy or something. Jumped at me like a mad man. He didn't have no call to do that, talk to me like I was just a nobody; all I did was tell him what I thought, just told him what I was worried 'bout; he went nuts. Damn fool. 'Ta hell with him too. All nonsense as far as I'm concerned. I tried to tell Terry anybody could see they were really arguing over Mr. Saunderlake cuz Martha, well, you could tell she still thought the world of him." Finally, he took a breath. "Women? Beats me."

George reached into his pocket and offered Cloud Cover a sugar cube. "Wanna give him one?" He said as he placed one in my hand. "Sure he'll like it, just don't hold it with your fingers or you'll get nipped. That's it. Hold your hand out flat and he'll take it."

Cloud Cover took the cube. His nibble tickled and made me smile.

"He looks like a nice horse."

"Nice?" George said in mild amazement. "He's a damn site better than nice. Gonna win The Vanderbilt next weekend if we can get him to the starting gate."

This was more in my line. My mind was singing. Maybe the God's had forgiven my unworthy soul.

"Really?" I whispered.

George looked at me, "You play the horses?"

"Me," I said softly, choking my words through a large muffler, "once in a while. I usually bet grey horses to show, you know, just to have something to cheer for." (Please dear reader, don't laugh).

"Well, this boy right here should be worth a five-er. Don't go broadcastin' that around, but Cloud Cover's sitting on a big race, I can tell you that, a big race."

"Really?" I was almost suffocating.

"Won a nice allowance last week under wraps, totally under warps. Went the six panels in 1:09 and change. My boss told the jockey to lose the whip. Yup, he never used it once all the way 'round."

"That's good?" My heart was in my throat, but I knew I was on the verge of a genuine coup, so I kept mum and buried my greedy impulses in a deep, dark cave.

"Big. We got our fingers crossed he stays good till Saturday. Course he didn't beat much in that last race, only a seven horse field, but a runner is a runner. Yup, if I heard it right, the racing secretary's gonna post his morning line at 12 to 1. Can you imagine, 12 to 1? Just because he ain't never run 'gainst graded stakes company before. Damn fool could be makin' us rich. Winning The Vanderbilt would help lots of folks around here . . . help us pay some bills." George kept reciting the odds and the possibilities he offered more and more candies to the happy stallion.

I watched the horse crunch his way through the treat, but my mind was riding an Arabian carpet, there was light at the end of my dark dreary insolvent tunnel. What if it went up to twenty to one; twenty to one could mean a nest egg, a reserve that would carry me through to the end of the meet. My brain's calculator was reeling. A hundred to win on a twenty to one shot meant two thousand bucks in no time at all, just a little over six furlongs. Five hundred clams meant ten thousand. Magic. I was beginning to breath. All you need is one good hit in this game and you're back on top.

Cloud Cover nuzzled up to George, but after a while he could only offer an open hand. We both smiled at each other as the stallion let out a whinny and snorted at us.

The horse turned away and took the first few easy steps the way only a thoroughbred can. You have to admire God's sense of symmetry and form, I thought to myself as I watched the cadence of the enormous muscles fluttering beneath his cinnamon coat. The legs seemed too slender to power him over a racing surface at forty miles an hour, and the ankles, it's actually called the fetlock and pastern areas, no wonder they were wrapped, the ankles, so thin.

My eyes stopped. Just that quickly the tale was right in front. The wrappings on his left ankle were stained, tiny spots of deep amber red, the color of dried blood. Even the right ankle was be-speckled with the same sad décor. I was cold for just a second, inhaled, and renewed my thoughts. Cloud Cover had been there, Cloud Cover knew how she had met her grizzly end. He was a witness. If the thing in the dog's house was what I thought it was, and if the stuff on Cloud Cover's ankles was what I thought it was, I had the story right in front of me; I knew, no one else knew, and I didn't understand any of it. Someone had to be told.

"Nice talking to you George."

"Pleased to meet you too."

"Guess I'll go inside and see what the boys are up to?"

"Well be careful in there. This is bad business and when things go bad you never know who's talking to you straight. Don't trust that Terry fellow too much, I can tell you that; he'll turn on you like a rattlesnake. I know. Don't trust him."

As I was heading back toward Terry's office two more police cars stopped in front of the main house and several officers went inside. Just as I was reaching for the door handle Terry and Aaron came through the office door. Terry was laughing as Toby reemerged and circled Aaron. He was yapping away like a tobacco auctioneer. Aaron made a gesture of bravery with his left shoe and muttered something rude, but Terry only laughed the louder.

"Ha, Toby's got your friend's shoe lace, got it good," he said leaning onto the car.

"Damn dog." Aaron put his foot up on my front bumper and began to retie the laces.

"See him jump?" Terry continued. "Came out of his skin. Yeah, Toby's a smart little guy, Miss Patricia trained him to do everything but make the morning coffee. Smart as a whip. And dogs are smart you know, real smart."

"What's he doing here anyway?" Aaron asked.

"Who Toby? Look around there are lots of animals around a horse barn, always. Yeah horses don't like to be alone. Cats and chickens and dogs always around these guys. Helps'em stay calm, especially at night when they got nothing to do. We had a horse once adopted a goat, yup a goat, Aneta's Pride, he loved that goat."

Aaron dropped back into the passenger seat. I smiled and reassured him the world, with or without canines, was a still good place. All he could do was mutter some things about Bullet and Rin-Tin-Tin. I tried not to laugh.

"Terry, you busy right now?" I asked.

"Not really, just have to wait for the police I guess. Not suppose to leave until . . . why?"

"Get in, just for a second; I don't want nobody to hear this."

I got behind the wheel and turned so I could see both of them. "Look don't laugh, but I know what happened this morning."

They looked up at me and smiled.

"Seriously, I was just out by that horse, Cloud Cover, now don't laugh, but the horse did it, or at least had something to do with it."

Both men looked at each other, but they didn't laugh, at least not out loud.

"And I think this dog, Toby, is covering up for him."

Aaron's smile turned to disgust. "The horse is a killer and the dog is his accomplice? Stranger! You got your flask on you?"

"Well it sounds weird when you say it like that but give me a minute will 'ya. Terry, can you take us out into the corral area where the horse is?"

"Sure."

"Then without making a big deal of it, let's go; I'm going to show you something."

"Like what?" Aaron asked.

"Like the horse has blood on those cloths on his back legs. It ain't mud, and it sure looks like blood."

We spoke for a moment more and then strolled to the corral. Terry led Cloud Cover to us.

"You might be right," he said in a quiet voice, "I didn't notice it before, but it sure looks like blood."

"I thought so."

Aaron bent down to look at the wraps more closely. He pushed his straw hat off his forehead and scratched away at his receding hairline. "Blood," was all he said, "I'd bet my life on it."

"I better get the cops," Terry said. Aaron and I took that as our cue to leave, but I stopped him.

"Wait a minute," I said, "there's more. Come out behind the barn."

The three of us peered inside Toby's shabby little hut. He barked at us until Terry picked him up and held him quiet. We looked and looked while Toby whined. The pointed instrument was still there, stained and in plain sight.

"What 'ya think?"

"Dunno?"

"Might be blood?"

"Dunno?"

"How'd it get here . . . Toby?"

The three of us stood up, I scratched my head, Aaron pulled on an earlobe, and Terry stared as he muzzled Toby's ear.

"That thing is a trocar," he offered.

"A what?" Aaron asked.

"Trocar, vets use'em to lance boils and swellings and such. But what the heck is it doing here; the grooms sure wouldn't have anything like that?"

"And where'd Toby get it?" he said out loud, "And that looks like blood near the handle thing."

Terry was quick to remind us. "A vet would clean a tool like that if he had to drain something, and keep it in his bag. What's it doing here?"

We resumed our posing. It got us nowhere.

Aaron looked around as if to see if someone else was listening, "But if this is the murder weapon and the blood on that horse is Martha Victor's . . . ?" We all stood in silence a moment more.

I was confused.

Terry put Toby down. "I gotta tell the cops about this." Aaron nodded in approval, and I knew it was time to leave.

"Time for us to go. I'll call later, or you call me." And with that we were off.

The drive back into Saratoga was a quick one that took us back into the deep grey sky and the persistent drizzle. Aaron knew

I hadn't told him everything and I now knew that this was too serious not to. It didn't take me long to dish out the entire story of Diamond and his deal with Martha Victor, and his car, and the library.

"You know this could make you an accessory if it turns out this friend of yours is mixed up in this?"

"Don't remind me."

"And I am not risking my neck."

"I know, I know, neither am I, but the dog and the horse?"

"Well, step on it, I want to touch base with a friend on the police department; let's see what this old blunderbuss can do."

Aaron went to his office to check his paper's archives in an attempt to dig up something about the Saunderlakes and the marriages and divorces. Plus, we had pushed our luck with Terry and the police about as far as we could, and they'd certainly be asking some tough questions soon enough. It is a common truth known to anyone beyond the age of consent that the problem with tough questions is always the same, tough answers.

I took a quick spin by the library. Thankfully, Diamond was nowhere to be seen so I jumped inside. The main floor and the top floor were both Diamond-free. The bottom floor was not so fortunate. There in the middle of the children's section was Diamond Chelm, deeply engrossed in a Spider-Man comic book. His eyes were wide open and his mouth agog. There was a collection of hard cover Peter Rabbit novellas on his lap and another stack of Golden Book classics on a table next to him. Grown women were eyeing him suspiciously and whisking their little ones into other aisles. Hopeless.

He seemed to be happy to see me. I fixed that. "Diamond, you can't hang out here with a bunch of little kids."

"Huh? I found some stuff to read, good stuff, and it's nice and bright in here. Look," he said waving a comic book before me.

"An old pervert like you doesn't belong here."

"But . . ."

"Upstairs and now," I said as firmly and as quietly as I could through gritted teeth.

He followed me like a brow beaten puppy. He pouted, he actually pouted; it was all I could do to contain myself. I was tired and a little scared and I had no patience for this sewer rat. I bought him a coffee and a cookie from the snack shop, (he still wouldn't go in) and found him a place far away from the main desk where he could read his comic books and not come in contact with regular human beings. I got him settled in and reassured him I would be back within the hour to give him the news, good or bad.

Escaping the library was a pleasure. I was filled with thoughts, plus, tucked securely away in a corner of my suddenly rejuvenated mind was the image of Cloud Cover surprising all the pundits this weekend at twenty to one with me, yours truly, waiting by the cashier's window for the race results to become official. The mind soars like a hawk when the odds are in one's favor.

Back at The Saratogian I found Aaron standing at his desk, phone in hand. His eyes told me to wait.

"City Hall, right now," was all he needed to say. I had a bad feeling about this.

"What for?"

"Got a tip the Saunderlakes are going to meet with the D.A."

"Really? But, but, why?"

"Cause Sgt. Kelly wants me at City Hall. If he wants the entire story of how I got mixed up in this mess, and you are going to tell him everything you know."

"Sure, sure," was the best I could do, but my legs were melting into my shoes.

"I tried to tell him, but I don't know if I got it all straight. Come on, we've probably got some explaining to do. From what I could tell the cops know almost everything and if Kelly has it right, the Saunderlakes are coming in to hear the bad news."

I spoke not a word, but I was imagining interrogation methods not even dreamed of in the Middle Ages. I was in for it, sure.

At City Hall I found Aaron and the good Sergeant Kelly huddled together near a water fountain.

"What's up?" I asked after the officer went into an office.

"Not sure. Paul tells me they already tested those horse wraps; it was blood all right. They're waiting for more tests to be sure it's

Martha's. And he also tells me her arm; her left arm was broken, just above the wrist."

"Somebody beat her up too?" I asked. My legs were gone, first quality genuine Vietnamese rubber.

"All I know is what Kelly told me."

"And the Saunderlooks?"

"Lakes dummy, Saunder-lakes. Not sure, but something else is stirring."

"Like?"

"Paul wouldn't tell me, he just said I'd get the story as soon as the Saunderlakes are told what's going on."

"Sounds heavy."

"I know."

At the top of the hour the Saunderlake entourage entered with all the charm and charisma of a conquering army. First three middle aged men wearing ink black suits with pink ties threw open the large oak doors, followed by two smaller, athletic-looking men, and lastly a tall grey-haired gentlemen, painfully under-weight, lumbered by an enormous valise. The six entered and immediately stood aside in silence. Seconds passed before I caught my first glimpse of the often mentioned Andrew Saunderlake himself. I couldn't help but notice that his suit hadn't seen a hangar since it was delivered. It was difficult to find a fault with his tonsorial or sartorial acuity, and his fifty years of living appeared to have been well managed by a regimen of physical training and extended vacations near the Equator. His presence was worthy of admiration; it spoke of self-control, influence, and power. If he was a thoroughbred, I'd bet on him. I noticed Aaron surveying his own arrangements, the seersucker suit, bow tie, and straw hat suddenly seemed rather tame.

Patricia Saunderlake was close behind, but this was not the charming debutante I had envisioned. She passed through the doorway with all the temerity of a golden eagle. Broad shouldered and nearly six feet tall, she walked quietly and stood motionless once in the deep dark of the building. She looked about and then to her husband, demanding assistance. She didn't speak at first, but her posture spoke of a person prepared for combat.

Mr. Saunderlake's first words could have been heard over the blast of a jet engine. "Adams, see if this LeGrand is here, and find out where we are suppose to meet. Quick."

She spoke. "Adams . . . stay right where you are. I mean it." Her gaze went straight to Mr. Saunderlake. "If you want this LeGrand fellow, have one of your men get him."

Saunderlake was struck silent for only a second. "They're all my boys damn it and they'll do what they're told. Adams!"

The afternoon sun framed a brilliant rectangle on the wooden floor and threw two angry cameos deep into the building.

"Don't move Seth, stay right here." She charged toward Saunderlake with the eyes of the crepuscular fisher, "If it's important, get . . . him . . . your . . . self."

I really thought she was going to deck him, and she could have done it by the look on her face. It didn't take Phillip Marlowe to see how things were here. I sank into an old Victorian chair and did my best to study the Pink Sheet.

They stared at each other, neither blinking nor giving an inch.

"Get out of my face," he said with remarkable reserve.

"Get out of my life." Her voice rang with authority, and at that very moment I could believe either one of them was capable of violence.

"Soon, Patricia, soon. You will be sorry, you will be sorry."

"Me? Ha, the only thing I'm sorry about is the way this stupid state threw out the death penalty."

"Miserable witch, you're not going to turn your dirty work on me."

After that the language got rough, the details of which don't need to be recreated. Obviously, these two had spent a good deal of time accusing each other of doing something unthinkable. There were no sign of tears in Patricia's eyes, only disgust and judgment. And there was no less resolve in Mr. Saunderlake's countenance; his was the look of a man about to break something. Two black suits gathered enough courage to approach the combatants, but that was as far as they got, neither dared enter the skirmish. The exchange went on, punctuated with stamping feet and pointed

169

fingers, each assaulting the other with new-found disgust. And the language, oh, the language. I re-read my paper.

A rotund gentleman appeared in a doorway and beckoned them inside. The entire mob shuffled its way into a room to my left and was gone. We listened for half an hour. Police officers entered, left and reentered. Doc Keller went in and then came out a few minutes later. The place was a beehive. The best Aaron and I could do was roll our eyes and wait. A teenager came through hawking The Daily Racing Form. Good news for a guy like me. I read it three times before the entourage exploded from the meeting room.

And explode it did; the Richter scales at R.P.I. must have been doing a jitter-bug. Mr. Saunderlake was bellowing something about treachery while the older, malnourished gentleman kept gesturing with an upturned palm. One of the black suits was shuffling papers, trying to put them into Saunderlake's hands, but all he accomplished was to have them litter the floor and get trod upon. Patricia charged right past us, so close I knew her perfume. She stopped for only a second.

"I'll see you in hell first, damn coward, you lousy selfish coward . . . in hell."

And she was gone. The men gathered around their boss, but he burst through their circle and went flying into the street as well. I watched closely, she turned right, he turned left. Interesting.

My friend's eyes darted from left to right. Officer Kelly approached, absorbed in a ream of letters. "Congress Park, three o'clock," was all he said and he disappeared into another room.

I drove every back street I knew of and got us to the southern part of town. I looked around for signs of alert police officers and, lacking that, parked my Classic Taxi by the spring water pavilion near the park's entrance. I was getting brave, but I was too distracted to take all the duct tape off. I'd have to risk it.

Late in the afternoon I found myself fading behind the steering wheel of 'Old Faithful'. I could feel the arms of Morpheus moving in to shelter me. Outside children ran and cried while lover's strolled holding hands, and women chatted over trams and shopping bags. Nearby, a fountain's running waters pushed the day's cares out of my heart and into an unlit dungeon. The very humming of Broadway was becoming my hypnotist. What a day.

The sun sank behind the buildings to the west and the darkness of day chilled me. My stomach, and the lengthening shadows, told me it was supper time, but where was my friend Aaron? I was warm and comfy, I didn't want to move, but the image of Earl Chelm's tortured face got my blood flowing. With more than a little difficulty, I walked through the park, circled the memorial, and then looked behind the Casino museum. I wondered, for just a second, if my old friend had forgotten me, had gotten so caught up in a story, or a by-line, that he had dashed off to the paper and left me to worry on the streets. What if this was so bad he knew he needed to avoid me, not be seen with me? What if I was in so much trouble he had to make a police statement?

I shouldn't have worried. I was about to return to the car when Aaron and the good officer emerged from the Casino itself. I found a park bench and waited. Aaron was smiling, Officer Kelly was smiling, and I was breathing. They spoke and then went their separate ways. Aaron watched him leave the park and sat down.

"Well, no by-line for me on this one."

"Really?" was all I could say.

"Well, this'll kill you."

I didn't like his choice of words, but I listened.

"She wasn't murdered."

"Huh, no murder?"

"Nope, an accident of sorts."

"An accident?"

Officer Kelly had kept his word; Aaron got the story first. The official report would be released to the media until six that evening. The police reports and coroner's findings were all in and the only story that made the pieces fit was so strange it had taken over an hour to accept. It seems that Martha Victor, at some ungodly hour before sunrise, had saddled and prepared Cloud Cover for a workout or a ride or something. Quite unusual, and, at the very least, suspicious. Was she stealing the horse, preparing to ride it away from Tomlin's farm? Was she out for a joy ride with a full blown thoroughbred? None of it made sense but that was how it appeared.

Doc Keller had confirmed the time of death as around four in the morning. No one was sure where she got the odd tool, but her finger prints were on it, and it was her blood on the handle of the grizzly thing. Then, when the police technician found shreds of cloth in the horse's hoof that matched the material of her shirt, along with the broken wrist, the only scenario that the police could come up with was she must have been behind the horse with the trocar, the horse kicked her, and accidentally gave her the wound.

"The horse did it?"

"In a manner of speaking, looks that way. Why in hell she was poking around a horse's back side with a sharp thing like that trocar, no one can figure; she'd been around horses all her life, she had to know better, everyone knows not to get behind a horse."

"But the trocar?"

"Cops think the little dog must have found her and took the damn thing to his hideaway. Had blood on it and you know as well as I a dog can smell blood."

We spoke some minutes more until I began to yawn.

"Supper?" I asked my friend.

"You buying this time?"

"Bailey's? Let me run one quick errand. Meet you there in thirty minutes."

My last task was not unpleasant. Diamond required retrieving and as luck would have it I found him on the bottom floor of the library, again, reading a Green Lantern comic book. It fit. I told him as best I could that despite being around cops and newspaper guys all day, no one had mentioned seeing him or his old Thunderbird and he might be off the hook, at least for now.

He thanked me, a little too much, almost kissing my hand, and I hurried him up to the Ford dealership as quickly as I could. I would have preferred to have made him walk to route 50, but riding myself of this pestilence was too important for any exercise of self-indulgence. Bailey's would wait. Heavens how I celebrated when I saw his taillights dwindling away toward the Northway. My luck had turned. May he never darken my door again? I knew it was too much to ask, but horseplayers always dream.

Late the following Saturday I was leaning on the wall next to Patrick's window, waiting to cash in my wining ticket. Cloud Cover had been as good as advertised, he had run away with the race, a clear winner by over two lengths. Of course he went off at five to one, not the twenty to one I might have hoped for, but good news always travels fast around the barns and big chunks of smart money had crushed the odds. Still I was a winner and had reason to smile.

As I waited for the band to start up at Siro's, my mind retraced the previous week. How strange I thought. I had picked up enough cash to survive another week at the races and I was content, at least for now. But a woman had lost her life, two old friends were now enemies, and a marriage had apparently broken up and it and its fortune was headed to the courts. How easily this sad misadventure had brought out the worst in so many people. I couldn't complain much, I had lost some sleep, but the others had peeled open their dark suspicious hearts and were all the worse for it.

I counted my winnings and left Patrick a twenty, it's bad luck if you don't tip your cashier. I stood in the breezeway, enjoying the air when two dedicated punters, Mel and John, walked up to me.

"Had the winner," Mel said in his heavy Boston way.

"This time," I said with subdued pride.

"Well then be sure to get the next one," John said gently in his soft Texas way.

"Yeah, got a little cash, at least there will be a next time. Things were getting pretty tight last week."

John smiled, Mel smiled, "There's always a next time in this game."

"Always," I said, recounting my bills, "always."

Brianna

I

The taxi trade was beginning to pay off. I was even enjoying some dependable repeat customers who needed to get to work on time, or get home on time, or get to the pharmacy on time. I was their hero. One of my best customers was Eddie, a little old man, and I do mean old, who required transport, on almost a daily basis, to his girlfriend's little hideaway in Greenfield while his wife used the family car to play mahjong in Glens Falls. I really enjoyed his company as he seemed to know everything there was to know about anything. During our little jaunts I discovered that during the Revolutionary War Benedict Arnold was not our worst commander, nope, we won despite a General Schuyler who, according to Eddie, was a simpleton. We were supposed to fight the Battle of Saratoga at Fort Edward, but the darn fool knew nothing about artillery ranges and tactics. Almost lost the war for us, according to Ed, except for the Polish kid who saved the day. History he claimed was a catalogue of mental cripples. Karl Marx was a drunken egomaniac who kept a slave girl, some egalitarian he was, and General Custer was a bumbling insubordinate who was suppose to wait for General Terry before going anywhere near Little Bighorn. If he'd survived Little Big Horn, he should have been court-martialed. And Henry Ford never invented the assembly line, Ransom Olds did. All phonies! I even discovered I had been driving a car with a nail head engine all these years, I never knew that, but I did now. The old guy was a walking talking compendium of information, some of it useful, some of it otherwise.

"Damn straight young fella, damn straight. This is a good car, yup, good old boat, but they never shoulda stopped making the Corvair, never. They got the suspension crap fixed, fixed good with Corvette parts and half shafts and then quit on it. Stupid. Had a hell of a car the last year they made it, hell of a car. Turbo charged, independent suspension, quick, light, great mileage, air conditioned. Cowards!"

He made a speech like that every time we went to Greenfield.

"Yup, they had it, right in front of them, maybe could've been the best damn car they ever made, dollar for dollar, and what did they do . . . what did they do? Screwed up, that's what they did, walked away from a good thing and left us with the damn Pinto. Milksops!"

"Not good Eddie?"

"Stupid. Some jackass lawyer makes a stink in the newspapers and the bosses fold up their tents like they was running bootleg liquor. Bunch of quitters! No faith, God, how can you live this life without any faith, without some courage? They chickened out, right when they should have been crowing like roosters."

"Gee, I didn't know."

"Milquetoasts, every damn one of them, milquetoasts! General Motors my foot . . . Scaramouch Motors if you ask me. Can't be a pessimist in this life, no sir sonny. Pessimism is just another name for self-hatred. If you're a pessimist, you're already half dead."

Had to like the old guy, he loved everything he did.

And on one bright Wednesday I ended up with even more reasons to like him. He was my only fare that morning and as I was heading back toward his apartment, quietly admiring the glint in his eyes when he stopped the trivia parade and leaned toward my ear.

"Say young fellow, can I ask you a favor?"

"Sure," I said.

"I'm taking myself shopping, got to get a birthday present you see. Would you drop me off by the bus depot?"

"Course Eddie. How you gonna get home?"

"Well, could you come back for me in an hour or two, maybe up by Congress Park?"

I thought a second, as timing is crucial when you have to make the fifth race. "Yeah I can do that, it's a deal. I'll be there, give you two hours to do whatever it is you gotta do, just be out in front of the Canfield Casino so I don't miss you, and don't be late Eddie, got a lot to do later, don't be late."

I pulled into the parking lot, reviewed Eddie's plan one more time and began to pull away when I spotted someone I had not seen in years. It was Brianna, one of my favorite people at the race track, unmistakable in the afternoon sun. A little older of course, and a little heavier than I remembered her when she was a part of the race track's security team, but it was Brianna. There was no mistaking the eyes, or the smile, or the statuesque presence. She was a giant of a woman, tall and broad shouldered with a piercing gaze that had intimidated me several times, before she let me discover her soft heart.

It took her a minute to recognize me.

"Is that who I think it is?" she said as she reached in through my passenger window to shake hands, "it's been a while. Glad to see you."

"And it's nice to see you too. Where have you been? I haven't seen you . . ."

She smiled, "It's been a while, I know."

"Here for the races?"

"Heavens no, I never bet."

"Really," I quipped, "really? Well, I've heard of that."

That made her laugh. "I'm sure you've heard of that, but never met someone that doesn't bet." We both laughed.

While we spoke, I learned she was waiting for a bus to take her to Albany's airport.

"Well, it's quite a story, you see I came up here last weekend with some friends, but we got separated, they got jobs back in the city, and . . . well, I'm retired now and I met an old friend and . . . well, I stayed. But now family, back on the island, come down sickly, and with my friend up here in charge of a big reunion thing . . ."

The light went on. "Well hop in, I'm in the taxi business now, as you can see. I'll get you to the airport, free, if you tell me this story you say is so special."

"Oh, I couldn't."

"Yes you could, it's only twenty miles, I insist."

In seconds her case was in the trunk and old faithful had a passenger headed to the airport, pro bono of course, but the story she shared was worth every inch of the journey. As best I can remember, and, as best I can put it all back together, it went something like this:

It started a few days previous when Brianna found her self at Reflection's Aquarium in the Staten Island Mall while her friend Barbara did some last second shopping in a pharmacy. The aquarium housed rows of glass tanks filled with a rainbow of aquatics and bubbleators dominating the quiet rhythm of the building. At the front of the store, a large tank held one chubby goldfish and one miniature gray castle. Brianna was hypnotized.

"Got'em," Barbara's voiced whispered into Brianna's ear.

"Really?"

"Yes," Barbara said as she waved a subtle finger toward the aquarium, "and what are you doing, staring at that fish, or looking at yourself in the glass?"

"Hush," Brianna responded with an equally quiet gesture, "You've got no place barking at me, not today, not after talking me into this crazy day trip, and then making us stop because you forget those things."

"Oh hush yourself, at least I still need them. Come on, no more; don't want to hear no more. We're going, this'll be fun."

"I don't know, it's such a long drive," she said as she returned to the fish tank.

"Please, Sherrie's driving, and we need you, you know your way around that place; you're going be our tour guide."

"I'm too old to be a tour guide."

"What!" Barbara's voice jumped with alarm as she spun around to face her friend with her fists planted firmly into her hips.

"I just saw myself in the glass, I look old. I don't like looking old."

"You look fine, now, no excuses."

"Fine, for an old lady of fifty-something you mean." She couldn't bear to say fifty-six, it didn't sound real.

"Ladies," it was a young salesclerk, "Can I help you?" He was blond, and, pale, and seventeen at most. The two women looked into each others eyes and smiled.

Brianna interrupted before her friend could start one of her performances. "I was just wondering," she offered quietly, "why this fish keeps going back to this castle thing in its tank, you know, round and round. Why it doesn't get bored or something?"

The young boy looked intimidated and shy for a second. "Well it is a gold fish; the books say they forget just about everything in a matter of seconds, not much memory they say."

"And no regrets," Barbara interjected.

"Truly?" Brianna added.

"That's the myth anyway, that's what they say."

"In a matter of seconds?"

"Yup, see, he never gets bored; every time he comes across that castle he gets all excited because he thinks he's found something new to explore."

"No memories?" Brianna mused quizzically.

"Come on, we're running late," Barbara said taking her by the arm, "we're off to Saratoga."

The salesclerk was left standing there, still relating his gold fish legend, wondering where the women went.

Far up the New York Thruway, Brianna lost herself in the green-blue depths of the Catskill Mountains. She had thought about this trip for weeks, ever since Barbara, Sherrie, and their friend Toni, had discovered the idea at the bottom of a large bottle of White Zinfandel. They insisted that going back to Brianna's 'old stomping grounds' because it might be a 'fun' way to celebrate her retirement. Twenty years with the Nassau Police Department had been enough, but it had all started with the New York Racing Association and the security department, and the racetracks, and Saratoga. It seemed so long ago.

"Your mind plays funny tricks on you, doesn't it?" Brianna said out loud.

"Say what?"

Her giant brown eyes flashed open and she smiled at herself, "You weren't supposed to be listening."

Everyone smiled.

"Brianna's gonna be our tour guide. Aren't you?" Sherrie said from the steering wheel.

"I'm retired, I'm tired and retired, sweetheart, once you get to that crazy place, you are on your own." And she said it with decisive finger pointed directly at her friend through the rear view mirror.

"You watch, you watch, Brianna'll get us around," said Barbara, "she knows that place like the back of her hand; she'll show us all the good stuff, horses, handicappers, ice cream, cotton candy, all the fun stuff. Oh yeah, maybe we'll meet one of those rich mucky-mucks that hang out there in August."

Brianna rolled her eyes in disbelief and returned to the distant mountains. Her friends were waking up and getting excited as the miles rolled beneath them. So many memories, yet, in a way, she was lucky that her friends were giggling and laughing and making rude jokes; their noise and prodding kept her from remembering too much.

"I'll bet you Brianna, I bet you lots of your old rich friends are still there. Brianna had lots of friends there, some of 'em real rich too."

"Really?" Toni asked.

"And none of them will be looking for any of us, unless one of their maids died yesterday."

"Don't listen to her, she's just being stubborn. She's probably afraid she's gonna have a good time, and then she'll have to admit she was wrong."

"Barbara is always looking for some kind of romance, a real dreamer this one. Stick close to her and she'll have you chasing stars," Brianna said quietly.

"Oh yeah," Barbara jumped from her seat and turned to her friend in the back, "do ya think that Johnson guy might still be there again? Maybe you two will have a reunion?"

"Come on, that was a long time ago."

"What's this girl?" Sherrie asked.

Barbara was jumping out of her bucket seat at the opportunity to tell a story, "Oh sweetie you don't know, Brianna was a model once."

"Hush!" Toni squealed.

"She's crazy," Brianna said with a disgusted wave of her hand.

'Yes she was, yes she was. This guy Johnson met her at the races one day and got her to do some modeling. Her eyes were used in some make up commercials, Revlon or Avon I think it was, um-hmmm, her pictures were in Jet magazine and, and what was that other magazine?"

"Only he wanted a lot more than pictures," Brianna offered.

The girls laughed.

"What he got was an education."

They laughed more.

Barbara was bursting at the seams, "Yeah, she had to put him in his place. He probably still remembers."

"Oh yeah girl. Did you really?" Sherrie said.

Brianna nodded, "Should have known what he was, but he got his, and that was that."

"And what else haven't we heard?" Toni queried, "Sounds like we've haven't heard the really good stories yet."

"You just drive and don't get us lost, all right." Brianna commanded, "Get me to Route 87, and I'll get you to Saratoga. You'll all probably end up with more stories than me, that's for sure."

Brianna returned to her mountains. Rolling clouds shaded their peeks with acres of deep blue that highlighted the green forests. They looked peaceful and silent. She couldn't help but think that she shouldn't have come. There were so many memories up there, so many which had been safely put away, silent for so long.

+

"Lieutenant Mathers, got a minute?"

"Sure Brianna,"

"If this guy we're looking for is as bad as you're saying," she was interrupted as the troop of guards shuffled out of the conference room, "don't you dare stick me with no candy ass little college boy like that duty last week."

The lieutenant never really nodded yes or no, he just waved his great skull back and forth, "Don't worry, no college kids on this detail."

"I mean it, no horse . . ."

"Brianna we can't play games here. If I could find us some bullet proof vests I'd hand them out. The tip we got from the folks at Monmouth ain't no joke, this guy's bad news and the state police are sure he's in town."

"Insurance?"

"Maybe?"

"What?"

"Could be blood feud between the owners, family jealousy, who knows, all we know for damn sure is the guy, DePaolo, is here and he's here to put that horse down," he said with emphasis as he peered into his shirt pocket to see the name of the horse again, 'Equinox', yeah 'Equinox' He's goin' down if this bastard gets close to him and then our necks are on the line."

"Why don't they just move him out of here?"

"Cause this guy would just go to wherever that place is. We're the lucky ones cause it looks like this thing ends here," and with that he turned to look Brianna directly in the eyes, "and it ain't goin' wrong on my watch. The city cops are here, the state police are all over the highways, and we are going to cover these barns like a new coat of green paint. Ain't we?"

"Lieutenant, don't give me no candy ass; I want somebody at my back."

"Trust me, just trust me. The boss says he's got a guy from the Troy Police Department for you. Just out of the Army I hear. Trust me."

II

Hours passed. The sun reappeared from behind a mountain's cloud and Brianna was back in Toni's car.

"What's the matter Brianna?"

"Oh, we got off at the wrong exit."

"Jesus," squealed Toni, "are we lost up here in this place?"

"No," laughed Barbara.

"Where are we Brianna," asked Sherrie from the driver's seat, "you sure you know where we are? Oh Lord, look at this place, just miles and miles of woods. What would you do if we broke down, oh Lord, out here in no-where?"

"We're not lost, just didn't have to drive through the city and all the traffic. No matter, just keep going. Stay on 9 and we'll get there."

"You OK now Toni?" Barbara mocked.

"Don't say nothing, I just want to see this gosh almighty fancy place you're always talking about. So far I haven't seen anything but a couple of trucks, some ugly old woman in a Cadillac, and cows for over an hour. Did you really work up here, really?"

"Sure she did," Barbara offered, "I use to come up here every August to meet Brianna and we'd go out, and woo-ee, did we have some fun."

"I bet the two of you weren't running for saint either," Toni said over her sunglasses.

Everybody laughed.

As soon as the foursome entered the Nelson Avenue gate, her friends started the interrogations.

"Brianna, Brianna" Toni kept calling to her, "this is the prettiest place I've ever seen." Her eyes were roaming over the rows of oaks and elms and maple trees. "Where'd they get all these flowers, look at all them all? This don't look like no race track I've ever seen."

"I don't remember those escalators," Barbara said beneath squinted eyes.

"I don't know," Brianna answered, "something's different. I don't think there was a clubhouse gate back then? I think that used to be open to the grandstand."

"What's up there, what's that little house out there?"

Brianna smiled and winked at Barbara to be silent, "That's spring water."

"Really," answered Toni, "how much for a glass?"

"Free I think. It used to be."

"No way," Toni said as she led the four women toward the Big Red Spring pavilion, "Look no doors and free cups, this wouldn't last long in Brooklyn, whole damn thing would be gone and on its way to Brazil. Free water!"

"Have some," Barbara said as she and Brianna pressed their chins into their chests to keep from laughing. Their restraint didn't last long. The cup was filled and taken in one huge gulp. Toni's eyes bulged, her cheeks ballooned, and she made the most pitiful whimpering noises. Sherrie was about to take in her cupful when she saw her friend's misfortune and froze.

Toni spit it out, gagging. "What was in it," her eyes were pleading for help, "that poisoned or something? I'm not gonna be sick am I? Am I gonna die?"

Strangers around the pavilion enjoyed the harmless joke. Barbara explained how Brianna had gotten her with the same water on her first trip to the Spa, and even Brianna had to admit that her old boss, Ross, had gotten her on her first day.

"I am gonna be sick." Toni was pleading for sympathy.

"Stop that girl; it's harmless," Barbara said through her smile, "mineral water is all. Everybody who comes here has to go through the same initiation. Now let's see the track where they race. Where's the track Brianna?"

Her friends laughed, but as Brianna was about to offer directions to the racing surface, her eyes focused beyond the steel fence into the rows of parked cars. Beside an ancient elm tree stood a face that seized the back of her mind and ambushed her tongue.

"That way, that way," she gestured meekly, "through those big square archways, that way. I'll catch up with you at the rail, the fence, you'll see it."

Her friends were bemused by the tone of her voice. Brianna, after years of police training rarely fumbled with her words and was never distracted.

"C'mon Brianna."

"I'll catch up, you go and, find something . . . to ask me about . . . quick, go."

The three women paused, but Sherrie was anxious to see everything, and they all wanted to see the horses.

Brianna stalked through the assemblage of picnic tables and laughing faces. She withdrew into the shade of a giant oak and sidestepped some small children at play in order to keep a small shrub between herself and the parking area. She found the face again standing in the sun. Her mind refused to admit what her eyes were telling her. She looked again. The face carried years of living, the hair seemed thin and graying, but it was his face. It was Joe's. Joe of so many years ago and in the summer heat, she froze and shivered and held herself still, too vulnerable to defend herself from an ignorant world and her chest of memories.

++

The head of NYRA security and the Lieutenant, motioned for Brianna to join a group of officers beneath the street light at the back of Horse Haven.

"Brianna, I want you to work with Joe Cronley tonight. Joe, this is your partner."

Her first reaction was never spoken. Her tone said 'this kid is huge', but her tongue simply uttered "You're Joe?"

"Hi, nice to meet you," was his simple response.

She thought to herself that it was nice to finally have to look up at a man; most of the guards were shorter than herself.

"Joe's from the Troy Police Department, getting' some extra work, aren't ya Joe?"

"Right Lieutenant, I'm really looking forward to this, working with your security people I mean."

"That's all I needed to hear, we've got this place covered, and I'm sure you two will carry your part just fine."

"Does he know the score here?" Brianna asked.

"Everybody's briefed, we're as set as we can be. Did you see the state police out on Union Avenue, and the extra lights? Yeah that's the way it's gonna be."

Brianna eyed her boss and raised her eyebrows. The Lieutenant took his cue and sent Joe off on a mission to get some extra flashlights and their radios.

The Lieutenant smiled, "Well, did I give you a candy ass this time?"

"Where did you ever find that kid? Those arms, he looks deformed. But does he know his stuff? Looks like he's about twelve years old."

"He must be thirty, done two tours overseas as an MP, played some college football, and passed his exam for the police academy last year.

He's fine. His Captain told me some good stuff about the kid; you won't be alone tonight."

"Damn good thing."

"That's why I'm putting the two of you out on the fence near the Yaddo."

"You're what? Out there with the mosquitoes and weeds and no coffee or tea or . . . Lieutenant, come on, wouldn't Marty or Sandman be better?"

"They're going over to the Oklahoma training track, back by the BOCES building; I think the horse is over there?"

"You think?"

"Yeah I think, nobody but two or three people in this whole damn place know where the real 'Equinox' is. The owners wanted him moved around for a little extra protection. This is serious. Now get ready and get along, you'll be fine. See the size of those arms, you'll be fine."

Brianna smirked and grimaced, "My grandma said there'd be days like this."

III

Next to the walking path children were playing a game of hopscotch. It moved Brianna into the sunlight.

"Brianna, Brianna," a plaintive voice called from between the rows of artist's tents and jewelry merchants, "Brianna, is that you, is it really you?"

It was Mary Kohn, different now, heavy and stooped shouldered, but it was Mary Kohn's eyes and smile and strange crackly little voice. She use to serve up cupfuls of coffee and orange juice at the breakfast tent. Mary had been considered old when Brianna worked here years ago, yet here she was, moving to greet her old friend in front of Attwaters' Little Hat Stand.

"Oh my gosh, I remember you, Oh my Gosh, Mary, are you still here?"

"Yes, it's me and bless you, bless you for remembering. How are you, how are you? Oh come here and give me a kiss."

The two women stood out in the noonday sun to share selected moments from those long ago days. Sadly, Mary had lost a son to cancer, but her daughter was doing well, living in Kentucky. She was coming to visit next week with her new husband Robert. Mary marveled at Brianna's stories and congratulated her over and over again.

"I didn't know, honest to Pete I didn't know."

"Well, Nassau was good you know, but it was time to retire and move on, you know, find something else to do, while I can still do some things."

"Oh, gosh that sounds so exciting, really, you've had some life. I knew you would do something special, I knew this security stuff wasn't enough for you."

"It wasn't that really, no it was just other things going on in my life then and when I passed all their exams, well Nassau just offered so many new challenges and a faster pace. Things worked out."

Oh. I'll bet luck had nothing to do with it, I'll bet you've got quite a few stories under your hat. Golly, did you carry a gun and everything?"

Brianna laughed, "Mary, of course, I was an officer."

"Oh gosh," Mary said without thinking or recalling adequately, "Did you ever have to shoot someone or really, you know . . . use it?"

"Mary, you devil, there were times I wished I had, but no, I never used it once!"

"Oh, come here, sit down, sit still and just tell me everything."

Their conversation was overtaken by the siren of an ambulance headed toward Broadway. Brianna's mind was flashing back and forth, from image to image. She winced, noticeably.

"You feeling Ok?" Mary asked.

"Me? Fine. Just thinking is all. Tell me all about your daughter."

So she sat and Mary talked and Brianna tried to listen.

+++

The woods darkened beyond the glow of the barn lights. A rush of cold wetness that collected around her thighs and buttocks panicked her. The undergrowth was very thick, and dampness had started to work through the trousers of her uniform. Brianna remembered thinking that if this duty ruins this uniform, and I get stuck with a cleaning bill, there would be trouble. At the very least the Lieutenant was going to hear about it.

She spoke into the night. "Joe, where are you, Joseph?"

She tried their radio one more time. She removed the batteries and rubbed the contact points clean again, replaced them and tried again to no avail. She found a tree and put her back to it, holstered the radio and peered as far into the blackness as her eyes would allow. Part of her mind was rehearsing the lambasting her boss was going to get. Last week he gave her that goofy college kid to work with, and now he comes up with a muscle bound version of the Lone Ranger.

Again, into the night, "Officer Conley, report and NOW!" she called into the device.

The brush to her right began to crash and rumble. Brianna squatted quickly into the shadows. She touched the revolver on her hip, but didn't unholster it. There was a thud, and a small yelp of pain as Joe emerged from the underbrush. "Where the hell did she go?" was all he could mutter before Brianna stood up to confront him.

"Don't you ever do that again, don't you ever do that again," was the way the monologue started. Brianna surprised herself at all the resources she found right on the tip of her tongue. She shared paragraphs from The Riot Act, The Subversion Act, The Alien & Sedition Acts, as well as a few old homilies her grandmother had laid on her whenever she made a serious mistake. Brianna didn't care what he had seen crawling through the bushes, or how much it reminded him of things he had seen in the army. She reminded him in no uncertain terms that 'partnered up' meant they were never to lose sight of each other. She actually enjoyed reaming him out a little, but at the same time a strand of confidence formed behind her eyes, like the opening hymn in a church service. The big guy stood still and took it. He nodded yes, and looked her straight in the eye. After all he hadn't been slacking off or treating this duty as a lark; he had simply been too enthusiastic and was trying to do too much.

"Clear!" was how she ended her part.

"Clear Sarge," was all he offered in reply. She waited for him to turn away so he wouldn't see her smile.

Joe lead the way. The two officers tromped through the underbrush and over the perimeter fence in pursuit of Joe's sighting.

"I know I saw something, somebody low, wanting to move, but in a way hunters move when they don't want to be seen. I know I saw something."

She was a step behind him. "I'm not doubting you, maybe you did, maybe it was something and maybe it was some kid snooping around or . . . or maybe it was one of these grooms hiding out from the immigration folks? Jus' don't go running off on your own."

Brianna froze, looking to her left was an unobstructed view of barns and sheds and storage bins. "Joe," she whispered, "don't move, I saw it too, way over there behind the hay, a man, looked like he was changing his shirt. Who gets dressed in a hay mound at this time of night?"

"Radio?"

"Dead!"

"Got flares?"

"Please, we aren't Rangers, we're security."

"So?"

"We follow, at a distance, and try and get someone. These barns have phones in them, just got to find one that's open so we don't scare the horses."

"Who?"

"Anybody, who cares, barn hands, grooms, all these barns got phones. Maybe we can find somebody with a good radio, Stan and Armando are down this way somewhere, but I don't want to lose sight of whoever this is, just in case."

The two guards moved as quietly as they could to the pile of hay. They circled it, but found nothing. "Now I'm seeing things?"

"Naw," Joe said, "look in the hay, push it aside, here, look here Brianna," Joe whispered, as he pulled out a full body camouflage suit from the hay. "And you tell me lady, who sneaks around a race track in full camouflage, and then hides it in a stack of hay?"

"Damn, we might have the guy, good Lord; we might be sitting right on top of him? C'mon, we've gotta get some help, but I don't want to lose sight of him."

The two guards walked slowly and quietly between barns. Horses snorted and wheezed as they walked past. Ancient streetlights stretched into rows of darkness and then replaced with long channels of thick blackness. At the opposite end of each barn they looked, straining into the darkness. There was a radio playing somewhere in the distance, and trucks could be heard whirring up and down the Northway.

"I don't like it," Joe said

"I know. Hear that radio, somebody's awake near here, come on."

"I just don't like the way we lost sight of this guy so fast."

Brianna looked left and right. "Damn radio! Stuck out here by ourselves. Let's get some-back up here. Stan and Armando gotta be down this way, down near the big storage shed."

The two strangers-partners stood and listened and began moving to their left. "All barns have phones, any phone, look in these barns, one of them must have an open office, something we can use."

It was all Brianna was able to say. As they stepped off the wooden walkway but were stopped by a faint rattling of chains. Immediately, a heavy timber swung out from the darkness. It struck Joe squarely in the head with a deep wet thud. Brianna saw the legs of her partner move, jerk and watched his weight began to sink toward the ground. He never made a noise. Her right hand moved to her hip but the board was coming again, cutting the air like a saw. It speared the point of her shoulder and sent her reeling backward. From the ground she saw the man, smallish, with long thick black hair spraying out from a baseball cap. He was standing not five feet from her, smashing the two by four into the ground, trying to split it. Brianna went to rock herself to her feet when the timber caught her again and rolled her through the dirt. The nightmare that awaited her when she turned on her back could not have been imagined. Instinct had made her kick and roll, trying to catch her attacker from behind, but when she turned over one last time the splintered board was already through her uniform and flesh. He had made the board into a spear and she was impaled. A terrible clenching fist seized her, a hysteria of pain. Hate, rage, and fury poured out of his eyes. She could feel things tearing and snapping below her skin, deep within where she had never felt anything before. He thrust the weapon at her again and then a third time, it seemed to delight him and enrage him all the more.

There was more blackness; it took her sight, and her hearing, and any sense of her own skin. It released her and recaptured her, returning the world to grays and light and then back to darkness. Fear challenged her to stop him, grasp the spear, pull it away from him, demand she stay alive, but the black silence returned and beat softly through her skull, pounding her sense of self, and time, and place into the cold earth and out of her consciousness.

There was a heavy noise, a strong thud that came out of the darkness and blurred across her sight. The lance fell from her stomach and for the first time she saw colors swelling through her fingers, pinks and blues and maroons and reds, it took her but a second to realize that all the colors were her. "Oh God," was the only cry she could muster rubbing her brown face into the dark dirt. One fist pounded the air. Years later she would tell her friend Barbara about that moment, her angry fist, not certain if she swung it out of fear of dying or anger and disappointment that she had allowed this monster inside her arms where he could hurt her.

She took deep breaths and tried to stop the wetness. She gasped over and over again knowing she was forcing life back into her senses. Where was he? She looked up to a sight that both confounded and shocked her. Her attacker was on his back, face up, writhing and screaming, like some rabid animal. He flailed and kicked, but couldn't move. Those were Joe's arms around him, lying under him, bear hugging his chest from behind. The two men rolled back and forth, the screaming rose, until Joe was above the assassin. Brianna forced herself to move on all fours to the struggle and, with more weight than strength, fell on the madman's legs to keep him from kicking her partner. They rolled far to the left one more time; there was an ominous first sound, an audible crack. Its sound was as clear and unmistakable, the same sound she had heard when her attacker had broken the board into a spear. There was another crack. His screaming became wet coughs; there was more cracking, and then silence.

The last thing she remembered that night, before the EMT's loaded her in the ambulance, was the crowd that surrounded them. Joe was seated next to her in a wheelchair, the side of his head swollen by his ear and his left eye closed shut, purple and thick. Her hands were over her wound and Joe's hand was over hers. He kept whispering "Hang on, hang on!", but all Brianna could say was, "Where were all these people a minute ago?"

IV

"Mary, I've got to go. I'll come back after I find my friends a seat. I'll introduce you and then we can really catch up on the old days."

With a simple wave Brianna bid Mary a soft goodbye and hurried toward the Union Avenue admission gates. She was thinking of her friends, probably lost or in trouble by now, but she had to be sure she had seen him. She found her pace quickening, her little chat had caused her to lose sight of that face she was sure was Joe. She kept thinking that a dark blue suit should be easy to find on such a sunny day, amongst all this green, under all these red and white canopies. People were streaming in toward the track, dragging coolers and lawn chairs and umbrellas. She remembered the insanity of crowd control, especially on days when they would give away t-shirts or beer steins. An ancient woman, too frail to walk, was being wheeled in by what looked like her daughter. They approached.

"Where's the elevator Mam?"

Brianna smiled, "I'm sorry I don't work here." She laughed inside thinking 'come on lady can't you see the way I'm dressed'.

"Sorry, I thought, you look like you knew."

She smiled, "Looks can be deceiving, especially in this place. But the elevator used to be in the clubhouse, way down that way."

The young woman said thanks and resumed her happy burden. Another couple, equally lumbered, crossed her path with tiny triplets in an extra wide stroller. "Sorry," the woman kept saying, "Sorry" as she tried to maneuver her tribe around patrons and the artist's tents. "I thought we'd never get here." was all the Mother could say, "six hours, six hours; Dennis said it wouldn't take more than three hours from Toms River."

"Dennis doesn't travel with triplets," the Dad replied. "Stop that; stop hitting your sister, all of you. Sit still!"

More memories; some things never change.

++++

"We are going Barbara," Brianna's voice was firm, "don't let me down, I've got to do this."

"You sure you want to do this?"

"Four hours, no more, now c'mon, get your things in the car and let's get out of here before the Belt gets all jammed up."

"I'm hurrying girl, I'm hurrying," Barbara said loudly as she dropped into the passenger seat, "and if you're really in a hurry, and determined to get your best friend in trouble, well then don't bother with Knapp street, just make a right here, and we'll sneak in the back way to the bridge and it'll be Sticksville, USA for Barbara."

The bridge was clear and crossing the Bronx was unusually easy. The two women sat in the car and enjoyed a long talk about old boyfriends, dim-witted bosses, and their plans for November. Their first and only frustration was a backup at the Harriman toll booth that made Brianna uncomfortable.

"I'll drive sweetie," Barbara offered, "jump out and I'll get us going again."

"Right here, in traffic?"

"This ain't traffic," Barbara reminded her as she reached for the door, "this is parking, now get out."

The exchange made, Barbara quickly changed gears from pilot to worried friend. "You OK?" The question was gentle, not wanting to intrude.

"Sore," was all she said.

"We got a long way to go girl, maybe you should try this next week when you're feeling better? You've only been out of the hospital a couple of weeks . . ."

"I might not be feeling any better next week, or the week after. Who knows?"

"I mean did they take out all the stitches?"

"Course, all the ones they could. Some of them are, you know, inside, they just dissolve or something."

"Hurt?"

"Yeah, what do you think? Course, a hundred stitches hurt, but that's all, it just hurts, everything in there is clear, no infection, no nothing."

"Sure?"

"Doc said so, yesterday."

"Brianna?"

"Drive Barbara, I want to do this, dumb kid could lose his job."

"I don't get it; I mean I really don't get it. How the hell did this guy get busted for stopping this other guy from, you know, killing you and that race horse?"

"I don't know, politics probably, and lousy lawyers."

"And this guy DePaolo, his family is suing, suing like in court."

"Yup." Brianna sat in silence and let a deep chill shiver through her. She looked out the window while thoughts and images careened through her mind.

"Brianna?"

Brianna collected herself, "You would not have believed the hate in that man's face?"

Barbara listened.

"The hate, he didn't even know me. He was like a great mad dog, with his black oily hair and those red eyes. I was a complete stranger to him. He was mad or something, crazy, you wouldn't have believed it." Her voice was trailing off.

Barbara's hand found her friend's arm and squeezed.

"But he's gone."

"Lord what a face, I see it in my dreams."

"But he's gone, gone forever now."

"Thank God."

"I like Joe already."

"Good guy, most everybody likes Joe. You gotta see the arms on this kid, bigger than your . . . ."

"Easy girl."

"God what a night. I still see it in my dreams. Joe kept squeezing and squeezing, trying to get him to pass out I guess. Joe wouldn't let go, we were both hurt, he just kept squeezing; he wasn't given up his advantage, and then everything was quiet."

Barbara heard her friend's voice cracking. Brianna's arm was cold and damp.

"Never saw a man killed before."

Barbara felt helpless, not knowing how to change the subject.

"And now Joe's suspended. They're busting Joe because of that pig."

"Dead. Those arms, crazy kid must lift weights all day every day."

"Have you talked to him, Joe I mean, since . . ."

"On the phone is all; he sent me flowers in the hospital, but I was so out of it with all the crap they shot in me. I don't remember if he was there or not. My mother even got mad at me for tying up the phone the other night. We talked for over an hour, he said he was just happy to hear from me, you know, out of the hospital and we talked."

"Really?" Barbara offered with a chime in her voice.

Brianna knew what her friend was saying and she smiled, "Yeah, and I owe him, a good guy."

"So?"

"So nothing, we're driving north so I can say thank him the right way let him know that I want to go to court with him, testify, and get him off the hook if I can."

"That sounds right."

"I remember how my Lieutenant always saying, whatever it takes."

V

Brianna moved behind the counter where programs and racing forms were sold into the dark arena beneath the grandstand. The face was lost for the moment and regret nearly panicked her. To her right, more parents lead little ones toward a small playground of swings and slides and to her left, couples strolled along a walkway that formed the perimeter of a large open pavilion. She remarked to herself that this pavilion was new; it hadn't been here when she worked the grandstand. Behind her was the hustle of tellers finding their place for the day's trials. She asked herself several times if she couldn't be mistaken, if this was really Joe, but all doubts were discarded when a large group of men emerged from the Union Avenue ticket booths and started walking toward her. Some were dressed in military uniforms, others were in civilian jackets, they talked amongst themselves and shook hands and in the middle, unmistakably in the middle, was Joe.

Unconsciously she found herself sliding toward a large steel girder, her brain afire again. It kept praying for time, she didn't know what to say, she knew she didn't want to see him yet.

A coarse laugh and a sawdust filled voice broke the moment, "Bay what? Bay number? Skinny! What the hell am I looking for, for Christ's sake Skinny, what are we doing?" It was two grimy mechanics in search of a work order, pushing a steel cart of tools and dragging a large red ladder.

"Aw shut up, it's right here, I wrote it down," a little gray haired man in green overalls hissed back at his companion. He was struggling and digging through pockets and zippers.

"Ka-Rist," the other man scowled as he put down a tall ladder and watched in mock annoyance. "Don't hurry or nothing, I get paid by the hour."

"I got it, I got it, Bay 23. The bay number is 23."

"Damn, over there, out near the gable end, pain in the . . . come on, grab the lousy ladder and let's see what's screwed up this time."

Brianna had moved aside to give the workers room and still keep an eye on Joe. She watched as the older man, who looked too heavy to be climbing ladders, struggled through a crawl space to examine some wiring, while his partner held the ladder and observed the people coming to the races. He made eye contact with Brianna and nodded.

"I'm suppose to catch him if he falls," he said with a wry grin.

Brianna grimaced at the thought of catching a guy that size, from any height.

"Fat chance, I'm gonna risk catching his fat butt flying through the air."

Brianna turned aside to hide her smile.

"What did you say, you little muskrat?"

"Nothing Tiny, just get to work and get those TV sets working so we can take a break."

And as she watched the repairman teeter on the edge of extinction, she continued to peer out into the bright paddock hoping to find Joe's face. For the moment he was gone. She looked and looked again, until a voice broke in upon her silence. It was Joe, he was right behind her, inches away, saying hello to other men, exchanging formalities and fulfilling introductions. The last thread of doubt vanished when she heard someone introduce Colonel Conley, Colonel Joseph Conley. Her Joe, the baby faced police rookie was a Colonel, an Army Colonel. She couldn't believe it, how was this possible? There must have been ten or twelve men at this mini-reunion, and in the middle, directly at her back, so close she could feel the warmth off his jacket, was Joe Conley, after all these years. She put on her sunglasses, folded her arms, and made herself small. An entire gallery of mislaid ghosts reentered.

+++++

"Here, Barbara, here, exit 14 and then take a left at the stop sign."

"Bee, if I'd a known this was gonna take this long you'du've been taking a bus."

"Left, right here take a left and then clear this bridge and take your second right."

"Sure?"

"I'm sure, keep going, there it is, there it is, see the house on the lake with those guys on the roof."

"You sure, are we safe here?"

"Shush, just pull in that driveway. I called his lawyer; he told me he was up here working on a friend's house. This has got to be it."

Barbara felt like she was stepping out on to the stage. The two women left their car and stood before four thoroughly bemused men in shorts, tee shirts, and tool belts. She stood by the car with her hand on the door handle, but Brianna stepped into the middle of the sawdust and black asphalt shingles to ask for Joe.

Barbara watched her friend shake hands with each of the workers, throw her head around casually, and then turn to look back at the car with a huge grin. Barbara was almost ready to be insulted by that smile when she saw her friend, stitches and all, start to climb up a steel ladder toward the roof.

"What the hell do you think you are doing girl? Get off that ladder. What the hell is going on, get off that house?" she muttered under her breath as she left the security of her car and charged toward Brianna. She looked at the workman, they at her, and she called to Brianna.

"Don't think she can hear you," one of the carpenters said to her, "he's running a pretty big saw up there."

"Joe is up there?"

"Yeah," another man said.

Barbara kicked the ladder lightly, "This thing safe?"

The group smiled and chuckled, "Safe as the guy who's on it," he said.

Another man approached her, getting a little too close for Barbara's taste. He was young, tall and a wall of muscles. Barbara, against her own best intentions, found herself thinking he looked like a model and should be wearing more clothes out in the open.

197

"You brought Brianna?" he asked with an alarmingly gentle voice.

"Yeah," she answered skeptically.

He offered her his hand," I guess we all want to thank you a little."

Barbara was tentative, but they shook.

"All Joey's been able to talk about is your friend."

Barbara looked around at the others and saw, to her relief; they were all smiling and shaking their heads up and down. "Really?'

"Joey's kinda special to everybody around here, to all of us, and from what he tells us, your friend's why he's still here."

"Brianna?"

"Guess so, but I don't care what you call her; she saved Joe's hide, one tough lady."

"Brianna?"

"Yeah, your friend, didn't she tell you what happened that night? That guy DePaolo was kicking his way out of Joe's grip, gonna get away, and you friend, hurt like she was, got back into the fight and jumped on him. She gave Joe a chance to get another grip."

"Brianna?"

"It's awful hot for September lady, want a beer?"

On the lofty perch, Joe and Brianna shared a reunion. They laughed and embraced, reviewed each other's condition, shared compliments, laughed again and sat to talk. They spoke of Joe's suspension, she scolded him for working so hard after all that had happened, and he scolded her for climbing up a ladder so soon after her discharge. She told him about her grandmother's stroke and her worries, he told her about his friend's house, its leaky roof, and a reluctant insurance company. They laughed in the wind.

"Come on, I know a great place for dinner, I'll buy."

"Oh no, Barbara's got to get back home and all."

"No way, you aren't going to drive hours just to spend thirty minutes listening to me tell old jokes, and then drive all the way back at night, no way."

"Thanks Joe, but I really just wanted to tell you, you know, thank you, just for being there, you know, with all that happened, I want you to call me if your hearing goes to court, I mean it, whatever it takes, I'll testify, anything."

"Well I got the union lawyers, but if this does come up in court, I can use all the friends I can get."

In one soft motion, Brianna saw her new friend blush and look away. His eyes were filling. Her heart jumped and she smiled in light amazement. He was sentimental. She leaned in to hold him and her hug grew stronger and lasted. His face remained motionless sensing her warmth. They pulled away and stared into each other's eyes, taking a moment to smile, conceding both delight and flight. Joe broke the spell when he jumped up to say, "Nope, no debate, we're going to The Wishing Well and dinner's on me."

"Oh damn," Brianna said quietly, "how do I get down?"

Brianna actually tried to debate dinner as they descended the ladder, but when they alighted they found Barbara working on her third Budweiser, and entertaining everybody with her best imitation of The Supremes.

"See," Joe said with a sun-splitting smile, "you're staying for dinner."

Barbara put down her brown bottle on the hood of an old Ford pick up truck and took her friend by the arm away from the workmen. "Brianna, where did you find all these pretty boys?"

"Are you drunk Barbara?"

"No I am not, but I'm gonna be something else if you don't get me out of here, right now."

"Well, you're in no condition to drive, and Joe wants to buy us dinner."

"Really?" She was smiling a smile Brianna had seen before.

"And that means we'll have to find a place to stay tonight."

"Oh damn, we stay here, there could be trouble?"

"Stop," Brianna demanded, "he's taken us to a nice place, and I don't want no vaudeville act in The Wishing Well."

"I mean it, we better leave, these boys think I'm funny and I think, well don't ask what I'm thinking."

"Barbara, get yourself together and do not embarrass me.

VI

The U.S. Army band charged through the grandstand with a volley of brass coronets and the relentless cadence of snare drums. Brianna stood next to a great white pillar watching Joe and his friends step out into the sunlight and saunter toward the clubhouse. Brianna paralleled their path from the darkness of the aged pavilion. Some of the men stopped to examine jewelry, others looked at historic paintings and photographs but Joe, with two others, seemed content to wait and look and point.

Their path brought her closer to another newsstand and Brianna obeyed the impulse to purchase a program. She flipped through the race schedule, examining the names of owners and trainers. The name Conley didn't appear anywhere, not as a trainer, nor an owner. She looked up from her reading, and saw Joe's group meet yet another assembly of veteran's in full uniform. One last look at the program gave her the answer, the feature race was The West Point Handicap, and she remembered clearly how the New York Racing Association always put on a big show to honor the armed forces. These retired officers were to be honored today. He had gone back into the Army, it was plain now. The air left her lungs while she rehearsed the idea. Names ran through her imagination, names like Panama, Somalia, Iraq.

Two small children ran between the rows of chairs and park benches in a desperate conflict to see who could get to their Mother's cooler first.

"The orange juice is mine."

"Mine, you get the chocolate," Ma said.

"No, you do, I want the orange juice."

One of the imps looked up and found Brianna's eyes peering over her sunglasses. She felt obliged to shake her head at them as if to say 'Don't fight' and then moved silently away.

When Joe's friends took the long path beyond the old betting shed, she was forced to leave the anonymity of the building. She settled in with a large group of picnickers collecting around the walking circle. She didn't like walking through all this grass and dust with her new shoes and was soon tiptoeing to avoid the blankets and sandwiches and beer. Some of the military men broke up into smaller groups, each examining a different entertainment, and Brianna found herself drawing closer to Joe's back as he watched small children climb the fence. A little boy was screaming at his sister but the mother sat and chatted, oblivious to the wordy warfare that was going on right behind her. Brianna stood still and watched in silent fear. Once more long interred phantoms escaped their shrouds.

++++++

"Mother," Brianna said, "get away from that window and step in here."

"I am just sitting for a minute, I am tired. Can a woman not sit and watch the street when she is tired?"

"You always stare at the street,"

"I am tired."

Brianna charged into the room, "And I am sick of your son . . ."

"Step son."

"Whatever. Benjy's mouth and his language."

"He means nothing; it is just talk, never mind him."

She could hear music from Benjy's room jarring the air, and she had to close her Mother's door to keep from hollering. "It is not just talk, it's hate, he's mean and crude and just awful. Didn't you hear what he just called me? Come on mom, is this your place or not, you've got to do something."

Her Mother looked up with flat unemotional eyes, "Ignore his noise, you have got to stop being so thin skinned. It is just noise. That boy likes to hear himself talk and thinks it makes him sound big. Ignore him."

"Mother, you can not ignore that, not in your own house, something's wrong, something's wrong here."

"Quit talking about me," Benjy's voice broke in through the door, "I could hear your fat mouth through the walls."

Brianna smoldered; her eyes flared. "Mother!"

The older woman raised herself and went down the hall to the kitchen. The eighteen-year-old was raiding the refrigerator and slamming cabinet doors. The older woman worked her way close to the young man and spoke quietly.

"I'm being nice," he said with a raised voice, "she just don't like me telling her the truth, and that's just too bad. You know. She wants to talk, she's gonna hear it too."

"Well then just leave her alone, you have said your piece and I think we can leave it at that. Can we not?"

"If she will?"

Brianna stepped into the kitchen picking up her sweater and purse. "Nobody talks to me like that, Mother, nobody, least of all family." She took three great strides toward the front door.

"Good, get the hell out."

Brianna lost it for a moment and returned to the kitchen with a warrior's fury, "Benjy, you are the most messed up, screwed up . . . and you don't know how lucky you are right now." She was too close to so much anger.

He mocked with a pointed finger and rolled his upper lip in a false sneer.

He grumbled more obscenities under his breath, ending each clause with a caustic smirk.

"I know what you just said," and she slammed the purse into the table and took one step toward him.

"No Brianna. Ignore him, it is just talk."

She hesitated as her Mother grasped her left arm and stopped her path, "Who taught you to be such an ass, who taught you to be so stupid?" She was boiling, "Where do you get off?"

"Brianna," her Mother said up to her, "stop it, stop it."

Benjy's sneer turned to a laugh.

"You are so damn stupid," she railed as she picked up her things and returned to the door. "I'm not staying in this house until he apologizes."

Her Mother turned to her step son, "Why did you have to say stuff like that to her? Causin' this noise, all for nothin'? This would have all blown over if you had just stayed quiet."

"Bull. What's she gonna do? Get back on her train and go cryin' to her boy friend."

"Mother!" Brianna called from the hall.

Her Mother trudged to the door.

"I'll be at Barbara's if you need anything."

Her Mother put her hands on her hips and looked at her daughter with unrelenting eyes. "No you are not, you are going up to see this Joe you have been seeing."

Brianna was silent.

"Are you?"

"Maybe, tomorrow, why?"

"Brianna!"

"I told you, we get along, he's been good to me."

"Brianna, you are playing with fire spending this much time with this Joe what's-his-name. Fire, you are playing with fire."

"Mother," she said as she heard her step brother continuing to rant and rave from the kitchen, "at least I can talk with him and he talks with me and . . ."

"Oh yes, I am sure, I know what else. You be careful girl." and with that she closed door and left her alone in the unlit hall.

VII

Sherrie and Barbara's squealing voices brought her out of the reverie. They came running out of the main building, away form the racing surface, all smiling and laughing.

"Hey, where you been?" Sherrie asked with larcenous eyes.

"What have you been up to?" she answered sarcastically.

"Oh, nothing too much!" Barbara offered.

Sherrie couldn't hold it in; she looked like a tick about to pop. "Oh, did you see that little jockey guy? Oh, he's so cute, makes you just want to eat him up."

"Boots and all!" Barbara laughed.

"What's his name Saint Andre something? Oh, Brianna, he saw us and he was flirting with us and oh sister, I'll bet . . ."

"Yeah," Brianna offered, "I'll bet your crazy."

"Naw, no way, he liked us. I think maybe he liked Barbara a little more than me," she was laughing more than talking now, "but give me an hour alone with that boy and I'll get him to change his tune."

"Hey little one," Barbara laughed pushing her figure around, "the man knows a good thing when he sees them." They laughed again.

"And what, Brianna, might I ask, have you been doing all this time?" asked Barbara suddenly changing gears. "Who have you been talking to?"

"Nothing, just taking it all in."

"Please! C'mon Brianna, where do the jockeys hang out?" Sherrie demanded.

Brianna looked over her sunglasses again, "The jockey's room used to be on the other side of that building there, on the other side. If you go past the hat store, and that Barbecue thing, look to your left, you'll see it."

And with that, the two were off in a dash to the jockey's room. When they turned the corner Barbara looked over her shoulder as if to suggest Brianna should come with them. Her eyes were worried; Brianna had never learned how to hide behind a brave facade, at least not with her friend. She shook her friend off with a smile and stood quietly for a moment. She was oddly alone, suddenly deserted beneath the ancient canopy.

+++++++

The two sat in silence under the patio umbrella that looked out toward Saratoga Lake and watched a baseball game on Joe's little black and white television. He got up at the end of the fifth inning when the Orioles loaded the bases. "Popcorn?"

"I thought we were going downtown to D'Andrea's or something?" Brianna whispered as she gazed down at her lap.

"Sure if you want, after the game. You want to go now?"

"I just don't want to sit around too much. Maybe there's something going on at Cafe Lena?"

"Cafe Lena, are you kidding me, you?"

"Why not, sure, we could see what's doing?"

"Brianna, the only thing we can agree on, with music that is, is Ray Charles. Everything else is off limits, and now you want to hear some off key folk music all of a sudden?"

She rolled her eyes and settled back into the soft sofa.

"Come on, what gives, what's so bad about the two of us spending tonight with each other?"

Brianna looked down again, her enormous brown eyes sealed shut. It was a look Joe had only seen when important matters were at hand.

"I don't know Joe," she looked at him the only way she knew how, "I don't know . . . I've been thinking, thinking a lot and, well, if we're not going out I guess tonight is as good as any to have a talk. Truthfully, I think I should be going back to the city in the morning."

There was weight in her words, a ponderous ominous weight. He had never seen her cry, but her eyes were filling and struggling for expression. Her difficulties made him aware of how desperate this conversation was going to be.

She shook her head up and down at him and said, "I think that would be best."

"Like that, all of a sudden? Tell me you're kidding Brianna, is this a joke?"

"Joe," she said after a long pause, "I've been thinking Joe, and I can't help but be a little scared." She couldn't look up at him. "And, well, I think we've let this go about as far as we should. Maybe too far? I'm afraid if we go on it's going to get bad, or worse. I don't know, but I've been thinking."

The night went, back and forth, memories, pleasures, adventures and long drives through New England, short drives in the city, and then a wave of fears and questions and doubts and frustrations. There was an ugly reality sitting in her mind she wanted him to know about, one he seemed unaware of. A reality awaited them, but the more they spoke, the more her friend seemed determined to hold on to a very different truth he had built around her. They spoke again and again. Brianna, the cynical realist, Joe the transcendent dreamer. The words wore each other out.

Joe paced back and forth across the room. Brianna sat motionless in the sofa watching him twist in a disbelief. His face and voice wounded her.

"This can't be real, this can't be real. Where did this come from, why didn't you give me a clue, just a clue this was coming last week? Damn, we spent three whole days together and there was none of this."

"Don't Joe."

"Don't Joe! What do I do with that?"

"I'm sorry Joe, I was thinking."

"You've got to be kidding. Why?"

"Joe, we'll still talk and call and be there for each other, I don't mean I want you to fall off the face of the earth or go away, I just think we've gone too far maybe?"

"That, let's be friends crap, never works, not for us it won't."

Brianna looked away.

"Brianna you're way off base here, no way you were thinking about this last week. No way you were thinking all this nonsense last week. It was the best time I've ever had, we spent half the weekend alone, just us, and we talked about everything, everything . . . no way."

Joe's raised voice was muffled when she turned away and the first tear escaped. Sunset blued the lake out of the corner of her eye. She felt like she was in a fishbowl. She got up, pulled down the blinds and stood before Joe without looking.

"Don't make me say any more."

"Damn it, you better say something."

She drew in her breath for strength. "It's just that, Joe, being with you has changed me in a lot. I've done things I never thought, but I also know how very much I want some things, you know, a family, a home on the island, children, my own children, my own place, you know."

Joe sat in a state of befuddled innocence and unknowing. He sat and listened with his mouth open in silence. "So?"

"Do you see what I'm trying to say?"

"You've lost me again."

"I need you to understand." Her tears were flowing now, but she was determined to finish what she had to say. "I know I'll be a good Mother, I know I can raise a family and I know, I really know my children will have a fighting chance."

"You'll be a great Mom, I know. We've talked about this."

"And you know . . ."

"And you know I want to be a Father, but I'm getting older and I was getting worried, you know before you, I'd ever . . ."

But as he spoke Brianna sat at the desk, twirled a pencil for a moment and then dropped her head into her hands. She sobbed. "I know Joe, you will be a great Dad," Her hands and arms were shaking, "and I know you need a son."

Silence took the room and brought it through the seasons in an instant. Brianna couldn't stop sobbing now, sitting alone at the desk, sobbing into her hands, refusing to look up. Joe laid his head on the back of the sofa and exhaled into the ceiling. He rehearsed sentences that would win the day, words that might break through her citadel of silence and resolution, but none would form in his throat. The clock moved on.

"An hour ago I had it, I had the best friend I've ever had at my back and a future, I thought, and now, Christ I don't know anything."

"You're just not facing it."

"What? What kind of crazy crap is that woman, where did that come from?"

She turned to face his eyes. "Can't you see Joe; can't you guess what I'm seeing, down the road for us?"

"Tell me."

"There'd be kids, mine, my children and I want them to have a chance, a real chance at something great in their life. Around our house they would be ours, around our house, Joe, but not where they live, not when they left our house, not at school, not on the job. They'd grow up with us, but they'd have to live, out there."

"Brianna, where did you get all this crap, you've got to be kidding me."

She paused, "Joe I want my children to have everything, I want them to be everything they want to be, but I don't want anybody, anybody, whispering behind their back. Can't you see what I'm worried about, what I can see the kids will go through?"

After a moment of stunned silence all Joe could offer was "Who put these ideas in your head? Tell me who? I want to know."

"Joe, people talk, life hits you in the face, it's right there. Come on Joe, there's no changing the way people live, and the way life is."

"I don't believe you; I'm not going to believe you until you start making some sense."

"We can't do this to children, and if things go any further, between us . . ."

They pled their cases to no avail, and before midnight she left the lake in silence.

VIII

Brianna hurried toward the clubhouse. The Traver's Porch was buzzing with patrons looking for table space and a waiter. She listened for that voice, but a Dixieland band drowned out everything around them. She looked over the hedge and along the rail, but no uniforms, no Joe.

And as she walked inside the final fears found her in a library of 'what if's'. She couldn't help but wonder if, after all these years, and all this gray hair and, the extra pounds she carried, if he would even recognize her. What if he didn't know who she was? Worse, what if he didn't remember her? Sometimes thoughts have a life of their own. What about all the adventures he must have had with other women? What if she was just an addendum in his biography?

She moved beneath a massive television screen she couldn't remember from her working days and then remembered The Jim Dandy Bar. Everybody meets in The Jim Dandy Bar, but when she got inside with the crush of customers, the only face she recognized was Barbara's friend Toni, smiling and laughing and toasting three older gentlemen with a mixed drink and a kiss. Brianna shook her head in her direction and smiled. How did that girl manage to meet so many men wherever she went?

"Oh, Brianna, come here girl and meet my new friends. This is Robert and Christopher and this is, is I'm sorry but . . ."

"Dan," a man in a three-piece suit offered.

"Have a drink Brianna, really, Mr. Tarver here won nine thousand dollars yesterday, and he needs a little help celebrating," Toni's eyes were alive with fantasy and extravagance.

"Sorry Toni, gentlemen, but I've got to meet you know, other friends, they're over at the jockey's room and . . ." Brianna knew she was stumbling over her words.

"Good, go get them, the more the merrier you know, go get the girls and we'll make a regular party out of this."

And with that weak excuse, Brianna escaped the Jim Dandy Bar and stood beneath the old scratchboard not knowing which way to go. Softly she allowed the worst of her fears to surface. What if Joe did recognize her but didn't want to speak to her, was angry with her for what had happened all those years ago or worse, was ashamed of her and didn't want his new friends to know he knew her, to know she was a part of his past. More memories. This was why she knew she shouldn't have come on this trip. All she could think to do, at least for this one moment, was to escape to their car and wait for her friends to reappear.

Her heart walked toward the clubhouse exchange just as a new river of patrons poured through the turnstiles. They made her hesitate while some of the partiers waited to get their hands stamped for readmission. She stood aside when, just behind her ears, a voice broke through her thoughts,; she bolted upright, startled through her fears.

"Brianna? It is Brianna isn't it? Remember me?"

There are gestures that direct our lives and speak for us, gestures that clarify moments and speak to our tomorrows. Some are generally understood, while others are known only to the few. Those like traffic officers, doctors or school teachers speak with their hands and eyes that are universal. Others, like the youngest among us can communicate in ways known only to their peers. But lovers have a private language that grows out of moonscapes, midday coffee, and the warp and woof intimacy. They speak with a silent music composed by tiny rhythms born in the shadows of midnight.

And so it was on that day, near the Nelson Avenue turnstile and the 'May I Help You' customer service stand. The man reached out to sweep eyebrows standing guard above large brown eyes, while the woman raised her hand, not to take his, but to grasp a bicep and make him smile with her nails. The hesitation lasted only a second; a second required for reassurance and acceptance, a second to understand and risk the embrace that placed her warm face in the bottom of his neck and a hand upon his shoulder.

Near the Nelson Avenue turnstile, not far from the clubhouse betting windows, and directly before the information booth, hundreds passed by, desperate with gestures of their own, and they missed the eyes, never saw the tears, never heard the whispers, never noticed the stillness. No one saw, but two reknew.

"Maybe I will see you next week," she said as she jumped out of my car and got her case before I cold put it in park.

"I'd like that."

"If everything goes all right back in New York, I'll be back Friday morning," she said as she looked in through the passenger window.

"I'll be in the breezeway lady, right by the escalator. Find me if you can."

"We'll do that."

I watched her virtually jump into the terminal and disappear. I was impressed, but as I wound my way toward the interstate I kept hearing her words. She had said 'we', that woman had said 'we'. Son of a gun, Brianna, you are full of surprises. I realized her story was more than romantic, it was a romance. And if she could enjoy such an advantageous and benefic turn of fate, well, maybe a phone call might still be coming my way. You have to positive in this life, pessimism is self fulfilling fate, Eddie told me so.

He Stoops To Conquer

It must seem to most civilized citizens that the precise date of national holidays and celebrations might be beyond my domain of expertise, and on any given Monday the odds would be well in your favor if you choose to bet against me in some modified quiz game or Jeopardy audition. Moments such as Flag Day escape me, as does St. Patrick's Day and Valentine's Day is a mystery beyond comprehension. I usually have to consult my driver's license to get my own birthday date correct, really, and my sister's birth dates are lost in the cyber ditch of my cerebrum. But before you throw in the towel on me I must say, in my own defense, that on some subjects, namely Easter, Mother's Day, and Father's Day, you would be wise to back me to the limits of your wallet as you would be very much a winner. There were days in my extreme youth when I would sit in an old wicker rocking chair on my grandmother's stoop, watching the comings and goings of the world around us while she snapped beans, and she would complain about my grandfather, who was wise in many things such as poker, handicapping, and bathtub gin, but who knew little of the things she thought truly important, such as birthdays, anniversaries, and holidays. And it was at these times that she would share little mnemonic devices so that I would never appear as uneducated and thoughtless as Grandpa Pete.

Easter was a snap if you remember a simple code, '321FMS'. You see Easter is always the first Sunday after the first full moon after the vernal equinox, which is always the 21st of March, or 3/21, as it is written on most government tax forms. And according my Gram's code the 'S' naturally stands for Sunday which comes after the 'FM', which to her was shorthand for 'full moon', which is right after 3/21. Easter is the first Sunday after the first full moon after the equinox. Easy! Why that contrivance sticks with me I do not know, but it does.

There was also a Grandma code for Mother's Day and Father's Day. 2SM3SJ. She always admonished me to keep this in mind so that my Mom and Dad would never be forgotten, no matter how much foolishness my Grandpa Pete got me into. Mother's Day was easy because Mothers are very special people because without them none of us would be here to make the world right and save the planet from each other. Mothers, she would always said, never let the field get away except possibly when it comes to her children which any good Mother would give her eye teeth for as children are always winners with Mom's. In a right world Mothers only settle for place with their children, so it followed that Mothers should be given the second Sunday in May to reminded them how special they are. 2SM, see what I mean.

All of which meant that Dads were going to show, if this was a horse race, as they are the next most important person in the world and since they were due a day and month to themselves they should get the third Sunday of their month, or June. 2SM3SJ. Always thinking was my Gram.

However this little adventure isn't about Grandmothers or miscreant Grandfathers, but rather it concerns a very good friend of mine, a gentleman the local punters know as Vegas, a person much respected about town for an abundance of intellectual resources and an equal measure of style. His given baptismal name was David Anthony Napolitano Andriani, but he had been branded with this celebrated dub many years prior when he had summoned the courage to leave the safe confines of small town America and reemerge in Las Vegas, there to make his fortune as a professional gambler. And while this grandiose contrivance may have ended badly, merely a 'somnium interruptus', its singular audacity had long since earned him the quiet respect and admiration of those privileged with his acquaintance.

One particularly sunny afternoon I happened to park my car, quite by accident, next to Dave's in the Hawthorne Spring parking lot on Phila Street. We both laughed and while catching up on old times and new campaigns, we began sharing biographic vignettes.

"But what brings you here?" I finally asked.

"Forgot to get my Dad a present for Father's Day."

I was amused. "Will he care?"

"Course he'll care," he said through his giant laugh, "why wouldn't he?"

"Dave, Father's Day was two months ago."

Immediately we were embroiled in a full fledged debate. It was like old times.

"Truly, it was the third Sunday in June."

"Naw, August, come on Stranger, don't tell me I missed it."

"Vegas, this is too easy a bet. I will feel bad taking your money."

"You, you feel bad about taking money? Christ, did the sun come up in the north?'

"Tell you what," I said attempting to settle things in the most civilized manner I could muster, "let's go into Baileys over there. I know the manager, Stefanie, she's got all that stuff written down in a little organizer thing. She will know, she is an encyclopedia of useless information."

"Eh, eh . . . who 'da hell is this Stephanie, your twin? This some stooge you keep in clothes just to back up your stupid bets."

Even I had to laugh at that. "You'll see. Come on, her joint is right over here."

And right on cue, Stephanie emerged form the kitchen of her little eatery, lithe and fashionably svelte as always. Within moments of hearing about our harebrained wager her appointment ledger was retrieved and the master calendar put before us. There, in the middle of June was the notation 'Father's Day' affixed at the bottom of the month's third Sunday. Stephanie grinned, I gloated (just a tad) and Vegas admitted defeat with a counterfeit smile. I was a winner and we proceeded to use my winnings to continue the flow of ale across the bar. Yes, that was how I won my first bet that day, but it was hardly the best part of the day.

When Cyd, our bartender came back, she asked me if I knew anyone who might have clubhouse seats for the upcoming

Saturday. This was happy news to me as I am well acquainted with a Mr. Too Tall Teddy, a unique character who makes extra cash by wheeling and redealing his grandstand seats to folks with fallen arches or sore backs. I was quick to share his phone number and forewarned her of the prices she might encounter. She thanked me over and over again, as apparently a new man had entered her life and, if his parents were in town for the weekend, she wanted to show them a good time. I had done a good turn. Good for me. But then Vegas chimed in and set the wheels of a most engaging chronicle in motion.

"Damn, wish I'd known about your seat connections last week."

"Really?"

"My poor brother could've used'em."

"I remember your brother, real good football player."

"Almost got himself into a hell'uva fix over there."

"Really? He OK?"

"Oh yeah," he said with his muffled laugh, "he ended up all right, but what a mess."

"Your brother Chris? You gotta be kidding me."

Dave's brother worked in a local plastics factory with his wife and daughter. They had settled in a small village up north in a quaint little cottage on a little back street near the school. They lived with two cats, a dog, a goldfish and their, of course, their daughter Phyllis. And, as so often happens with little girls, she had become the apple of her father's eye, and more than somewhat. To say she was spoiled might be stretching the truth a little, but anything Phyllis asked for she usually got, and she always asked Dad first.

According to Uncle Dave, little Phyllis had started ballet lessons after a class trip to The National Museum of Dance which is parked on the south end of Saratoga's Broadway. Like so many of her class mates, she was dazzled by the colors and the music and the costumes. Her eight year old eyes could barely take it all in. Late in their visit, just as Mrs. Fitzpatrick was gathering her brood to reenter their school bus, one magnificent ballerina, tall and spectacular in full dance attire . . . hair, mascara, tutu, tights, ballet shoes . . . approached little Phyllis and looked her straight in the eye. She bent down slightly and in a quiet womanly voice whispered to the little girl she knew Phyllis would be a great ballet dancer some day. She could just tell.

That did it, Chris's daughter was hooked. That very evening, her imaginary playmate, Sandy, 'dis'-appeared, and demands for ballet lessons 'a'-ppeared. Her parents smiled, knowingly, and the lessons started the very next week in Glens Falls. According to Uncle Dave the little imp really liked the ballet, she'd been 'cabriole-ing' around the house all year.

Now dedication usually comes at a price of course, and according to the Uncle, the little whirling dervish had worn out two pairs of ballet shoes by the Fourth of July and new ones were needed. However it had been a difficult season for the Andriani's as the refrigerator had gone on the blink some weeks back, their Mercury station wagon had chewed up its transmission on a trip to visit the in-laws in Atlantic Highlands, New Jersey, and then the hot water heater refused to heat. With all the regular bills and their anniversary coming up in September, Chris had found himself doing more than the usual amount of creative bookkeeping.

It was then that Dr. Fate stepped in. While at work, Chris and his partner, Roger Proter, were about to mount a new print roll in a machine when Roger noticed a sizeable flaw in the surface.

"Good grief Charlie Brown," Roger said, "look at dis thing . . . who 'da heck ok'ed this for production." Chris looked. "Here right here," Roger repeated," next to 'da flower petals in this engraving, look at 'da size of 'dat scratch." He was laughing now. "Somebody's gonna get their butt kicked over 'dis."

"Get Jarvis down here," some one said.

The flaw brought Cyril Jarvis, production supervisor, to the floor and after reviewing the blemish, ordered the machine to be refitted for a new pattern. There would be lost time, and it would cost the company some money, but they couldn't use the bad roll.

"Nice job fellas," he said to the group as they waited for the new roll to appear, "nice job. Who spotted the chip?"

"Roger did," Chris offered.

"Good job."

Roger broke into an enormous toothy grin. "Really," he laughed, "how 'bout a raise?"

Jarvis smiled. "Well I don't know about that," and then he paused, "but come on over here."

Roger nodded for Chris to follow and just that fast the three men were by themselves outside on a walkway that over looked the Hudson River. The sun glared and made the men squint.

Jarvis held his forefinger to his lips and drew the men near, "Not sure about a raise fellas, but I might have something for you." He waited for the men to acknowledge the secrecy of his offer. Chris and Roger shook their heads appropriately.

"Alls quiet wid me," Roger whispered.

"Ever go to the races?"

"Once in awhile," they both said.

"Well I own a couple of nice fillies with Doc Rosenberg. Kabish! And this Saturday should be very good for us . . . very good. Get my drift?"

Roger was smiling like an Ipana toothpaste commercial.

"Shade Tree . . . third race. Look at her twice before you throw her out. She will be, I repeat, she will be on the board. Promise."

"Odds?" Roger asked.

Jarvis rolled his eyes and looked around to be sure no one was eavesdropping, "Long."

"Long?" Roger repeated.

"Very long. Now keep it under your hat fellas, don't ruin the board for us. She's been out seven times with no luck, but we cleared an abscess in her throat some weeks ago and our trainer says she is going to run big . . . real big." The three men spoke and thanked each other and eventually Jarvis returned to his office.

"Did you hear that Chris, did you hear that? We are on the inside rail this time."

"Think he's on the up and up?"

"You cracked or something? Why would he give us a bum steer? Why? Course he's shooting straight, he thinks he's gonna get his picture taken in the winner's circle just as sure as night follows day. Getting' your picture taken is big to guys like him, and if Doc Rosenberg's in on it you know it's legit."

"And if the odds are long, that means it might pay pretty good?"

"Good? Long to a guy like Jarvis means ten or twenty to one. At those odds ten bucks turns into hundreds pretty quick."

"And fifty bucks?"

Roger's eyes flared and he rubbed his enormous midsection in warm circular motion as if he had just devoured a gourmet dinner. "A touw-sin maybe. 'Dats a one wid tree zeros, hear me? We could be in 'da pink?"

When Chris returned to his work station he was awash in visions, teetering on a vortex . . . water heaters, anniversary presents, and ballet shoes . . . Lord yes, ballet point shoes.

And that was how this little adventure got started, at least according to Dave, just two working buddies trying to have a little fun chasing a hot tip while hoping to pay some bills and possibly buy some ballet slippers.

They got to Saratoga a little before noon, found some free parking on George Street and walked a mile or so to the grandstand. Chris's eyes were swimming, he never dreamed the place was so big and filled with so many people.

"Saturday's usually like this. Travers day even worse."

The two conspirators shard the price of a program and quickly located their objective, Shade Tree. She was entered in the third, just like Jarvis said, and she was listed as thirty to one. Roger howled. All the other entrants, Society Max, Regret, Big Louie, Little Miss Marker, were five to one or less. Shade Tree was the longest shot in the race, by far. He played with the numbers over and over again. His fifty dollars wager could be worth fifteen hundred dollars. Christopher's mind boggled, it was hard to consider all that money, all the problems it would solve. He shook quietly and tried to remain calm, but his mouth went dry.

They considered a quick beer, but balked at its five dollar price tag. The lady at the snack counter told them to try the spring water at The Big Red Spring, it was free. So they wandered through the backyard maze of picnic tables and pop-up canopies to get a free drink of water. Its odor shocked them, metallic and alkaline. Roger forced his down, but Christopher couldn't take the smell.

"Wow, what's in this stuff. It's not really sulfur but it sure is strong." He tried more than once, but the scent curled his nose every time.

An old man, cane and all, chugged up to the spring, filled a tumbler using all three spigots of the fountain, and threw it down in one artful torrent. He let out an enormous gush of air, smiled and went back for a second glass. Chris looked at Roger and Roger him. The old man caught their intimidated glances. "Ahhh, good stuff guys, good stuff. Brings 'ya luck. Drink this and never have a bad day, least not here."

Chris gestured to him, "Ok mister, it is all yours. Go for it. If you can enjoy that stuff, you're my hero."

The old timer waddled away leaving the two accountants rechecking the odds and the arithmetic and their would-be profits. Conspiratorial audits were at their zenith when Tom Durkin introduced the field for the third race. They listened and heard him call out the name, Shade Tree; they reviewed the tote board one more time, thirty to one, and they both knew it was time.

Chris felt a pang of reluctance and an instinct to not bet, not risk his hard earned dollars and simply remain content with what he had, but it soon left him. He jumped into the betting line, the one that said $50.00 minimum, and waited his turn to join the brave elite. He almost chickened out a second time as he shuffled toward the window, but the look on his friend's face in the adjacent line kept him focused and unafraid. The only discomfort came from the little colorless man who stood directly behind him; breathing and wheezing too close for comfort. He could smell the Vicks. Chris looked back once or twice, trying to get the little guy to give him an inch of space, but he never took the hint.

A minute later Christopher left the teller's window clutching a $50.00 win ticket on Shade Tree. His mind was spinning, a mild euphoria of disbelief, almost afraid to see what he had done, so he shoved the ticket into his side pocket without looking. He had bet all that money on a horse, on a tip, money he could have used for something, anything else, but for the promise of his boss and the wild mathematics of his friend Roger. He was shaking a little, mostly astonished by his own brazenness, in a rapture that had left him more than a little off balance. This was all new and he didn't know how to handle the moment.

He waited beneath an enormous elm tree until Roger appeared. He showed Chris his ticket with more than a little pride. He had wagered one hundred dollars, fifty to win and another fifty to place on their horse. Chris laughed; he had never seen his rotund friend dance before but Roger had happy feet today.

"Rog, you're crazy, a hundred bucks.?"

"Had to, had to," was all he kept saying. "Damn C-note was burning a hole in my pocket. You know what I always say, go big or stay home."

They looked up at the television monitor. Shade tree was listed at fifty to one. Christopher's mind went racing again. Roger kept running new numbers, wild with excitement. The odds were going up and the longer they looked, the longer they got.

"Sixty to one, Chris 'O pal, damn, sixty to one. We're gonna be rich." His eyes were bulging, veins were popping across his forehead.

Tom Durkin announced it was three minutes to post time when Chris spotted something odd. "Rog, see that guy by the garbage can?"

"The old guy in the plaid shirt? The one picking through the garbage?"

"Yeah, why?"

"What's he doing, picking through garbage cans? He's the one that was standing behind me in the betting line, acting kind of weird, kept pushing up next to me, breathing down the back of my neck."

"Maybe he liked you?"

"Funny."

"Maybe he was hawkin' you, ya know, tryin' to see your program, what youse was playing?"

"Don't know, just didn't like him being so close, he made me . . ."

"Hey buddy," said a tall man with a long mane of reddish hair, "buddy, the teller wants you, over there at the fifty dollar window."

And as he had said, the teller Chris had placed the bet with was standing up and waving.

"He wants you Chris, he's waving at you," was all Roger had to say to get his friend back near the window.

"Buddy, didn't you hear me calling for you, didn't you hear me?" the teller said frantically. "The stooper got your ticket, over there, the guy picking through the garbage, the stooper." Confusion claimed the moment. "Didn't you see him, just a minute ago, the ticket you bought from me, the fifty dollar ticket?" Chris continued his blank stare. "Check your pocket man, check it, it looked like you went to shove it in your pocket, but it fell out and the stooper got it."

Chris slapped at his pants pockets and raced through the contents. Keys, a drug store receipt, five nickels, two quarters, a penny and a Saint Christopher medal, but no fifty dollar ticket. He looked at Roger, "It's gone." His voice was empty with pain.

"Check again, Ya sure it's gone?"

The teller interrupted, "I'm telling you the stooper's got it. I saw it fall. The old guy snatched it soon as it hit the floor."

"What's stooper?" was the best Christopher's mind could come up with at the moment.

"The old guy? He's a stooper. Every big track has these guys, this place has a dozen. They walk around and look through garbage cans and pick tickets up off the floor looking for a good one somebody has thrown away by mistake. They cash them in for some quick dough. They are lower than mud turtles; I can't stand those guys."

'You're kidding?'

"No way," the teller was almost yelling now, "go get him before he gets your ticket canceled. He'll get you money."

"He can do that?"

"If he works it right?"

"Damn," was all Chris could say.

"Hurry up and get that guy."

Chris and Roger turned as one, but the colorless man was gone. They dashed around the corner to the canopied porch, the Turf Terrace Restaurant, The Carousel Restaurant and then back again to the upper club betting bays. No gray haired stooper in a faded plaid shirt. They circled the clubhouse again. It was only when they returned to the front of the clubhouse for the second time that they found their mark. There he was, clam and smiling, not twenty feet in front of them, tucking crisp new bills into his wallet.

Roger almost leaped at him, "Hey, you, that's my buddy's money."

The stooper's face was sickly and growing paler with tiny translucent eyes. His lipless mouth was quivering.

"Come on, that's my friend's fifty bucks."

"Get away from me," he said in a heavily calloused voice.

"Get back here," Chris hollered as the man tried to mingle away into the crowd.

The three combatants ricocheted up and down the second floor clubhouse. They exchanged a stream of barbs, insults, and epithets that entertained everyone they passed by. The clubhouse was cheering for the third race just as two Pinkerton's intervened near Manny's service bar. The horses were charging to the finish line, in deep stretch, three thoroughbreds noses apart, feet from the finish line, but the people in the breezeway were following the argument that rocked back and forth.

"Look pal, all I'm telling you is that I can't take fifty dollars out of a guy's pocket just because you said to. I just can't, understand. I'm only a security guard and I just can't do it. I can tell you think you're right, but I can't take money from people."

The burly guard in the white uniform was growing impatient and losing his diplomatic demeanor when he tried, for the third time, to explain his point of view.

"But this bum . . ."

"Look son," the lady guard offered, "this is a big place, lots of money flying around here, millions some days, all my boss is saying is we can't tell who is lying and who's telling the truth. We don't know. Her deep brown eyes were pleading with him to be reasonable and not make a 'scene'.

"And if you don't drop this, calm down right now," the other guard said in a not-as-friendly voice, "We could throw you out of here. Understand, off the grounds."

"Us, throw us out?" Chris pleaded, "He's the thief, we didn't do anything; he's the one who got my ticket."

Nothing helped. The unpleasantries only got worse as each side abandoned civility. New volleys of anger devolved into swearing and after a minute the guard's patience ran out. The next thing Chris and Roger knew, they were on their way toward Union Avenue. The lady guard escorted them to the gate.

"I'm sorry, but I know how my boss is. He doesn't want any trouble, and he isn't sure. Look, he didn't take your picture or I'D' did he? No? Ok, so you're not banned or anything, you can come back, just be more carful with your money and stay away from that guy."

The men thanked her for being civil. They apologized as best they could and began the long trek back to their car. Things got worse for Christopher. As they walked along the steel fence of the picnic area they could hear the track announcer announcing the results of the third race. There had been a photo and a steward's inquiry, but the results were in . . . Shade Tree by a desperate lip. Someone behind them muttered, "Forty to one, gonna pay telephone numbers; why didn't I play that horse, why didn't I?"

Roger looked at Christopher as if to apologize. "Not your fault," he said to his sheepish friend, "not your fault. How you going to cash that ticket?"

"They give you six months to cash a good ticket. Aubrey's down here most every Sunday, he'll cash it. You'll get half?"

"It's not your fault Rog, thanks anyway, but it's not your fault."

That night Christopher tried to listen to a comedian's monologue from his tortured posture on the worn divan. The television was on, but Chris heard nothing. His wife had given up her hold on the day an hour before. On other evenings that might have inspired him to take an early shower, but tonight he was fighting with shadows, dark gray memories of the lost ticket, the colorless little stooper, and ballet shoes.

After Sunday mass, Chris and his family made their way into The Yorkland Restaurant to share a hot fudge sundae. The children played, the women talked, and the men hitched up tortured belts while everyone shared the latest news. There was one exception to the social gathering, one disgruntled soul who sat silently. His wife looked at him now and then. She worried, not understanding the distance in his eyes, but returned to her friends as a matter of faith. There was depth in his eyes and she knew from experience that look had consequences. Christopher's mind was in a trundle, tumbling through a catalogue of aphorisms about kindness and forgiveness his Father had taught him in the middle of plumbing projects and camping trips. He had learned them well, but there was one axiomatic principle, one ominous truth that grew out of a spinal intelligence that never needed to be taught. It went like this: 'If you value your future, never, but never, come between a Dad and his daughter'.

The following Friday, Christopher and Roger were once again surrounded by print rolls and frustrated bosses, "You're going to the races again?"

Yup," Chris said, as he waved a lift truck into position.

"Get out. Didn't we learn our lesson last week? I told ya I'd give you half of what I won."

"No, no, you won it fair and square. That's yours, that's not why I'm going back anyway."

"Come on, it's just fun money. Found money in a way."

"Not the point. I won my bet too; I just got robbed, and my little girl got robbed."

"Don't go making yourself crazy over 'dis, it's only money."

"Nope this isn't bout money. I'm going back, I'm going to get even. I'm not sure how, but this is going to be made right . . . You'll see, you'll see!"

Saturday afternoon, Christopher used the admission pass he'd found at a Stewart's convenience store to get into the track. He found a discarded newspaper in a trash can and spent some time looking through the entries. This was Sword Dancer Saturday, a big day on Saratoga's racing calendar, and although the weather was warm and more than a little humid, the racing officials were expecting a good crowd. Chris saw a rotund man reading a pink newspaper with Sword Dancer Day in its headline banner. "Not really, not really," he said out loud, "Here I come you God-awful little sewer rat, this is Get-Even Day."

Once inside he toured the grandstand, several times, taking a different route each time. His quarry was not to be seen so he coughed up the extra five bucks and paid his way into the clubhouse. He couldn't remember his senses burning like they were, at least not since his days on the firing range in the Marine Corps. Today he would miss nothing.

Two coffees later, just prior to the fourth race, Christopher, the Dad, spied a grimy little man in a faded grey shirt picking through a garbage can near the clubhouse elevator. The Dad's eyes dilated and he looked again to be sure. He smiled within. The game was afoot.

He unfurled his newspaper and hid his face within it. He watched the little man with a silent concentration known only to snipers and big game hunters. It is a singularity of purpose that dissolves the rest of the world into oblivion and everything else slips away behind thick veils. From now on there was to be nothing in his field of vision except the disheveled man in the sad shirt. "You're mine," he whispered.

The stooper moved from trash can to trash can, with the Dad following at a safe distance. He rifled through every can, bending over occasionally to pick tickets from the floor. The two circulated time and again until an apparently valuable ticket was found lying next to the napkin dispenser at Cass's bar. The stooper seemed pleased; he snapped his fingers and smiled a little as he read and reread the results board. The Dad felt his mind flame with but one thought, 'not today' he kept thinking, 'no you don't, not today'. He followed the stooper across the clubhouse and into a betting line. He stood right behind him, his face still sheltered by his newspaper; he stood so close he could smell mothballs and stale beer rising from the tattered shirt.

They paced in place, rocking back and forth as the line shortened toward the teller. The stooper was holding a twenty dollar win ticket on the upcoming race. He was going to cancel it and take the twenty, no matter what it might be worth if the horse won. Instantly the Dad's resolve took shape and was forged into action.

Finally at the window the stooper held up the ticket, as if on the precipice of an eloquent gesture; Chris struck. He had reached behind, into his back pocket and found his wallet. He looked about to be sure no one was paying close attention, shuffled his feet a little to be at exactly the right angle, and then charged straight into the stooper. All hell broke loose in the clubhouse.

Christopher slammed against the man before him. There was a fleshy crack as the man's ribs struck the teller's window ledge, and a gush of air went out of his lungs. One of Christopher's arms went around the stooper's waist and just as quickly he fell backwards pulling the little man down on top of him. They wrestled and rolled across the floor, hollering as they went. Patrons screamed and tried to jump out of the way, two young girls tripped and somersaulted backwards. Beers went flying into the popcorn stand and tellers stopped everything to witness the pandemonium.

Christopher cried, "Help!"

The stooper bellowed.

Chris called for help as loudly as he could.

The crowd backed away, giving the two grapplers room to roll about. Feet and arms thrashed until Christopher spotted a security guard coming their way and he released his hold.

"What the hell is wrong with . . ." the little gray man sputtered from the floor. He raised a fist over sunken eyes and tried to get to his feet. "What are you up to?" He was regaining his breath and an ounce of recognition was beginning to form; the face of his attacker was emerging into the light.

Christopher yelled again as two security guards arrived. One guard pulled the pale faced man away but Christopher pursued him, only to be stopped by the other guard.

"Cut this out here, what gives, what's going on?"

"Key-Rist, there's no nonsense in the clubhouse, stop this."

Christopher saw his chance and round three began. "This guy robbed me, he robbed me," he said as he flailed away with a pointed finger.

The stooper was stupefied; he rolled his eyes back and forth and examined the ticket he was still holding in his hand.

"What do you mean he robbed you?" the first officer said.

"He did, he robbed me!"

"Of what?" the other guard said maintaining a firm grip on Christopher's arm.

This guy, this scummy rat picked my pocket, he's got my wallet, just as I was about to pick up that ticket I dropped, he did it, he did it, he pretended to bump into me and he picked my wallet."

The stooper looked at the ticket again, more confused than ever.

"You sure mister, you're talking serious stuff here. If you're bluffing or something you could be in big trouble."

"What about it mister," the other Pinkerton said, "Why does he think you stole his wallet?"

"Me?" said the main in the sad plaid shirt, "he's nuts or something."

"Don't believe him," was Christopher's best reply, "check him, check his pockets, he's got my wallet!"

Too many bystanders were gathering. The guards moved the two men away from the betting windows toward the relative privacy of a sheltered staircase. They radioed for assistance, more guards would be coming and that might mean the ones from last week. Christopher knew he had to act fast.

"I mean check him right now, you'll find out."

"Buddy we are security, the police usually do the frisking if there's real trouble."

"Huh, like robbery ain't real trouble?" Christopher blurted out.

"How about it bud, we can settle this if you'll agree to empty your pockets?" one guard said.

Far out in the paddock, Chris saw a guard from last week's jumble hurrying across the yard toward the stairs. She was holding her hat in place, running as best she could through the crowd. It was time to win the day. "Here, I will, here's my stuff," Chris said as he emptied his pockets and held the contents up to be reviewed. "See, keys, change, gum and no wallet. This thief has it."

"What about it bud, mind if we look?"

"Damn no," he said as he reached into his side pockets and left hip pocket. All he pulled out was cash, car keys and an old cloth wallet, badly worn. "The wallet's mine," he said.

"Your wallet?" the guard asked Christopher and Chris shook his head no. The third guard lighted on the top step of the staircase. She saw Christopher and immediately recognized him. Her shoulders sagged a little, but her tiny smile told Christopher he might be safe with her, at least for the moment.

The little man almost jumped out of his shoes when he saw the guard, "That's her, that's her, this broad's the one who saw the trouble this jackass caused me last week, ask her."

But the guard held up diplomatic hands as if to say she wasn't part of last week's drama. Chris saw the opening.

"Check his other pockets; he didn't check the right one did he?"

The guards looked at the man and gestured for him to look again. His left arm and then his right arm swept behind him and suddenly his sinister look of triumph disappeared. The officer followed his arm's path and then looked the stooper straight in the eye, "Come on buddy, let's see what you got."

In awed disbelief the stooper withdrew a second wallet from his hip pocket. He stared at it in disbelief, looked to the Pinkerton's, and then to anyone around him, desperate for an answer. One guard tightened his grip on the old man's smelly shirt while the other took the wallet from his hand. He opened it and looked to Christopher.

"What's your full name? Where do you live? How much money you got in here?"

Chris had the correct answer for each question. "Here," the guard said with some finality, "it's your wallet."

Slowly the stooper began to realize what had happened to him.

"This ain't happening, you aren't goin to get away with this, you son of a . . . I'll kill you, I'll . . ."

"Quiet pal, you aren't going to be killing anybody, you got enough problems. You want us to call the state police?" He turned the old man around and made him face the stairs. "Take him to the office Kurt. We'll have to show him to the Lieutenant and get him processed."

"He is lying, lying, this is bull and this bi . . ."

"Hey," the officer bellowed, spinning him around, nose to nose, "watch your mouth little man, or you will have problems you can't solve."

The stooper fumed in silence as he was led down the stairs toward the security office.

"You want to go with them, you know, to press charges Mister Andriani?" one guard said.

"I don't know . . . what will happen?"

"Probably have to go to court and testify, takes months sometimes for these things to get worked out. After all, you got your wallet back."

"And what will happen to the guy, the thief?"

"Him? Lieutenant will take his name and photocopy his I.D. and then they'll probably throw him off the track."

"For the day?"

"Pick pocket? Probably the whole meet, maybe more, who knows?"

Chris thought just a second. "I'll let you guys handle him then, especially if I won't have to see him again."

The guard gave an approving nod. "Sorry about all the fuss, it's usually a pretty nice crowd here in the summer, especially in the clubhouse. But say, you better let me have your name and phone number, just in case, you know."

"Sure," Chris answered. While he was giving his information to the guard, the other officer bent down and picked up a ticket that the old man had been holding. As the trio was about to part she moved close to him and said in a quiet voice, "This must be yours too."

"Huh," Chris said to her.

"The one horse, it won. Paid nine dollars. You're a winner. You can celebrate."

"I don't know," Christopher said trying to thank her with his eyes. He found a smile, the first real smile he had enjoyed in days, "I've got some shopping to do."

"Shopping?" she asked.

"Yeah, know where I can find some ballet shoes in this town."

When David drove away I fell back into my old car and caught a glimpse of my own smile in the rear view mirror. Good guy, Christopher, great guy, my old friend David. I began to wonder how my own family was doing, and I decided to spend some time up north to check on the sisters and possibly catch up with the nieces and nephews. They would have stories to tell and maybe they might even need a taxi ride somewhere. I'll go Tuesday when the track is dark. Might be fun? Hey, you never know.

No One Smiles Like a Winner

I almost forgot to note one worthy adventure that spanned a goodly portion of the meet. It all started back in late July when the Spa traditionally hosts The Jim Dandy Stakes, a prestigious race for the horses who were on their way toward The Travers stakes and, at the same time, recovering from the Kentucky Derby and Triple Crown. I remember I was perched atop the once resplendent fenders of my once beauteous Buick Invicta, waiting a message from the bell boy of the Adelphi Hotel concerning the possible presence of particularly attractive woman I have known for quite some time, and who, it was rumored, had registered therein the day before. And as I am doing my very utmost to not appear like a fish out of water or in any other way out of my depth, I raised my chin to the warm Easterly breeze swaying up Phila Street, inhaled slowly, and took in the peculiarities of Saratoga's main drag, Broadway. It is a glorious human experiment, as one might expect, on such a fine Saturday morning, especially as it was the morning of the Jim Dandy Stakes to be held out at the old race track on Union Avenue. Crèches and Limos trolled softly between jaywalkers and baby carriages as the swirl of entrepreneurs, and some ne'er-do-wells, navigated the walkways and doorways of this ancient 'Berg's'.

In fact, I thought, I was preparing myself for a lovely afternoon beneath the pines when the very peace of the day was taken from me. Out of Impressions Gift Shop appeared the unmistakable visage of none other than Turtle. Yes, that is very correct, you read it right, or heard it, if someone is reading this to you; this gentleman is called "Turtle", and not The Turtle, or Turtle Man, or, Turtle Soup, or any other appendage one might normally associate with such a sobriquet.

You see, Turtle is a very well known individual around gaming places like Monmouth Park, Keenland, and Santa Anita. He is also quite famous as a man who knows his way to the windows and is never shy about 'sending it in' when he sees advantage. But he is also a rather strange man with an even stranger history. During his youth he spent many days rummaging through the back alleys and neighborhood bars of Taylor, Pennsylvania, after graduating number three in his high school class. The people of his hometown expected the good Turtle to go off into the world and make quite a name for himself as he was so heavily armed with great intelligence and wit. But Turtle did not agree. You see Turtle, while having many great qualities to be sure, also had one unmistakable flaw, one deep dark unforgivable spot on his soul not even his grandmother could over look. He was lazy. And by that I do not mean to imply he was slow to start or slower to rise. Nor do I mean to suggest he was the kind of simple selfish soul who could only muster enough adrenaline to burn away a calorie if there was risk to his own neck or checkbook. No, Turtle had mastered the very heart, soul, and neural fabric of the sedentary lifestyle. Not even Mycroft Holmes, Sherlock's older, smarter brother, could outdo him when it came to the finer points of inertia. Some who polished the walls of the local pool emporiums maintained he was so lazy he could not beat an asthmatic tortoise across the width of a standard size tennis court, if his life depended on it. Lord, Turtle was lazy.

So to see him actually moving his immense bulk, all three hundred pounds of it, across the Broadway's double yellow line was an exceptional occurrence indeed. And as he avoided on-rushing bumpers, I had time, in fact, I had more than enough time, to reflect on our previous meetings and, despite my best efforts, I could not remember one moment in the past fifteen years when I had seen him doing anything else but sitting in his chair in the top row of Section F of Saratoga's aged clubhouse. I had to speak to him.

"Turtle, is this really you I see, dashing around in the middle of the road?"

"Of course it is Stranger, my toothy friend, who else?"

I had to laugh, he was so windswept and breathless, "But?"

"But what," he growled through a very well chewed Dutch Master Palma, "What?"

"Oh nothing, I was just . . . nothing, forget about it. What brings you down town?"

"You my good man," he said with heightened pitch in his voice, "you, and every other plunger I can think of who might be foolish enough to waste this day sitting around some filthy O.T.B. parlor or . . . or . . . Betty Boop-ing in some sleazy Albany bar."

"Truly?"

"As true as a man can be," he said as he tried to relight the soggy stogie he had been chewing.

"How so?" I asked distractedly as I was still looking around for my bellboy.

"Haven't you heard? Today my good man, today," he was drawling with all the bravado of P.T. Barnum himself, "if you contain wisdom, you will appear in the lower clubhouse of the old racetrack, before Patrick's window, you know the one, and there you will see a wager with cosmic implications, cosmic I say . . . a wager like none other . . . like none you have ever seen, nor has any other living human being of any epoch, ever witnessed, ever." His excitement was growing as he spoke. His face was beginning to accept a faint shade of pink. It was the first time I had ever seen his complexion leap beyond French vanilla. Remarkable.

"Ever?"

"Ever. Are you listening? I am telling you today there will be a wager on the eighth race unlike anything ever invented. Yes, the first and only wager of its kind known to civilized, or your uncivilized, breed of barbarians."

"Truly?"

"Truer words were never spoken Stranger old chum."

"And will witnessing this wager cost me any hard earned scratch?"

"Not a shilling, not one dratma, not even a wooden nickel, unless you are more foolish than I suppose. This is an adventure of the highest order, for one like yourself, one who understands the hazards and rewards of this magnificent game we play."

"And this involves a bet?" I shared with a stammer.

"Without question."

"Really?" I mused softly.

"Really!"

"Is this a bet on a horse race or some shell game? Is this about which bird will fly off the fence first kind of stuff?"

"My good man, you disappoint! No, this is a bet on a horse race, pure and simple, today's eight race."

I puzzled but for a minute. "Some new form of the Chesapeake Parlay, like in the 1938 Preakness?"

"Please, your hook lacks a worm."

"Hmmm, the Caliente five-ten pool?"

"Child's play Stranger, Caliente . . . you are in the wading pool."

"A Penultimate, like they play at the Curragh?"

"Sad, very sad."

I was confused, but chose to ignore his condescension and renew my investigation, "A pick ten, full card bet?"

"Hah, come on now, seize the day Stranger, carpe diem, my boy, carpe!"

I thought harder, "A Doctor Z show bet?"

"Pathetic, truly pathetic, you are adrift on a silent sea"

I hated hearing him quote Coleridge, "The Mike Illich secret play"

"Avast!" he said with great emphasis and a terrible Russian accent.

I was beginning to develop a curious nose, "A new bet . . . like nothing ever seen . . . and you say this will be a bet on a horse race?"

"Lord man, this parlor game is wasting my time. Can't you understand any part of what I have been telling you?" he blasted between gasping for volumes of summer air, "can't you get anything through that thick noggin' of yours? Listen and try to fathom my drift . . . would you please! Now stay with me. Indeed, today, the eight race, here at the Grand Old Dam of racing herself, The Spa, a bit of wagering history, a bet . . . a real honest-to-goodness horse racing wager, and it will be one you never thought you would ever see."

"And are there some big potatoes to be had?"

"Don't know?"

That stopped me, "What?"

"That's right, I don't know and no one else knows."

"Come on, no one. How about the betters?"

"Not even they."

"Turtle, I know when my leg is being pulled."

"It might seem that way Stranger, but I assure you I do not jest."

I had to admit Turtle was luring me in. He seemed utterly earnest. A bet that no one had ever witnessed. I was moved.

I pondered a minute. "Got the time?"

"Not today, friend, my Timex is kaput."

I could tell by the sun and the length of the shadows across the parked cars that it must be getting close to noon, and as such, if I was to witness this wagering adventure, we needed to be heading toward Union Avenue shortly.

"Will you give me a minute Turtle?"

"Minutes I have, if you would be good enough to give me a lift to said same racetrack I will share the details. Go to my good man, proceed with you errands, and I will await your return in this fine auto-mo-beal."

Quickly I found myself in the archaic lobby of the Adelphi Hotel, looking for my well tipped co-conspirator and just as quickly discovered that no one answering the description I had given him was to be found wandering around the hotel's grounds. My disappointment was heavy, but temporary, and I quickly returned to Turtle. He was well anchored in the front seat, recumbent and still, a posture I had seen before.

"We are off Turtle."

"To the races I hope."

"To the races!"

"And a new page in the gambling history books."

I had to admit, the old guy had me thinking.

We were trying to make a left on to Phila Street, never an easy task, when Turtle renewed his apologue.

"Are you acquainted with Doctor Dan?"

"No," I muttered between belching truck horns and waving fists as car after car cut me off.

"Ever enjoy the company of the accountant, best known as CP?"

Again the answer was in the negative.

"How about Philadelphia Phil from New York?"

Strangely, this was a name I seemed to recognize. "Maybe? Average height, dark thinning hair, always wears a baseball cap, drives big cars?"

"You may have him."

"Hmmm."

"Well, these three fellows lie at the heart of our adventure."

"Hmmm."

"You see they are old college chums, so to speak, fraternity brothers, classmates; they went to school south of here, Sienna . . . monks, priests, nuns, and such, and then went on to their own pursuits."

"I'm with you."

Well, Doctor Dan made his fortune after navigating his dental practice into a little hole in the wall called Lakewood, New Jersey. Ever been there?"

"Don't think so?"

"Pity. But Doctor Dan has found the folks around Lakewood to be in great need of his services, and so he is a gentleman no way strapped for cash. Get my drift?"

"Certainly."

"And Philadelphia Phil is another hombre whom dame fortune has smiled upon. Started out delivering fish and sea water and such with an old truck he won in a poker game; quickly parlayed that into quite a lucrative enterprise caring for the aquariums and pet shops all over Long Island."

"Good for him."

"And last there's CP, Mr. Carl Petronius, an accountant by trade."

"Hmmm, CP, Carl Pet . . ."

"No, his name is not the real reason they refer to him as CP. His friends always wear a sardonic smile when they use this label on the poor chap. Let me be clear so you understand when you make

234

his acquaintance. Sadly, CP tried several times, unsuccessfully I must add, to pass a special exam and become a Certified Public Accountant. Flunked every time. He therefore lacks the 'A' from such a title. Sad but true, never got the 'A'. He has been working all these many years for some detective agency in Easton, Pennsylvania, doing their books and such."

We both were distracted by the gate of a remarkably turned out red head striding down Union Avenue toward the racetrack. Her enormous yellow sun-hat sheltered bare shoulders and highlighted her crimson mane. I forget highway etiquette and was only salvaged from sideswiping some innocent parked cars by the cries of an irate traffic warden. There was a moment of silence and then Turtle cleared his throat to continue. "So these old friends reunite each August to tell tales and party a little, you know the game."

"Certainly."

"And when they do, naturally there is more than a little wagering and alcohol involved, which by any measure of civilized behavior is easily understood."

"True."

"Well, apparently for the past few years, how shall I say it, some one-up-man-ship has crept into their game. Private wagers have become quite the game amongst these three and the wagering, has become, let us say, spirited."

"Private betting?"

"Oh, you know."

"I'm not sure," I said as we made the right hand turn into the Union Avenue parking lot.

"Sure you do. Let's say I like General Assembly in the Travers and you like . . . , oh let's say, Strike The Gold. You bet your horse to win, and I bet my horse to win. Now what always happens when bettors disagree . . . hullabaloos of one kind or another . . . usually friendly, but energetic insults and innuendos are sure to follow?"

"Huh, you are being polite."

"To say the least," Turtle squirmed in his seat as we shared a chuckle. "You get it, and before you know it one bettor says to the other bettor, 'your horse couldn't beat a rug' and the other replies with some caustic insinuation challenging the former's sanity, or genetics or worse . . ."

"Or worse," I offered.

"And as the course of human events often dictates, the combatants end up saying things like I'll bet you your horse dies in the middle of the race."

We chuckled, "Or . . . or . . . I'll eat your left shoe if your plug gets out of the starting gate."

We chuckled again. "Or . . . how 'bout . . . You don't know nothing 'bout pickin winners . . . you couldn't pick out a gold fish at a dog show."

"Well spoken my ingenious friend. So you see these three have been in town a week or so and Doctor Dan has been having a run of luck to be sure, while CP's luck dried up two days ago, and Phil, hah, he hasn't cashed a ticket the entire meet."

"Bummer!"

"Don't reach too deeply into your sympathy-wallet, he's got it, and a lot more to lose if he likes. Anyway, for the past two days, just to get away from the windows and change his luck, Phil has been trying to get his chums to focus more and more on some private side wagers. Get my drift?"

"Ok." I said as we stopped by the red light at the corner of Union and Nelson Avenue.

"So yesterday Phil falls in love with a horse in the third race that is so fast he is willing to go three figures on it at the windows. But when his friends, CP and Dan, offer some gentle criticism of his judgment, Phil becomes a bit irate and states that if his horse in the third race does not win, it will at least come in far ahead of the nags his friends have selected. Well, verbal sparks began to fly and the wagers began to flow like Niagara. First a hundred dollars, then two, and then more. And as the Fates would have it, when the race was over, there was a miraculous reversal of fortune. Phil's horse looked like War Admiral coming down the stretch, and just that quickly he was walking mighty tall, what with all the money he had stuffed into his shoes, which of course left Doctor Dan grumbling, and their hapless friend, CP, approaching poverty."

"Oh yes, I've seen that," too many times I thought to myself.

"True enough, but all of that leads us to this momentous day."

"I've been waiting for this," I said as I wheeled into a shady parking place close to the fence by Siro's Restaurant. I got out from

behind the wheel and hurried around to the passenger side to help
Turtle to his feet. It wasn't easy.

"Damn, did you have to park out here in the weeds? Where the
hell are we, The Ukraine?"

"Come on," I offered, "it's not that far, main gate's right around
the corner."

"Corner of what," he grumbled, "Cape Horn?"

We chugged and wheezed our way toward the gate, Turtle
cursing and grimacing every step of the way. He even threatened
to send me the bill if this unnecessary experiment in hiking caused
any damage to his knees or wear on his tennis shoes.

"They're eleven years old damn it, eleven years old, and they
look as good as new."

"Amazing," I said to myself. They did look new. I wondered
if he ever stirs in his apartment or room. How did he feed
himself . . . or bathe? I began to shudder at the thought of Turtle
bathing and demanded my mind regroup.

"That is until I fell in with you and your abysmal docking
practices. This sucks."

But we did, eventually, after three stops to let Turtle's coughing
subside, enter the Nelson Avenue Gate. I paid Turtle's way in, mea
culpa, mea culpa, mea culpa, and then sprang for two programs.

"Thank you my good lad, I'll not forget your generosity."
Turtle's moods were as empty and transitory as the promises that
flow from Washington politicians.

"Ah Christ, I need a chair, I need to sit. Where was I? Oh, say,
accompany me into that cozy retreat over there," his eyes were
suddenly shinning, "the Jim Dandy bar, where we will rendezvous
with some other witnesses, and there, play our small part in
wagering history."

Turtle truly had me; curiosity is a germ that spreads
exponentially.

There were five other gentlemen waiting for us just out side
the bar. Each was leaning with quiet confidence on pipe railings
beneath the enormous red and white awnings. Turtle became the
master of ceremonies and immediately organized the introductions.
I never got to know their real names, just nicknames. First there
was Powder, the Coppertone salesman from New Hampshire, My

Cousin Vinnie, the undertaker from Illinois, Vinnie's close friend Mad Max, a broker from the Chicago Commodities Exchange, Shiner, who owned a shoe store in some mall outside Meriden, Connecticut, and a strange little fellow only known as Topper, whose claim to fame was working on the set of several Clint Eastwood movies some several years ago. Seems that every living soul who crossed into The Jim Dandy bar immediately lost their identity and assumed another known only to fellow gamblers.

Beers were bought, consumed, and refilled, while insights were shared concerning yesterday's card. Turtle continued to rail louder and louder for a place to rest his aching back, as standing was ill-advised, while the seven intrepid Ripleys managed to slowly relax and settle into shades of familiarity.

After another round was well abused, I could hold my peace no longer. "Vinnie, Powder, anybody, has our friend Turtle let you in on this afternoon's big bet, this historic event?" The assemblage grew quiet. "Shiner, somebody, tell me what this is all about?"

"You mean," Powder said directly to Turtle, "he hasn't been told?"

"Turtle," My Cousin Vinnie piped in, "you disappoint."

Turtle quaffed down the last twelve ounces in one sustained pour and, smacking his lips in exaggerated satisfaction, looked up and down the bar reviewing his audience. "Gentlemen," he began, "if one of you old frauds will just get me a lousy chair, I shall share the details of this afternoon's triumph with our friend. I was planning on divulging all the magical details in one grand moment, a spectacular gesture of eloquence, but as it would appear, conspiracy has robbed me of that pleasure, I suppose I must unlock my chest of secrets."

"Please," I said.

"Yes, let us all in on it," said Topper.

And again resorting to the feigned bravado of a circus barker, Turtle summoned three legal sized envelopes from his vest pocket.

"Here you have it my good fellows, here is the bet."

He waved them in the air as if he was holding the Magna Carta or Shakespeare's lost folio. All of us, even Powder, who seemed to know the details, stared with reserved awe. Vinnie looked dazed, and I for one was about to get one of my headaches.

"I see, you doubt my veracity," Turtle postured, "but I tell you simply and straightforwardly, here is the bet, neatly sealed and locked tightly within. Here is the bet like no other."

"Go on Turtle," Powder demanded.

"Yesterday, just before the daily double, CP, our sad accountant, told Doctor Dan, our eloquent drill master, and Philadelphia Phil, that their handicapping was all wet and of course, there ensued a series of generous and aggressive, shall we say, challenges."

"So, who among us has not had such an afternoon?" Mad Max offered, "Why all the dramatics?"

"Because, my good fellow, near the end of the day Dr. Dan upped the stakes and the three gentleman suddenly found themselves on the precipice of this spectacular gesture. It seems the three debaters got into quite a brouhaha involving the late pick four. CP was trying to get his friends to pool their moneys and cover most of the horses in the four races. They argued, naturally, but by the time civility had returned to their ranks the ship had sailed, gone, was out of the harbor. The sixth race was out of the gate and all their shenanigans turned out to be a waste of time.

Most of us nodded having at one time or another suffered the same indignity. Few things humble the erstwhile handicapper as completely as being 'shut out' at the window.

Turtle continued, "Now all of this was accompanied by gestures of mock-anger, disbelief, and worse of course, but here I believe the seed was planted."

"What'ya mean?" someone asked.

"Phil said the magic words first, 'I'll bet you anything'. Listen closely old friends, he said 'I'll bet you anything'. Hear me, these are the words everyone says, but no one really hears."

"And?" I said.

"And what followed was this, these three envelopes. By the end of the day, the three friends were puzzling over today's card and working their gray cells when they lighted upon the Jim Dandy Stakes. Each saw the race differently, so to speak, and private challenges ensued. Phil said it again, 'I'll bet you anything' . . . and this bet took form in their superlative imaginations."

"I don't get it," Max said plainly.

"Look . . . will somebody get me a chair . . . and while you're at it, see if they've run out of beer. Look, the three of them, Dr. Dan, CP, and the good Phil, all decided they would bet each other absolutely anything they wanted to bet, hear me, they'd bet *anything*, over the outcome of today's eighth race. The bet would be sealed and no body would know what the bet was because it didn't matter. They all had agreed to bet **any-thing** against the others wagers. Get it? Remember, it doesn't matter what the details are. It wouldn't matter because everyone agreed they were willing to bet anything. So it would not matter what the bet actually was and nobody needed to know what the bet might really be."

Six of us stood in awkward silence. Moments of bewilderment became barely perceptible layers of numbness and each, in turn, tried to speak, gestured with a finger or a waving arm, but then fell back silent.

"Each of the three bets is housed within these envelopes and I, Turtle, have been charged with holding them in safety until our intrepid plungers appear, today, right over there before Patrick's window."

"What do you mean no one knows the bet? How can that be?"

"It can be . . . because it is be. It is here in my left hand, right before your eyes, you bottom dweller."

"But what did they bet on?" I asked.

"Besides the Jim Dandy stakes . . . no one knows."

"Huh?" was the best Shiner could come up with.

"I mean what I mean old chum, now stop being the bottom button on an old stuffed shirt and open your ears."

"Huh," Powder spit out, "but how big is the bet?"

Turtle's eyes grew even brighter, "No one knows, I told 'ya, they were so sure of themselves they could bet 'any-thing'."

"Damn," Max sputtered, "this is sounding, weird."

"Real weird, to say the least," My Cousin Vinnie muttered.

"But, but, but," Topper interjected, "what if the whole thing is bogus? What if one of these sharks wants the losers to get him . . . a . . . a . . . date with Raquel Welch . . . or . . . or a nuclear bomb . . . or."

"Or what about the winner wants the planet Venus or something stupid," Powder said.

"Yes, I thought you might come to that," Turtle said with his usual reserve calm. "Why would someone ask for something they knew was beyond the other man's reach? The planet Venus? Your eel-like brain should tell you it had to be something they knew the others owned or could pay for or come up with, it had to be possible but, and here is the beauty of the thing, like 'Bet-A-Million Gates' said many decades ago, it had to hurt. It had to be worth losing some sleep over."

I was laughing inside, enjoying a private moment of absurdity; the impossible bet had to be 'possible'. Damn.

The silence that ensued lasted only moments. I was actually beginning to perspire. "I need a beer on that one." I said. "Me too," the others muttered. We leaned against The Jim Dandy's time worn bar and puzzled, each gazing at the yellowed walls. Some scratched their heads, others flipped through the Racing Form, but mostly each man stared and considered the 'possibilities'. On occasion, between refills, I looked with horror and admiration at the envelopes that peered over the top of Turtle's vest pocket. There was a living-breathing ember of both empathy and veneration twisting through the scullery at the back of my brain. What gall, what nerve, what unabashed egotism? For the life of me I couldn't understand if these three plungers were fools or heroes, but I was hooked good now, and I had to see it out.

A cheer rattled through the bar from the lower club. Powder peered around the corner but could only shrug his shoulders. "Nope, the race ain't gone off yet."

"Yes," Turtle exclaimed, "I believe they are here."

As swiftly as Turtle's laborious strides would allow, our group moved toward Patrick's window where, as promised, we discovered the glowing faces of the three daredevils. I reviewed them with a forensic eye. They were the most ordinary looking group you would have never noticed in Saratoga's lower clubhouse. Dr. Dan was a beefy rugged looking man, Phil smaller and less imposing, while the man in the back who must have been CP, was so unimposing he would have been missed in a wading pool.

We introduced ourselves to the teller in bay 0667 lower club. He sat there in a white shirt, combing salt and pepper hair, and peering over his reading glasses with polite suspicion as the assemblage kidnapped his window.

"Turtle old friend, what's going on?" Patrick queried while fostering a subdued smile.

"Give us a moment and all will be revealed."

Patrick looked at me, "Are you in on this?"

"Well, we all are, sort of," was the best I could do.

"What's up?" he said.

"Nothing, I hope."

"Something's is," Patrick said shaking his head. "I can usually tell the rookies from the plungers, but this crowd, I don't know, this bunch is up to something."

I nodded and gave him a look of mutual confusion.

"Usually," Patrick returned, "Rookies, they're easy. They are smiling and singing, because they don't know any better. And the losers, well, losers are what you guys look like . . . usually. But today, everybody here seems happy in a way, but not smiling like real winners. I know, I've seen real winners, I can spot one a mile away; nobody smiles like a winner. But you lot, I'm not sure what you're up to."

Truer words, I thought to myself silently.

CP piped up suddenly and spoke, over, through, and around an ancient splintered corncob pipe that he chewed on like a cud. He actually spoke with some clarity despite never missing a chaw on the well-gnawed stem; I don't know how he did it.

"Turtle, you old pike, I knew you wouldn't let us down," he said. "Damn, Turtle you got the envelopes, great!"

And about that time Dr. Dan stepped forward and proclaimed, "Let's see them, let's see if the seals are busted or anything."

"Not to fear," Turtle assured immediately, "not to fear, I have no interest or investment in the outcome of this little enterprise, I take my place as purely a historian. God, where's my chair? Here, examine the goods."

The doctor stepped forward, took the envelopes and held them up to the light. "They look all right," he muttered under his breath.

"They are my good fellow, perfectly in order."

"And no one has seen what's inside them?" Phil asked.

"Not a soul, not myself, or Patrick, or the Stranger, or Powder, or anyone else, that I can assure you."

CP fingered them for a second and confirmed their unsullied condition. He was chewing on his pipe as if it was bubble gum and seemed to grumble and growl more than speak when he uttered. "I'll buy it, they're OK." He gazed over his pipe and shook his head toward Phil and answered with a simple upturned thumb.

"Then," Turtle offered, "can I assume the bet is on? As the arbiter I feel it is my duty to give each of you the chance, here and now, to speak, or forever hold your peace."

"Go for it Phil," the good Doctor said plainly, "Now's your chance to shut it down. Or you CP, what do you say? All in or all not?"

Each in turn looked at the other. Heads nodded, but not a word was spoken. We all surveyed the faces of the three players and each seemed steeled for what was at hand. We looked to Patrick, who sat behind the betting counter adjusting his glasses and smirking. He never gave any of us a chance to speak, he simply interjected, "This better be good."

We all laughed a little and Turtle stepped forward, "Patrick, you will be our judge?"

"And jury if I have to. Come on, I'll do what I can," was Patrick's diplomatic reply.

"Then it is done," Turtle proclaimed, "Gentlemen shake hands."

One by one CP, Phil, and Dr. Dan shook and sealed the covenant. We, the admiring seven, couldn't help ourselves; we applauded politely and patted each man on the back with cheers of respect and veneration.

The day went smoothly, but only rarely did anyone seem to enjoy their winnings or loses. Each time I returned to confess my incredible lapses of racing judgment, I was mildly surprised to see the big three with bright smiles on their faces. I wondered if I would have stayed with this crazy bet. What if my supposed friends asked for the moon, something at least something I could barely afford? What if they were asking for my savings account or my car, or . . ." I swallowed a hard grizzly swallow and thanked the stars I hadn't been around when this adventure was conceived. Knowing me, I couldn't have resisted.

Before the fifth race I found myself behind Philadelphia Phil in Patrick's betting line. "Phil," I asked him, "how'd you get into this anyway?"

"I don't know, but isn't it great?"

"I do not know if great is the word I would be using right now."

"Sure it is, I'm going to clean up."

"And if you do not?"

Suddenly his eyes drew narrow and distant. He paused and then muttered the only thing a man like Phil could say could possibly say, "Hmmm, I never thought of that."

These ancient mariners were taking me to school.

When I got to Patrick's window to place my wager he looked behind me to be sure I was his only customer and then printed out my ticket. He grabbed it and pulled me in so as to whisper. "Did I get this right? These three numbskulls are betting against each other but . . ."

"You got it, no one knows the bet."

"Or the horses?"

"Or the horses . . ." We entertained each other rehashing the details and shared some quiet moments of subdued admiration. "This whole thing could backfire and some old friendships might go right down the drain."

"I know. Gotta hand it to them."

The day went quickly until it was time for The Jim Dandy. The horses were called to the post and Saratoga's ancient bell told the crowd the race was seventeen minutes away. I watched them parade past the Travers Porch, and then to their outriders care. The horses were at once majestic and at ease with curious eyes that snapped from side to side, each glaring with hard won confidence. In the far corners of the lower clubhouse stood, equally still and confident, the heroes of the moment. Phil was speaking with the now seated Turtle, CP was standing close by chewing on his pipe, and Dr. Dan was hosting a roundtable discussion that consisted of Powder and some new characters who had learned of the secret bet. I watched as each made their case to audiences at hand about what was about to happen. If my Grandmother were only here, I'm sure we would have all been on the receiving the end of a lecture entitled "Smart People are often the Dumbest.".

To make a short story a bit longer, the Jim Dandy proved to be a spectacular affair with Macho Again besting Pyro at the wire in a terrific stretch duel that had 30,000 fans thundering rabid approval. It was a glorious race, a fitting testimony to the artistry of horse and rider, but each of us had little time to enjoy it. Quickly, before Patrick's window, fifty prying eyes peered over shoulders and awaited the verdict. I marveled at the size of our assembly. I looked to Powder, but he didn't know who these people were either.

"This is getting out of control." I said to Turtle, but he didn't hear a word. With the true flare of a newly elected politician he drew out the envelopes.

"Are we ready gentlemen," he asked? "Yes? Well then Patrick old friend, could you print the 'O'-fficial, I say again, 'O-ffical results of the last race, please."

And with a puckish smile Patrick did exactly that, struck all the right buttons and handed me the paper. I, in turn, forwarded it to Turtle.

Turtle made the pronouncement. "The results of the Jim Dandy Stakes are now here and 'O'-ficcial. Listen carefully one and all. The winner of this race was 'Macho Again' . . . Macho Again' the winner." He paused as if to await some legal debate. "And it states here 'Pyro' ran second and 'Tiz Now Tiz Then' showed. Do we all agree? The final order of finish was 'Macho Again' . . . 'Pyro' . . . and then 'Tiz Now Tiz Then'."

All agreed in silence.

And just that quickly his pencil tore through the first envelope. Its shearing echoed through each conscience. Turtle read aloud with more than a little style.

"I, Phil Breber, bet Dan and CP the cost of my youngest son's education . . ."

A subdued howl rose up behind me.

". . . at Sienna, that 'True Aspen' finishes on the board, first, second, or third and ahead of which ever horse my ignorant friends have chosen."

We were dumbstruck. We tried to comprehend the magnitude of the bet that had been laid before us. The cost of a private college education could be huge. Powder's eyes were the size of Susan B. Anthony dollars, and Topper had to turn his head away to review the finish on the big electric board. Phil's bet was a loser; 'True Aspen' was off the board and as such, everyone assembled knew he was vulnerable.

"Settle down gentlemen," Turtle said quietly with a wave of his arm, "there is more." And with that he produced the next envelope labeled 'Dan'.

Quickly the paper was retrieved and read; "Dan Wrust bets Carl and Phil, a year's professional services, a year's, that 'Tiz Now Tiz Then' will be the clear winner of the Jim Dandy Stakes. Sworn to on this day, August . . . etc., etc., etc."

Again Patrick did the honors, reviewed the results and declared the bet bogus. 'Tiz Now Tiz Then' had finished a well beaten third and as such, Doctor Dan knew he too was vulnerable. The good Doctor shuffled his feet and looked at the results again. We studied him, waiting for some crack in his countenance but, to his credit; he proved to be a true stoic.

"So what if none of your bets are any good," Vinnie said?

"Then there is no bet," Phil interjected.

"Yup, no bet," CP said through his pipe, "that's the way it'll be." But it was difficult not to see that CP's beaver-like pipe gnawing had increased to a feverish pitch. His eyes gleamed, and I knew we had a winner.

Turtle lifted the last envelope, and whisked the paper from its sleeve. His eyes suddenly glared with astonishment. We all watched as he reviewed the contents several times.

"What?" demanded Dr. Dan.

"Damn it Turtle," Phil yelped.

"Gentlemen, I think we have a winner?"

A cheer went up.

"Indeed," said Turtle.

"Oh man," snapped Powder.

"Out with it," said another.

Turtle cleared his throat and said with admirable calm, "The first paragraph of this note reads as follows: I, Carl Petronius, being of sound mind and body, and after long and complicated mathematical calculation have concluded that the horse known as

'Pyro' will finish on the board, win, place or show, and I further submit that Pyro will finish ahead of whatever plugs my addle brained friends have backed.

We all stopped and stared, could this be, was this a bet on a real horse race? Just being on the board was a bet? Was betting the other fellow was wrong a form of betting? After reviewing the pari-mutuel rules with Patrick, our resident wagering scholar, and with some debate, it was generally concurred that CP's wager was a bet, as good as any other. He had risked everything and, at least to all appearances, had been prepared to hold up his end of things had one of his friends chosen more wisely.

Turtle, with style and uncommon energy, declared CP the winner. A new cheer went up, right there in the middle of the Lower Clubhouse. Patrick laughed and slapped his knee, over and over again. Phil threw his program on the floor and cursed mightily under his breath, "This is going to cost me, isn't it?"

"There's more gentlemen, there's more," Turtle declared trying to quiet the crowd. "There's the wager itself . . . remember?"

"Give me that," Dan demanded, and pulled the paper from Turtle's swollen hooks. He read in silence while the rest of us peered over his brutish shoulders to see the bet. CP had won, but only as we read the intricate details did we realize what he had won.

"Damn," Vinnie said.

"Well, for Christ's sake," Powder announced, "Patrick did you read the bet?"

The teller only shook his head and adjusted his glasses, "Let me see it, and I'll clear this up so you fellows can finally get away from my window and go celebrate somewhere."

I took the note from Dr. Dan's fingers and handed it to Patrick. I didn't look at the details at all; somehow I was enjoying the suspense.

Patrick read aloud: "I Carl Petronius being . . . oh, ok, we know all that . . . ah, here it is . . . Carl Petronius bets that both of his friends have cast losing bets." Patrick paused to eye each of us and confirm the correctness of the note, "If he is wrong, Carl agrees to pay his half of the winner's demands and will offer a complete security alarm system to be installed in their place of business as well. But if Carl Petronius has won and his two friends have, as usual, been unable to distinguish a runner from a rug, he entrusts his oral health, oral hygiene, and all his dental needs to his old school chums. He knows they will be honorable men and do the right thing."

The cheering hurt my ears. The applause reached decibels that must have reverberated on the third floor. Phil kicked his program and began to slap the support beam with his baseball cap. Dr. Dan glared at CP. The good Doctor had been reeled in, and he knew it. He glared, but CP only raised his eyebrows in acknowledgment and for the first time all day, smiled, a smile filled with deeply yellowed pipe worn teeth. His mouth looked like a topographical map of Yellowstone National Park. The teeth in his lower jaw resembled some moonscape at a NASA museum. I stood in silent amazement. Fixing that mouth was not going to be cheap.

"You're carrying your half Phil," the good doctor exclaimed across the room.

When all was said and done, each of us had to congratulate the genius of the thing. What a wonderful day and how ironic. Racing history? Well, I would have to let the historians decide that, but for myself I walked out on to Union Avenue a much wiser and happier individual. I would certainly have a story to share, but given the condition of my wallet, it would probably have to be shared over fish and chips at King's Tavern.

As things worked out, Dr. Dan and Philadelphia Phil turned out to be very honorable gentlemen. I survived the meet with some small measure of dignity and even found myself a few dollars up on Labor Day. I was roaming around the upper Club on the last Sunday of the meet and decided to go downstairs to say hello to Patrick when, who did I see climbing Saratoga's well oiled stairs, but Carl Petronius himself, rather nattily attired in a new seer sucker suit and wearing a nifty straw hat. He looked like something right out of the Great Gatsby.

I had to stop him in the middle of the staircase to say hello, "CP, remember me?" He raised his face to greet me, and puzzled for a second.

"I was here . . . I was here for the 'bet'."

I offered my hand and we shook.

Quietly his eyes opened and he shook my hand more vigorously, "Turtle's friend."

"Well, I'm not sure Turtle has many real friends, but yes, I was with Turtle when you won your big bet."

He nodded with confident contentment. "I won," he said, and with that, as if to make a compelling gesture of triumph, smiled a smile for the ages. His teeth were brand new, a perfect row of glowing porcelain, a magnificent vision of whiteness and symmetry only Steinway could have imitated. I stared but held my composure. Dr. Dan had done his work well. We chatted for a moment or two and then parted company. He was off to join his two friends who were enjoying lunch on the third floor. I turned at the bottom steps to wave so long just as CP looked back, his smile beaming once again. I had to admire the magnificent way he looked.

Every inch of me was smiling. Patrick was right; no one smiles like a winner.

A Picture Framed By a Tale

On any given Tuesday the racetrack is closed up tight as a French nunnery, what the media folks call dark, so that plungers, folks like myself, can take a short vacation from the turmoil and excitement of chasing thoroughbreds and the bays of conquest. Yet it needs be said that even when the Nelson Avenue gates are closed, Saratoga still has more than its fair share of distractions to offer the lonely high roller, what with an amphitheater that acts as a summer home for all sorts of big time ballets, orchestras, and music concerts, a second racetrack, a casino, and eighty three pubs within walking distance of City Hall.

So to take full advantage of this respite I slept in, rising promptly at the crack of noon, took a cup of instant coffee and my Classic Taxi into town to enjoy the day. After hurried stops at the post office and the bank, I left my car parked behind Suave *Soave* Faire and spent the next hour reviewing the window displays of a dozen quaint little shops. The dress shops looked interesting. Good reconnaissance can be very valuable especially when one is trying to arrange a romantic weekend should a certain lady call. This is a racing town and optimism always rules the day. Even the little Irish store offered a collection of curios and bric-a-brac that might engage a lady's fancy, if the timing is right. I love to wander.

The day got even better when I popped into G. Williker's little toy store to reconnoiter a birthday present for my nephew Liam. I was working my way through wooden tractors and train sets when I looked up and found an old friend, Michael Kell staring back at me. I hadn't seen his most likeable mug once the entire summer.

He looked as amazed as I. We quickly shook hands and tried to catch up.

"Well, tell you what, I'm pretty much done here. Let me pay for these things and you can give me a lift back to the lake, let me show you the cabin I bought."

"Love to," I said, "my taxi awaits."

"Well, when did you buy this little place?" I kept asking.

"'Bout five years ago," Michael answered.

"Five years. And why wasn't I told of this big adventure?"

"Gosh I, I don't know, did we ever talk about real estate? You're always so busy during August and all."

"True enough I suppose," I said, "but I still think I should have been told? This is quite an investment."

"Investment? You think so?"

"I know so. Can't miss! Time, tides, and the affairs of men, as the poet once said."

"You ought to consider buying one. Would be the smartest thing you ever did, except for Yvonne of course."

"Always a lawyer looking for an angle," I laughed quietly. "So what . . . now come on, show me around."

The two of us followed a crushed stone driveway to tour a smallish English garden, a large deck, a simple brick patio, and then inside, with an enthusiastic, yet humble review of the seven rooms in the old Saratoga camp, recently remodeled with salvaged hardware and Montgomery Ward furniture. We were standing before the dusty red wood stove, reviewing mementos and knick-knacks over the hearth, when my eyes fell upon the south wall and a photograph.

"What's this?" I asked quietly reviewing the photograph in a dark corner. Within the 8 by 10-inch frame there were four small photographs from a day at the races. Each was drab and forbidding, with figures glaring out from a Gothic gloom in the subdued flare of a flash. One was of a racehorse, wearing number-one on its saddlecloth. It was crossing the finish line in a yellow cone of light. Next, the same great animal, now showcasing its large white blaze, was being lead to a winner's circle and posing with a small crowd of onlookers. Photographs taken under a heavy gray sky looming over a featureless roofline while golden trophies glistened in the foreground and a small well dressed group gathered around a small red table.

"Just a picture."

"Yeah, but it's a picture, a racetrack's official photos for a race. What's it say here, what's it say, damn glasses, it's so dark, a night photo? The Meadowlands? But that looks like, what's his name, the old governor, Carey. Is that Hugh Carey?"

"It is," Michael offered taking the picture out of the shadows, "and it says the 1979 Travers."

"The Travers, 1979, at night?"

"No it wasn't run at night. Saratoga hasn't got lights."

"But the picture?"

"It was raining, a pretty good rain that day."

I looked at the picture and the room that surrounded it. There were racing prints in every corner of the room. Some by Cortez, some by Montgomery, and many others I didn't recognize. His sitting room was a mini-museum to the sport, cluttered but impassioned.

"So what's this picture all about?"

"What do you mean?" Michael said as he returned the picture to its nail.

"It's the only photograph in the room. Everything in here is some kind of art, or print, or etching isn't it? But this is mechanical, a photograph."

"Well," Michael replied as he poured me a fresh cup of coffee, and settled into a wicker rocking chair on the front porch, "that is General Assembly winning the 1979 Travers Stakes, in record time, I might add, two minutes flat. Not even Man O' War ran that fast. The General was, and is, my favorite horse."

"Man O' War?"

"No! General Assembly."

"Really?"

"Really . . . of all time!"

"Absolutely. Not Easy Goer or Go For Wand? How about his old man, Secretariat, there was a good one."

"To be sure, but General Assembly is number one in my book. My all time favorite."

"Becasue?"

"Well, as Dr. Jung said, there is a reason for everything, but . . ."

"I knew it, there had to be a but in here somewhere."

I was intrigued and nodded for my friend to continue.

"And," he said with a grin, "as another old writer also said, a story goes with it. So if you want to know why I think so much of that animal, you are going to have to hear the entire tale . . . from start to finish."

Proudly I looked at the watch I had not been forced to hock, not yet, "You've got twenty minutes; I've got to be at the train station this afternoon."

"Expecting?"

"Maybe," I said with a grin, "a guy can dream can't he?"

"Give me thirty, I love telling this one."

"Twenty-five."

"Come on then, let's take a walk down by the lake. I've got a couple of Adirondack chairs down there, you'll want to be comfortable for this one. It starts back in the early summer of '79 when I was getting out of grad school, down in Jersey, and well, everything was beginning to calm down after finals and all that stuff."

I was listening closely as we crossed out on to his dock and fell into the two wooden chairs secured in the shade of a large ash tree. "Harmless enough I suppose."

"Ha, just wait, you'll see. Anyway, at the same time I was working on my friend Karen to come north and see Saratoga. We were talking . . . you know."

"And who is this Karen?"

"Well, she was a grad student, we were in a lot of classes together, and she was already teaching, French in a local high school or something."

"Spare me the details, especially if they're sordid."

"Oh they're sordid, very sordid indeed."

"Please," I said quickly.

"Well, like I said, I'd been working on her, exchanging calls and letters and such, trying to get her to come north before the summer ended. I actually had given up hope of seeing her about the same time I got a job at Finch Pryun Paper. It was just my first full week of work when she finally called, a Wednesday late in August. I remember the weather had been awful, heat, humidity, and an endless parade of thunderstorms."

The story of what my old friend went through to have a chance of meeting up with this pot of pulchritude was all the testimony I needed to continue listening. She must have been a 'lot-a-girl' in more ways than one. First he had to call off from work and get someone to cover his shift at the plant, then take a shower, find some fresh threads, locate his old umbrella, and finally drive into the city . . . all in forty-five minutes. I mused. The things we do when a great female is at hand. I had nothing but empathy for him at the moment, as I understood too well such extremes. What he didn't understand was that Karen wanted to meet him in an alley on Caroline Street next to the folk music emporium, Café Lena. Even as he spoke he felt that was a strange rendezvous.

"I know, felt like I was in some Humphrey Bogart black and white. It was all dark and gloomy and shadows. I kept thinking I was going to run into Peter Laurie or Sydney Greenstreet or . . ."

"Staring in your own Film Noire," I said.

"Uh, yeah. But I found some parking and sure enough, I found her in the alley, just like she promised. The odd thing was she was standing next, or actually a little behind, a big blue dumpster. She was hiding, that was obvious, but from what or . . . ? I told her how happy I was to see her and she seemed happy to see me, but I had to tell her the alley was kind of weird."

I was becoming more interested. Romance, summer heat, and a femme fatale hiding in back alleys; my friend Michael had gotten himself involved with a mystery lady, a schoolmarm Mata Hari. It seems he found her, right where she had said and after a time he was able to talk her out of the alley and into Congress Park. The rain and wind was letting up so they were able to walk slowly under his umbrella around the park in complete privacy.

"We walked and I told her all about Morrissey's Casino, and all the rich folks that use to tear this town up every summer. And of course she had to hear about the religious fanatics, and potato chips and hot fudge sundaes, but I could tell she was only half listening and spending most of her time looking scared. So when we got up near the Franklin Spring I made her sit down and demanded some kind of an explanation."

"And, did she give you the whole story?" I mused over my coffee.

"Yes she did, and you could have knocked me over with a well placed breeze. Wait till I tell you. She looked up at the sky, made about a dozen stumbling starts and finally, when I was about to get up and walk away, she just told me. Yes sir, she looked up at the tops of the trees, and blurted out that her husband was in town."

Michael was rolling his eyes as if he was reliving the pain and confusion of that moment all over again.

"You sly dog Michael, you little home-wrecker."

"No, no, no, wait a minute, neither did I. This was the first time I had ever heard about this husband thing."

"Truly?"

"Truly! We had been seeing each other for maybe six or seven months, and I had never once, not once, ever heard of, or ever thought, there was even a hint of a husband. And to make matters worse he was not only a foul tempered hunter, with many rifles and shotguns, but he was in town. He'd followed her up to Saratoga and was driving around town in his big red truck looking for her."

"Looking for her? Hunting for her more like it, but you're not kidding."

"Wish I was, but there you have it. I must have turned six shades of corpse-gray. We talked, and argued, and went round and round, but the fact was she was married, and I was on the spot."

"Hey buddy boy, you could have been in real trouble."

"You don't know the half of it, I already was and I didn't even know it."

"She started balling. Tears, real big alligator tears"

"Crocodile," I offered.

"What?"

"Crocodile tears, I believe is the expression."

"Oh yes, I'm sure, but then it got worse.

I started to laugh out loud which annoyed my friend a little. I mean he was sitting in front of me, as healthy as I'd ever seen him, so I knew this story must have a happy ending, but back then, when he found out this Karen had a husband, one who owned scads of

artillery, and he had followed her to Saratoga. I should have been
more empathetic, but I was having too much fun.

"Man, I was mad as anything. I couldn't believe my ears, but
I couldn't get her to stop bawling. I let her cry for a bit in order to
get my brain back together. Clearly, there were three things I was
sure of. First I was in trouble, two, she was getting out of Saratoga,
and three, I didn't know what to do."

"Understandable."

"So we talked some more and I buried an impulse to just leave
her sobbing away in the park. She looked so helpless and pathetic
and well, just awful. Didn't take Copernicus to realize we had to
get her, and her car someplace where this crazy nut job husband-
with-a-shotgun couldn't see us."

"OK."

"So, we drove out past the hospital, toward Greenfield, where
we found a little bar and shared a cheap beer. We parked her old
Chevy out back and sat in a corner booth to relax a little and talk. It
took an hour and three beers, but we came up with a plan to rent a
room in Albany, and then she would be going home."

"Not very creative."

"I know, but she was as frightened as I was, and by the time we
were getting into our next beer, she was willing to go along with
me. So we went to leave and guess what? Her car wouldn't start."

"You're kidding?"

"Nope."

"Battery?"

"Nope. That would have been too easy. The motor turned over
fine, but it just wouldn't run. So one of the old timers came out
of the bar to look at her car, and one says it's her timing gear, and
something about the valves aren't working."

"The what?"

"I don't know, all I know is it's busted and we're stuck."

"Damn," I said as I quickly checked the time.

"Stop watching your watch, you're gonna like the ending,
I promise. So the bartender sends us off to this greasy garage
down the road, and the guy tows the damn car, and in about thirty
minutes he tells us he can fix it, but it's going to cost us $350.00."

"And?"

"And nothing. I haven't got more than about a hundred bucks on me, remember, I just got a job, been working only a week, and she's only carrying a hundred as well. And even if we had enough for the gear thing, we still had to find money for food and highway tolls and gas."

"This is getting better," I offered as he rolled his empty glass between his fingers, "I wish I could have been a fly in her car with all this skullduggery."

"Wait 'till I tell you. So she's crying, and I'm trying to figure out how the hell I got into this mess, and why I'm not home sitting in the air conditioning watching Clark Gable sink half the Japanese navy, or the Mets on channel 9, and why I'm scared puke-pink by every red truck I see, and how I'm going to get my head blown off with a shotgun. But I tell the guy to fix the car and we'll be back for it in the morning, even if we don't have the money. And of course she starts crying even more, and the mechanic guy is starting to look at us like he doesn't want any part of whatever is wrong with us."

"Yes, I'm sure."

"OK! So we're back in the bar, trying not to be too scared, and we're getting a little drunk and silly, so as it was getting late we took a walk back to her car. The garage was closed so we used her spare keys and sat inside to listen to the radio, and before you knew it, we're both sound asleep sitting up, and then it's the middle of the night. So yours truly is sitting there, sort of thinking."

"You slept in the car?"

"We sure did."

"Cozy!"

"Lousy you mean, ached all over for days. But just after dawn I woke Karen up and told her I wasn't gonna let her stupidity, and her stupid husband, screw up my vacation. Nope! I wasn't gonna have any part of it. She could stay with the car, or she could come with me, but it was Travers Day in Saratoga and I wasn't going to spend my day in Albany in some no-tell motel hiding from some Mr. Shotgun. Besides, Saturdays are big days there and not only would we be hard to find, but he wouldn't dare do anything in front of thousands of witnesses. No, I was going to the races."

"Really?"

"Yup, I just couldn't stand all this double-oh-seven nonsense, sleeping in that cocoon of a sedan, feeling scared, and unwashed, and not even really knowing why."

"Proud of you."

"Well that's the way it was. I remember walking over to a little Stewart's Shop down the road, got a cup of coffee and some chewing gum and I knew exactly what I was going to do."

"And?"

"Well, she said she understood, and so we were off to the races. We took a taxi to town to get my car and then we went straight to the track. We walked around, had a beer, watched some races, grabbed some lunch, and talked about the good times. She told me about her crummy marriage and the bum she was married to, and mostly we pretended we didn't have a care in the world. Then, late in the afternoon, I went over to King's Tavern and called up the mechanic to see how the car was doing and we got the bad news. The water pump and the timing gear were both gone. Yup, the bill came to four hundred fifty bucks."

"And you two had?"

"I don't know, maybe a hundred and fifty between us. But I told the guy we'd be out before nightfall to pick it up. Didn't know how to pay for it, didn't have half enough, but I knew I couldn't get her out of town without that damn car, and she was going, as soon as I could manage it, she was going."

"My old friend, why oh, why didn't I ever hear about this before?"

"Wait until I tell you the rest."

"The rest? You mean there's more?"

"General Assembly, remember!"

"Ok, let's hear it."

"Just as we crossed Union Avenue it started to pour again. Buckets. My old umbrella got us as far as the clubhouse escalator, when I ran into a guy from the old high school, Jerry Monte. Hadn't seen Jerry in years, but he was always a real good guy who was also known to one and all as quite a perspicacious handicapper. I offered him the shelter of my umbrella and he returned the favor by telling me there was a good bet coming up in the seventh. It seems that in the seventh race there was a horse named Dumbo who liked the grass a little wet and kind of soft."

"Dumbo?"

"Yup, Dumbo. Sounds like the horse was named for me, doesn't it? So I look, a second and a third time, and with five minutes to go, it's pretty clear that the officials are going to leave the race on the weeds. Dumbo is 3 to 1."

"And?"

"And I bet on Dumbo, and sure enough, he comes flying down the stretch and wins by two, maybe three lengths. Suddenly I've got $300.00 dollars in my pocket, and I think I can see light at the end of the 'We-gotta-get-this-girl-out-of-town' tunnel."

"You do?"

"I do because the next race is the Travers and the Travers is always a good betting race, but I did feel a little uneasy just then, like maybe someone was watching us. She was still as nervous as I knowing we were still short so when the rain seemed to let up a bit we started walking and talking, trying to be happy and find another winner for the couple bucks we needed. In the paddock, we walked up on tree number one and what do you think I see?"

"A horse?"

"Oh gosh, my God man, one hell'uva horse. The most magnificent animal I have ever laid eyes upon. The horses were being saddled for the Travers and this one animal looks spectacular, strong, arrogant, calm, with all four legs resting squarely on the ground. He just looked like a winner. There was quite a crowd gathering as the trainers prepped them, so we meandered our way through the crowd and ended up next to an expensive looking group of ladies admiring the same animal. I don't know what all the buzz was about, so I ask this one particularly elegant looking woman for the horse's name. And guess what, she laughs and tells me this is General Assembly, you know, like everybody knows that, except me of course. And when I ask her if she thinks he's as good a runner as he is a looker, she laughs again."

"You've got people, rich people in the paddock, laughing at you." I said.

"A little, but wait. This woman starts telling me her friends used to own his father, Secretariat, 'The' Secretariat, the King, and this General Assembly is his first son, you know, off spring, and she is down here in the walking circle, under a tree, braving lightning strikes, in the rain, in wet grass just for sentimental reasons. Can you imagine that, a sentimental soul at a racetrack?"

"Remarkable indeed."

"So that does it, how can you ignore great Karma like that. I mean the writing was on the wall."

"Or in the mud?"

"Yeah, mud isn't the word for it that day. So up I go to the windows, and I put it all on Secretariat's first born."

"All of it? You just won $300.00 dollars, you are almost out of the woods, so to speak, and you bet the whole load?"

"Yup. And in case you haven't figured it out, not only did General Assembly win, he set the track record, in a driving cold rain, two minutes flat, two minutes flat, not even Gallant Fox or Man O' War went that fast. And nobody's ever come close to breaking his mark."

"Really? I didn't know."

"I was rich."

"You're saved!"

"In more ways than one. We left the track like the devil himself was chasing us, drove out to the Greenfield Garage, paid the bill, and got her car out of hock. We had a quiet teary-eyed dinner that night in a little place called Dee Dee's near Albany and about eight that night, I watched the taillights of her lousy sedan fade into the sunset."

"And that was it?"

"Not quite. I mean I felt so good at that moment. It was like Christmas, and Birthday, and Stanley Cup, and first kiss, all rolled into one. If I knew how, I would have danced a jig. I jumped around, sang songs, and said a dozen thank-you's to the big guy upstairs. I drove back into town with a happy, happy heart. I spent the next two or three hours sitting in King's Tavern, watching the replays of the days races on the evening news and especially watching General Assembly save my life over, and over, and over again. I didn't want to stop watching. Today, if they show a replay of that race, I still stop and watch. What a great horse."

"I have to admit, that is a story. I guess I understand."

"Not quite, wait 'til I tell you."

"You've got one minute, I've got to run."

"So I'm sitting in King's, getting ready to put my change away and take a long walk through downtown, when three guys come in, and they end up at the bar right next to me. Turns out they're cops, just off their shift, and they're all talking about this guy they arrested."

"You're kidding me?"

"Nope. Earlier that day they had to arrest a crazy man, some real lunatic, according to Sergeant Cohen. It seems this guy had parked his big red Ford pick up truck right in front of the racetrack, just under a no parking sign. Can you believe it, a no parking sign? And when the officers told him he couldn't leave his truck, he copped an attitude; he gave the cop some lip. He told them he wasn't blocking anyone's way, and he should be left alone. He starts screaming about he's just going inside to get someone and at the same time the officers are noticing a stack of rifles hanging in the rear window of his truck and they naturally asked questions. And before you know it the cops find out that the shotguns are loaded and off safety, much against the law, and within a few more minutes three hundred pounds of blubber was wallowing around in the dirt, right in front of old Saratoga racetrack, wearing a pair of handcuffs."

"Buddy boy, you are kidding me."

"It gets better. It turns out, Sergeant Cohen is really put out, because by the time he gets the wild man processed and under control, the Travers was over and he had missed the race."

"You mean while you were inside chasing a tip, and a sentimental selection from a total stranger, with your assassin just a few hundred yards away, toting a loaded shotgun, and the only thing that saved your sorry butt was a no-parking sign, a little red framed parking sign?"

Michael raised his eyebrows and smiled.

"Old friend, you were walking around lucky, and didn't even know it."

"But like I said, that picture you saw is more than a just a picture. A story goes with it."

Travers

An outlandish party, a genuine first rate Saturnalia, is often accompanied by one of life's most ignoble adventures, a hangover. And if I might clarify my point a bit further, these 'hangovers' are not solely restricted to excesses of alcohol. They can be blamed on food, dance, song, or any such overindulgence that my sainted grandmother used to refer to as jollification, which is very much the right word if one attempts to plum the very depths of one's stamina and hedonistic creativity. Lovely days with spectacular nights!

It should also be noted there are times when entire communities are subject to these hangovers as well as individuals. Sometimes a population gets caught up in a moment of history, or importance, or joy and, acting as one, they dive into frenzy and frolic the night away. Been there, done that, and more than somewhat . . . scandalous evenings!

Truth be told, the little town of Saratoga Springs can cook up just such a party several times each August when the thoroughbreds come to town. The recipe usually requires a Grade 1 race at the old race track, a measure of some crazed performance at Saratoga's Performing Arts Center, and an endless frosting of merry making at the harness track's casino and the clubs downtown. Pubs remain open till dawn, serving a spicy breakfast in unlit barrooms behind politely locked doors. What's better than that, as Too Tall Teddy used to say? Blissful, albethey, exhausted dawns.

And the weekend of the Travers Stakes, the oldest and most prestigious of Saratoga's Grade 1 races, is easily the grandest of the summer revels. The music never stops, parties never end, parades (both official and impromptu) litter old Broadway, while tourists clog the side streets, and the whiskey flows like Victoria Falls. Some of the regulars wish for it to be over, but it never is until Monday's sun comes up.

And on Travers Sunday, my Classic Taxi was back in service and enjoying the residue of all this jollification. I was pulling away from the gas pumps on route 50 in old Ballston Spa when I noticed a woman on the side of the road. She was hard to miss, this was no ragged runaway, rather, she looked as though she had just left a fashion show or was imitating an expensive department store mannequin. She was wearing a petite black cocktail dress and fashionable heels with a white linen wrap thrown over her left arm and spectacular diamond pendant earrings that flashed from behind her shoulder length sloe-black hair. She was magnificent and she appeared to be hitchhiking. This was too good to miss; I had to stop.

"Are you for hire?" was all she needed to say.

The possibility of picking up some much needed gilt summoned my smile. I put down my cup of cold coffee, my cinnamon swirl pastry and said, "Certainly miss. I like to call this Classic Taxi, a classic car makes for a classic taxi." I was doing my best to appear charming and harmless. That's me, the harmless charming Stranger.

"Thank you."

"Where to?" I said, as she landed in the back seat.

"Canterbury Restaurant, you know where that is, The Canterbury?"

"Certainly, by the lake on 9P. But it's called Longfellow's these days."

She seemed to sink into her seat, "Well whatever it's called, can you get me there?"

"Happily."

We drove quietly, she never offered her name so I didn't offer mine. Mostly I was admiring the view in my mirror. She caught my eyes studying her, but didn't seem to mind. This woman was comfortable with esteem. Conversation warmed after we turned left on to the lake road. We both noticed the rather bucolic simplicity of the view. The lake was still, a deep electric-blue mill pond.

"Pretty here," she said, "been years since I've been up here. I'd almost forgotten how nice it is."

"Do the races?"

She exhaled a smile I enjoyed. "I certainly did, and Siro's, and The Horseshoe, and Lillian's. I must have been out of my head; I'm getting too old for this stuff. What was I thinking?"

"Well, you must have been thinking more than this fellow," I said pointing toward a ridiculous sight I discovered through the front passenger window. There, draped neatly on a hangar, swinging from a tree limb was a man's silver-blue tuxedo jacket.

"What the . . . ?" she muttered from the back seat.

"No slacks, just a jacket, Hmmm, if it's rented, that's gonna cost'em."

"Cost him plenty," she said.

We almost stopped in the middle of the road to study the garment swaying in the morning breeze. It looked positively unruffled with no sign of a stain or damage, but it certainly was an orphan. We shrugged shoulders to each other as 'Old Faithful' got back up to forty.

She was hunting through her purse for something, so I didn't have a chance to turn on the charm and begin one of my classic trip shortening conversations. I didn't have to.

"Look at that," I said

"What is it?"

"A beach ball, I think. It's enormous!" And indeed it was a big beautiful, red, blue and white beach ball, nearly six feet across, sitting in the culvert on the side of the road. I slowed again; it had something written on it in thick black marker.

"I love . . . you . . . Martin . . . Wilson," she read out loud as I managed to dodge oncoming traffic. "Oh dear, poor boy, I'm afraid he didn't get his love note." She was smiling.

I smiled, "Or the fool threw it away."

"Oh dear, poor girl," she said as she turned to take one last look at the plaything. "Wonder, hmmm, half mile from the water?"

This was my opening, "Probably came with the tuxedo." We both laughed, but not for long. The road took us down a steep grade, first left and then right, and as we survived another of route 9P's jaw shaking potholes, I found more entertainment on the side of the road.

"What is that?" she asked.

"A car jack, all the way up, like somebody was changing a tire."

"But where's the car?"

"And where's the tire," I asked? It sat there, miniature statuary, shining in the sun, proud as a peacock, all by itself. "How the heck . . . ?" But I only could grin and drive.

We went past Mangino's Restaurant and then Panza's without distraction. My fare was rummaging around in her purse again, looking more and more frustrated. We followed the macadam for a mile or so and I let myself enjoy the sapphire vista of the lake when route 9p did it again. We were approaching the road that leads to the Revolutionary War battlefield and there, in the island of the intersection, was a wheelchair, a complete solitary wheelchair, all alone.

"My Lord," she said. "No one around, no one. Do you see anyone?"

"Not a soul."

I had to stop.

"I hope they're all right," she kept saying as she gazed out her window.

"Not even a 'For Sale' sign. I don't get it."

"Oh dear, I hope they're all right."

"Maybe they had a spare somewhere." I tried to laugh.

"Oh, you're awful, just awful." But she said it with a grin as I got back on the gas.

We pressed on, curiosity my king, and the rest of the drive did not disappoint; the highway was well decked out today. We passed garbage cans in the middle of the road, two on the middle white line, two others lying on their sides in the gutter. They looked like they had been put there purposefully, possibly a slalom course for mischievous skateboarders. And near Fitch Road there was a pile of ladies clothes, rolled in a heap, and then a clump of towels with a solitary boot, yes, one lonely ladies boot, a yard high, brown leather and zipped to the top. It looked ready for sale at Macy's. Then further on, a giant stuffed animal, five feet high, Tweedy, big and yellow, leaning on a mail box.

"Ready for this?" I asked, pulling her eyes to the front. "Take a look." It was a boat, a rather large boat, nearly on the asphalt, in front of a smallish cottage. All I could do was laugh. It was prostate on the shoulder of the road with no trailer, no tow vehicle, no sign, just a small red flag, clearly a distress signal for curious police patrols.

She came up to the back of my seat and whispered, almost in my ear, "How the hell did it get there? There's no trailer. Was it wrecked or something?"

We gazed, we chuckled, and shared theories, each more comical then the next. The roadside refuse had loosened her speech. We spoke and laughed about racing and gambling and losing and, of course, leaving too much information on the side of the road for all the world to see.

Finally we arrived in Longfellow's Hotel parking lot. I rolled up to the front entrance and put the Buick in park.

"There it is, damn thing," she exclaimed with great relief, and she pulled a hotel key out form the bottom of her handbag. She jumped out and pushed a twenty dollar bill through the passenger window. "That cover it?"

"Sure." Truth be told, a nickel would have covered it. She was lovely and charming and witty and my Classic Taxi hadn't smelled so good since it left the factory.

"Keep the change, it was fun. Let's see, we found a wheelchair, a dress, some hotel towels, ummm, a boot."

"Don't forget the tuxedo and the car jack, can't forget them." We both smiled once more. "Looks like it was a good Traver's day."

"And night," she offered with raised eyebrows.

All I could think was the rather obvious fact that if the shoulder of route 9P was any kind of a witness it had been a very good day, and night, indeed.

The twisted corner of her smile was a suddenly confessing to secrets of her own. "Oh it was," she said calmly, "it was." She flashed her eyes at me and was off, sauntering blithely into the hotel lobby.

I was struck silent. Yes, I had found a unique mix of 'stuff' on the side of the road, but suddenly I realized I had found nothing as unique and mysterious as this lady, this magnificently turned out woman, who just disappeared inside Longfellow's. Travers Day!

Getting Out

I swear, no matter what you may have heard, horseplayers remain a notoriously stoic breed. True, their reputation has been sullied by certain behaviors at the conclusion of an ill considered wager which might have given rise to an outburst of uncivilized frustration, but usually, within moments, composure is restored and universally recognized standards of decorum resume. Stroll through the clubhouse of any major track, or find your way to the small warm pub next-door, (there's always one close by), and you will be hard pressed to distinguish the barons from the beggars at the end of the day. Men and women, ladies and gents, each will be gathered near the bar displaying the same unmistakable air of optimistic determination horse players share. There is, after all, hope in tomorrow, and one must abide today's indignities with style and grace; some things are expected.

In fact, few things ever cause these intrepid students of Marcus Aurelius genuine emotional distress, or besalted eye-floods, save the closing day of the race meet at Saratoga. That day, and it's usually a Monday, is dreaded and denied like few others. Ardent plungers fortunate enough to stroll across Saratoga's sacred lawns in August, are enrapt in a timeless calendar of suspended mental animation. Each August they shroud themselves in an imaginative umbrella woven from self-imposed ignorance, oblivious to the outside world, the movements of clocks, the shortening of days, the lengthening of shadows, or the early tincture of reds and yellows on aged maples. They live for this month, as this is the grand gesture of their entire year. They waited through the long drab gloom of winter, snow, rain, and the like, then survived the inhospitable moments of spring, pollen, tax collectors, insects, and more, to finally arrive beneath the hallowed boughs on Union Avenue, just to indulge in its purity of pure excess. August should never end; Saratoga should never close; just ask them.

One of the dreamy-eyed players I had grown to admire was a character known to us as The Coach. His mother knew him as George, but to all other living, breathing, 98.6 human beings, he was The Coach. He had been a police officer in a small town on Long Island for many years, but when chasing down desperados no longer rekindled his imagination, games of chance, particularly the thoroughbreds, took him in tow. Early retirement afforded him the opportunity to travel, and travel he did from Hialeah to Pimlico to Woodbine and beyond. And after a few successful seasons cashing tickets he became an owner of some interesting state bred runners who usually could be relied upon to supply more treasure from Finger Lakes or Aqueduct. They never made him rich, but they were able to pay their own barn bills. And during the height of summer, he traditionally set up residency on the second floor of Saratoga's aged clubhouse where he would remain, as long as the sun was shinning, to entertain his close friends and play 'the game of games', as he called it.

On the Thursday of The Hopeful weekend, I discovered, by way of a head spinning phone call, that I was suppose to join him and another friend, the almost famous 'Dreaded Fred' of New York, for a day chasing winners. Apparently Fred was driving in from Floral Park, to rendezvous with a new lady friend, who had abandoned her responsibilities out West so Fred might have the opportunity to spend some money on her and show her off. A day at the races with The Coach and good friends and a great lady filled my imagination: romance, intrigue, guile, and possibly, profits were sure to follow. I showered with a smile that failed me rather quickly.

With fresh clothes on my back, some folding money in my pocket and a Racing Form in my back pocket I charged into the morning light, prepared for a great day but was greeted by non other that the fleering face of the good Officer Kelly, standing next to the Buick. I was in for it, as sure as night follows day, I was in for it. I became a statue in Wentworth's parking lot.

"I know you, you are Aaron's friend," he said as soon as we made eye contact.

I was unable to reply.

He stood erect and pushed his cap back from his forehead, "Remember me, we met at City Hall. I remember you."

Silence was my barrister, the Fifth Amendment my cohort; he'd need pliers to get a confession out of me, big equine dental pliers.

He offered to shake hands and I accepted . . . with foreboding.

"Yeah, we've met, but buddy, is this your car?"

"The Buick?" I was astonished at my own verbosity.

"Well yeah. I mean do you have any papers from DMV or anything for this, uh, taxi?"

I was sinking and the quicksand was warm. "Papers?"

"Well yes, we got some complaints of a car like this, an illegal taxi, uninsured and all, driving around town."

"Really?" I should have been concerned at how easy it was to appear stupid, but the moment saved me from self recrimination.

"Well yes. Is this your car?"

"Well yeah," I knew my reply was barely audible, but it was the best I could do.

"But are you using it for a taxi? We've been getting complaints form the real taxi companies about some counterfeit hacks running around town."

He said 'hacks', I had heard plurality in his words . . . 'HACKS'. There was opportunity in this, and my feeble brain sprang into action.

"Well my friends and I," I started off, stalling for time to let the scenario form, "thought it would be cute to decorate the old car. I was giving them a ride to the airport and," (more stalling, more stalling) "they put all that on the car as a joke. Am I in trouble? Should I have taken it off?" What innocence I thought, as the words fell away, as natural and calm as a flower asking for sun and water.

The good officer looked down at the Invicta and then walked around the entire car. "Well, this could be a problem I suppose, but you're free and clear with Maryland's DMV. Why don't you take this silly tape off before you get into real trouble with a real taxi?"

I toasted this invitation to freedom with the only bit of vernacular that seemed appropriate, "Done said the Devil, done said Tom Walker."

Officer Kelly returned to his patrol car, but stayed long enough to see duct tape being pulled from the passenger door of 'My Classic Taxi'. I reminded myself that even Secretariat had to retire eventually. But at the same time, as much as I had lost my foothold on commerce in The Spa City, I was not under arrest, I was not ticketed, and Old Faithful had not been towed away. Like a better than average day at the races, I did not lose. Such a fortuitous event often foretells grand days at the windows.

I hurried into town, parked on George Street and sauntered ever so happily into the clubhouse, none the worse for wear. I found my friend, The Coach, in his accustomed office, beneath a television by Marty's service bar. He looked grand as ever, larger than life, with hard set eyes that were following the replays of yesterday's races. We laughed a little, spoke of my close call with the law, and eventually reviewed the day's scratches just as his other friend Fred came wobbling up the escalator. As promised, he was a sketch, with his Yankee baseball cap pulled down over badly dyed hair, an Armani sports jacket and a gold tie pin. I had been warned he would be complaining about the traffic in New York and the 'clowns' who start highway projects during Saratoga's racing season.

We introduced ourselves, as Coach was too busy with his research for politeness.

The Coach whispered, "At least you're here."

"No thanks to that jackass going fifty miles and hour in the left lane the whole damn way up the Thruway."

"The whole damn way?" I had to ask.

"Just about. My God, I blew the horn, I shook my fist . . ."

"Did you wave your baseball cap out the window, The Coach asked, "that would've got him over."

All Fred could do was groan as he shuffled a collection of papers.

"Got the Wizard's picks?" Coach asked without looking up from his Racing Form.

"Yeah," Fred grumbled, "and Lawton's too. You know me, I'll bet all the numbers on both sheets."

"Frederick, you disappoint."

"I know," he said under his breath, "probably end up betting against myself, again."

"Well, don't be too down-in-the-mouth old friend."

"Why?"

"Because it might be contagious and I gotta stay positive. Some of us need, I say again, *need* a winner!"

"Ha, who doesn't?" It was the best I could offer at this early hour.

"No! For a man who has earned many advanced degrees in prestigious institutions, you fail to understand. We NEED a winner." The Coach's earnestness was impressive.

"Truly?"

"Very truly indeed."

"And your twenty grand?"

"Hmmm! Not so far."

"The horses have not been kind?" I asked.

"Have you tapped out?" Fred asked shyly.

"Lord no, course not."

"Still in the game?"

"But I didn't come here to leave with 'some' money. There is no way I am leaving here unless I am up."

"Up twenty grand?" Fred asked.

"Well come on, here at Marty's's, let me buy you another beer so we can talk it over." Beer was all I had to offer.

"A beer would be nice, but a winner would be nicer."

We leaned against the end of Marty's counter, sipped draft beer, and reviewed our latest exploits. Crowds slowly filtered in, each exiting the escalator beglittered with exquisite tonsorial creations, larcenous hearts, and bewildering eyes. Occasionally, a face from the past emerged from beneath the canopy desperate to find either seats in the clubhouse or an open betting window. For half an hour we enjoyed our tales and the glamour of this year's second floor fashion show.

We shared a pretzel and started to relax when a truly magnificent woman materialized before us and startled us back into consciousness. Even Marty had to look again. The dark haired beauty stepped off the escalator and stood stationary for only a second. Piercing coal black eyes burned through designer glasses and her navy blue sweater clung to a figure from a Vargas drawing. She collared every eye, a work of accessible art, painted and prepared in perfection for her day. I smiled my aged smile. Such splendid women can make living worth while. Fred gazed but could only manage silence.

"Well," The Coach mused, "and she's by herself?"

Fred studied his friend and whispered quietly, "Coach, do not tell me you think she might give you a chance? Now we know you are not thinking real good, no wonder you are short twenty grand."

"Maybe, but I'm not giving up," the Coach scowled under his breath as he tried to return to The Form. "There's always a way to make some kind of a score at this place. Always."

Fred and I confirmed our new friendship with smirks and disbelieving eyes.

We looked over our newspapers to watch the raven-haired beauty stride through the breezeway. She stopped for a second to inspect her diamond pendant earrings, threw her tresses back across her shoulders, examined a glittering clutch, and then disappeared into the clubhouse.

"I've seen her before, somewhere?" I offered. It was the best I could do at the moment. The face and the hair and the jewelry were all ringing faint bells in the back of my brain, but I was too happy to remember.

"That's not fair," The Coach kept muttering, "I am telling you, not fair. Women like that mess me up; they screw up your equilibrium, nothing's the same. It's not fair. How are we supposed to keep our mind on our work with women like her prancing around?"

Fred soon regained consciousness with some stern wisdom for his friend. "Back to work lover boy, and don't share any of your ideas with me, they're probably contagious, and I don't need your bad luck sticking to me."

The Coach eventually cleared his thoughts and revived his dialogue.

"I'm telling you I'll save this meet yet, I just need one saver."

"A saver?" I said.

"Yes, it only takes one, or two, good hits in this game; this isn't roulette or poker, that's all you need, one good hit and you can be back on top," he said, his voice filled with dark sardonic sarcasm, "a real score."

"Some feat of genius, an imaginative contrivance to restore your bank accounts," I said with a wink and a nod to Fred.

"And what, may I ask, is the sex of this little brain child?" Fed offered.

"Not sure Fred old pal, not sure."

"Good enough."

The next minute our day got even better. The one and only Erwin Montalabano appeared. Things were looking up.

Erwin had been a long time employee of the New York Racing Association. He retired on his seventy-third birthday to start a new career photographing New York City bridges and turning his photographs into refrigerator magnets . . . at five dollars a piece. His brilliant eyes still shone with an electric clarity few younger men could match. He quickly took over the conversation.

"Coach," Erwin said with a crushing handshake, "hey, how'va doing? Really, good to see you. How ya hittin'em this year, really, how'ye hittin'em?"

"Well, you know," The Coach said in a whisper.

"Yeah, I know, I know. You guys bet too big for my blood, too big, but 'ya got anything good . . . for today . . . tomorrow?"

"Not yet Erwin," The Coach said in his ear, "but check in with us later, I'm working on something."

"Something good I bet?"

"Could be?"

"Really good, like really, really good?"

"Worth your shoe leather."

"Ah dat would be great; I could certainly use 'da money." He paused and looked over his shoulders, as if privacy was a scarce commodity. "You see 'dese refrigerator magnets haven't quite caught on, at least not yet, and I'm workin' on something that, well, kinda personal 'ya know, so I needs money."

"Really, like what?"

Erwin placed a soft finger over his lips, "I'm working on my night moves. Know what I mean?"

The three of us stared.

"Coach, don't be dense," Erwin's whisper was beginning to chuckle, "I'm here with my new girl friend." There was subdued glee in his voice. His robust chest was bouncing with quiet guffaws.

"Your what?" The Coach exclaimed with an impolite laugh, "You new what?"

Erwin moved in closer, "Girlfriend, I'm sure 'ya heard 'da word before. Girl-friend. And, let me tell 'ya, she is something. Know what I mean?" he said with an enormous lecherous grin. He made me laugh the way he smiled and shook his hand like it had fallen against a working wood stove.

"Fred," The Coach said turning to his friend, who was trying unsuccessfully to ignore the conversation, "Freddy, help me here. Please. Erwin's got a girlfriend, a new one. Come on, a real girl, like a living, breathing, eats a good meal once in a while kind of girl?"

"Why of course. What else?" Erwin said in mock amazement.

"What else? Like maybe she is made out of latex or something? Maybe you see her in Macy's window on Sunday mornings, or you take her down to the Mobil station for 35 pounds of air, you know, to get her started or something?"

"Hey, don't be daft, you're sounding weird . . . ya know, the women love me. The women can hardly control themselves. I am just covered in animal magnetism."

"Animal what? I thought that was moths!"

"Baaa, you're crazy, I'm telling you she is maybe, just maybe, 'da best one I ever knowd. Oh yeah. Da best. She uses me a little, I use her, and we just have a great time. No rules you know, we're too grown up for that. Nobody cares."

"Too grown up? Erwin, at your age you are past grown up. Come on now, what are you doing with this woman anyway?"

"What the hell do you think I do? Didn't your daddy ever have a talk with you? Hey buddy . . . you . . . buddy."

The Coach couldn't stop chuckling, "Fred, wake up, Erwin wants to talk to you."

"I'm sorry," Erwin said with a polite nod, "I am Erwin, and I have known dis guy here, your friend, for what, twenty years?"

"Since grammar school," said the Coach.

"OK, more than twenty years, and I never once, in all that time, ever heard him sound so ridiculous," Erwin was pleading like a frantic politician.

"Why's that?" said Fred, giving up on his numbers and racing program.

"Does he, or does he not, appear to be a full grown man?"

"That is in the affirmative," Fred said readjusting his baseball cap.

"And yet, he does not know what I am doing with my girlfriend. A full-grown man should be so ignorant. Please mister, take this poor excuse aside somewhere, out by the stables or something, and tell him all about the flowers and the bees, please."

Fred laughed. "Flowers, flowers? What about the birds?"

"Birdies? What birds? 'Dis is a racetrack."

"No, no Erwin, I didn't mean to get you mad or nothing. I just was wondering why a guy your age should . . . ?"

"Should what? Know what? Hey, I am telling you, when 'ya meet her you are going to be impressed," he declared with utmost confidence.

"But Erwin," The Coach said," I mean how old are you?"

"I am seventy-six years old this October, seventy-six, and I don't need no Viagra."

Fred spilled his beer and Coach had to breathe slowly to get the next sentence together. I just laughed.

"That's mighty useful information Erwin, I'm sure I'll put it to good exercise some time soon, but . . . I mean, you look great for your years, and you are still strong and all. But a woman?"

"And every inch of her is all girl."

"Really. And where did you meet his bubbling cauldron of pulchritude, if you don't mind me asking?"

"In the hospital, last January."

Fred spilled his beer again. I spilled some of mine.

"Yeah, I had a tough winter, I was getting my knee drained and she was in the next room."

"The next room? Visiting a friend I hope?"

"Naw," he said after a pause, "hip replacement."

Fred put his beer down on the counter . . . there wasn't much left.

"Erwin, a hip replacement, is that how you catch your women these days? You wait 'til they can't walk or run and then you pounce?"

"You son of a gun, she had to get it done. When she was younger she was a dancer and, you know, that profession is tough on the legs and hips and things."

"A dancer?" Fred asked, waiting for Marty to refill his beer. "What kind of a dancer?"

"She was a real showgirl in New York, for years, Broadway even."

"When, the Roosevelt Administration?" Fred shot out as he mopped beer streams off his shirt.

Erwin scowled.

Even I couldn't keep quiet now, "Teddy Roosevelt's!"

"Hey you guys, I'm telling you she danced on Broadway."

The Coach burst out laughing, "Which Broadway? Newark, New Jersey."

"Ah you guys think she was a stripper. Please. Do I look like the kind a shmo who would be seen in public with such a person?"

"Erwin?"

"In private maybe," he laughed, "but out here in public, please."

We all enjoyed Erwin's lighthearted diplomacy.

"And how old is this . . . um . . . exotic dancer?" Coach asked.

"Let's see, I think, if I remember correctly, she once told me she was going to be seventy this December, at least that's what she told me."

"Seventy, she admits to being seventy years old. Erwin, how could you, with a bummed up hip, I mean, Erwin?"

"Yeah, I know, she's a little older . . . not as spry as she used to be . . . and that damn cane."

"The cane?"

"I mean she's' lively, oh yeah, she, you know, she still, you know."

"Know what?"

"You know," he spoke with renewed courage, "she still likes a little sparking on Saturday nights."

Fred spilled his new beer.

"Sparkin'? . . . sparkin'? On Saturday nights. Erwin, a seventy year old woman with a hip replacement and a cane?"

This was getting better and better.

"Yeah," he began to admit. His smiling face was taking on with the ruddy redness of a child caught with a hand in a cookie jar, "I mean, we slip away every chance we get, but, well, truth be known, 'dat damn cane does get in the way."

The laughing wouldn't stop. Even Erwin couldn't hold back his own belly laughs. We waited for the tears to subside before trying to renew the conversation.

"Erwin, you are priceless," the Coach offered through desperate breaths.

"Have a beer Erwin," Fred said.

"No, no thanks, you know I don't drink," he replied.

"Really," The Coach asked, "no beer, ever?"

"Nope, not one drop in years, not since 1962."

"Really?"

"True, it was a night in 1962 I stopped drinking. Yup, 1962, A bunch of us left Belmont Park with our pockets full of money. We ended up in your old neck of the woods, at Nancy's out in Floral Park, you know, and we was celebrating and I got bombed, I mean bombed. Stupid me, I tried driving home in a horrible thunderstorm. It got me so scared and confused with all 'da flashes and rain, I ended up side-swiping' a cop car at a red light just off the Belt Parkway."

"Erwin, you hit a cop?"

"Yup, right near Knapp Street. Talk about trouble. Yup, 'dat was it for me."

"Well then how about a coffee?"

"No tanks neither, I've got to go down to lower club . . . to meet Monique."

"Monique, your lady friend? She's here?"

"Of course she's here. I was trying to tell ya that, she's meeting a friend of hers from the city. Her friend, Bonny, she's dating a jockey, and we're all supposed to . . ."

Fred and The Coach both jumped in amazement, "Erwin, put a lid on it. Hold it! Your lady friend has a friend who has a friend who is a jockey. Erwin how could you keep this from us? We are some of your oldest and dearest friends, and we are all looking for a way to get out, as the saying goes, to make a nice score, and go back home in style, and you have a contact and you do not tell us."

"Coach, I just got here, and you wouldn't give me time to tell ya nuttin'. All 'ya wanted to do was make fun'o my love life."

"Forget about it. Let us find this friend of a friend of a friendly jockey, and maybe we will all be better off," Coach whispered to Fred, "I am suddenly overcome with renewed religious fervor. We don't need a simple saver, I believe we are closing in on a savior."

Fred looked up from his paper, "Savior! You should swim in the River Styx for a comment like that."

The four of us sauntered, shoulder to shoulder, out to the walking circle. Dozens of people, some laughing, some reading papers, some strolling arm in arm, stopped our way. Everybody knew Erwin, and they all had a tale to share or questions to ask. He even sold a refrigerator magnet to a little girl who wanted one for her mother. Fred recognized some old friends who also shared quick hellos, or a friendly wave on their way to the windows. Near the back of the paddock area Erwin put his hands up and the caravan came to a sudden halt.

"I think dat's Monique," Erwin said pointing to a woman in a deep pink dress walking under the gazebo of The Big Red Spring.

"Where?" asked Fred.

"I ain't got no glasses. Maybe not, where's her friend? Real tall chickee in a white dress."

"Christ, is that the friend, up there by the barbecue pit?"

Some fifty feet away from the gazebo stood a tall thin woman walking hand in hand with a smallish blond man.

"Gotta be 'dem," Erwin said with an enormous grin.

"Who's she with?" The Coach asked.

"Oh no," Fred said, "oh no, that's Jessie Pellitier."

The very name stopped us in our tracks.

"Jessie Pellitier. I thought he was banned or in jail or something?"

"I thought he was dead," Coach offered.

"Who," said Erwin, "who is Jessie Pellitier?"

"Just one of the biggest crooks on the East Coast, that's who."

"A crook?" The word fell from his tongue like an old cigarette butt.

"If it's Pellitier? He was thrown out of Laurel a few years back, careless riding or dangerous riding or something, and then showed up drunk at his hearing and made a total fool of himself on some crummy news broadcast."

"Yeah, yeah, and he even tried to move his tack to Kentucky, but that didn't work either."

"I remember now, yeah, couldn't get no mounts, started drinking, couldn't make weight, ended up sandbagging some claimers in Oklahoma and . . ."

Erwin stood wide eyed, "Bonny's guy is dat bum? Naw, can't be."

"The one and only, if my eyes are still in my head?" Fred said.

"Come on Erwin," Coach said quietly, patting him on the back, "let's meet her. This could get very interesting."

Erwin's friend Monique proved to be as advertised. She was trim and frail, but stylish, wearing great sheets of blue eye shadow, while her equally blue locks framed the face of an elderly Saxon queen. Her friend, Bonny, was many years younger, but just as chic. She sauntered more than walked while clutching Jessie by the hand. Everyone said polite hellos and smiled about nothing in particular. A surreptitious interrogation ensued.

"Certainly I'm riding here. Don't you have a program? Look in the ninth race, that's me. I'm riding for Betancourt and Max Titus," the diminutive jockey announced with more than a certain amount of pride.

"Well that's' good news, isn't it fellas," Erwin said winking at us.

"Who else are you riding for up here?" Fred asked.

He shrugged, "I'm looking for more rides right now. You know, trying to pick up some clients before Belmont."

"Oh," everyone returned in choral agreement.

"They'll come my way; I'm showin'em I can still ride like a professional. Sometimes, when a guy like me has been away awhile, just riding professional is important."

"Congratulations, we missed you riding here," Coach said.

"You did?" Jessie queried, "I've never ridden up here before."

"Oh," said The Coach while straightening his belt and tucking in an already neat shirttail. "You know, I meant watching your rides, you know, Laurel and Maryland and all."

"Oh," he said suspiciously.

"Tell you what," Fred announced, "why don't we all have a cold drink, on me."

And as an offer like that can not be refused at any racetrack north of the Tropic of Cancer, the seven new friends strolled toward the Shake Shack bar and found a table for the ladies. Beers for Fred and George, champagne cocktails for the ladies, while Erwin and the jockey shared a coke. The conversation came quick and easy as Jessie recounted some of his most daring rides and spectacular triumphs. Everyone smiled and applauded his intrepid feats while rumors of unscrupulous behavior were meticulously shelved. It was then that I noticed a new look moving across George's smiling face. He was thinking even though Jessie's was in the middle of a heart pounding stretch duel he once had with Herb McCauley at Hialeah. The Coach's eyes were wandering. I could tell he was half listening and I knew, instinctively, he was on to something. Only Erwin's soft elbow brought him out of the gossamer mineshaft.

"Looka 'dat. Do you see it?" Erwin said out loud.

"See what?" Fred answered half-heartedly.

"Look, on the monitor, the three horse going back to the winner's circle. Look at those shadows, you can always tell by the shadows when it's getting late in August."

I looked as well, "Autumn's closing in."

"Some days left, a few," Jessie offered, "a few."

"September be here soon" Monique said.

"Too true," The Coach answered, "this place closes after Labor Day."

Jessie slipped away to prep for his race later that day while Fred, The Coach and I put our heads together to scope out the fifth race trifecta. Our tickets ended up beneath our beer cups and then the seventh race broke our hearts when a treacherous photo emptied everyone's pockets. Nice day, good company, but it was clear to me we weren't going to get to the end of the rainbow this way. Erwin excused himself to walk Miss Monique and her ever present cane back to her car, she needed a nap. Her friend Bonny begged off returning to the hotel, she wanted to stay and watch Jessie ride the ninth race. My friends and I also parted company near the Union Avenue gate. Fred was headed to his summer cottage on a nearby lake, hoping to spend the night watching the Yankees and waiting for a romantic phone call. Coach and I waved goodbye and drifted unobtrusively across the street into King's Tavern.

Inside we took a table and watched the last two races on the television. Jessie's horse finished a professional, but well beaten fourth. We both noticed he rode well off the rail as if he didn't want to take chances or get into a bumping war with another rider. His technique was odd to say the least. He was riding safely, staying clear of trouble, but even I knew that's a rough way for a jockey to make rent.

Outside you could hear rock and roll bands tuning up from nearby clubs and taverns. The nocturnals were back and streams of young people, freshly washed, and groomed for vespertinal chicanery, were populating the streets. I watched The Coach return to his beer and a bowl of snacks. King's patrons had finished reliving the day's adventures, and they were excusing themselves to join other friends for dinner and dancing downtown. The Coach rubbed his hands together as if to drive off a cloud of loneliness and mentioned a stroll down the length of Lake Avenue for a nightcap at The Parting Glass. I was too hungry to hike across town, but I promised him a ride to Lake Avenue as soon as my stomach was silenced. I looked closely at my friend. I was intrigued by a mysterious patina within his eyes. For that moment, he was not of this earth and yet was on it.

"You OK big guy?"

"What am I doing?" he mumbled.

He instantly broke into a monologue I will never forget. He knew he was about to accept an unprofitable day and return to his room with little more than a stomach full of beer to show for his day's pains. And yet another part of his mind knew he could do no such thing. He had seen the shadows of August, time was most certainly running out, and if he wanted to regain some dignity he had to turn things around starting now. I tried to empathize and listened as well I could.

A waitress appeared with menus in hand. "You fellows want something to eat?"

We took the menus and spent a few minutes letting her charm us.

"Here for the races?"

"Sure. Who isn't?" was our only reply.

"How're you doing?"

George only nodded with a frustrated smile.

"Maybe things will go better tomorrow? You never know."

"True, true, you never know, you never know," he said pointedly.

"Tomorrow will be better for me."

"Really?" I asked.

"Yeah, my last day here. I go back to school tomorrow."

"Where do you go to school?"

"Lemoyne, in Maryland. My boyfriend and his folks are driving me back."

"Long drive, probably seven hours."

"Eight the way Andy drives when his Mom's along."

"Andy? Your boyfriend?"

"Sure. We've been seeing each other a lot this summer."

"Must be a good guy," Coach added with an enormous grin, "if he doesn't treat you right just send him over to us and we'll set him straight."

She smiled.

"Yup, driving into Maryland tomorrow, early, but with Andy's Mom I don't think we'll be setting any speed records."

"Your boyfriend goes to school there?"

"Well no, actually he goes to high school here."

We couldn't contain ourselves. "High school? Younger man?"

"Stop, I've heard all the cradle robber jokes I need for one summer."

"Understood young lady, understood. Don't let us kid you, we're only kidding. I'm glad he's a good guy. But you do like Lemoyne?"

"Well, I will. I'm a freshman, but my grandparents are from Potomac. I know the area pretty well. I really like it there."

"Oh yeah, I know Maryland too," I continued.

"The summer sure went fast . . . autumn's closing in, as the song says," she said softly.

"Honestly, that's the second time someone has said that today."

"It's the truth though, the nights are getting cooler."

"And more fun I'll bet," George remarked smiling.

She returned a gaze that belied her innocence, "Well yeah, my friends call it practice for college."

"True."

"Oh not me," she said, "but my friends, my friends are out every night. I don't know how they do it?"

"Don't say any more, I remember those days . . ."

"And nights?" she said with a laugh.

He smiled again, "And the nights, I remember, I remember."

"But there is a big race tomorrow. And if you pick it right and win some money you will have new things, better things, to remember." Her voice was impressive, calm and strong.

"The big baby race? Could be, we'd love to hit that."

"I do know one thing," she offered with her tray on her hip and a strong well pointed finger before her, "Maybe you can explain it to me? It seems kind of strange that every night I see guys in here, at my table or at the bar, and they all seem to be dreaming up some weirdo way of cheating their way into a fortune."

"Yeah, well, you know how guys are, trying to be wise guys."

"But in some of the races they're only six or seven horses, right?"

"True."

"So it always seemed to me that if they spent all that time and brain power just playing the game right, and not being greedy, they'd have a real chance to pick a winner, you know. I mean six or seven horses doesn't seem impossible."

"Well, it's a tough game, but maybe you've got something there?"

"Would it really be that hard to just play the game right?"

"I'll give it some thought," Coach answered with a smile.

"Well, I'll give you guys a minute to look things over. The chicken picatta's real good tonight."

"Thanks," I said as we watched her move back toward the kitchen.

George sat there. Flirting with the young woman had been pleasant, and she did make him think. We had heard this all before. It was a question all horse players ask themselves from time to time. Why didn't people just play the game straight, and steer clear of all the dark intrigues.

We sat there a few minutes more and just that quickly The Coach said something about having an idea. It had been throbbing in his mind off and on all day, but this time it would not go away. With the grace of a Lippizan stallion he completed a curvet away from his table, stood straight up, and smiled down at me with blow torch eyes. He was thinking, I gawked, he sighed, and I knew, I knew he knew, what he was going to do.

He charged toward the kitchen where our waitress was waiting for an order. She recognized him and smiled only to drop her tray when he put a twenty-dollar bill in her hand. He blew her a kiss, said thanks, and wished her well at school. Just that quickly we were through the door, streaming into the darkness of Union Avenue where he sketched out the plan he was going to try in the morning. It was more than a little outlandish, thoroughly unique, but I was intrigued and couldn't wait to see how it all played out.

His cabal was remarkable for its simplicity but, like most things in Saratoga, it involved money, and while he had enough to get it started, he knew he would have to work it smart, real smart and more than somewhat, if he wanted his twenty thousand potatoes. And because of that he needed someone he trusted to make it work, which is where I came in. Yes, Coach thought he had found his 'savior', and, as often happens in August, salvation was as close as the next betting window. The next morning we met at the coffee stand outside the Traver's Porch.

"Stranger, looking' for a winner?"

No reply was necessary.

"Ready to get on a hot jockey?"

Again no reply was necessary.

"Well, Stranger old pal," he said as he settled into a handy chair, "if you can find your way to The Bread Basket for the next few mornings, we should be on the inside rail and driving for home?"

If the Coach had it right, he was going to get out, and that meant I was going to get out as well. What could be better than that? The crazy scheme seemed too outlandish to work but since I didn't have a better idea, I knew I had to jump on.

Coffees in hand, we found our way to a small green bench beneath a tree by the main horse-path. We waited a few minutes when Jessie Pellitier came walking past in his riding gear. George stopped him within earshot so I listened.

"Sure I remember you. Yesterday. You're Erwin's friend. You are . . . ?"

"Name is George, but most people call me The Coach."

"Yeah, yeah, George."

"Sure, that was nice of you guys to stop and stay hello. Nice morning. Hope you didn't bet too much on me in the ninth?"

"Came in fourth?"

"Fourth was the best I could do on that one. She's got some bad knees and the boss wanted her ridden kinda soft. She'll run down at The Bell, and she'll make Titus some money there."

"Down at the Bell? Well, I've got something for you right here and now," The Coach said in a low breath. "Sit down Jessie and let me make you some real money."

A suspicious eye could not keep the word 'money' from finding a home in the jockey's imagination. George laid it all before him with great alacrity, energy, and charm. I truly admired his tact and diplomacy. Jessie Pellitier, to the contrary, sat with his mouth hanging open for a solid minute.

"So let me get this right," the jockey said, pushing the riding helmet off his eyes, "every time I ride a winner, a winner, you are going to pay me one thousand dollars. And if I lose a race . . . ?"

"You owe me nothing."

"Nothing? I owe you nothing. And all I have to do is find your . . ."

"Do not worry; just be at the Bread Basket in the morning, and my man will pay you. I own horses; security might ask some unnecessary questions if they see me, an owner, giving good money to a jockey that doesn't ride for me. If we do it my way, there will be nothing, absolutely nothing for security to get worried about. My man will be in the parking lot sitting in a gigantic old Buick, you won't be able to miss it. All you have to do is say 'Hello Stranger' and the envelope will be there."

Jessie sat and thought. "Are you a cop?"

"A what? Why would I be a cop?"

"You look like a cop."

"Of course not, and besides, I'm not asking you to do anything illegal. Why would a cop be worried about you doing something legal? Think about it, I'm asking you to win; I'm willing to pay you to win, not lose. No stinkin' boat race, no sponges, no meds . . . . just win. It's that simple."

"You sorta sound like a cop. I don't know? You sure you're not a cop?"

"I'm not a cop; I'm just a player. Simple!"

"Too simple." Jessie stood still in the morning's gray-mauve light, as silent as a Florentine statue. "You are going to pay me one thousand dollars every time I win, and all I have to do is win."

"Win. Look Jessie, I read the Saratoga book last night. You are riding mostly claimers up here, even maiden claimers. Right?"

"Well. Yeah, so far."

"And you are getting your act together after making quite a mess of things down south. Right?"

"Easy now, I wouldn't say that."

I was suddenly concerned that Jessie was going to bolt from our negotiations or loose his temper, but he just sat there.

"Jessie, your bad habits are known far and wide. They are none of my business here. What is my business is making money. Here, you are riding very nicely, very safely, and very much under Mr. Titus's thumb."

"Professional."

"OK, you ride professional. But you are not in the big races. You are riding for twenty thousand dollar tops. Correct? And from that, if you win, your owner gets maybe ten or twelve thousand bucks. Are we on the same page?"

Jessie nodded, "Close."

"And from that sum of money ten percent goes to the trainer and another ten percent is supposed to go to you."

Jessie nodded again.

"But knowing the way Max Titus does business, he has let you know he is taking a big risk letting you ride anything faster than a lawn mower. So my instincts are telling me that you are not getting your ten-percent, maybe five at best. I do not want to use so crude a word as kickback, but there it is. Keep you nose clean, be reliable, don't take any chances with your mounts, play it safe, and maybe you get your full cut down at Belmont or Florida when the races set up for a big score. Too many unknowns here. Too many horses from out of state, right?"

Jessie looked away for a second, "You're guessing." He was sounding angry.

"Hear me out, please. So at best, if win you are getting maybe a thousand, but since anyone can see you are riding under wraps, you're coming in third or fourth at best and these plugs are getting you just a few C-notes at best Think about it, I am willing to double, hear that, double or triple your take with no risk to you what-so-ever!"

Riders and horses passed in silence while the negotiations continued. I was hypnotized by the little drama playing out behind me.

They spoke for some ten minutes until a small fellow in grimy denim came for Jessie. He rose, looked skyward and then shook George's hand. Each smiled. They looked like newlyweds about to escape the reception. All was right with the world, and redemption was at hand.

The very next day it became more than a passing curiosity as Jessie Pellitier suddenly was riding like he was on a suicide mission, skimming the rail and splitting other horses like a bull in a china shop. He found his way to the winner's circle twice that first day. And for the next few days I would meet my friend The Coach at Compton's Diner for ham, eggs and enormous smiles, and then, make my way over to The Bread Basket with the prize. The abacus in my head told me how much better we were all doing. Every time I handed over the envelope to him, he looked confused and a bit paranoid, but he always took it. Soon there was an article in The Pink Sheet that mentioned how Max Titus had dropped Jessie as his regular rider, but the jockey was now riding for some new connections and doing very well for himself. His smiling face even managed to find its way into the sports section of the local paper. Still we met at The Bread Basket and each evening The Coach and I drifted toward Siro's with heavier and heavier pockets. Life was good!

On the last glorious Sunday of the meet, when so many of the players were moping around in a denial and depression, I was invited to join The Coach on the third floor of the clubhouse. Fred was back in town and this time he was with his Arizona friend Susan. Such fine company insured a delightful afternoon. Good times, great friends, and the champagne flowed like one of Saratoga's infamous summer cloudbursts.

"Well old boy," Fred grinned as he adjusted his napkin, "you certainly have rediscovered your smile since I've been away."

"Very nicely, thanks. Things are much better."

"But I don't get it, run all this past me again. You, of sound mind and all that, are giving this guy a grand ever time he wins and, and he owes you nothing."

"Correct."

"And he doesn't have to tell you if he's going to win?"

"Why should he? This is totally legit. No insider trading. No shenanigans. No illegal drugs. I merely bet on him, heavily of course," he said with a wily grin, "when I think he has a quality horse under him, one that fits the race. I haven't bet him every time, just when I think he has a shot."

"And?"

"And since he is riding for me, in a way, I know I am getting a first class ride every time. And at the same time, the owners and trainers are very happy to be sure, except for Titus of course. Granted, they might not be happy with the way our boy uses the whip and skims the rail, but he is wining and that means they are stuck and we are happy."

We each looked at each other.

"So now, I believe I have a jockey who is trying every time! Hear me! Every time he is doing his damndest to kick his horse across the finish line? He is no longer content to finish a safe third, no matter what anyone says, not when he can double his money. I am paying good money to keep a jockey on the hump so to speak, and I am making money doing it. For the past few days, and maybe one or two more, I have an edge. I wish the meet was longer, but this will do."

"You found your savior in a banned jockey," I said.

Fred pushed his ball cap back and scratched his head. He looked at his lady friend, and she looked at him. "How'd you ever come up with this?"

"Divine inspiration," he said with a laugh, "and a lovely little waitress,"

"Really?" Fred asked.

"Uh-huh, little school girl got me thinking. That day we met Erwin, remember?"

"Really? But what about his money, can you afford this?" Fred had to ask.

"Oh yeah. He's had six winners in the past four days, and I was on all of them. On them good!. I'm finally up nice for the meet, and if he wins two or three more, I can't tell you what I might make."

"Well," Fred said pushing his ball cap off his brow, "I have to admit, I never heard of this one. No one's stiffing the players, nobody's drugging the horses, nobody's lying, or playing a shell game or . . . Hmmm! A jockey trying to rebuild his reputation is trying hard to win, all the time. What a good idea! The most unheard of thing I've ever heard of." We all smiled, enjoyed our ten-dollar sandwiches, exchanged high fives, and celebrated a plan so filled with paradoxes and irony I couldn't wait to tell someone, but no one would believe me, so I stayed mum.

Fred's eyes froze. The Coach noticed his friend's change. "What?"

"Over there George, over there next to the stairs."

Everyone turned to look, but only Fred saw.

"It's that woman, the one we saw that day, that day with Erwin."

"Where?" George's eye's burned until he spotted her.

Even I was impressed. The woman was stunning in an electric blue dress and a soft white sweater that defended her shoulders against the chilling breeze. Enormous sunglasses protected her eyes, while a bright red flower highlighted her white hair ribbon. She was leaning against the ancient wainscoting, balancing on one leg with ankles crossed. Her raven tresses glowed like brilliantine in the afternoon sun.

"Excuse me people," George announced, "but that woman is good luck. I think I'm going to say hello to her."

Fred objected, "Have some of your lunch first."

"Food?" The Coach said to his friends with a wink and a smile. "Please! Look at the maples, the colors, those shadows." He said pointing to the horses crossing the racing surface. "Who's got time for food? Time and tides, as they say."

Susan looked up and winked, "Good luck."

The day after the track closed, I paid my bill with some happy Jessie Pellitier money, and told Abigail I would be leaving for home the following morning. Leaving Saratoga is always bittersweet; it's the end of something grand and one knows full well that tomorrow will not be as much fun as yesterday. It was a long drive to Maryland, highlighted by one flat tire and rough ride on the Cape May Ferry.

But that is not the absolute end of the story, so to speak. The next day The Coach called me. He was residing comfortably alone at the end of the bar in The Olde Bryan Inn, ensconced snugly beneath the painting of Leda and The Swan. He was working his pencil through the arithmetic of a bountiful bank account, rehashing his profits and asking how much our jockey plan had earned me when Gentleman Dave, the restaurant's owner, appeared and started talking to him.

I listened.

"Good news?" It was the voice of the restaurant's owner, Gentleman Dave.

"What?" was all The Coach said.

"You're pushing numbers around."

"Well yeah, the thoroughbreds were kind to me this year."

"Oh . . . well," Dave said, "the horses. Congratulations. Hope you get them again next year? Next year? Doesn't seem possible does it? It's autumn. The place is closed already."

"I know it always goes by so fast; it always does."

"Winter will be here quicker than you think."

"I won't. I'm heading to Florida."

"Nice here in the fall."

"Yeah, but, you know, it's closed, and I have a friend I want to see. She has a place in The Keys. I'm kind of anxious to see it."

"Understood."

"And it's getting late. Look how dark it is already, not really night, and yet it's getting dark."

"Not even shadows left at this time of the day."

"I know," he said.

"Well, good luck in Florida," I heard Dave say, "be sure to drop in next year and say hello."

"I'll do that . . . I'll do that."

"We'll be here."

And maybe we'll be here next year, next August? There's always hope, right Yvonne, hope and the promise of next year. Please call if you can.

The End